ALSO BY
DARCY COATES

GALLOWS HILL

DARCY COATES

Poisoned Pen
PRESS

Published by Poisoned Pen Press, an imprint of Sourcebooks
P.O. Box 4410, Naperville, Illinois 60567-4410
(630) 961-3900
sourcebooks.com

Library of Congress Cataloging-in-Publication Data

Names: Coates, Darcy, author.
Title: Gallows Hill / Darcy Coates.
Description: Naperville, Illinois : Poisoned Pen Press, 2022.
Identifiers: LCCN 2022011069 | (trade paperback)
Subjects: LCGFT: Ghost stories. | Horror fiction. | Novels.
Classification: LCC PR9619.4.C628 G35 2022 | DDC 823/.92--dc23/eng/20220310
LC record available at https://lccn.loc.gov/2022011069

Printed and bound in the United States of America.
WOZ 10 9 8 7 6 5 4 3 2 1

1.

The casket lids remained closed for the funeral.

Margot had seen beneath them. Just once, that morning, four hours before the guests were expected to arrive. The mortuary owner had led her into a cool, dusty viewing room behind the funeral home, where two heavy caskets had been positioned below the sole window.

Margot blinked furiously. Her eyes were dry, but her throat felt rough, as though she'd tried to swallow gravel. She fixed her gaze on her clenched hands as she willed her stuttering heart to calm. There had been no question of whether her parents' funeral could include a viewing.

Around her, old pews creaked. A lot of people had shown up. More than she'd anticipated. She'd found a seat about halfway back in the dim, cold church and sat surrounded by an ocean of black-wrapped strangers.

Ahead, past the rows of gently shifting heads, the two caskets had been positioned on the raised platform. A pastor with a soft, well-creased face stood behind the lectern and read from loose pages of handwritten script. He talked about how the Lord was taking his children home. How they would be missed by all, how we might not understand why loved ones had been taken so suddenly but that it was not for us to know.

He wasn't telling her any of the things that really mattered. The last time Margot had seen her parents, she'd been eight, and she remembered none of it. She was desperate for the gentle-voiced pastor to tell her about her only family. Whether they laughed often. Whether they'd had tempers. How often they visited their friends.

Even what they'd looked like.

What they looked like before death at least.

There were no photos on the caskets, just wreaths filled with carnations and roses and hydrangeas, ghastly bright in the dim room, held in beds of ferns and placed on the sealed lids as though necessary to distract from what was beneath.

Under the stream of gentle platitudes, Margot was left grasping for any hint of what kind of people her parents might have been.

A lot of guests had shown up. They were liked in town, then. Or at least, they were entrenched enough that acquaintances felt obligated to attend.

The caskets—bought as part of a funeral plan years before—were solid and carefully crafted, but their design was simple. They looked expensive but not gaudy.

The pastor paused and looked up from his notes. There was something in his eyes. Margot frowned as she tried to read the expression. Some kind of…distress? The pupils, hidden behind thin-rimmed glasses, were more constricted than the dull light should have caused. They seemed to flicker, staring into the audience without actually seeing, as though some unpleasant idea gnawed through his mind, drawing his focus.

Did he see what they looked like too?

He cleared his throat, his long fingers resting on the loose papers. "Would anyone like to say a word?"

Margot waited. The pastor's speech, although handwritten, had been hollow. But a close friend or a neighbor would have stories to tell. Fond memories, even bittersweet ones, that might give Margot some small taste of who they had been during life.

The silence pulled onward, and onward, and onward, until her skin crawled from it. No one stood. The heads around her were bowed, eyes averted.

Why? So many people came. Someone must have known them. Even if they weren't well liked—even if they'd been bitter and irritable—surely someone would want to put in a word.

Margot swallowed again and felt her throat ache. Speeches were most often given by family. That meant her. But she had nothing to offer. Hugh and Maria Hull had been as much strangers to her as the nameless faces filling the church.

The silence ached in her bones. In that moment, it seemed to Margot that the guests were even holding their breath. The pastor cleared his throat. "Let us pray."

She bowed her head, but her mind was racing.

The funeral was tearless. The mourners had maintained a somber mood throughout, and no one had brought children or babies into the hall. Every face she'd been able to glimpse had been respectfully attentive to the service.

But no one cried.

Again, she realized, that duty should have fallen to her first. She was the daughter after all. Her throat ached with dust and stress, but tears were impossible, even if she'd wanted them.

"Amen," the pastor said, and the word was echoed back in soft murmurs from every corner of the chilled stone chamber.

As she lifted her head, Margot felt eyes on her. She turned. Two rows back and on the opposite side of the church, a man stared at her.

Dull-gray eyes, half-hidden beneath heavy brows, caught flashes of muted light through the nearest stained-glass window. She could barely see his lips behind the salt-and-pepper beard. Shaggy hair had been combed away from his face and clung to the back of his neck. He'd dressed in dark colors, like everyone else in the room, but his clothes were the least formal there: a faded button-up shirt with a dull pattern of crisscrossing lines and navy blue jeans that were so dark they might as well have been black. Margot had the impression that he might not have owned a suit, and this outfit was the closest he could manage from his wardrobe.

The stranger didn't look away when she met his eyes. Nor did he smile or nod; he simply stared. His expression was impossible to read. Margot's skin crawled as she turned back to face the caskets.

A woman—the pastor's wife, Margot thought—climbed the steps to the platform. Curtains had been concealed at the edges of the stage. She pulled them in, one side at a time, the thick red fabric rattling its runners as it moved. Heavy shadows fell over the smooth wood caskets as the first side was closed. Then the second side was pulled in, tugged to where the two met in the floor's center, fully hiding the back half of the stage. And that, Margot understood, would likely be the last time she ever saw her parents.

The pastor braced his hands on the lectern and released a long, slow breath. "The Palmers have arranged for refreshments in the hall and would like to invite all present to join them there. Thank you."

A soft murmur rose from those gathered—not exactly conversation, but a mingling of sighs and single-word acknowledgments. Bags and jackets rustled as the guests stood and flooded into the aisles. Margot, feeling caught, rose as well. Bodies bumped her sides and back. The swell pressed her along the church's length, and she only managed to break free at the doors.

When she looked behind herself, the church was empty. Even the pastor and his wife had left through a side exit. In the distance, the dark red curtains seemed to absorb the growing shadows. A wall of crimson, cutting her off from the last of her family.

Cold wind caught at Margot's jacket, and she pulled it tighter around her chest. A spit of rain, funneled under the doorway's arch, hit just below her eye. She swiped it aside with the back of her hand.

The guests moved away in loose clusters. Some stomped feet, a few others pulled out umbrellas in defense against the steel-gray sky and its threatening rain. Indistinguishable conversations rose.

There was a new emotion around the guests. Not joy—they were still maintaining the softly muted reverence that accompanied a funeral—but some kind of tension had eased.

Relief. Margot ran her tongue across chapped and cold lips. The guests were grateful to be away from the church. Away from the *caskets*. She was struck with the sudden idea that no one had volunteered to give a speech because not a single one of them wanted to stand any nearer to the bodies.

A marquee tent stood a little way from the church in an empty patch of field between the ancient stone building and the wall dividing them from the dirt road. It hadn't been a recent construction; the canvas walls were faded and stained with age, and one of the posts listed. The mourners moved toward it in clumps of twos and threes, and Margot realized this was likely the "hall" the pastor had said would offer refreshments. The church was too small to hold a milling congregation after Sunday services, and the building was too historic to build an extension, so the cloth tent served as a gathering point.

Margot raised her shoulders to hold the coat's collar closer to her throat as she followed, her shoes leaving imprints in the damp ground. She felt faintly lost. There had been so little time to do anything—*prepare* anything—that she'd mostly flown on the idea that she would figure everything out when she arrived at Leafell. Now she was here, and she felt more painfully untethered than she ever had in her life.

The call from a lawyer had come just two days before. He'd said he was contacting her to share some unfortunate news. Her parents were dead. He didn't know the full details, but he'd been told they had passed of heart attacks. The funeral was already paid for, and a close family acquaintance was making arrangements for the service, so she wouldn't need to do anything at that time.

Margot, still reeling, had leaned one shoulder against her kitchen wall as the call continued. He explained that her parents' sudden deaths had left Margot the sole recipient of their estate. That included their family home. The home she had supposedly grown up in—the home she couldn't even remember. And the family business: Gallows Hill Winery.

The funeral had been scheduled for Wednesday, leaving Margot with just enough time to pack her cases before getting into her car for the two-day drive across the country, stopping at whichever motels had vacancy signs out front and eating at whatever fast-food places didn't require detours.

She'd managed to arrive that morning with just a few hours to spare and had gone to the funeral home first. The director hadn't seemed surprised. If anything, she had the impression that he'd been waiting for her. And he'd taken her to the back room for the only viewing of her parents that would be allowed.

"We did the best that we could, but…"

Her breath caught in her lungs. She quickened her pace, lifting her chin to catch some of the ice-laced wind to cool her suddenly burning skin.

She'd been so focused on making it to the funeral in time that she hadn't given much thought to what would happen after. There would be loose threads to tie up, but she didn't even know what they were yet.

She'd been bequeathed their home and their business, but they wouldn't actually be hers until the estate had been settled. She wasn't sure if she would be allowed to stay in the house until then. If she wasn't, her options were limited to retracing her journey across the country to return home or somehow pulling together the money to stay in a motel.

Someone close to her parents had arranged their funeral. A Mr. Kent, the lawyer had said. He hadn't been able to give her any contact details. He hadn't given her much at all except a location and a time for the service.

The marquee's canvas sides quivered in the wind, creating a flapping sound that nearly drowned out the conversations beyond. Margot hesitated for a heartbeat, then ducked her head and stepped through the opening.

Inside was warmer than she'd expected. Standing heaters had been erected, and they not only took the bite out of the air but cast a soft golden glow across the space. Folding tables stood along one of the walls. The legs dug into the soft dirt, and paper tablecloths rustled as the crowd brushed past them. Platters of sandwiches and cakes cluttered the surfaces.

Closer to the door, another folding table held thermoses filled with boiling water beside bowls of tea bags and jugs of milk. Margot took up a paper cup, added a spoonful of instant coffee, and filled it. The acrid odor promised it would be bitter, but she didn't care. She was just grateful to hold something warm.

The subdued tones from the church had almost fully dissipated. Chatter flooded from every direction. Many groups stood near the standing heaters, shuffling as they tried to get feeling back into their limbs.

They all knew each other well. Leafell was a small town.

A woman, eyes trained on Margot, covered her mouth as she whispered something to her companion. A man nudged his friend and nodded toward her. They knew who she was, Margot realized. It must be obvious. She would be the only person there who wasn't from town.

Maybe, like the funeral director, they had been waiting for her.

Her mouth was dry. She couldn't bring herself to meet the curious glances but pushed through the gathered, searching for a corner that might offer somewhere quiet to stand.

A dense group had collected near the tent's back wall. Margot had assumed it was another food table, but as she drew nearer, she realized it bore stacks of plastic wineglasses. A man and a woman were behind the table, uncorking bottles and pouring generous measures to those who had clustered around them.

Of course. My parents owned a small winery. It makes sense to have wine at the reception.

The bottles were dark, which let the stark-white label stand out. The logo was simple: a tree's silhouette, leafless, its dead branches twisting into unfathomable and arcane shapes. Below that, in a formal serif font: *Gallows Hill Winery.*

That logo touched something at the back of Margot's mind. A memory. Or perhaps the impression of a memory. Maybe even a dream. Dark and dead branches, enormous, twisting, writhing—

She turned away from the table, her heart racing as she tried to catch a hold of it, a fleeting memory from the first eight years of her life. It flowed away from her like water between her fingertips, and the harder she tried to hold on, the faster it vanished.

A cold, bony hand landed on her forearm. Fingers dug in. Any noise Margot might have wanted to make died in her squeezing throat.

The woman before Margot had to be at least eighty. She barely came up to Margot's midchest. Her skin was an unsettling white and heavily creased, and Margot had the impression of bleached, crumpled crepe paper. Long, white hair had been plaited and then pinned into a knot behind her head. The only respite from the white came from her green eyes, blurred with cataracts, and the loosely layered black clothes.

"I'm so very sorry." The hand on Margot's forearm was so translucent that blue veins were visible as they pulsed beneath. The grip tightened a fraction. "You're the daughter, aren't you?"

She struggled to smile. "Ah, yes."

"Ooh." She made a faint shushing noise. "Poor thing. I am so sorry."

I am so sorry. Those were common enough words at a funeral, but something about the way she said them made Margot's skin crawl. As though it wasn't just a platitude. As though she was *apologizing*. "What…"

"I should have been there that Friday." A rasping, coughing noise caught in her throat. The woman closed her eyes and leaned nearer. "Should have. But I was sick. Pneumonia, yes? Couldn't get out of bed. Couldn't be there. And now…"

Margot's pulse beat hard, a tempo that pushed until she thought her very veins would burst.

"Such an awful thing," the woman murmured, and the coughs returned, deep, slow, and rasping, like a saw drawn through dry wood. She struggled to speak through them. "They weren't perfect people but they didn't deserve *that*."

"Do you…" Margot's voice cracked. She was acutely aware of the bodies around her. The glances. The whispers. The pressing heat of a hundred strangers crowded inside the tent. "How did they die?"

The woman lifted her head. Her eyes were narrowed and, beneath the cataracts, sharp. One hand came up and pressed against Margot's cheek. The flesh was cold. Clammy.

"Be careful," the woman said. Her final words were drowned inside the gasping, wheezing breathlessness. "Be safe."

She turned and vanished into the milling crowd, leaving Margot abruptly lost in her wake.

No more. The tent's heaters had been a relief when she'd first entered, but the packed bodies were turning the space oppressively warm. The flapping tent wall beat its tune without pause. The scents of coffee and churned earth and wine burned her nose as they flooded down to her lungs. She needed to get out.

Margot pressed through the crowd, acutely aware of the way people's eyes followed her when they thought she wouldn't notice. The space was packed, and the gaps between black-clad mourners claustrophobically narrow. Someone behind Margot laughed, the sound jarring.

She dropped the half-full cup of coffee into a bin. The exit was close. Margot fixed her sight on the slice of natural light between the tent's loose door flaps. Bitingly cold air wormed across her skin as she drew near.

A man moved in to block her path. Margot pulled up short, feeling a sting of shock as she recognized him. He'd mussed his shaggy gray hair out of the damp, combed arrangement she'd seen in the church. He stepped toward her, and Margot noticed a slight limp.

"Hello, Margot." His voice, like his clothes, was rough at the edge—slightly cracked, slightly gravelly. His head tilted as his gray eyes searched hers. "It's good you made it in time."

Margot's palms were damp. She felt exposed under his quiet scrutiny. Someone bumped her shoulder as they passed. Someone else near the tent's back wall laughed again, the sound a little too loud, a little too urgent.

"Hope it was okay." The man's wide shoulders shifted in a brief shrug. His voice was soft and nearly swallowed under the rapid conversations around them. "I'm not good at...planning things. The Palmers helped with a lot of it."

"Oh." Margot took a sharp breath, reassessing him. Pieces clicked into place. "Mr...Kent?"

"Kant," he said.

"Sorry. Mr. Kant."

"Just Kant is fine." He blinked slowly. "I suppose you'd want to see the home."

My parents' home. My home now, I guess. As foreign as that idea sounds. "I… Yeah, I would."

He glanced toward the tent entrance. "You're ready to leave." It was a statement more than a question, but Margot still nodded. "You have a car?"

"Yeah."

"Then follow me. I'll show you the way."

2.

The wipers made rhythmic thudding sounds as they swiped the spitting rain off the windshield. Margot had the heat turned fully up but still hadn't shed her jacket.

Ahead, Kant's pickup moved at a steady pace. Its steel-blue paint was unmissable in the browns and dusty greens of the road. The area would have been beautiful and lush in summer, Margot thought, but they were in the early weeks of winter and the shrubs and trees had withered into stark, barren angles.

The pickup's left indicator light flashed, and Margot slowed. On the side of the road was a wooden sign supported by two posts: *Gallows Hill Winery.* The twisting, silhouetted logo caught the sparse rain and funneled it downward. Beneath, in a smaller font, it read *Award-Winning Small-Batch Vintage Wines. Public Storefront.*

Margot searched the image of the twisted, dead tree and waited for the flash of emotion she'd felt when she'd glimpsed it on the bottles, but this time it was barely a flicker. The black-rendered branches appeared cold. Grim. And although Margot opened her mind to it, no images came.

She turned into the driveway, following the blue pickup. Trees flanked the path. They would have provided shade in summer, but the bare branches now formed lattices over the sky, slicing it into a thousand jagged pieces of gray.

The storefront appeared to her left as the driveway widened, leading into a parking bay with room for a half dozen cars. The store, built of wood and steel, appeared modern. Wide windows faced the drive. Barrels were stacked around the entrance. A second sign, suspended on two posts, read *Public Storefront*. The door was closed, though, and the windows were dark; everyone would be at the reception.

They followed the drive as it narrowed and turned in a slow arc. Her small hatchback lurched as it passed over a dip in the road, then rose onto a single-wide bridge passing over a small, slow-moving stream. Margot had just enough time to glimpse clusters of dead leaves and slimy debris catching along the banks, then she was past it and following the pickup as they climbed a hill.

The *hill. Gallows Hill.*

Barren trees continued to flank the drive. Most of Leafell had appeared flat or with gradual undulations. From what Margot had seen, this might be the only truly significant hill in the region. It wasn't sharp, but rose steadily. A break in the trees gave her a view of the top. From that angle, it seemed immense.

A hazy glimpse of something man-made—the house—appeared through the drizzling rain. Margot, hungry, *desperate*, strained forward over her wheel. She had an impression of a broad roof, but then the trees closed back in and smothered her view of the home.

Kant held his steady pace, his pickup rocking over the road's uneven patches. Margot's hands itched as she flexed them on the wheel. She'd told herself not to expect anything. Not to daydream, not to imagine scenarios, because there might be nothing for her in Leafell. But every time she thought she might have stamped down hope, it rose again, aching in her heart and in her bones until she could barely breathe from it.

Hope for what?

She couldn't answer herself, but it throbbed through her again—a deep, desperate want so powerful she felt like she could tear her own chest open if she could just be rid of it.

A side road split off from the driveway. Kant bypassed it, but Margot twisted to see down its length. There were more buildings in that direction. She caught glimpses of peaked roofs and fences, but then they were gone, and she focused back on the road ahead.

They continued to climb. The path was never too steep; her tiny hatchback was made for the suburbs, and even though the engine became growly, it didn't struggle. But Margot was conscious of how far they were rising, even though the bends in the driveway worked to disguise it.

The drive turned one final time, and the flanking trees vanished behind Margot as she passed through an open gate. She tried to draw a breath, but the air caught in her throat. The wipers flashed past her eyes as they worked to smear the fine rain across the glass. Beyond, she had her first true glimpse of her childhood home.

It rose above her, broad and dark and heavy with shadows. Although it had a second floor, it was still wider than it was tall. Rooms sprawled out to both sides, jutting at inexplicable angles.

A wide porch wrapped around the building. Wooden posts supported the roof, rising out of the porch railings at regular intervals. Dark windows interrupted the walls. The roof was broad and ran at a low angle, and its gutters dripped excess water in a steady flow.

The car resolutely piped hot air toward her, but Margot felt the cold invade her bones.

This is…home?

She waited for something. *Anything.* Memories. Emotions. Even a sense of distant familiarity, like reconnecting with an old family friend.

The house offered her nothing.

Maybe they changed it—added extensions, renovated. It might have looked different when I was a child.

No, she realized. The house was old. Far, far older than Margot herself. The wooden walls were a map of cracks and stains. The boards might have held rich colors once, but time and sun had bleached them to gray. The roof had been maintained—smatters of new tiles intersected the mottled old—but Margot was hit by the impression that the building had not seen significant change in any recent generation.

It was old enough to belong to the hill now, as much a part of the landscape as the ragged rocks poking through sparse grass.

The blue pickup drew to a halt near a set of stairs that rose to meet the porch. Margot couldn't bring herself to drive that close. Instead, she pulled her car off the path several dozen paces away.

Thin weeds grazed her ankles as she stepped out. Funneled by the wind that cut through patchy trees spaced about the house, the rain flicked across her face, catching in her lashes. Margot hesitated at her car's side, one hand still holding on to the handle, as though half-prepared to step back into her car and let the house shrink in her rearview mirror.

Kant waited at the base of the stairs, his weight resting on his right leg. His expression was unreadable. Margot had the uncomfortable feeling that he was gauging her reaction. That he wouldn't try to stop her if she turned around and left.

No. You wanted to know about your family. You wanted it so badly that you cried yourself to sleep in that motel last night. It's too late for cold feet.

She stepped away from her car. The wind pulled at her coat and snagged strands of hair across her face. Kant dipped his head slightly, as though accepting her decision, and turned to climb the stairs.

There wasn't enough sunlight to define the shadows, but Margot still felt it when the estate's layered shade fell over her.

Grass crackled under her shoes. Margot couldn't stop herself from watching the cold, dead windows as she approached. No lights were on inside the home, and it left the glass with a vacant, dark sheen.

The steps leading up to the porch were worn down, a discolored, scuffed dip showing where countless footfalls had eroded the thick boards. They groaned as Margot put her weight on them. To her left, a porch swing shifted in the wind, its metal hinges creaking. There was a scent in the air that she couldn't fully place. Dry age. Dusty soil. The sickly undercurrent of old potpourri. She ran her tongue across her teeth and tasted it there, building like a residue.

The juddering wind softened as she stepped onto the porch. The air felt a degree or two cooler. The porch swing creaked again, the dark shape shifting restlessly in her peripheral vision.

Kant waited at the door. She met his eyes, and he turned the handle, pushing it open for her.

The gap looking into her home was a queasy kind of dark. Very little light made it inside to highlight the edges of walls and distant furniture. For half a second, Margot pictured it forming the edge of a figure waiting down the dim hallway, but then she blinked and all she saw was a shimmer of dust caught in the air.

Kant waited. He was silent, his expression inscrutable.

Margot dabbed her tongue across her dry lips. Her fingers were numb, but the nerve endings still prickled when she clenched her hands into fists. She drew a breath, bracing herself, as though she were preparing to plunge into an ocean, and leaned forward to step inside her home.

3.

A clock ticked somewhere deeper in the house, meting out small slices of time that couldn't quite match her heartbeat. A hall speared ahead, with open archways and closed doors on both sides. Limited light streaked through windows that had gathered years' worth of residue.

A floorboard creaked as Kant shifted past her. He ran his fingers over a set of switches just inside the door and the lights flashed on in bursts, starting above her and shooting down the house's length.

The gold glow wasn't as strong as she would have wanted. It should have been enough to chase the shadows away, but instead it barely made them retreat; they clustered in corners, around furniture, along the walls.

"Kitchen's this way," Kant said, shifting toward the open archway to their left.

Margot didn't immediately follow. Her eyes tried to drink in the house's details, but even with the lights, they seemed to merge in unnatural ways. There was too much to take in at once, too many lines and curves and corners. A flash of a paisley-patterned armchair to the right. *A sitting room?*

Wood-paneled walls here; painted walls farther along. Old floorboards ran through the house. They were all worn down; only the varnish closest to the edges had survived.

The sound of running water broke Margot's hesitation. She moved forward, tiny flecks of dust spiraling around her as she stepped into the archway.

The kitchen was dated, its cabinets and appliances all harking back to an older world and chipping around the edges, but it still struck Margot as very much *alive*. The clutter felt suspended in some kind of shrine-like state. The wrinkled towels hung over the oven handle, the kaleidoscope of magnets scattered across the fridge, the half-empty jars of pecans and dried apricots pressed against the splashboard—they all told tiny pieces of a narrative that Margot badly wanted to hear.

Kant had shed his coat and draped it over the back of a chair. He stood at the sink, refilling the kettle. The window wasn't large, but it did its part in highlighting the wrinkles across his face. His gaze didn't waver as he watched the water flow.

Margot stopped just short of entering the room. Her legs felt strangely unsteady. "You knew my parents, didn't you?"

"Yeah." It came out as a short syllable—*yah*—closer to a grunt than conversation. He looked at her over his shoulder, and his eyes softened a fraction. "You'll want to know about them. But I need something to drink first."

"Right. Sure."

He placed the kettle back onto its stand, then indicated the kitchen cupboards. "Mind if I…?"

"Go ahead." She watched as he fetched two mugs from an upper cupboard and a jar of instant coffee from the rows of bottles beside the fridge. He was familiar with the kitchen. She wondered how many hours he'd spent in there, if he had a favorite seat at the small, white-painted table, if one of the mugs was *his*. He wasn't family, but he belonged in the space so much more than she did.

She struggled to put a smile into her voice. "It's kind of weird to be asked permission in a building I don't even know."

"It's only polite." He gave her another glance. "Your house after all."

She leaned her shoulder against the doorframe, the prickling ache filling her throat all over again. "I mean...is it? Probate won't finish for another few weeks, so I'm pretty sure the court owns it right now."

It had been an attempt at humor, but when she tried to laugh, the sound came out ragged and uncomfortably loud. She clamped her mouth shut to quiet it. The silence that followed was painful.

"It was Hugh and Maria's house," Kant said gently. "They're gone. And that means it's yours now. No one would argue with that."

She didn't know where to look and fixated on the worn rope rug beneath the table. "You're sure? I'm not... I mean, I don't exactly belong here. In this town. I don't even remember what the place looks like."

Kant's hand flicked aside in a cryptic gesture. "House is still yours. Both the good and the bad parts, I suppose. D'you drink coffee, Margot?"

"Yes. Thanks." She watched him as he opened a draw to retrieve a teaspoon, then shifted slightly, pulling her shoulders higher. "How do you know my name?"

"You don't remember me, I guess." The spoon clinked as he dropped both it and its load of instant flakes into the mug. "But I knew you when you were small." He held a hand at waist height, indicating her size.

Margot's stomach dropped, her heart beating too fast for the conversation's gentle tones. Her early childhood had felt like such a thoroughly separate, thoroughly detached event that she'd never considered that Kant might have been present for it. "Oh?"

"You'd follow me around while I did my work, asking questions. So many questions. I used to pretend to be exasperated." A hint of a smile entered his voice, but it vanished as soon as Margot detected it. "I didn't really mind it, though. Things felt too quiet once you left."

Once I left. As though it had been her decision. As though she'd had a choice.

He crossed to the table and placed the two cups of coffee down, pushing one toward her. "No milk. It went bad," he explained, nodding to the dark hue. "Suppose it was on the verge of expiring even before…"

Even before they died.

"That's how I like it. Thanks." She took the closest seat, pulling her mug nearer, while Kant lowered himself into the white-painted chair across from her.

He exhaled as he stretched his legs out. One hand closed over the mug's rim, though he made no move to lift it. He stared down at the drink for a moment, watching the tiny eddies, then said, "You'll have questions."

"Yeah." Even now, Kant's face was unreadable. The speckled gray brows were heavy, the beard disguising the edges of his mouth. He met her eyes, but it felt uneven, as though her own thoughts were laid bare before him while she got nothing in return. She shifted, uncomfortable. "You've known my parents for a while, I guess?"

"Near thirty years. They hired me to be a manager for most of the practical half of the business. Live in the employee accommodations." He tilted his head toward the window, and Margot knew he was indicating the clustered buildings they'd passed on the drive up the hill.

"Oh." She'd guessed he must have been close to her parents in some way to be put in charge of their funeral arrangements, but she hadn't realized they worked together. It made sense, though. He probably knew them—their routines, their preferences, their plans—better even than a friend would have.

She tried to remember what she'd seen of the buildings on the climb up the hill. The view had been obscured by the rain and mist and scrubby trees, but she was certain there had been more than a couple of rooflines.

Margot ran her tongue across her teeth. "Do other people live here too?"

"Andrew does bookkeeping and sales work." His short fingernails picked at the edge of his mug. "Nora and Ray run the public store, but they live in town and drive in each day. Otherwise, we have eight full-time workers staying on property, plus seasonal employees. They bottle and ferment the wine, fill the casks, keep on top of the daily work. And…" His gray eyes flicked up to watch Margot's reaction. "They're wondering if they still have jobs."

A faint tinny noise rang at the far back of her ears. She didn't know where to look, and her eyes settled on the kitchen table, where the shadow from her mug fell. The wood's grain was still visible even under the sloppily thick paint: weaving lines, uneven around the edges. She let her gaze track over them, following the rivers and eddies they formed, as her mind raced.

The lawyer—the one who had called to tell her about her parents' deaths—had said the estate came with a business. He'd said very little about it except it was a boutique winery. There had been no time to dig or question, and Margot, so focused on just making it to the funeral, had let herself imagine it was just a two-person affair—her parents handwriting labels and sticking them onto bottles that had fermented inside a kitchen cabinet. She'd been expecting a handful of loose ends to tie up, bills to settle and supplies to sell, little more.

Twelve full-time employees. It was larger than she'd ever expected. Twelve people waiting on her decision. Twelve people wanting to know whether their next paycheck would arrive.

"I can't…" Margot caught herself, swallowed, and tried again. "I'm not the sort of person… I haven't ever…"

Kant didn't try to hurry her but waited as she fought to gather her scattered panic response into words.

"I don't...know how to do any of this," she finally managed. Twelve employees. She barely had enough in her savings to cover her own living expenses for the next six weeks. "I can't, uh, afford—"

"Business has its own bank accounts." Kant raised the mug to taste the coffee. His brows scrunched together at either the heat or the bitterness, but it didn't distract him from continuing. "Andrew manages the wages. Doesn't impact you."

"Okay. So...okay." She ran a fingertip across the thick white paint, trying to ground herself in small ways. "It's just that I haven't... I've never *run* a business before. I don't know how it's supposed to work. Or how wine's made. I know it's grapes, but you need to add something to them, right? I don't..."

As he watched her flounder, his features softened a fraction. The mug touched back onto the table with a soft click. "Margot. You'll need to make a choice. But not tonight."

"Okay. Right. Okay." When she drew a breath, it was tight, whistling.

"I can manage things." Kant folded his arms on the table, resting his weight onto them. "Gallows Hill pays for itself. If you want, we can keep it running the way it has. Nothing needs to change for the next few weeks at least. I'll show you around the business, teach you how it works. And you make the decision in your own time."

"Okay." Her fingertip continued to scratch at the white paint, but her mind was clearing in increments. *If it doesn't work—if I can't stand it—I can always sell, can't I? Kant says it's profitable, so surely someone would want it. They won't have to lose their jobs.*

"I can show you around the winery and introduce you to the folks tomorrow," Kant said. "I imagine you'll want to spend tonight getting reacquainted with your house."

She could feel it at her back, this sprawling monster of a home, rooms stretching in every direction, all of it foreign, all of it supposedly *hers* now.

"You'll have questions," Kant repeated. "I can't guarantee that I'll always have the answers, but I'll do my best for you."

"Please." The coffee was cooling. Margot couldn't bring herself to drink it. Her question, the most important question, had stuck in her throat so long that she felt like she would choke if it stayed there another moment. "How did my parents die?"

The light from the window came in at a sharp angle, highlighting the creases and weathered pocks across Kant's face. Some unreadable emotion moved behind his eyes, then was gone again.

"What did Walter tell you?" he asked.

The mortuary owner's words had been hushed and bordering on apologetic. Margot fixed her eyes on the table as she tried not to let frustration bleed into her voice. "He said they both had heart attacks while they slept. That it was a fluke that they happened on the same night."

"That's what he told me too."

Margot swallowed and tasted a bitter, stringy flavor at the back of her throat. At least she hadn't been the only person given that story. And based on the edge to Kant's voice, she wasn't the only one to be dissatisfied with it either.

At the time, she'd thought the funeral director must have been hiding something from her, some real cause of death that, for one reason or another, he'd thought would be too distressing to share with Margot.

Now, though, she wasn't so sure. There had been a hesitancy in the director's voice that made her think that he was at a loss to fully explain what had happened—that he was trying to convince himself as much as Margot.

Kant took up his mug, his eyes downcast. "I was the one who found them."

Margot's heart thumped. She leaned forward, a slick kind of dread pooling deep in her stomach.

He was there. He saw them.

"What happened?"

"They hadn't shown up that morning, so I came into the house." Kant tilted his head toward the hallway. His voice dropped until the rattling windows and tight whistle of wind forcing its way through narrow cracks nearly drowned out his words. "I called but didn't get an answer. Went upstairs. Found them in their room. In bed, on their backs. They…must have passed in their sleep."

That last part was a lie. Margot didn't doubt her parents had been in bed, but they couldn't have been asleep when they died. Not after what she saw in the brief viewing that morning.

Kant's shoulders shifted uneasily. "I touched Maria's neck. Wasn't entirely cold yet but was close. They must have been gone for hours at that point."

"Did…" Margot hesitated and wet her lips. She didn't want to pry too aggressively, knowing the questions would be painful. But at the same time, she needed to *know*. "Did they look…like…"

His eyes flicked up to meet hers, and Margot had her answer without ever finishing her question.

Yes. Yes, they looked like that.

Kant drank deeply, then put the mug down. He leaned back from the table, the chair's legs scraping as he reached for the fridge behind them.

A colorful mesh of magnets and papers coated the old, white surface.

Kant picked a photo, which he tugged free from a sink-shaped magnet advertising plumbing services.

He placed the photo on the table in front of Margot and turned it to face her. It was old. The left-hand side had been torn, as though it had originally been part of a larger image, and the corners had grown dog-eared and discolored.

A man and a woman smiled out at Margot. The woman leaned against the man, one hand touching his chest, while he held his arm around her back.

Something sharp stung in Margot's chest. She leaned forward, her arms clutched around her. She felt alarmingly close to collapsing otherwise, as though her body were made up of a Jenga tower of bricks that had been nudged too far.

These are my parents. The image was small and the colors faded, but she hungrily searched the two smiling faces for hints of herself. They were there. Her mother's hair—she'd cut it short, but the dark curls had been gifted to Margot. So had the dimples on either side of her father's smile and the high quirk to his eyebrows. The photo was old, but he'd already begun to bald.

My family.

"You wanted to know about them," Kant said. "We didn't talk much about our personal lives. Mostly focused on business. But I know they married young and waited some years before having you. And I know they loved each other."

She was suddenly desperate to not let him see how wet her eyes had become. "Yeah?"

"They both liked working. When things went wrong, Maria would be the first to figure out what needed to be done to fix it." Kant finished his coffee and pushed the mug aside. His voice, deep and soft, only made the prickling inside Margot's chest worse. "Hugh loved jokes, both telling them and hearing them. They didn't have to be especially funny ones. He just liked to laugh."

Margot clutched at each word, using them to build an image of her parents. She couldn't tear her eyes away from the faces in the photo.

Kant hesitated. When he spoke, his voice had grown softer, less certain. "They cared a lot about you."

The coal of warmth forming in Margot's chest abruptly turned cold. She fought to keep her faltering smile in place as she leaned back in her chair, putting some distance between herself and the photo. "Not enough to keep me apparently."

She'd half expected Kant to argue, but he didn't. He only watched and waited.

Margot rubbed at the back of her neck, fingers grazing through hair sticking to a slick of sweat forming there. "What…" She knew what she wanted to ask, but the question seemed so horrible and misguided that she tried to swallow it. Kant didn't provide any break in the awful silence, though; he simply waited, and the words flew out of Margot before she could stop them. "What kind of parent sends their child away like that?"

He breathed in slowly, resting his crossed arms on the tabletop. "You lived with your father's mother, didn't you?"

"Yeah." Margot had loved her. She'd been warm and patient and fair, and had raised Margot from the age of eight as though Margot had been her own. But it didn't overwrite the knowledge that Margot had parents and that they had apparently been physically and financially capable of caring for her and yet hadn't. "They never called, never—"

Never visited. No birthday cards. No response to the invitation to my eighteenth birthday party or to my graduation, or when I broke my leg and spent the night in the hospital. I thought they might come to Nanna's funeral, but not even then.

Her smile felt as though it was going to break her face. "Didn't they want me?"

This time, the silence that followed her question was horrendous. Margot lifted her head. Kant slightly opened his mouth, then closed it again. He looked lost.

Flaming heat rushed up her throat and across her face. *Stupid.* She'd overstepped. Kant barely knew her. He was trying to view her as his potential employer. And she'd dropped *that* on him. Her own words echoed in her mind, growing more childish and whinier with every iteration. *Didn't they want me? Didn't they want me?*

"Forget I said that." She stood too quickly. Her hand slipped and hit the mug; warm coffee poured across the table's surface, running to the edges and dripping over. "Damn it—"

"I'll get it."

"Sorry. I'm really sorry."

"It's fine." Kant had already grabbed a cloth from the kitchen and run it along the table's edge to stem the overflow.

Margot's face burned. She found a dishcloth at the sink, hung over the handle after its last use. It had become stiff as it dried, and crinkled when she flexed it. She knelt by the table, pressing the cloth into the spills before they could stain the rug.

"No harm done," Kant said, running the towel across the tabletop. She couldn't tell if he was talking about the coffee or her faux pas. The heat in her face refused to fade. She felt like she was burning alive from it and shoved the sink's tap on as far as it would go to rinse the cloth.

The kitchen had a second door, close to the fridge, letting out directly to the porch. It seemed rarely used, based on the clumping dust caught around its edges. A black dog door had been added to it, the rubber flap barely flinching as the wind whipped outside. Margot latched on to it, desperate for a change of topic. "Do my parents have a dog?"

"They did." Kant had come up behind her and placed the tea towel in the sink. "A long time ago."

"Huh." She swallowed thickly. "I like dogs."

Kant leaned back against the counter while Margot rinsed the towel. He was watching her again, frustratingly inscrutable.

As she wrung water from the towel, he said, "I imagine you'll want some privacy to settle in. Do you need anything? Soap, spare toothbrush?"

"Oh. No. My bags are in the car." *He's making his excuses to leave. Honestly, I can't blame him.* She swallowed. "Thanks, though."

"Sure." He pushed away from the counter and picked up his coat off the back of the chair. "I'll stop by tomorrow morn to show you around the cellar. If you need anything before then, this is me." He indicated a slip of paper fixed to the fridge by a magnet painted to look like a cartoon sun.

The paper was old, yellowed, and curling around the edges, but it held a handwritten phone number. Margot had the sense the paper hadn't been needed for many years; her parents would have known Kant's number by heart, but they'd never gotten around to clearing it from the clutter. Now, it was being passed down to her, along with everything else.

"Margot." Kant, coat held loosely in one hand, had stopped in the doorway. He didn't turn to look at her but shifted his weight uneasily in the silence. "Your parents were always hard workers. Except for September seventh. Your mother always stayed at home on September seventh. The few times she came down to the business, I could tell she'd been crying. I don't know if that makes any difference."

Margot faced the sink, her fingers growing numb from the beads of water drying across her hands. In the distance, the front door opened and then closed with a muffled click as Kant let himself out.

September seventh. My birthday.

Slowly, Margot approached the kitchen table. The photograph waited in its center. A drop of spilled coffee had landed on it, tingeing one corner brown.

She brushed her hands dry on her black dress's skirt and carefully raised the photo. Two smiling faces stared out at her.

What does that mean? Did you miss me as much as I missed you?

The photo's left side was torn, showing where it had been ripped from some larger image. Margot ran her eyes down the ragged edge. A wisp of black, curling hair, almost too small to see through the faded colors, grazed across her mother's dress.

Margot frowned and held the photo closer until her eyes threatened to blur.

It really was hair. A lock of it, pulled in from the torn side of the photo by some invisible breeze. Margot was fairly sure she recognized it. She'd fought with that black hair her whole life.

The dark curls had come from her mother's side. Her grandmother had been gifted with smooth hair and hadn't known how to deal with them as Margot grew up. She'd been in her late teenage years before she'd figured out the combination of products and microfiber towels that kept them presentable most days, but if she ever skipped her routine, those coarse curls would frizz again, just like in the image she was looking at.

Margot ran her thumb along the ragged edge of the picture.

She'd been in the photo. And they'd torn her out.

The tears that had been absent at the funeral appeared, burning her eyes and stinging her throat. She tried to breathe, but it came in as a choking gasp. Margot pressed her sleeve across her face as she tried to stop the flow.

The photo felt heavy. She brought it back to the fridge and forced shaking fingers to pluck an unused magnet and pin the picture back where it belonged.

As she stepped back, she realized that wasn't the only photo among the clutter of leaflets and paper scraps. The fridge was covered with them. Some photos showed her parents posed with other men and women, possibly employees or friends. But most often they were just her parents. Many had a ragged side.

She dreaded what she would see, but Margot couldn't prevent herself from bending closer and examining each image. There—the edge of a sleeve belonging to a young girl's dress. More traces of flyaway curly hair.

Near knee height, Margot found an image that showed her mother and father from their shoulders up. From what she could tell, this was the oldest photo on the fridge. Her parents looked young; her mother's hair was long and wild, her father lacking the creases that had grown across his face in his later years.

In the image, her mother's shoulders were lifted slightly, as though she were carrying something against her chest. That something was gone, though, the lower half of the image torn away. The only hint left was a flash of pink peeking above the ripped edge. If Margot wasn't wrong, that was the top of a baby's fist, reaching toward her mother's face.

Margot backed away, her arms loose at her sides, her heart fracturing into painful shards that seemed to stab the pulpy flesh inside her with every movement.

"Why?" she asked. Her voice echoed in the space, coming back in hollow loops. She swallowed a thick, unpleasant lump as her voice cracked. "What did I do wrong?"

The empty house gave her no answer.

5.

The wind snatched Margot's breath away as she opened her car's back hatch. Two luggage cases were nestled in the tight space. She hauled them out, propping them upright by her side as she slammed the hatch closed again.

The sound ricocheted across the hilltop like a gun blast, and small, dark birds burst from a clump of tightly grown trees behind the house. Margot shielded her eyes against the cloud-muted glare and the spitting rain as she traced the birds' path into the sky.

She felt very small and very alone.

The luggage cases had wheels, but they got bogged down in the soft dirt as she crossed the space between the car and her new home. Her breath came in sharp bursts. It would have been smarter to leave one case by the car and come back for it, she knew, but the empty stretch of lawn left her feeling uncomfortable in ways she couldn't put into words, and she didn't want to spend any more time on it than was necessary.

As she neared the stairs to the porch, a sharp whirr of wings made her pause. Another cloud of dark birds had exploded from their sheltering trees, this time a cluster growing closer to the wooden fence that circled the property. Margot watched them tear away in erratic jags, racing as though hell itself were on their tails.

She couldn't blame herself for the disturbance this time. She knew she wouldn't see anything, but Margot still let her eyes drop to the trees that had housed the birds. The trunks, thin and twisted, were a pained manifestation of poor soil and harsh winds. A multitude of heavy shadows crisscrossed the growth's insides. She couldn't see what had caused the birds to flee.

The luggage thumped with each step Margot climbed. She moved faster than she should have, and a stitch had formed in her side by the time she maneuvered them through the door. She bent over, inhaling stinging cold air.

Okay. Take a minute. Figure out the next step.

Margot left the cases against the hallway wall and gently closed the door behind her. She felt like she'd been living in a constant daze of *one step at a time* for days. No future plans were allowed because the future was a blurry, amorphous thing, so she'd reduced her life to a string of singular goals, each being plucked out of the ether one after the other: Get to the funeral. Find someone who knows where the house is. Get the luggage inside.

And now?

Now, she needed to find a place to sleep.

Margot pressed her hands into the dip behind her hips and stretched her shoulders and back. The house, left unheated for days, was dark and chilled.

She crossed into the kitchen first. Mud had splashed onto the hem of her dress, and she leaned close to the sink as she dabbed it off. The photos dotting the fridge blended into a multicolor mirage in the corner of her eye, and she deliberately focused on the room's other details to distract herself.

The kitchen looked as though it had last been renovated in the eighties, with wooden counters sagging from age and cracks running through the small tiles forming the splashboard, but vestiges of older history still clung in areas. The metal hooks by the door had collected smears from many fresh coats of paint, showing they had likely been a part of the house for generations.

Near the doorway was a tarnished bronze bell the size of Margot's palm. A wire ran from it and disappeared into the wall. Margot approached it as she squeezed dampness from the dress's hem. She'd never seen that kind of bell in person before, but she recognized its design. Somewhere else in the house would be a cord that the home's owner could pull. The bell would ring then, alerting the staff that they were being summoned.

She tapped the bell's side. It was stiff with age but still swung on its support, releasing a faint chime.

Most likely, the bell system hadn't been touched for decades.

Margot left the kitchen. Opposite its entrance, across the hall, was another open archway. The room beyond was dark. It had windows looking over the porch and the field where Margot had parked her car, but thick curtains had been drawn across them. Margot could make out the faintest edges of the fabric where cold light bled around it. The rest of the room was lost in shadow.

She reached through the opening and blindly felt across the wall for a light switch. Her fingertips grazed wallpaper so old that cracks had begun to marble the surface.

As her eyes began to adjust to the dimness, she thought she could make out the thin outlines of furniture. It was some sort of sitting room, she thought. Ahead and slightly to the left was the swollen corner of an armchair. To her right was the sharp line of a bookshelf. And ahead…

A figure.

Something stood against the opposite wall. It faced Margot, its head nearly grazing the ceiling, its shoulders stooped, its hands folded ahead of itself. There was a face, she was sure, but it was impossible to see beyond the narrow glint of one eye.

Margot's breath snagged in her throat.

Have they been here this whole time? No. Stop. Calm down.

It couldn't be a person. There was no way a man could stand that still. He was like a statue, not so much as a millimeter of give to him.

The single visible eye glittered.

Margot's heart felt ready to burst with each pulse. Her fingers, desperate to find the light switch, reached farther and finally touched plastic. She didn't dare take her eyes off the motionless form as she turned the switch.

Dull light flooded the space from the overhead bulbs, wrapped in tulip-shaped shades. The glass's curling edges sent shadow patterns running across the green wallpaper and off-white ceiling in an unsettling mesh of swirls and scoops.

The figure opposite dissolved under the light. It was only a patterned gray cloth, draped over a tall, narrow shape that reached nearly to the ceiling. Some kind of ornate coat rack, Margot thought.

She felt tension drain out of her that she hadn't even realized she'd been carrying. A faint nervous chuckle escaped, but the room was so cold and so unwelcoming to the intrusion of noise that Margot pressed her lips together to cut it short.

She was in a living room. Couches and armchairs clustered around the left-hand side, all facing the opposite wall. Two curtain-shrouded windows were divided by a strip of wall, which housed a television so old that Margot felt as though she'd fallen back into a vintage photograph.

Margot herself was used to outdated technology. Her budget had always been tight, and neither she nor her roommates had watched a lot of TV, so their television had already been about a decade old when they bought it.

That was nothing compared to the television ahead of her. It was a box kind, with two antennas pointing out from its dusty top. The thick-framed screen was smaller than a lot of laptops, and the whole thing fit on top of a stand with shelves underneath.

Margot approached the television and crouched to see the contents of the console. The lower two shelves all had VHS tapes with handwritten labels. The script was faded and hard to read, but Margot caught some phrases: *Comedy special. Perfect sticky date recipe. Cartoons.*

The highest shelf held the VCR player to one side and a stack of several dozen TV guides squeezed in beside it. Margot pried the top guide out, flinching as part tore from where it had become jammed in the back corner. The paper was dry with powdery dust. Margot found the date in the upper-right corner: 1997.

It's old. The TV is outdated because they never watched it. They must have never seen any point in trying to replace it.

Now that she looked closer, she saw a sheen of dust across the TV's slightly curved screen. She eased the TV guide back into its narrow gap.

Still crouched, Margot turned to examine the room behind her. A closed door promised access to deeper into the house. Once, many years before even her parents' time, this would have been the heart of the home. There were signs that two rooms had been joined to form a larger space: a line ran across the ceiling, showing where a wall had once existed.

The house must have been relatively modest when it was first contracted, built with small rooms and sturdy doors to retain heat in winter. With each new generation that prospered, though, the house was made larger: an extension on one side, a wall knocked out here, an extra wing added there. Over time, it had sprawled. Margot had gotten some sense of its size from the outside, and it overwhelmed her.

Her eyes were drawn back to the shadowed shape on the wall to her right. She'd thought she'd lost her fear of it when the lights came on, but a sticky, prickling unease continued to needle her. When she looked directly at it, she could see it was simply a woven cloth draped over some tall, narrow stand. Every time she looked away, though, the form remained in her peripheral vision. And it slowly morphed. The coils of fabric pooling around its base grew darker. The top began to look uncannily like a face. And its single, narrowed eye glittered…

Margot grimaced and stood. She folded her arms across her chest as she moved closer to the cloth-draped shape. It loomed above her, its top just inches from the ceiling. The fabric had been embroidered. A line of shiny thread ran across the part she kept mistaking for a head. That accounted for what she kept seeing as an eye.

What's underneath? She'd assumed a decorative coat rack, but that didn't make sense, she realized. She'd never seen a coat rack go to the ceiling before. Or to have its top curve in just the way that a bare skull would be shaped.

As long as she looked at it, she could see it for what it was: a misshapen form covered in loose fabric. But as soon as she tried to turn away, it solidified again. A man with stooped, sloping shoulders, his hands folded ahead of himself, his cold eye fixed hard on Margot.

If this was in my living room, I'd give up on watching TV too.

Margot's palms had become sweaty. She flexed her hands, feeling the chilled joints click, then reached for the pooling edges of the cloth.

The room had been swept often enough that the rest of the floor was clean, but whatever brooms had moved through the space had avoided disturbing the fabric, and clumps of dust clung around its edges, peeling up in fang-like strands as Margot dipped her head to look underneath.

Her heart missed a beat.

Trapped inside of a tangle of wires and string, the empty eye socket of a bird's skull met her gaze.

6.

Thick dread coated the back of Margot's tongue as she met the skull's dried, fissured eye socket. Holes had been bored into the bone to allow tarnished gold and bronze wires to be threaded through, lashing the skull to something much larger underneath.

She lifted more of the cloth. Tendrils of dust floated outward as they were disturbed for the first time in years. As the fabric moved still higher, the shapes beneath shifted. They set up a discordant rattle: bone against metal. Stone grinding across wood. The noise ached in Margot's ears.

Still higher. Margot stretched her arms overhead, gripping fistfuls of the gritty embroidered material. As the center of balance shifted, the fabric's own weight dragged it over and down. Margot let go of the cloth with a gasp and let it pool on the floor behind the shape.

It's a person after all.

At least…it's an effigy of one.

The figure was monstrously distorted, but the inspiration was clear. It was a body. Wider at the base, perhaps to imply some kind of robe or maybe simply because it needed the support, then tapering upward to narrow shoulders and an elongated head.

Is it supposed to be art? It has to be, doesn't it? Something postmodern, made entirely out of...

Her mind blanked. Part of her wanted to call it *trash*. Or perhaps *nature*. But it wasn't entirely either of those things.

Bones were incorporated, mostly small ones: bird skulls, hip bones from what might have been a possum or a fox, and, most uncomfortably, teeth. Pieces of wood were woven between them. There were signs that the wood had been chosen carefully. Willow branches, longer than Margot was tall, had been braided into a cord used to lash other elements together. Shards of long-dried driftwood held elaborate carvings along their length.

It wasn't all organic, though. Keys hung from it, interspersed with old, rusted spoons. They would have caused most of what Margot heard when she removed the cloth. Small pouches, some leather and some fabric, were hidden behind larger objects.

The whole shape had been held together with wires. They looped through and around each element, tying into incomprehensible knots, turning it from a scavenger-hunt collection into one solid form. Smooth river stones were dotted across it, clamped down by the fine, sharp metal.

A deer's skull formed the figure's head. It loomed over Margot, all empty eye sockets and yellowed, elongated teeth. More wire threaded through it, tiny rivers of bronze sprouting out from gaps in the bone and stretching across its bleached form.

Margot tried to swallow, but her mouth was dry. Everything she'd seen about the house up to that point had suggested a comfortable, if mundane, life. She couldn't fathom why the couple who had been content with an aging kitchen and sagging couches might want something like *this* in their home.

When she'd first tried to categorize it in her mind, she'd called it modern art. But that wasn't true. It was the opposite of modern—like a regression to a wilder, older world. Some arcane figure dragged forcibly out from history, powerful and patient and not quite dead.

Gooseflesh rose on the back of her arms, and Margot grabbed for the fabric. The embroidered threads prickled at her palms as she hurled it high, casting it back over the macabre figure. The material was heavy, and her aim was poor, and she ended up with a gap near the floor where parts of the effigy were still visible. She didn't want to fiddle with it, though. The structure was old and, even woven through with wire, looked liable to break if she tried to pull on the cloth. And she didn't want to break it—partially because it must have been in some way important for her parents to keep it in their living room for so many years, and partially because she felt as though damaging the form would invite some kind of horrific misfortune.

You're being superstitious. It's a decoration. Maybe a gift from someone my parents didn't want to upset. Maybe a misguided crafting project by a now-gone relative. My parents didn't seem to like looking at it any more than I do if it was always covered.

She'd have to decide what to do with it eventually. Margot doubted she could let it stay in such a visible location. That meant breaking it up and throwing it out or hiding it somewhere less intrusive, like a shed.

But that would be a problem for another day.

As she turned her back on it, Margot was once again struck by the unnerving way the cloth-covered shape seemed to morph into something human, something *real*, once it was only in her peripheral vision.

Other than the archway to the main hall, the living room had one other doorway: at its rear, behind the row of couches. Margot approached it. She'd half expected it to be just a linen closet, but it opened into another hallway clad in desaturated wood paneling.

Lights hung from the ceiling, but Margot couldn't see a switch. She squinted as she moved into the narrow passage. Her path was lit solely by the glow from the living room at her back.

This part of the house seemed less used. Dust was thicker on the floor and the air tasted stale. Occasional doors broke up the lines in the paneling, but she didn't try to open any of them. She was starting to develop the irrational fear that, if she took too many turns, she might never find her way back to center.

The hallway ended, with new offshoots splitting to the left and the right. Margot turned left and was rewarded by the shape she'd been searching for: the dark angular lines of stairs leading to the second floor.

The wood groaned as she stepped onto the stairway. Margot held one hand just above the railing, in case she might need to catch herself, as though at any second the stairs might begin to writhe and coil in on themselves like a snake.

A small amount of filtered light came from the upper floor. Warm air was supposed to rise, she knew, but the higher she climbed, the colder she felt. The wooden steps gave way to a landing and Margot stopped there, waiting for her eyes to adjust to the new environment.

The wind was louder on the second floor, even though Margot couldn't see any windows. It shuddered across the walls and rattled against the roof above. The landing bent to the side and split into several paths: closed doors, more hallways, and to Margot's right, the source of the light: a large wooden door that hung open.

Its hinges groaned as it shifted backward and forward on air currents. Margot, cautious, moved toward it. This was the first open door she'd seen in the house, she realized. The entrance to the kitchen and the living room had been open archways, but every other door was sealed tight.

As she neared the room, Margot could see the edge of a dresser and, farther back, a window with slowly drifting curtains.

Prickles ran over her skin, flaring across her fingertips like a thousand needles. She knew what this room was and why its door was open.

The master bedroom. Their *bedroom.*

Every other door was closed because that was how her parents had preferred it. Only this room—the room last entered by paramedics when the bodies were removed—was left exposed.

A cold dread dampened Margot's skin and stuck her tongue to the roof of her mouth. She tried to focus on the things Kant had told her: her mother, the hard worker, the problem solver; her father, always delighted by a joke. They were warm thoughts. Not quite a balm on this crossroad between hesitant grief and confusion, but *something.*

Other images cut across those pleasant thoughts—the torn photographs, the caskets in the mortuary's viewing room, and the sights contained inside. She remembered the mortuary owner's soft words. *"We did the best we could…"*

She blinked furiously. The corners of her vision had turned hazy, and Margot realized she wasn't breathing right. Too fast and too shallow, like bellows desperately trying to keep a fire alive.

She pressed one hand to her mouth as she tried to reel herself back to some safer, central place. An unseen window frame rattled as the gale beat at it. Her legs felt weak, her stomach queasy.

You came for closure. And you came for answers, if there were any to be had.

Her shoes scraped across the dull wood floor as she forced her feet to move her forward. A faint, tinny ringing noise had taken up residence in her ears. The door creaked as the wind pulled on it, and Margot reached out a hand to keep it from hitting her. It rolled back under her touch, revealing the room beyond.

Her parents' room. The place where they had breathed their last.

7.

A queen-size bed took up the room's center. Its frame was made of heavy, old wood, much like the rest of the furniture.

Opposite it was a chest of drawers. Beside that, double doors that most likely opened into a closet. A standing mirror was propped in the rear corner. It reflected a glimpse of Margot back to her, the heavy black dress and thick coat. Her dark, curling hair, going frizzy at the ends in response to the humidity. And her face, pinched and sunken and vacant, as though some part of the soul had already faded away, leaving a hollow vessel in its place.

She didn't like seeing herself like that and frowned as she turned away.

The window on the back wall was flanked by curtains. Thick brocade formed dense lines of muddy green to the floor. Behind those and pulled across the glass panes were thin white curtains, designed to let filtered light through. They rippled in the wind, billowing toward Margot like waves.

Another of the service bells hung beside the bed. That was strange, Margot thought; the master bedroom of all places should have a cord to summon the staff, not a bell to *be* summoned. Maybe the rooms had different uses when the system was installed.

She took another step into the room. Her mirror self moved closer in response.

The bed had been stripped. Only the mattress remained, faded and uneven from age. Two indents, one on each side, marked the positions her parents had slept in most nights.

The prickling, stinging sensation in her throat was back. In a strange way, those indents made her parents feel far more real than the photographs had. This was a stamp they'd left on the world. The shape and size of them, forever formed into the mattress, a tangible memory built across thousands of nights.

Margot's hands shook as she reached toward the mattress. It was old and likely at least a decade past needing to be replaced. The stitching had come loose in places, and the colors had faded into a murky gray blur. She touched it and felt a spongy kind of give.

The sheets and quilts, unsalvageable, would have been removed along with the bodies. The mattress had been left, though. Someone must have decided it was too good to throw out, but Margot doubted anyone would want to sleep on it after it had cradled two corpses. She couldn't. Even if the house didn't contain a single other bedroom, she would rather sleep on the sagging couches next to the wire effigy than in the room where her parents had died.

Some people believed that death stained a place. Margot didn't like to think of herself as superstitious, even though superstitious behaviors had a way of creeping into her habits: the slight skip over cracked pavement, the wariness during full moons. She would laugh at herself every time she knocked on wood. But it was hard to deny the unnatural sense of stillness in her parents' room.

Their heartbeats had thrummed through the space every night until they'd abruptly stopped. Their bodies had remained, waiting to be found by Kant that following morning, but their selves—their lives, their souls, their personalities and hopes and fears and most private thoughts—had faded into the ether during that night, sometime between two and four in the morning.

And it almost felt as though part of that essence was still there, suspended in the air, waiting to be breathed in.

"Who were you?" Margot's voice came out as a whisper. She leaned closer to the bed, dropping her voice even further. "Did you know you were going to die that night? Would you have done anything differently if you *had* known?"

She glanced behind herself, paranoid that she was being watched. The bedroom door hung open, but the house was empty and still. Margot swallowed and carefully, gingerly climbed onto the mattress.

The springs creaked as they took her weight. Margot climbed across the space until she reached the shallow bump between her parents' indents, then lay down, her head next to where their heads had once been.

The bed was stiff and smelled of must and age. The mattress, its springs soft, rocked under her with every small movement.

Kant said they were on their backs when he found them.

Margot rolled to face the ceiling. The plaster, a dull shade of white, stretched across the space, interrupted by the molding for the hanging ceiling lights.

Directly above the bed was a crack. It started over Margot's torso and spread out in jagged fissures. And at its center was a stain.

The discoloration was dark, the shade of fetid water and fungal decay. It bloomed like a flower, its overlapping petals showing where it had seeped and dried multiple times.

Its center still looked fresh. Moist. Margot stared at it, her eyes unblinking and her breath whistling between tightly pressed teeth. The fading light through the window seemed to catch on the dampness. She felt certain that, if she lay there long enough, a drop of sour, greasy water would land on her.

She sat up. Her heart ran fast.

It's nothing. A leak. This house is old enough to have more than a few of those.

It was immediately above the bed, though. And according to what Kant had said, her parents both slept on their backs. They must have been staring at it every night as they tried to fall asleep. And they hadn't tried to repair it.

It could be fresh. Maybe it only formed in the last few days, after they passed.

That was impossible, though. She'd seen the countryside on her drive to the house. It was parched. The spitting shower that morning was the first rainfall for some time.

She suddenly hated the idea of being on the mattress. She'd thought it would be an intimate moment, a way to draw closer to her parents. Now it just felt macabre. Margot crawled toward the bed's edge. Before she could reach it, motion made her look up.

The standing mirror had caught her reflection again. Its frame matched the rest of the room's furniture: solid and sturdy. The glass had aged, though. Tarnish spread in from the edges. The reflection was just faintly blurred—not enough to say the mirror no longer worked, but enough that, when looking at a reflection, it wasn't possible to say you were *really* seeing yourself. The reflection was an imitation, an inch off, a convincing replica that distorted around the edges.

Margot looked at herself then, and her heart turned to ice.

The mirror showed her crouched on the bed, one arm reaching toward the edge. The black coat clung to her form. Her hair, dense and dark and just starting to frizz at the edges, framed her face.

And her face…

Her skin had shrunken and puckered. Swollen wrinkles spread over the cheeks and forehead. The eyelids had peeled back. Her eyes were swollen round orbs, barely fitting inside the sockets, bulging and bloated and swallowed in a sick gray tinge. Her lips were shrunken away from the teeth, exposing grimacing yellow bone and gray, pulpy gums.

She appeared dead.

Margot flinched back, her eyes pressed closed. The staccato rhythm of her heart beat through the wind's low howl. Her skin burned with sharp fear, too hot and too cold at the same second.

She opened her eyes. The reflection was how it should be. Her face was her own again. Pinched and wild eyed and the cheeks drained of blood, but familiar.

Margot half threw herself off the bed. She staggered as she hit the floor. Her legs were shaking, and she clutched at the doorframe when she reached it.

Don't look back. Don't—

She looked. She couldn't stop herself.

The bed's mattress held two depressions where two bodies had lain over the years. Margot's own brief moment in the center was already erased, the mattress forgetting her as soon as she was gone.

Past that, the white curtains rolled in huge billows. In that second, they almost seemed to be like white hands, reaching out, stretching toward her.

In the far corner stood the mirror. It captured Margot in the doorway, normal and whole. At least, as close as she could be when she leaned on the house for support to stay upright.

The phantom reflection—not quite in focus, not quite clear—stared back at her. Margot kept her eyes fixed on it, unwilling to turn away, as she reached for the doorknob. She leaned back, watching, waiting for some trick of the light or shimmer in the glass to give her an explanation for what she'd seen. She kept watching until, at last, the latch clicked, and the only open door in the house was once again sealed.

8.

Margot followed the hallway for a dozen shaking steps, intent on putting some distance between herself and the master bedroom, then leaned her back against the wood-paneled wall.

She slid down the surface in increments until her legs poked out at odd angles and her hands could lay loose in her lap. Then she waited.

For what?

For her heart to slow. For her mind to shake free from the sharp panic. For some kind of rationality to give her relief from the image in the mirror.

I saw myself as a corpse.

She ran her tongue across her teeth. Her eyes were half-closed, leaving the opposite wall in a vague, fuzzy blur.

There were plenty of excuses she could conjure to explain the vision. She hadn't eaten since breakfast. The day had been stressful. She was in a new environment, surrounded by new sights, and her brain had malfunctioned for a second.

That could happen easily. One of her roommates had explained the phenomenon to Margot the previous summer. At any one time, the eyes are only taking in a small portion of an environment, so the brain would fill in the gaps from memory. It explained why switching a photo on someone's desk could go unnoticed for days or why a friend's haircut wouldn't register until it was pointed out.

Besides, the sun was close to setting, and the room had been dim. Twilight did strange things to eyes.

They were good reasons. Plausible. Solid.

Margot pressed her hands over her head, a shuddering breath scraping the insides of her lungs.

She might have just believed her own excuses if it had been a glimpse from the corner of her eye. But she'd looked right at herself. Made eye contact with those blurred, grayed pupils. Watched the shrunken lips twitch above the yellowed teeth.

It had not been some accidental glance. It had been real. She'd stared at it, and it had stared back.

A delusion of some kind. Maybe a temporary mental snap. Stress can manifest itself in many ways.

But Margot doubted it could manifest like *that.*

She'd watched her share of horror movies. She'd seen plenty of fictional portrayals of death, both modern and campy. She had to assume, if her mind was intent on tormenting her, it would have plucked inspiration from something it had already seen.

She never in a thousand years would have imagined a corpse looking like the figure in the mirror. The skin had a strange appearance, both shrunken and wrinkled, but the wrinkles had a fullness to them that felt achingly unnatural.

And yet, the moment she saw it, she knew it was a more accurate visage of death than any of the movies had managed. It had resonated. For the first time in her life, she'd seen a corpse, and it had been her own.

Margot knew she wasn't capable of imagining that. Not in her nightmares and not in the waking hours either.

What does that leave?

She lowered her hands and stared at the palms. The creases running across them were barely visible in the darkened hallway, but she'd seen them often enough to remember the shapes. Her life lines were short.

Superstitious. Superstitious.

But maybe it wasn't wrong to open herself to superstitions a little more.

The master bedroom door would stay closed. That was a certainty. If anything was in there—bad air or some darkness from the memory of her parents' deaths—she wasn't going to invite it any farther out into the house.

Margot pulled herself up, using the wall for support. None of her theories could explain what she'd seen. It was possible there was still a rational explanation. She quietly, desperately hoped there was. But her cautious optimism about the house had been shattered.

She knew what the building looked like from the outside. Broad and built from heavy wood, it had stood steadfast for more than a hundred years. But as the wind raged against the walls and the old wood groaned under the pressure, it was hard not to believe the house was on the verge of crumbling in on itself.

Margot ran one hand across the wall as she followed the hallway. With the master bedroom door closed, very little light crept into the space. Thin lines ran from each sealed door, fading out across the wood boards. There had to be a light switch somewhere, but she couldn't find it.

Where are the stairs?

She stopped, squinting into the gloom. She should have arrived at the landing already. In her panic to leave the master bedroom, she must have turned in the wrong direction. Margot ran her tongue across her lips and looked behind herself.

A soft *tap tap tap* echoed at her back. She froze, her ears straining. The sound had been faint, filtered through the dense walls, but unmistakable.

It's the wind. Nothing to worry about.

Margot rubbed at the back of her neck. From the dim outlines she could see, the hallway continued on for another twenty feet before turning to the left. Heavy shadows clung to the wood paneling like cobwebs, playing with her eyes.

The sound repeated—three low, heavy taps. Like wood hitting wood. Coming from behind the closest door to her right.

She'd reached for the handle before she could stop herself. Adrenaline still ran through her, and the panicked terror clung to her nerves like static. Her mind painted pictures of what could be emitting the dull taps, so much like knuckles rapping on a window to be let in, but in that moment, she feared *not* seeing the other side of the door more.

The hinges released a slow, grinding cry as they turned. The door wasn't used often. As it drifted inward, Margot held herself stiffly, her legs slightly bent as she prepared to dart back.

The room was doused in grays as the cloud-smothered sun began to set. The walls were all covered in faintly patterned tan wallpaper except for a sky-blue feature to her left. Opposite, a french window overlooked a view of the field around the property that Margot hadn't seen before. Its right-hand pane had been unlatched and left open. As she watched, the wind buffeted it in, resounding with the three heavy, dull *tap tap tap*s.

Margot pressed a held breath out between her clenched teeth. She crossed the room, moving around a single bed that stood against the feature wall, and pulled the window closed. It was old and the wooden frame was slightly swollen, and it grated as she dragged it into place.

There was no sign of water damage on the sill or floor, except for a few drops from that afternoon. Her parents must have left it open recently to air out the room, then either forgotten about it...or passed before they had a chance to close it again.

A hasp lock had been screwed into the frames where they met. The metal was old, bleeding rust onto the wood. An open padlock hung from the left-hand side, with its key still inside. Clearly, the window was intended to be locked at night.

I don't understand. Why would you need such a heavy lock for a window?

She frowned as she leaned closer to the glass, straining to see over the porch beneath.

And why on the second floor?

Slowly, she turned back to face the room. It was sparsely furnished, suggesting an unused guest room. Another of the bronze service bells hung near the door.

The single bed against the blue wall was covered with a flowery quilt. The bed was adult size, but the quilt's colors made her think it had been intended for a child instead.

Margot gently touched the material. It was slightly dusty but not enough to say it had sat untouched for years. It felt more like a bed that was refreshed every six months or so in case it was ever needed.

A slow, sticky premonition grew in her stomach, making her queasy. Margot approached the double-door wardrobe inset in the opposite wall. Ideas of bright dresses and muddy child-size overalls danced behind her eyes, but when she dragged the doors open, the racks were empty. The only things inside were a cluster of mothballs forgotten at the wardrobe's back and two dozen wire hangers, jangling against one another at the sudden intrusion.

Margot slumped, resting her head on the door's cool edge as she stared at the barren wardrobe. A floor-length mirror had been attached to the back side of the door. It was milky and faintly tarnished, much like the one in her parents' bedroom, and Margot refused to make eye contact with it.

A small, white shape peeked out from between the mothballs. She crouched to reach for it, the wire hangers snagging at the flyaway strands of her hair as she plucked a small, folded piece of paper out from the back corner.

The scrap was small enough to be swallowed inside her palm if she made a fist. Margot unraveled the painstakingly folded sheet. Inside were sketches: the same shape over and over again. A butterfly, a smile on its misshapen head. Endless, uncertain patterns swirled through its wings, not quite perfectly mirrored.

"Ha."

Her voice felt foreign in her own ears. Margot walked backward until she hit the end of the bed, then sat on it, the paper cradled in her hands.

She remembered drawing that butterfly design endless times at school after she moved in with her grandmother. The design in the wings had been different each time, but the butterfly always had two eyes and a broad, curling smile.

The wardrobe had been cleared out completely...except for the drawing, fallen from a pocket or discarded there after a play session.

Margot lifted her head and examined the room with fresh eyes.

Her parents might have cleared it out thoroughly after she left, but they'd missed the paper hidden under the mothballs. Even Margot herself had forgotten the space. But it hadn't entirely forgotten her.

This was her room.

9.

The sun had almost set when Margot left her old room. She felt heavier, like time had found ways to creep into the creases and linings in her jacket and now pulled her inexorably toward the floor.

If she turned left, she would retrace her steps toward where she knew the staircase had to be. But that would also mean passing by the master bedroom. Margot pressed her lips together and turned right instead. The hallway continued on for another twenty feet before turning. Margot had no sense of where she was in the house's layout or even what might lie in that direction, but when she turned the corner, she was rewarded by the sight of a second staircase leading to the ground floor.

She followed it down. The atmosphere grew lighter with each step, and as she ducked her head to see under the ceiling, she discovered why. Ahead was a straight hallway leading to a large outside door. Light flowed through an archway to the right. And propped against the wall were her two travel cases. She'd followed an elongated loop and found her way back to where she'd started.

Margot retreated to the kitchen, where she feasted on something that probably shouldn't have been called dinner: two granola bars and a cold breakfast burger that she'd bought from a takeaway joint next to her motel that morning. The eggs in the breakfast burger had taken on a strange consistency and bacon grease oozed from the bun with each bite, but Margot hadn't eaten for most of the day, and it tasted delicious.

She'd bought the extra food under the suspicion—accurate, as it turned out—that there might not be much opportunity to go shopping. Already, the sky was black, and the kitchen was lit by a dim bulb above her.

As she folded up the empty burger wrapper and reached for the granola bars, her mind slipped back to the mirror in the master bedroom.

Already the image had grown dull in her mind. The distorted face had gained a slightly cartoonish appearance. She could still remember the utter, heart-freezing terror from the moment, but now the reaction felt overblown, like a nightmare that consumed her on waking but gradually faded with each passing hour until it felt irrelevant.

Margot pulled a face as she chewed through the sticky, crumbly block of oats and raisins. She'd expected something like that would happen. As her would-be-psychologist roommate was fond of saying, the human brain was an expert at rationalizing and diminishing things that it didn't fully understand.

That didn't mean she could safely discard the memory. But she *was* grateful. She'd have to sleep in the Gallows Hill house that night, and she didn't think that would be possible if the mirror image was still clear in her mind.

Once she'd cleaned up from her meal, Margot carried her luggage up to her old bedroom. There would be other spare rooms hidden behind the closed doors, but she'd run out of daylight and the idea of searching the aging house at night seemed like it would be tempting an unpleasant fate.

Besides, it felt appropriate to return to the old room. It had been hers once. It would be hers again.

She used her heel to nudge the door closed, then exhaled heavily as she placed the luggage cases on the floor. The ceiling light's thick glass shade had gathered years' worth of dust and discoloration, and it dulled the light more than diffused it. The shadows around the space were heavier than Margot would have liked, especially in the corners, but at least the bedding was relatively clean.

The house felt too large and too empty. Margot stood near the end of the bed for a moment, her eyes running over the faint tan patterns in the wallpaper, as she listened to the wind howling beyond the window.

She wasn't sure how her parents had coped with the building. Her grandmother had told her she was an only child, and there had been no other relatives mentioned in their will. They must have spent every night like Margot now was: alone in a house vastly too large for them, bouncing through a handful of familiar rooms while countless other spaces remained sealed and forgotten.

It would have been a lonely way to live.

Margot crossed to the window. Through it, she caught a distant blush of light, filtered through the patchy trees behind the property. That would have to be the town. She'd driven through it on her way to the church that morning but hadn't stopped to examine it any more closely.

See? People do live nearby. You're not entirely isolated.

She dabbed her tongue across cold lips. The lights seemed miles away.

They weren't her only company, though. There was the cluster of worker accommodations farther down the hill. Ten employees including Kant stayed on the property.

Employees who are waiting for my decision.

A distant grouping of trees, their scratchy branches barely visible against the dark sky, rocked in a dizzying loop. Margot closed her eyes.

She hadn't been expecting to inherit a business. Certainly not one that large. Kant had offered to show her how to manage it, but she still didn't know if she would be enough. She knew nothing about wine.

Businesses failed often and easily. Margot didn't know if she could forgive herself if she became responsible for killing this one.

She could sell the business. But there was no guarantee it would see a better fate under someone else's control.

My parents spent their life building this. They must have loved it more than anything. And they left it to me, probably hoping that I would continue it after their death.

A dark, bitter thought slipped in. *Maybe if they'd kept me, maybe if they'd raised me here, I'd have a better chance of not ruining it.*

Her throat was starting to ache again. Margot turned, putting her back to the window as she folded her arms. The frames rattled as chilled air worked its way through the cracks.

More than her own grief and guilt, she needed to think about the employees. Gallows Hill Winery was an unexpected windfall for her. She'd never factored it into her life plan, and she could have continued to live happily without it.

It was another story for the staff. They relied on its income.

Kant had said the business could pay their wages…at least for the short term. But a decision needed to be made, and sooner rather than later.

She didn't have much else waiting for her back home since her nana had passed. The junior sales position she'd held at a city clothing store had few chances for promotion and saw a high turnover. Margot had already been there longer than she'd planned. She'd asked for a week off for the funeral, but a simple phone call to the manager would see her taken off the roster permanently.

She'd rented an apartment with two friends from her class, but one had emigrated overseas and the other was talking about moving in with a boyfriend. Margot would need to find a new place to stay eventually; why not here, in Leafell?

And then what?

Then she would live at the Gallows Hill Estate, in this enormous house. She would try to learn the business. She would give it her best attempt. Four weeks seemed fair. That should be long enough to know whether she could survive in the business, and if, at the end of four weeks, she truly hated it, she would sell it instead.

Who knows? You might be able to do this.

You might even love it.

The corners of her lips twitched, but she wasn't sure whether she was trying to laugh or cry.

She was desperately aware of how rare opportunities like this were. A house and a business, each worth more than all of her current possessions combined, had been handed to her. She felt achingly ungrateful for the way she was shirking them.

Except that, sometimes, an unasked-for gift could easily begin to look like a burden.

She would try, though. For her parents. Whatever their reasons for sending her away, she must have meant *something* to them if they had left all of their worldly goods to her. And so she would try to do the right thing, to keep the workers employed, to keep the winery running.

And she would just have to hope that she was enough.

Margot turned back to the window. The panes were closed, but she hadn't touched the padlock. It hung from its bracket, the shackle open, the key still in place. For a second she considered locking the window, as had clearly been intended. It was a ridiculous thought. And a terrifying one.

What was she locking the window *against*? And why only in this room? None of the downstairs windows had locks, and if theft was any kind of concern, that was where they would be most needed.

She gingerly lifted the padlock. It was heavy. Like many things in the home, it seemed old, but Margot suspected its mechanism would still work. She let it drop back again.

The night was still early, hours before her normal bedtime, but Margot's sleep in the motels had been erratic and she was ready for the day to be over. She lifted the first suitcase onto the foot of the bed and began unpacking. She hadn't brought much. A lot of her old possessions—furniture, board games, and the television—had been joint purchases with her roommates and left at her old apartment.

That meant her life neatly fit into the suitcases. They could have belonged to a traveler: stacks of clothes, a bag of toiletries, a few of her favorite novels, and a spare set of sneakers.

Her bag held her cell phone, which in turn held everything valuable to her: hundreds of photos with her nana, her calendar—which would be shockingly bare once she asked to be taken off her old work's roster—and contacts, mostly for people she hadn't spoken to in years.

Everything else had been left back at the apartment...and could stay there. Margot chewed her lip as she considered how little her life had boiled down to. There wasn't much. Not enough to fill the house she'd found herself in. Barely enough to fill the wardrobe, even.

She hung her clothes on the clattering metal hangers, then carefully pulled off the black coat and dress. The coat was old, but the dress was new, bought from the store she worked at on the same afternoon she'd gotten the lawyer's phone call. It had been expensive and would probably live out most of its life in storage, but she hadn't owned anything that would be appropriate for a funeral.

As she hung the dress, she was faintly aware of her own movements in the mirror on the inside of the door. She glanced at her reflection.

White lines ran like rivers across her torso, threading from her collarbone, under her bra, and ending near her navel. They'd faded over time, but the scars would never fully vanish.

She remembered examining them at her nana's house, back when she was a scrawny child with sharply jutting elbows and knees. They'd been brighter then, harsh against her skin, but not quite fresh at that point either. She'd run fingertips across the jagged, overlapping lines like she was tracing roads on a map.

They'd never made her self-conscious. She'd shown them off to her classmates—usually to shrieks or recoiling fascination—but now, as an adult, she mostly kept them hidden under high necklines. There wasn't any shame involved. She just didn't like the attention they drew. People would look concerned or ask questions, or very pointedly try not to stare at them. To Margot, though, they were no more noteworthy than her toes or her ears: just a body part that she thought about rarely.

The one time she'd asked her nana about them, she had gently explained that Margot had been attacked by a dog when she was very little. But there had been something in the explanation—some lack of conviction—that left Margot with the sense that her grandmother hadn't had all the answers either.

This house has a dog door. She hung the dress absentmindedly. There were pieces of a puzzle there, but they didn't fit together quite right. She'd never been afraid of dogs. Even the snarling ones with huge teeth had only ever looked like possible friends.

Maybe I forgot I was supposed to fear them, just like I forgot everything else.

She sighed, then shuddered. The room was cold. She wished she'd thought to bring some kind of heater.

Her creased flannel pajama set was thick at least. She pulled it on with trembling fingers, covering up the myriad lines. In the quiet between her breaths, she could hear soft taps at the window, telling her the spitting rain was back.

Margot turned out the light and crawled into the bed. The old sheets were clean, but she still moved gingerly, as though there might be something old and rotten at the foot of the bed, waiting for her bare toes to press against it.

She lay awake for a long time, kept sober by the pervasive chill as she waited for dreams to claim her. When they finally did, they were queasy and upsetting, full of memories of that morning, of approaching the caskets, of seeing what remained of Hugh and Maria Hull.

10.

"It's just this way."

The funeral director walked only a few paces ahead of Margot, but his voice seemed to echo, as though it came to her down a long tunnel.

The scene was familiar. The funeral parlor: decorated in dark-stained woods and faded fabrics. Red carpet lined the halls but peeled up in patches, threadbare where thousands of feet had paced before.

A small bronze key came out of the funeral director's pocket. *Walter*, Margot remembered belatedly. His name had been Walter. A disarmingly comforting name. His suit was old but kept pristinely clean. Thinning hair had been combed across the top of his head. He had a gentle face. Almost too meek and soft to belong to someone who tended the dead.

The key went into the lock in a tall, dark door at the end of the hall. Margot knew what would be on the other side. She wanted to pull away, to walk backward until she was out of the funeral parlor entirely, but her muscles wouldn't move. Acidic fear burned in her veins as she realized she was trapped in the memory, unable to alter or escape what was about to happen.

The lock clicked and the door opened. Walter moved through first, then held the door as Margot stepped into the cool, dim viewing room at the back of the parlor.

Rows of coffins stood upright against the walls on either side, display units that, in the moment, had felt more like sentries. A physical manifestation of mortality, a promise: one day you will lay in us too.

Ahead, beneath a window set high in the wall, were two caskets. Walter approached them first, and his soft face sent Margot an uncertain glance. "The viewing is optional."

He'd already warned her—what waited inside the caskets would not be a peaceful representation of death.

And Margot, trapped in her own body, was incapable of stopping herself from saying, "Please."

The funeral director dipped his head in acknowledgment, then lifted the lids on both caskets. He stepped to one side, hands folded, to allow Margot access. She screamed inside her own mind as her feet dragged her closer and she craned her neck to see inside.

The funeral director was speaking again, though she barely heard him: "We did our best, but…"

A sharp alarm cut across the memory. Margot jolted upright, a gasped breath dragging through her choked throat, sweat-dampened blankets sliding off her and exposing her to the icy air.

She couldn't remember where she was. The walls were foreign, the window alien. She reached toward where she kept her bedside lamp but her fingers only touched air. Then the memories snapped back to her like an elastic band, and she keeled forward, groaning.

Home. This is home now.

The sound that had broken her dreams continued. A shrill, chiming alarm, loud and close by. The room was dripping in heavy moonlight. Margot squinted into the darker corners of the space and saw a flicker of movement.

The service bell danced on its hook.

Her pulse pounded through her, stirred into a frenzy by the nightmare. She clenched her teeth until they ached as she stared at the bell. It bounded wildly. Something, somewhere in the house, was pulling on the cord with such fury that it seemed close to breaking.

One twisted, frightened thought flashed through her mind: *I should have locked the window.*

She was out of her bed before she could stop herself. The cold padlock was heavy in her hand as she grappled with the key.

No. Stop. Think.

Margot slowly let the metal slide out of her grip. Whatever was pulling on the service bell wasn't outside her window. If she locked it now, she would be barring a possible escape from the house.

Slowly, she turned to face the bell. The moonlight flashed across its tarnished bronze. It jolted one last time, then finally fell still. The aching chimes hung in the air for a second longer and then they, too, were gone.

Her lungs ached. She made herself breathe again, but couldn't manage much more than shallow gasps.

What does this mean? Is someone in the house?

She darted her eyes across the room, searching its dark corners and lingering on the empty travel cases, as though the stranger might be there, crouching in the shadows, grinning as it watched her reaction.

Margot crept toward the door. Her back itched at being left exposed. Cold wood spread its chill through her bare feet.

If someone was inside the home, she had two choices. She could barricade her bedroom door and spend the rest of the night hoping and praying that whatever was outside couldn't get in...or she could leave her room and search the dark house.

She glanced toward the bed. It was the only item in the room big enough to hold the door closed. Maybe. Depending on how determined the intruder was.

And then what? Lie down and try to sleep, listening to every creaking floorboard as the night drags on and on?

The alternative was a thousand times worse, but at the same instant, it didn't seem like she had a choice.

I'd feel safer if I didn't have to search it alone.

Margot found her bag next to the bed and fumbled for her cell phone in the dark. It flicked on at her touch. Eight percent battery. She ground her teeth.

She should have entered Kant's number when she had the chance. Instead, it was waiting for her downstairs, still on the fridge.

The bell remained silent, but as she watched it, she thought she saw it twitch a fraction. It could have been a trick of the light. Or it could have been more.

Margot's pulse writhed like a live thing in her throat, swelling the skin with each pass. She slipped her sneakers over numb feet and then pressed her bedroom light on. Slowly, her movements silent, she opened the door.

She didn't know where the intruder might be. She'd seen multiple bells as she searched the house but hadn't yet found one of the pull cords used to activate them.

They're usually kept in the places where the homeowners spend their time. But...where is that exactly?

The bedroom's open door allowed a trapezoid of light to flow across the hall outside. Margot's silhouette blocked its center, but it still grazed across the wooden walls and the edge of another door.

She didn't have anything that could resemble a weapon. Her room had very little furniture, and Margot's own possessions were all small and soft.

With the house's other doors all kept closed and with the lightbulb in Margot's room muted by its layer of dust, the passageway in both directions remained nearly indistinguishable. She turned on her phone's flashlight function. It would drain the battery, but she dreaded the heavy darkness surrounding her and what it might hide.

The artificially white light spread out in a haze. It still wasn't capable of reaching the hallway's end. She held the phone out ahead of herself, as though that might do something to ward off an unwelcome presence, and left her room. Somewhere deeper in the house, a floorboard creaked. Probably the wood flexing as the night air cooled it. Probably.

Margot wet her lips, then called, "Hello!"

Her voice was absorbed into the home's deepest recesses. She received no reply.

Margot took another step out from the safety of her room. "This house is no longer empty! The new owner moved in this morning! You have to leave immediately."

Any authority her words might have conveyed was betrayed by the waver in her voice.

She wanted to believe the bell had been rung by some unassuming presence. A child or bored teen from the town, maybe, who wanted to explore a house they believed to be vacant.

But she already knew it wouldn't—couldn't—be that simple. The town wasn't large, and based on the glances cast at her during the wake, her presence there had been expected. Even if word of her arrival hadn't spread, the intruder couldn't have missed her bright-red hatchback parked in the front lawn.

Whoever had entered her home knew she was here.

Margot turned left, toward the stairs that would carry her to the ground floor. Her sneakers were soft, but every small flex and groan from the aged floorboards carried, magnified by the deep night air. She hung close to the wall, near enough that her shoulder almost brushed against it. She couldn't shake the sensation that something lingered in the darkness behind her, but every time she turned, her phone's light only hit the walls, the floors, and her open bedroom door.

Get to the kitchen. Get near an exit.

The labyrinthine house seemed to close in around her, its walls folding toward her and its ceiling sagging under the weight of the shadows. Heavy sounds carried from its depths: sighs and creaks, soft shifting noises that competed with her own labored breathing.

She reached the corner. Breath held, she extended the phone ahead of herself, lighting the passageway.

There was no sign of the stairs that should have been there. Just more hallway, more doors, and more turns.

She looked behind herself. The bedroom broadcast its band of light. The stairs should have been just around the corner from it, but somehow, the house had turned her around.

Focus. Rethink your steps.

Margot slipped around the corner, one hand pressed to the wall to remind herself of its solidness, its stability. She might have misremembered how far away the stairs were. The odds of that seemed more hopeful than the idea of turning back and retracing her steps into a different, darker corner of the home.

She held her tongue between her teeth as she followed the hall. The doors seemed endless. She didn't try any of them. Lights were set into the ceiling above her, but she hadn't found any trace of their switch.

Her ears strained to hear any foreign noises in the house. Only, the house *itself* was foreign. At her old apartment, she'd been able to tell in a heartbeat what was normal for the building and what was out of place. She didn't have any of that familiarity with the new home, and every sound felt like a warning. Its walls sighed. Its hidden window frames rattled. There were distant noises she couldn't even place—faint cracks and pops and creaks that left her skin prickling with unease.

Another corner loomed ahead. She felt on the verge of not being able to go any farther. Already, her room's light had all but faded. If she turned that corner, she wasn't entirely certain she could find her way back. A nauseating idea flashed through her mind: being lost, her phone's light dead, all but blind as she roamed the maze of her home by touch alone. She would be utterly lost and utterly alone... or, worse, stalked in the dark by something that lingered just a few paces behind.

She leaned around the corner. Her phone's light hit a polished banister, and Margot's breath hitched. She'd found a set of stairs.

Thank mercy.

She didn't know where they would let her out, but at least she would be on the ground floor. One step closer to the door. To Kant's number. To safety.

Set next to the stairs was a light switch, nearly invisible against the textured wood. She pressed it.

The bulb above the stairs lit up. It flared bright, brighter than Margot had expected, brighter than she thought the house and its aged-stained walls could tolerate, then burst with a sharp pop.

The darkness rushed back in, leaving Margot gasping in its wake. Her phone's light, which had seemed too bright when she first activated it, now seemed feeble. She checked its battery. Down to 6 percent. A *low power* warning had appeared on the screen.

She didn't have much of a choice. Margot angled the light down. It flowed across the steps and the dusty banister. She took a step forward, then froze. The light had glanced over something on the ground floor.

Something that looked horribly like flashing eyes in the pitch-darkness.

Just the wooden floor. It's polished. It'll reflect light like that.

She knew that, but her heart still thundered and her body ached with coils of fear wound so tight that she felt on the verge of breaking. The eyelike lights had only been visible for an instant. She tried changing the phone's angle, but they wouldn't return. She could see the top three steps clearly, the next four vaguely, and scarcely anything beyond that.

The acrid taste of fear coated her tongue. Margot didn't dare move, didn't dare to so much as blink, as her wild gaze stayed fixated on the place she'd thought she'd seen the lights.

It's nothing. Your imagination. An overactive mind stimulated by the dark.

But what if it wasn't? Someone had been in the house. It was quiet now, but she'd heard the bell ring. The cords were stiff and old. They wouldn't move to anything trivial like the wind. Someone had tugged on them, and tugged hard enough to wake her.

They might have left. Maybe they just wanted to spook you. A prank. A hazing.

She'd heard no car motors, though, and it was a long walk to anywhere of significance. The employee accommodations were the closest buildings she'd seen, and even they were a hike away.

But that still didn't mean she'd actually seen something at the stair's base.

She tried to make herself move, to take even one step forward, but her body had locked up. Flight or fight, her psychology roommate would have said, except she'd entered the third possible state: *freeze*. Her mouth opened in a bare-toothed grin that didn't extend to her eyes. She was being ridiculous. Her light didn't reach far enough to show her the stairwell's base, but there couldn't be a person standing there. There just couldn't.

And yet she still could not step forward.

Just go. Do it quickly. Run for the door and worry about everything else after you've reached it.

Her leg muscles ached from how tightly they were locked in place.

A horrible sense developed: that her focus was fixed on the wrong area. That, while she was staring down the fading stairwell and into the pit of darkness below, something was emerging from the glut of darkness behind. Inching out of the shadows at her back, moving on silent feet, its unblinking eyes fixed on the back of her head as she stood ignorant at the top of a pit that would drag her down to certain death should she be tipped forward.

She couldn't breathe any longer. She wanted to turn, to confront the darkness behind her, but the faster her heart pounded, the tighter her muscles clenched. She couldn't even take her eyes off the space below. In her peripheral vision, she saw her phone's battery hit 4 percent.

The bells started ringing again.

Harsh, clattering tones rushed around her as rusted metal beat out a warning. There was no longer just one but a dozen, chiming from every corner in the house simultaneously—inside rooms, along hallways, ahead and behind and below. The sound assaulted her ears, the clashing peals dizzying.

But it broke the spell. Margot lurched forward, her sneakers hitting each step with a heavy thud as she raced for the ground floor. Her light jarred with each bound, no longer fixed steadily on the stairwell but glancing across the walls, the steps, the ceiling, and occasionally flashing in Margot's eyes and blinding her.

She hit the ground hard, sliding on the old floor, before catching herself on the wall.

The bells were louder. She tried to place them, but there were too many, coming from every direction, and she no longer knew where she was in the house.

Margot hunched against the wall, directing the light first ahead and then to the left, and then to the passageway at her side. Her bedroom window had overlooked the house's rear. She'd turned left out of it and then turned left again...or had it been right?

The bells made it impossible to think, and the darkness distorted the space until she doubted she would recognize it even if she'd passed through before.

She thought the house's front must be ahead but had no context for how far away that might be. She moved forward. A bell, hidden somewhere in a room to her right, grew louder and then dulled again as she passed it. Her breathing was labored, and dust and the tang of mildew and cold decay dragged her throat raw with each inhale. She hit a corner and pushed herself around it, no longer moving cautiously but racing—racing the fading battery in her phone and racing whatever presence was in the house, perhaps behind her, perhaps gaining with every step.

The bells drowned out everything. Her own breaths, the pounding of her footfalls, even the croak of her voice as a rough, panicked gasp escaped her.

And then, ahead, light. Not much, but there was a blue-moon blush inside the acres of darkness. That meant windows. And windows meant she had found one of the external walls.

Margot lurched toward it, hope and growing urgency forming an aching concoction in her chest. She couldn't see much of where the light came from, only that it was blocked by curtains, leaving only a thin trace around the edges. She reached her free hand toward the cloth as she grew nearer, eager to tear the curtains back and bathe the room in moonlight, but she was still half a room away when her cell phone's light fell on something else.

A presence. Tall. Standing to her left, facing her.

Two black-socket eyes stared down at her from a deformed, ash-white face.

Margot rocked backward, a wordless cry dying in her terror-choked throat. Her ankle hit something hard and unyielding. For a heartbeat she grappled with her balance, trying to find her footing as she grasped at thin air. She fell, and she fell hard.

Her elbow collided with the floor first and sent a jolt of raw pain along her arm. The phone bounced free, tumbling over hard wood floorboards before coming to rest with its light aimed toward the ceiling.

Eyes blurred by the shock and pain, Margot blinked as she tried to see through the diffused light and the flecks of dust free floating around her.

The figure stood ahead, unmoving, the too-long face directing its empty gaze into her.

The effigy. She'd found her way to the lounge room.

Margot swallowed wetly as she crept onto her knees. Every flex of her elbow resparked channels of pain. She glanced to her right and confirmed the glint of the curved TV screen. The light crept in around the curtains on either side of it. And it wasn't entirely moonlight, she realized. The blue was slowly being tinted by the dusty, purplish flush of dawn. High up on the hill, her family's home would be first to see the new day's dawn.

The house was silent again, she realized. The bells had fallen still.

In some ways, that felt like a worse omen than listening to them chime.

Margot turned back to the deer-skull effigy. The cloth she'd used to cover it now lay pooled about its base. It could have slipped free on its own, she reasoned. But she didn't like how, out of every object in the house, *this* was the one that had been exposed.

At least she knew where she was again. Margot took up her phone and cradled it close as, moving more by memory than by sight, she crossed from the living room through the hallway and into the kitchen.

The dozens of ragged-edged photos on the fridge reflected her phone's light back at her. In that ephemeral gap between night and dawn, the smiling faces took on a strained quality. As though every posed photo had been forced, as though the eyes that stared up at her were filled with pleas for help, begging for her to notice, to save them. Margot, shivering, looked away.

Kant's number was still pinned where he'd left it. Margot had half typed it into the phone when she hesitated. Dawn was nearly here, and with it came clarity that hadn't existed in the depths of night. Was she really going to wake the winery's manager just because she'd had a bad dream and let a dark house send her into a frenzy of fear?

Yes. She resumed typing. *Someone rang those bells. Someone was in your house. Don't let daylight lull you into a false sense of security.*

Margot held her phone to her ear. The kitchen window overlooked the driveway. She caught a glimpse of her red car. Its color seemed to hold a sickly tinge.

It wasn't just her car, she realized. The whole world was tainted by that predawn gray-purple halo. It was the color of malnourished grapes, gone rotten before they ripened. The color of a freshly drowned corpse.

There was a click, then a calm, sleep-heavy voice crackled through her cell phone. "Kant."

"Hey—" Margot cut off. Something moved outside the window. Something that looked like rope.

She took a step closer, straining to see through the dirty panes. The rope shifted slightly, and she was sure she heard the deep, aching creak of fibers being strained.

Her phone was silent. Margot lowered it. The screen was black; its battery had finally been emptied.

Margot shivered against the cold saturating the kitchen as she pushed the dead phone into her pocket. The flannel pajamas were designed to keep her warm in bed; they did next to nothing to combat the early morning frost that wormed around the window's edges and under the doors. Her body was pocked with gooseflesh, each breath sapping more of her warmth away.

She moved almost against her will. Soft, padding steps carried her back into the hallway and toward the front door. Beyond, she heard the rope creak. Margot swallowed and tasted the tang of blood. She'd cut the inside of her cheek at some point. Mostly likely when she fell. She'd barely noticed the pain, but now the cloying metallic taste coated her tongue, nauseating.

She reached for the door handle. Her skin was already taut, the hairs standing alert, but as she touched the bronze handle, quivers passed through her like electricity.

Don't.

She didn't want to see what was outside. But a deep, crawling yearning need to *know* had boiled up inside of her. She didn't want to see. But she *had* to.

The door juddered as she forced it open. The night chill had infused it with moisture, getting through the cracks in the paint and swelling it. The hinges creaked as they turned, and beyond, the rope creaked in a matching tune.

The hazy, sickly purple light flowed across her. Cold air whipped in, dragging at the loose flannel around her arms and legs.

Margot tried to breathe but couldn't. Ahead of her, suspended directly in front of the door, was a length of rope. It was old. Dirt crusted it. Small threads wove around the twisting cords, likely loose fibers but possibly roots. Possibly hair. The rope looked like it might have been lying on a forest floor for months. No, years. It was age weathered, faded in places and stained in others, both heavy and fragile with age.

The rope had been tied to one of the beams on the underside of the porch's roof. It trailed down to shoulder height, then curled back and tied to itself, forming a loop the size of Margot's head.

She clung to the doorframe as her legs threatened to collapse. Her ears were clogged with a distant, tinny ringing noise. Even as she watched, the rope swung loosely, and a slow, aching creak rose from where it was fastened.

More movement appeared in her peripheral vision. Slowly, unwillingly, Margot turned her head. This wasn't the only length of rope tied outside her home. One hung near the kitchen window. One was farther down, near where the wall turned, draped nearly to the wooden floor. Another on her other side, catching the sickly dawn light.

Six in total.

Six nooses, suspended from the beams outside her front door.

12.

Margot sat on the porch's top step. Her feet were numb, and the skin around her fingernails had turned blue. She couldn't bring herself to move, though—not back into that home, not back past the row of nooses suspended like a barricade around the doorway.

She wasn't sure how long she'd sat there already but knew it couldn't be long. The sun was barely rising, just in the earliest stages of transforming the sickly purple into its more vivid golds.

In the distance, a figure moved toward her. She recognized the stride. Kant, moving in long, loping steps that made his limp more pronounced. He must have come because of her phone call.

Margot was faintly aware that she wasn't in a good state to meet anyone. Clad in pajamas, her hair clinging to the condensation that formed on her throat and jaw, unable to slow her heart or even think coherently. It still wasn't enough to make her turn around and go inside.

Behind her, one of the ropes creaked.

"Margot." He'd been moving fast, but it hadn't made him breathless.

Kant stopped when he was still a half dozen paces from her and turned, slowly, to survey the house at a distance. "Something happened?"

She wasn't sure if her voice would work, but tried regardless. "Bells."

The word was cracked and raspy. Her throat was parched. She tried to swallow but it only hurt.

"The bells were ringing?" He glanced at her, then looked away again, still surveying the property. "Did anything else happen?"

She wasn't sure what he expected of her but raised one numb hand toward the ropes hung from her home. "Look. Someone wants me gone."

He nodded once, calm eyes flitting across the nooses. "I suppose it would look that way to you."

Margot blinked furiously to calm her burning eyes. "They're...nooses. That's got to be meant as a warning."

"Maybe. But not toward you in particular." Kant exhaled deeply, his shoulders slumping. He closed the distance between himself and Margot and leaned one weathered hand on the stair's banister.

"But..."

"Nooses have been appearing around here for as long as I've worked the place. That's near thirty years. Sometimes you won't see them for a few years at a time, and then they'll come in batches. Like now."

Margot turned just enough to glimpse the ropes. Aged, frayed, clogged with dirt, they moved slowly in the wind. The knots where the nooses were tied appeared viciously tight. "But...why?"

"You don't know much about the place, I suppose." His gray eyes scanned her, and there was something in them. Sadness? Or regret? He turned away before Margot could get any proper reading on it. "Come up, then. Let me get you something warm to drink."

Kant knew the house better than Margot did. He found a thick blanket from somewhere and wordlessly passed it to her as she inched her stiff body into the kitchen. Kant turned the oven on and opened the door—presumably to heat the room—then set about making drinks.

Margot wrapped the blanket around herself, then slid into the same chair she'd taken the day before. The sounds—the kettle beginning to rattle, the soft scrape and slide of Kant's shoes, the way he sighed when he reached for mugs on a high shelf—were so commonplace, so banal, that it seemed almost impossible to fear the house in that moment.

Almost.

Margot leaned back in her seat. Through the open kitchen archway, she could see across the hall to the lounge room. The sun should have been hitting that wall but very little light made its way past the thick curtains. She could barely see the effigy, shrouded in darkness at the back of the room.

"Where do the ropes come from?" Margot asked.

Kant leaned one hand on the counter as he poured hot water with his other. "Can't answer that."

"It's been happening for years…and no one knows who's responsible?" Margot pulled the blanket tighter around herself. The cold had invaded her very core. "Hasn't anyone called the police?"

"Sure. Couple times. Not much they could do." Kant returned to the table and placed one of the mugs ahead of Margot. "It has honey in it. Will help with the shock."

She frowned at the drink. "But…"

"Why nooses?" Kant had somehow guessed her next question. He dropped into his chair, his shaggy, gray hair catching light from the window. "That's because of the place's history, I suppose."

"Gallows Hill," Margot murmured, suddenly making the connection.

He gave a small noise of assent. "Several hundred years ago, this land was used for executions. It wasn't much of a town back then, more like a wilderness with scattered houses clinging together for survival.

There was a lot of crime. Mostly out of desperation. Thefts and the like to put food on tables, but also murders when disagreements couldn't be settled with words. The lawmakers back then had only one solution. Hanging."

Margot held the mug close to her chest. It was hot enough to scorch her skin, but that was the only sense of warmth she had left in her body, so she clung to it.

"The hangings happened on this hill," Kant continued. "There was an oak tree here, a huge one, pretty close to where the house is now. When a person was sentenced to death, they would bring them up the hill, throw a rope into the oak's branches, and hang them. Left the bodies there afterward. It was far enough from town that the smell and scavenging animals wouldn't bother people, but you could look up and see the bodies each morning in the early light. They used them as a warning, I suppose, until the body began to fall apart, and then they would take them down and bury them."

His eyes had grown distant as he stared into the mug, and Margot almost had the impression that he was looking back at memories. That was what happened when you knew a place's history too well, she supposed. They stopped being distant stories and became something closer, something more real, almost tangible, as though he could reach back in time and touch the clammy flesh of a body hung from that tree.

"That went on for more than a hundred years. Eventually the town became more established. More civil. There were courts and jails and proper gallows, and the tree fell out of use. The land was put up for sale. Not many people wanted it; the deaths gave the air a bad taste, they thought. And it's said that a lot of the bodies may have been buried on the hill. No one wanted to eat crops grown through graves or meat that had grazed above the dead."

"But someone bought it," Margot managed.

"Yes. Your family. Of sorts. There were two brothers at the time. The older bought the land, but it eventually passed to the younger. You come from his line."

Margot frowned. "How long ago was that?"

"Seventeen sixty-one."

"Seventeen—" She tried not to let the shock show on her face. "That's…a long time."

"Sure." He paused to drink from his mug, then set it down gently. "The people who live here don't tend to leave. It was that family—the older brother—who first created the winery. He knew the land wouldn't be right for cattle or grains, but he thought he could build tunnels underneath that would be good for fermenting. He was right, I suppose."

She let her gaze travel across the kitchen. The tiles and cabinets from the eighties had seemed old when she'd first seen them, but what if this was only the latest rendition of the kitchen? She imagined the walls, built with stone quarried out of the hillside—the house might have gone through a dozen remodels between its inception and the current day, but the bones could very well be hundreds of years old.

Kant shifted, easing his stiff leg out at an angle. "The oak tree was still standing when the first Hull built his house beside it, though it had been dead for some time. It came down in a storm a few years after he bought the land. He worked it by hand into barrels. We still have them."

The imagery on the bottles rose in Margot's mind: a dead tree, its branches twisting in unfathomable patterns, adorned each label. "That's… morbid."

"A lot of folks thought so." The corners of Kant's mouth twitched up a fraction. "A lot of folks *still* think so. Can't blame them. Hundreds of souls drew their last breath on that tree. But the first Hull wasn't one to care about superstition, I'd say, otherwise he never would have bought the land."

"I guess that explains the ropes." Margot tasted the tea. She normally didn't take hers sweetened, but her throat was achingly dry and the blanket had done very little for the pit of cold in her chest. She swallowed it in one drag, breathing deeply once she put the cup down. "Is it like…some kind of tradition?" She frowned. "Wait, you said some people still don't like the winery being here. Maybe it's a protest."

"Can't say for sure."

"But it's not about me or my arrival?"

"I don't believe so. Best to my knowledge, those ropes would have been here with or without you."

"Okay." That was something. When she'd first seen the hanging nooses, she'd taken them at face value: a warning. Get out or this is what will become of you.

And she'd been prepared to believe it. Whether her parents had been beloved or reviled, a stranger moving into town and taking over one of its major businesses was going to upset some people. At minimum, they would be wary. At worst, she'd been prepared to face deep-flowing, bitter resentment.

Though it didn't change the fact that someone had come to the house—with the knowledge that Margot was now living inside—and left the macabre symbols hung across her front porch. And they'd rung the bells. Not just to be a nuisance, she thought, but to draw her out of her room. To make sure she saw the ropes in the dangerous hours of predawn, when she would be most easily frightened.

It wasn't exactly a generous welcome.

"I could get some night-vision cameras," she said. "The kind that turn on with motion. If they come back, we'll at least have footage of them. We could finally see who's been doing this."

"If you like," Kant said. "The electronics store in town is small, but there's a larger one about an hour away."

His words were supportive, but there was something about the way he spoke—no anticipation, no intrigue—that left Margot feeling that he was only going along with the plan because *she* wanted to, not because he believed it had any merit. She frowned at where her hands clutched the blanket to her chest. "My parents already tried cameras, didn't they?"

"Mm." He dipped his head in a slow nod. "Couple times."

"And?"

"They all died before they caught anything. But you could always try again. You might have better luck."

"If I'm going to stay here for any length of time, even another week, I need to do *something*."

"You do," he agreed, then indicated her empty cup with a twitch of his hand. "Can I get you more to drink?"

"No. Thanks, though." It was beginning to work in increments: the hot drink inside, the blanket around her back, and the open oven door nearby were slowly, achingly bringing sensation back to her limbs. All of the aches and bruises, dulled by numbness, were reemerging too, and Margot flinched when she rolled her shoulders.

Kant gathered the mugs and took them to the sink. "If you're set on staying, then, would you still like me to show you around the winery?"

"Oh! Right." She'd forgotten that this was the morning she was supposed to learn about the business. Margot glanced through the open archway, toward the effigy in the other room. Anything to get her away from the house for an hour or two sounded like an improvement. "Yeah. I'd like that, thanks."

"I'll sort this while you get ready," Kant said, turning on the taps, and Margot belatedly realized she was still wearing her pajamas. "Meet me back here when you're ready to go."

13.

Margot dressed quickly. Her room was chilled, and every second she spent inside it robbed more of the warmth she'd gained in the kitchen. Though her movements were hurried, her selections weren't. This would be the morning she met the business's employees. Her grandmother had been a firm believer in first impressions, and that was something Margot carried with her.

She picked dark clothes—the warmest skirt she owned and a top that ran high around her collarbones to mask the scars. The jacket from the wake went on top. When she clipped her hair back, she allowed herself a thin smile. It was understated but professional. She looked like she knew what she was doing, and although that was a stark contrast to how she actually felt, appearances could carry a person far.

Margot slung her bag over her shoulder and moved back down the stairs to meet Kant. With daylight aiding her, the path to the stairs was easily found. She still wasn't certain how she'd become lost the previous night.

Kant was hanging the dish towel to dry when Margot reentered the room. He gave her a single nod, which might have just been an acknowl-edgment of her presence but that Margot *hoped* was approval of how she looked, then wordlessly led her to the door.

He'd taken down the ropes while she was changing. They now lay in a loosely coiled heap beside the porch's stairs. Margot held a wary gaze on them as she passed. They truly looked like they had been dragged out of the forest floor; roots and loamy earth clung between the twisted fibers and the rope itself was beginning to rot in places.

The sun rose, slowly devouring the frost that clung to the sparse grass tufts. Margot thrust her hands into her jacket pockets as she put her head down. She'd half expected Kant to suggest they take her car, but he led her along the dirt track instead, his shaggy, gray hair whipped back by the wind.

"One of the upstairs lights broke last night," she said, more to make conversation than anything. "Scared me pretty badly."

"I'll come around later and fix that."

"Oh…no…I can take care of it. I didn't mean to—"

"It's fine." The ground began to lead downward, and although his gait became more pronounced, he didn't slow. "Used to do repairs for your parents too. It's an old house and needs more work than one person can keep up with."

She risked a glance at him. "There are a lot of rooms. Did my parents ever have guests stay?"

"No. Never. Liked the place to themselves." He shrugged, his knit turtleneck bunching up over shoulders that were slightly too broad for it. "Most of the house stayed locked up. It was built for a much larger family."

She'd guessed as much. At the time it was constructed, families of ten or twelve weren't unusual, and the building would have played host to other relatives who wanted a place to stay in return for working in the winery. The house was built to be crowded and full of voices. Now it lay all but hollow, filled with furniture that never saw use, slowly growing stiff and cobwebbed from neglect.

The driveway wove them in a twisting route down the hillside. They passed thin clusters of trees, the branches anemic as they strained toward the pale sunlight. Margot hitched her jacket higher around her throat.

Close to halfway down the hill, a side path led off to the right. Although the driveway to the house had been intended as the main road, it was clear that far more traffic took the bend to the side; the ruts in the compacted dirt were wider and deeper, and less grass managed to poke through. The tire tracks cut the corner, and Kant followed them, leading Margot toward a strand of buildings.

"Those of us who stay on the estate live back there," Kant said, motioning to a grouping of small homes—some two-story but most single—near the back of the cluster. His hand shifted toward a larger stone building close by. "And here's where we ferment the wine."

"Does…" Margot frowned, trying to pick her words in a way that wouldn't leave her sounding ignorant. "Do you grow the grapes here? Or, uh, buy them?"

"Ground's not so good for growing. We take in the grapes, press them, mix them, ferment them, distill them, and bottle them."

They were approaching the main building. There was already life inside, Margot realized. Lights glittered through narrow, paned windows, occasionally blocked by the movements of bodies beyond.

"Most of the crew is here," Kant said. "Told them to be ready to meet you."

The doors to the winery were massive and arched, made of solid, dark wood. They reminded Margot of church doors, even down to the black, ornate hinges that whined as Kant shoved an arm into one of them to force it open.

Margot had a split-second glimpse of movement before the crisscrossing bodies abruptly fell still. Any conversations cut out. More than a dozen expectant faces turned toward her.

The work area was below the door; three broad steps led down to a stone floor, which was occupied by clustered machinery Margot couldn't name and enormous steel tanks. Bodies filled the spaces between the machinery, some holding crates, frozen midtransport, and others with their arms full of paperwork. The heightened entrance made Margot feel as though she were standing on a podium, overlooking an expectant audience.

Kant scratched his fingers across his scalp, pushing loose strands of hair away from his eyes, then let his arm drop back to his side. "Everyone, this is Margot Hull. Owner."

It was a perfunctory introduction, and the gap of silence following it left Margot reeling. She tried for a smile and raised one hand in a tentative greeting. "Hi."

Public speaking had never given her more than a moderate dose of anxiety before. But there was something about the way the countless eyes had fixed on her that was desperately uncomfortable. There were too many faces, and they began to blur together, unreadable. She didn't know these people, but they knew her. And they were sizing her up, using these first few seconds to build an impression of her that she might never fully shake.

She was overdressed, Margot realized with a mortifying jolt. She'd put on clothes that would be considered professional where she came from, but that was a city, and this was the country. She didn't look in control, like she'd hoped. She looked clueless. And that was shamefully reflective of the truth.

Below, a few of the bodies shifted, waiting. Kant made no effort to fill the quiet, and Margot realized she might be expected to give some kind of speech, something introducing herself, and she had no idea what she was supposed to say.

Then a woman pushed through the group, arms outstretched, calling, "Of course! Margot!" and Margot could have kissed her.

Margot stumbled down the three steps to meet her halfway, and the woman grasped her by the forearms, a broad smile showing her teeth and part of the gums above. Thick, brown hair was tied in a braid that ran halfway down her back. "Nora," she said by way of introduction, "and Ray."

Belatedly, she realized a man had followed, stacks of papers still clinched under one arm. He thrust out a hand, which Margot quickly shook. They were familiar, she realized. She'd seen them at the wake, standing behind the table laden with wine bottles as they poured drinks for the guests.

"We run the retail store." Nora leaned back against her husband, who towered over her by at least a foot and a half. "I'm not sure if you saw it. Down the lane a little way, closer to the main road."

"Of course! The building with the barrels out front? I didn't get to see inside, but it looked lovely."

Nora seemed pleased by that, her smile growing broader. "I hope you'll stop by some time when you get the chance. Ray and I are always up for a chat. Plus, as many free samples as you'd like. Though I suppose you'll have no shortage of wine now that you live here."

"It's…a lot bigger than I expected," Margot said, gazing about the room again.

"The place isn't always this busy." Ray's voice was easy and warm. "But this is the hub. We call it the fermentation station."

"No one calls it that," Kant said.

Ray shrugged mildly.

"It's where the mixing is done," Nora said. "Happens once a year, after the grapes are brought in. Afterward, it's all moved to the lower levels to mature. Kant asked us all to be here to welcome you. That's why it's such a crowd."

"Oh." This time, Margot's smile felt more genuine. Nora's words had flipped something in her. She was being sized up, yes, but so were the employees. Their clothes were casual but clean and clearly picked with care. Hair was combed, boots scrubbed. Many of them held stacks of papers: reports and documentation, in case Margot asked to see them.

They were trying to make the best first impression they could. Just like Margot.

Kant took half a step forward and raised his hand to indicate the people gathered around them. "Nora and Ray Palmer handle tourist sales and sales to local businesses. You can usually find them in the store." He moved his hand toward a tall, ruddy-complexioned woman. "Sonya. In charge of showings at fairs, reordering stock, and sales outside of Leafell. Then we have the crew for fermenting, casking, and bottling..."

Margot smiled and nodded at each face in turn as they were introduced. The names blurred together. She wished Kant would slow down. Sometimes men and women reached out to shake her hand, and she lost the train of words entirely.

"That's it for the crew," Kant said at last. They'd come to a halt beside one of the massive metal containers. It stretched more than twice Margot's height. She thought she could detect the tang of grape skins and something yeasty in the air. A set of movable stairs had been pressed against the tank's side to allow access to the top, where a paddle was perched, to mix the concoction inside.

The steel, freshly cleaned, reflected Margot's image back to her. She was distorted, her shoulders pinched tight and the top of her head stretched as though she were about to explode. A funhouse mirror improvised in a fermentation tank.

Kant noticed her staring. "Merlot," he said, as though that explained its presence. He pressed one hand against the metal. "Our last batch for the year. Whites are processed first, then reds. This will be ready for casking soon."

"Right." Margot was too aware of the eyes on her back, watching her, taking the measure of her responses.

"You'll want to see the cellars." Kant turned from the tank. He crossed the work floor, and the bodies parted to let him through. Margot hurried to keep pace with him, her bag jostling against her hip, a coil of hair tickling the back of her neck as it came free from the clip.

She was aware of her own twisted image playing in the metal tanks she passed. She wasn't alone this time; Kant and the others were captured in the curving metal. None of the other reflections seemed as badly warped as hers, though. Her body stretched and broke, deforming repeatedly and never quite fitting back the way it was supposed to.

A set of double doors, very similar to the main ones, was at the back of the work room. Kant put his shoulder against the wood to open them. Margot fixed her eyes ahead, refusing to look at the reflections any longer.

The doors grated open. Beyond was a tunnel leading downward. Stone walls and floors faded into darkness. Margot blinked and saw the stairs in her own home the night before. The stairs...and the pair of eyes waiting at the base of them.

Kant flipped several large switches set into the wall. Rows of lights blinked on, one after another, leading down before turning to the side. The path was divided in half: a set of steps next to a smooth slope, all built out of the same stone.

"We have easier ways to get the barrels down these days," Kant said, "but this is the original entrance."

He led the way forward. Margot made it as far as the doorway before pulling up.

Steam and the press of bodies had kept the workroom humid and warm, enough that she'd been close to shedding her coat. That was a sharp distinction from the tunnel. The air was a breath of ice across her skin. It rolled out of the dim passageway, and with it came the smell of earth, of fruit, and of damp rot.

The tunnel would take her underground.

Fear, raw and hot like electricity, raced along her nerve endings.

Margot couldn't handle underground spaces. She couldn't remember how the phobia had started, but it had been a constant presence through her life. She could sometimes go months or even years forgetting about it, until the wrong circumstances collided.

It wasn't exactly claustrophobia. Elevators were fine…unless they carried her to a basement floor. Something about the knowledge that a thick layer of soil was suspended over her pushed her anxiety past the breaking point.

Once, as a child, she'd had a dream of being tipped into a grave while still alive. Lying in the soft loam, her eyes open but her muscles unresponsive, she'd watched as shovelfuls of dirt were dropped onto her. Each one heavier than the last. Smothering her face. Crushing the air from her lungs. Pressing and pressing, until she knew she would never be able to claw her way out.

She'd woken drenched in feverish sweat. The next morning she'd tearfully begged her grandmother to burn her when she died. She didn't like the idea of flames licking over her body either, but it was better than being buried.

The bulbs hanging from the ceiling were enough to light Kant's shaggy hair as he stopped, eight steps down, to look back at her. The light did very little to break the shadows that clung around his eyes. He didn't speak, but there was a question hanging in the silence. He expected her to follow.

And she didn't have much of a choice. She'd agreed to this—a tour of the facility, including the cellars, as part of learning the business. If anything, this was the bare minimum.

The staff behind her were still watching, waiting. She wished they wouldn't. She wished they could have just gone back to work after the introductions and left her struggle unseen.

Kant tilted his head a fraction. His expression was inscrutable, the eyebrows too heavy and the beard too thick to see the angle of the muscles beneath or to get any reading on his thoughts. The harsh bulbs glinted off the edges of his eyes. "You'd prefer not," he said.

It was only a cellar. A cellar that must be visited multiple times each day by multiple people. There couldn't be anything to fear, no matter how deep the tunnel led her down. Margot wet her lips. "No. Please. I'd love to see it."

He nodded once, then fell still again, waiting.

She had to do this. She had no excuse not to.

Margot took a short, quick breath and stepped forward, crossing over the threshold.

14.

Dirt crunched under Margot's shoes.

The passageway's angle was steep. Kant, leading, took the ramp rather than the stairs, so Margot followed his example. The stairs had probably been intended for foot traffic, while the ramp would have been used for transporting the barrels, but the incline must have been easier on Kant's gait. It left Margot feeling destabilized, though; she tested every new step, knowing a damp bit of stone could very well send her sliding down into the darkness beneath. Her skin crawled. It was all she could do to keep her breathing from growing noticeably panicked.

The lights suspended above them were high enough not to hit either of them, but Margot still felt compelled to keep her head low to avoid them. They were bare bulbs, an unkind shade of white that sapped warmth and color from the walls, and they were not set closely enough to eradicate the pools of shadows that formed between them.

Kant, familiar with this path, neither ducked his head nor struggled with his footing. He reached the floor below well ahead of Margot and waited at the doors for her to make up the lost ground.

The scents were stronger there. Although there was no dirt visible on the stone walls or floors, it hung in the air, heavy and loamy. Margot began to pick up the velvety, astringent strains of wine and, strangely, vanilla.

As she arrived at the level ground, Kant pushed the final set of doors open.

"The cellars," he said simply, and he moved to one side so Margot could see past him.

She felt her stomach drop unpleasantly. Despite all of her expectations that had been challenged so far—the number of employees, the above-ground facilities—she had not expected the cellars to be so *enormous*.

Stone pillars rose out of the ground, connecting overhead to form massive, interlocking archways. Between them were barrels. They were all arranged on their sides, held in place with wooden supports, stacked five to a grouping. And they seemed to go on forever.

All Margot could manage was "Oh."

"All oak barrels," Kant said as he closed the door behind them. "Some modern places use metal, but we've always been more traditional here."

Margot took a hesitant step into the room, both hands clutching the purse's strap as though it were a lifeline. The lighting was dramatic, highlighting sections like a spotlight while the ground between was absorbed by the heavy damp and dark. Margot took one more step forward to put herself under one of those lights. It felt safer there. As though the shadows were somehow alive. As though she would be consumed by them if she let her guard drop for even a minute.

"Kant..." She struggled to find words, but everything felt inadequate in the face of the place's scope. "How many barrels are there?"

His glance seemed to carry some empathy. "It looks more drastic than it is. The whites age for only a short while, but the reds can be here for years. A lot of these barrels are just putting in their time until they're ready."

Many had dust gathering on them, she realized. While the floor was kept swept, time had been allowed to settle onto the oak.

Moisture made the air thick. The ground was dry as far as she could see, though many of the stones had been stained. Spilled wine, she knew, although in the dim spotlights it could as easily be spilled blood.

Kant moved forward again, and Margot once more followed, shirking away from both the pillars and the barrels, fighting with every step to keep the quiet panic from rising over her.

The room had a weight to it. The great arched pillars held the ceiling up, but, at the same time, it seemed to sag toward her, as though it were slowly but inexorably crushing down the supports as it pressed toward the ground. The further they traveled, the worse the sensation became, until Margot could almost feel it pressing onto her shoulders, forcing the stale, scented air from her lungs.

And then they were at the opposite doors. She clung close to Kant—too close, near enough to hear his breathing as he unlocked the doors—as she waited to be let through.

At her back were hundreds of barrels. Identical, dark, clustered in stacks of five. They were oppressive. The stains on the flagstone floor felt less like remnants of an old history and more like a warning.

Then the door opened with a click, and Kant stood back to let her through.

Margot held her coat tight across her chest as she entered another passageway. She'd expected it to lead up, but instead, it carried her straight ahead. The walkway held no lights, but an open door at its other end was a beacon leading her forward.

"Go ahead," Kant said.

She had very few other choices. As she followed the narrow stone walkway, the door behind them groaned closed, then its lock clicked as Kant resealed it.

So far, none of the other doors they had passed through had been locked. Margot had expected the passageway to lead them back outside, but apparently there was another stop on their trip, and this one warranted security.

The room's light was a yellower hue than the harsh whites of the main cellar. It should have made the room warmer, but instead it set a sickly pall across the cracked stones. Margot reached the door and nudged it open.

The room held more barrels, but far fewer than the cathedral-like space they'd passed through. Only six existed there, suspended on a wooden structure that lifted them to chest height and locked them into place. They dominated the room's left-hand side, while desks, filled with papers, wineglasses, and an aged lantern, took up the right.

A tawny-skinned, spectacled man stood at the desk. He smiled as he saw Margot. "Ah. Margot, I'm guessing. Andrew. Glad to meet you."

"Andrew." The name was familiar. Margot cast back as she shook the extended hand. "Ah—the accountant?"

"That's him." Kant had entered behind her and closed and locked the door.

"I needed to fetch some papers, so I thought I'd save some time and meet you down here." Andrew, tall and lean and wearing a dark patterned vest, seemed wholly at home as he leaned a hip against one of the desks. "I'm sure your tour has been thrilling. Kant is such a talker, sometimes it's a challenge to get him to be quiet."

Kant grunted something inaudible. He moved around them, bumping Andrew's shoulder as he passed in a way that told Margot they knew each other well.

"Sorry about the lighting situation." Andrew nodded to the lantern at his side. "This was one of the earliest rooms to be built, and electricity hadn't been invented back then apparently. Everywhere else got wires, but they were so fearful of upsetting the chamber's balance that they never installed power here."

The lantern's flame flickered over the high walls in unsettling patterns.

Margot, colder than she would have liked, thrust her hands into her pockets to hide the way they shook. She felt edgy, itchy, eager to get back to ground level. "It gives it some charm."

"The place has plenty of that." Andrew, dressed only in his shirt and vest, seemed impervious to the chill. "Well, this is the chamber. That's what it was named way back when the Hulls settled this hill, before they built a *proper* chamber back there." He nodded to the passageway Margot had just come through.

"That's just called the cellars," Kant added.

Andrew's eyes crinkled behind his glasses as he smiled. "We got less creative with our names over time."

Margot turned to get another look at the space. While the cellars had been grand, this room felt small and narrow and imperfectly built. It had likely been a project by the home's original owners, dug out and put together with their own hands.

"Despite appearances, this is perhaps one of the most valuable rooms in the winery." Andrew indicated the six barrels arranged opposite them. "These darlings account for more than 30 percent of your annual income."

Margot frowned. The room she'd just come through held hundreds, possibly thousands, of barrels. She knew wine could vary in price—sometimes by a lot—but it was hard to imagine what could make *this* vintage so much more expensive than all the others.

"You remember what I told you about the old oak tree," Kant said, and Margot felt her heart skip a beat.

"He turned it into wine barrels." She carefully moved toward them. Now that she was looking for signs of age, they were abundantly visible. The wood was lighter than the oak in the main cellar—older, dryer. The wood's grain had pronounced texture.

The oak. The gallows. Hundreds of bodies breathed their last while suspended from this wood.

It had been changed—sawed and whittled and reformed until it was unrecognizable. But it still remembered, she thought.

She reached a hand forward to touch one but caught herself. She was being superstitious again, but this time, she didn't chide herself for it. Trapped belowground in a lantern-lit room with two near strangers and the barrels of the dead, a little superstition felt wise.

Then Margot remembered the comment about this room contributing a third of her income and recoiled. "You still put wine in them?"

"Yes." Andrew, candlelight flickering across his glasses, moved to stand beside Margot as he admired the barrels. "Each batch ages for five years. And the result is incredible. It wins international awards and nearly every blind tasting it's entered into. Critics sing praises for its rich tones and complexity. Our other wines are *good*, mind you; they're handmade from excellent grapes and nurtured with care. But this line is *famous*."

Kant stepped forward. He'd taken one of the wineglasses from the desk. A spigot was attached to the far-left barrel, and he released it, pouring a small amount of wine in the glass.

"We're very close to bottling this batch," Kant said. "Here. It's what your family is known for."

Margot froze, staring at the glass held with unexpected dexterity in his rough hand. A tablespoon of vivid red liquid swirled in its base, heavy, leaving streaks of crimson where it washed across the glass. She stared, fixated. It was beautiful. And sickening. A vision that promised hedonistic delights and horrors in a single taste. She pulled back, her shoes scuffing over the stones as she retreated from the temptation. "I…I'm sorry. I don't…drink wine."

Even as the words escaped, Margot knew how wrong they sounded.

The prospective owner of a winery, and she refused to partake in her sole product.

One of Andrew's eyebrows rose, but he made no comment. If Kant felt anything, he didn't show it. He made to turn aside.

"Don't throw it out," Andrew said. Kant passed the glass to him. Andrew tipped it back, draining the liquid, then put the glass back on the tray, his tongue lapping the taste off his lips even after he'd swallowed. "Damn. That's, what? The equivalent to a week of my salary?"

"Maybe more," Kant said.

Andrew chuckled, his voice soft, nearly inaudible. "It really *is* worth it."

They made no attempt to question her choice, and Margot was grateful. Maybe they thought she'd had a problem with addiction or maybe he believed her refusal was for religious reasons.

In truth, she drank most kinds of alcohol. Vodka, spiced rum, and cocktails were all fine. She didn't like the taste of beer but she could still tolerate it.

Wine, though, turned her stomach every time. Even the sight of it made her queasy.

"Is the wine that expensive?" Margot asked. She was feeling lost again. Too small, even in that cramped room, wrapped in the heavy blanket of shadows. The previous night, she'd imagined she might actually be capable of taking on everything that the estate entailed. She was starting to feel that she'd never before been so deluded.

"It is." Kant rested one heavy hand on the nearest cask. "We age it for five years before bottling. Two bottles are auctioned for charity. They fetch low six figures. The rest are sold to private collectors. Billionaires. People who require the very best, price ignored."

"The other wines have varying prices, but nothing like the dead tree line," Andrew said. "The bottles from the regular cellar are bought by locals, restaurants, and tourists. I take a few home myself. But these six casks are special. And they can't be replicated. The wood is over two centuries old and from a single specific tree. We can make a finite amount of each batch, and that's all that's available."

Earlier that morning, Kant had said many people in town still found the winery morbid. Margot now understood why. It was one thing to plant a business on top of a hill that was once designated for executions. It was another to still use the wood to create wine that would be sold and consumed.

Wine that, apparently, was valued above all others. Wine that couldn't be reproduced in any other barrel.

The damp, icy air stung her throat with each breath. Margot turned aside, trying not to let her discomfort show on her face.

"We maintain a very strict system to keep the wine consistent." Andrew still faced the barrels, hands propped on his hips as he surveyed them. "The same system that was designed when they first went into use. The barrels cannot be allowed to dry out; as soon as they're emptied, they're refilled. We keep them in the same room they were originally held in, with no electricity or other modifications, to preserve the intended temperature and humidity."

Margot faced the desks. Behind them, the stone wall was covered with slick, glimmering light from the lantern. All except for one section. At first glance it was easy to mistake it for a shadow, but as she stared into the dark, she realized, with slowly dawning anxiety, that it was a hole. A hole that led away so far that she couldn't see its other end. The desks had been positioned ahead of it to block it. "No modifications…what about that?"

"Ah." Andrew, his smile lopsided, rubbed the back of his neck. "Yes. This was the original cellar for the founding Hulls. As their business prospered, though, they expanded. But not without trouble. That tunnel collapsed only a few years after its construction. It was never filled in."

"There are a lot of those about," Kant said. "Some collapsed. Others abandoned. A network of old passageways connect them, with posts to mark the entrances. We keep clear mostly. Too dangerous."

Margot lifted the lantern. Its metal was cold enough to sting her hands, but she leaned forward, extending the light to see down the passageway. Its walls had once been paved with stone too, though much of it had collapsed. Roots extended down, hanging like tendrils from the ceiling, catching the light in unnatural ways. Margot put the lantern back down. She felt queasy. A cold sweat was forming across her back. She fought her body's reaction, willing her hands to be still, her heart to stop its palpitations.

"Ready to leave?" Kant asked.

She flinched at the words but fixed a smile on her face as she turned. Kant stood by a door opposite the one they'd entered through. An exit, she hoped. Her voice had become stuck in her throat like a blockage that couldn't be removed, so she gestured for him to go ahead.

"You go ahead. I'll pack up here," Kant said as the ancient door groaned open. He stepped back to let them through, and Andrew entered first, carrying the lantern. Narrow stairs led upward. They were steep and less well maintained than the passage to the main cellar, and despite how dry the floor and walls appeared, Margot swore she heard dripping. She glanced to her side and was just in time to see another pathway spearing off to the left. They turned a corner, Andrew murmuring "Watch your step," then Margot caught sight of a thin line of natural light far above them.

"I didn't realize we were so deep," she murmured.

"Oh, the old Hulls took full advantage of the hill. Passageways trail up and down through it, somewhat like an ant nest."

The image sent Margot's skin crawling. An ant nest. And they were the ants.

The steps grew steeper. She became breathless. The walls seemed to squeeze in at either side, until even Andrew's lantern couldn't compete with their oppressiveness.

And then, finally, Andrew hunched as they reached a ceiling. A thin line of light exuded from a trapdoor, tracing around three of its edges, razor thin. Andrew placed the lantern down on one of the higher steps and withdrew a key ring from his pocket. "You'll have one of these," he said. "You'll probably find it somewhere in your home. It'll get you into all of the buildings and any locked passageways. Though I wouldn't recommend exploring on your own. It's easy to get lost."

From far below, Kant's voice drifted toward them. "Sealed."

"We maintain an airlock," Andrew explained as he slid his key into the upper door's handle. "Just another precaution against damaging our main revenue."

The lock clicked. A rubber seal seemed to sigh as it was pried loose, and Andrew shoved the trapdoor up and open. It hit the loamy earth outside with a heavy thud, then Andrew climbed out and offered his hand to Margot.

She blinked against the unexpectedly bright sun as she let him help her up the final few steps. The day had warmed up since they'd entered the cellars. A tang of pollen hung in the air. Margot tilted her head back, the overwhelming relief of being *outside*, of being *free*, making her muscles weak.

The block of staff buildings—the place she'd entered the underground labyrinth—was far enough away that she could no longer see distinct parts of the architecture, but only the glint of sunlight off the roofs and a blur of dark glass windows. She hadn't thought they'd traveled that far.

Kant moved up the stairs behind her, and Margot stepped out of the way. He dusted his hands on his jeans as he exited, and Andrew heaved the trapdoor back over, letting it land with a resounding bang. The key went back into the lock and fastened it with a soft click.

"Right." Andrew fit his keys back into his pocket. "I'll need to get back to the office, unless you want me to stay around for a bit."

"We should be all right from here." Kant ran his fingers through his hair, getting it out of his face.

"Then I'll see you around, Margot." Andrew extended his hand one final time and Margot shook it. "When you're ready to take a look at the numbers, come by my office. Kant can show you where it is."

"Thanks. I'll do that."

He set off, snuffing the lantern as he traversed the gentle slope leading down toward the staff buildings.

Kant raised a hand to shield his eyes from the sun, then sighed. A tinge of relief flashed across his features before he hid it again. "Good. Witchety is here."

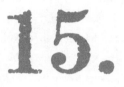

15.

"Witchety?" Margot frowned as she followed Kant's line of sight. The driveway wended across the property in the distance, and an older woman followed it, moving toward them, a huge dog leashed at her side.

Kant gestured for Margot to follow and set out to meet the woman halfway.

The sun was at the woman's back. Margot could make out very little about her except that a braid of white hair ran down her back and swung with each step and the dog beside her came up to her waist.

Margot, warming quickly, unbuttoned her jacket. Small insects flicked from the overgrown wild grass as she strode through it. Despite the sun, dew still clung to her shoes and legs.

The woman's details began to solidify as they neared each other, and Margot realized she'd been mistaken. The dog wasn't huge; the woman was just very, very small. And Margot already knew her.

The woman from the wake wore nearly identical, loosely draped clothes, just in different shades: earthy browns and forest greens, covered by an amber shawl. Her skin was shockingly, strikingly white, but there was no sign of powder in her heavily creased face. Blue veins threaded along her throat, pulsing beneath the crepe-thin skin. Her eyelids were heavy, and lines of red crept in across the whites, but there was a sharpness under a layer of blurry cataracts that gave the impression she was drinking in more about the environment than even Margot noticed.

At her side was a golden retriever, mouth open as it panted happily. As the woman neared, she squinted her watery green eyes, sizing Margot up. "Hello again. Poor thing."

Kant stopped beside her. "Margot, meet Witchety. We have her come by every few weeks."

"Hi. Nice to meet you, uh, formally." Margot couldn't stand it any longer. The golden retriever was smiling up at her, tongue lolling against off-white teeth, black eyes radiating warmth. "Um, can I...?"

"Go right ahead."

Margot dropped to her knees and buried her hands in the dog's silky fur. He responded immediately, haunches swinging from the force of his tail's reckless careening, tongue coming out to bathe her face. Margot, laughing, hugged him.

"His name's Marsh," Witchety said. "On account of how much he looked like toasted marshmallows when he was born."

"He's gorgeous." The force of Marsh's affection nearly toppled Margot backward. She stood before she could ruin her jacket but kept her hands on his head, scratching around his ears.

"Figures you'd like him." Witchety's voice crackled with barely repressed coughs. "You were thick as thieves with his great-grandmother."

Margot snapped up, surprised, her mind flicking back to the dog door in her home. "My parents...?"

"Always loved goldens. They had a girl, Clementine, when you were little. Gave me one of the puppies way back, and a few generations later, we have Marsh."

Her mind turned to her scars. They couldn't have been from the family pet, surely? Especially not if Clementine had been as friendly as Marsh. Margot buried her fingers into the thicker fur around his neck and kissed the top of his head. His breath wafted over her face, wet and sweltering with the scent of saliva and dog food, and Margot smiled despite herself.

"Witchety comes around once a fortnight to perform a blessing on the land," Kant said. "I thought you might like to continue the tradition, so I didn't cancel her."

A blessing?

Kant had seemed so comfortable around every part of the estate that Margot found it impossible to imagine him thinking that was necessary. He'd told Margot the place's history unflinchingly. Not even the barrels made from the hanging tree had fazed him.

But of course, Kant wouldn't have been the one to hire Witchety. That would have been her parents. Maybe Margot's superstitious streak had been inherited. Maybe they, like Margot herself, had felt deeply uncomfortable about the property's past.

"We pay her for her work," Kant added, "but you wouldn't need to worry about that. It's a business expense."

"Oh." She couldn't imagine what kind of gymnastics Andrew had to pull to make a blessing against evil tax deductible.

Then Margot's mind flashed to a different angle. Witchety was old. At least eighty. Her clothes, while not dirty, were worn to the point of growing thin in places. Her hands appeared arthritic. Even the shawl looked to have been mended many times over.

Maybe Margot's parents hadn't actually been nervous about the land. Maybe, instead, this was their form of kindness. A way to give some money to a widow who would have been embarrassed to accept charity. The property's reputation simply gave them an easy excuse to hire her services.

If that was the case, Margot wasn't going to turn her away. "Of course. I'd love you to continue, please."

"Smart girl," Witchety said. "It's bad land. A lot of suffering bled into this soil. You've got to do everything you can to keep the evil at bay."

Margot glanced at Kant, but he didn't return the look.

"Would you mind if I came along, or do you prefer to work alone?" Margot asked.

"I'm not alone. Not as long as I have Marsh with me." Witchety's smile was brief and crooked. "I'll never turn down some extra company, mind."

Margot fell in line behind Witchety, with Kant keeping pace. The older woman led them back toward the property's boundary. Margot let the silence hold for a few minutes before speaking. "I hope it isn't rude to ask, but is Witchety your real name?"

"Sure, it's real," Witchety replied. "Might not be the one I got at birth, mind, but I've been called Witchety for so long now that it's more my own than anything else."

Marsh, held at her side by the leash, bumped his black nose against Witchety's hand. She brushed her swollen knuckles over his head.

"My parents started calling me *witchety girl* when I was little because I'd brew up potions in old bottles. I'd make them from snails and moss and once the foot of a dead bird I found. They thought they were teasing me, but I liked the name. I've always been interested in the unnatural. Never studied. I believe these things are more intuitive than a lot of people want to think."

They reached the property's boundary line; a sturdy wooden fence ran along it, overrun by unmown grass and occasional saplings. Beyond that, past a row of trees that had started to twist and collapse from age, Margot caught glimpses of the road. There was no traffic on it.

Witchety wrapped the leash around her arm and then peeled back the shawl. Beneath, tied to her clothes, was a pouch. She opened it and withdrew a bottle that filled her palm.

"Holy water," she explained. "I get the local priest to bless it for me. You should have some too, in your kitchen somewhere. Let me know if you're getting low. It's not the kind of thing you want to run out of unexpectedly."

Again, Margot glanced toward Kant. This time he met her gaze, but his thoughts were kept well concealed behind his gray eyes.

Finally, Witchety withdrew a talisman from the folds of the bag. Suspended on a loop of crimson thread was a cluster of strange objects. Margot frowned as she tried to get a better look at them. She recognized a bird skull, possibly a crow's, the bones picked bare and sun bleached. Several old and rusted keys. Dried flowers threaded with dried herbs. Loops of scrap metal. Tiny bells.

Witchety held it in one hand, the threads trapped in her palm while the excess hung over her fingers, not unlike the way a rosary might be clasped. Then she began walking.

With each step, the clustered metals and bones knocked against one another and set up a faint, ringing tone. Witchety placed her thumb over the bottle's open top and let water fall one drop at a time, each one catching the light for a fragment of a second before disappearing into the long grass.

"Show us mercy." Witchety had her eyes closed. Margot's attention was torn between the ritual and watching the ground ahead, fearful that Witchety might misstep and break an ankle on the rocky earth. The woman coughed, the noise dragging through her chest like a rasp, before continuing. "Turn your anger from us. Let us have peace."

Kant, following behind both of them, walked with his head down. Whether he was in quiet contemplation or simply tired, Margot couldn't tell.

Strands of pure-white hair had come free from Witchety's braid. They coursed behind her like gossamer pulled by the earthy, pollen-laden wind.

A trickle of the blessed water ran down her thumb and formed a drip at her wrist.

"We mourn for your bones, lost in this earth. We wish only peace for you."

Kant said the convicteds' bodies may have been buried on the land. The realization hit Margot: if the remains had never been recovered, they would still be here somewhere. She might have walked over the unmarked graves without ever knowing. She might be walking over them right at that moment.

Marsh's low panting blended in with Witchety's labored breaths. She'd been sick only recently, Margot remembered. Pneumonia, she had said at the reception. Margot probably shouldn't have let her perform the blessing. At the very least, she should have deferred it.

But then, Kant hadn't told her to come back another day. He must have believed she was well enough for the visit. And he knew Witchety better than Margot could presume to.

"Show us mercy. Slumber another night."

They had reached the property's corner. Witchety stopped, flexing her shoulders back to loosen them. In the closest patch of trees, small birds bickered and then fell silent. Margot thought, unexpectedly, that the land was quieter than it should be. No insects hummed. No sounds came from the distant gathering of buildings. They had been walking alongside the road for close to ten minutes, but not a single car had passed in that time.

Witchety abruptly turned toward Margot. "Do you still have the Watcher?"

"The, uh…?"

"Big statue. Deer skull." Witchety placed her spread hands above her own head, miming the shape. "You can't miss it."

"*Oh.* The effigy. Yes, that's, uh, in the house."

"Good." Witchety shook the talisman in her hand, and the bells and pieces of metal clattered together. "Keep it close by. I made it for your parents years ago. It will ward away bad things."

I should have guessed. The talisman Witchety carried—made of bones and metal and scraps of nature—was like a little sibling to the hideous monster in Margot's home.

It also explained why her parents hadn't gotten rid of it. Witchety took her work to heart. She would have been deeply hurt if the effigy—her *Watcher*—hadn't been kept inside the home. Her parents had hated it enough to hide it from sight, but not enough to waste Witchety's effort.

"Does it have a significance? The deer skull, I mean?" She hoped that, at least in a small way, understanding the statue might erase some of the unease she felt around it. Just the memory of the shape made her palms itch with sweat. Marsh had approached her again, and she buried her hands in his fur, grateful for the distraction.

Witchety's hazy eyes seemed to hold countless secrets under their heavy lids. The corners of her mouth twitched in a near-imperceptible smile. "All things do. The Watcher is only made from things with the *most* significance, though. That's why it works."

Marsh, still panting, nudged Margot's hands, and she realized she'd stopped petting him.

"Some things are *special*," Witchety continued. "Keys to beloved places. The bones of an animal that never lived a day in captivity. Tiny gifts and unblemished flowers and stones that make you feel a particular way. They may not have much power on their own, but weave them together with care and they create a breathing tapestry. That's what the Watcher is." She lifted the talisman. "What *this* is. Things that are special enough to keep you safe. At least a little."

In that instant, Margot believed her. The bird skull's black eye sockets bored into her with something that felt too close to knowledge. She had to look away.

"Keep the Watcher close to your doors," Witchety continued, turning back to their path. "And don't stray too far from your home after dark."

They circled the property's perimeter over the following hour. Witchety's breathing was labored by the time they returned to their starting place. She poured a final few drops of the holy water and then corked the bottle, now mostly empty.

The trip had drained her more than Margot felt comfortable seeing. Witchety had been small when she arrived but seemed to have lost another inch along the way. Marsh, always hugging her side, gazed up at her adoringly, but with the tinge of worry that animals carried when they sensed something was wrong with the people they loved.

"That will do us for today," Witchety said, returning the bottle and talisman to her pouch and tucking it back under her shawl. "I'll return in another fortnight."

"Let me give you a lift back to your house," Margot said, remembering that Witchety had walked up the drive. "I need to go shopping in town anyway."

"That's kind of you, but I always walk. Don't want to risk any unwanted presences hitching a ride in a car. It's easier to shake them if you're on foot."

Margot turned to Kant. He caught her look. "I'll call Don to pick you up in the laneway outside the property."

"Don't bother that old fool." Witchety hitched the leash a loop tighter around her wrist. "He hates being near this place."

"I'll still call him."

She made a discontented noise. "If you're so determined. Take care until next time, understand? The earth feels bad. And it's growing worse. I can only do so much. You hear me, Margot? Stay safe. Don't go far from your home at night. Don't provoke anything you don't want to know better."

Margot didn't know what got under her skin more: the words or the complete sincerity they were delivered with. She managed a cracked smile. "Probably good advice for all of us."

Witchety turned her head a fraction, the heavy eyelids shielding her murky eyes as she surveyed Margot. The pure-white eyebrows twitched down a fraction. "I *am* sorry."

"What on earth for? You're very welcome here—"

"I was supposed to come last Friday. But I was sick. Couldn't leave my bed. Couldn't perform the blessing like I was supposed to. And now your parents are dead."

Margot's mouth opened and then closed again. She felt as though the breath had been stolen from her lungs.

Witchety's bony hand found hers. It was clammy and felt desperately fragile, but she still squeezed Margot's wrist tightly enough to ache. "Be safe."

Then Witchety turned, Marsh at her heels, as she made her way toward the driveway.

A breeze, warmed by the sun, tugged at Margot's loose jacket, grazing across her skin like questing fingers. She should have been warm, even overheated. But all she felt was cold.

The image in the mirror. The bells. The nooses.

Witchety's warnings should have been easily dismissed. Witchety was an unusual woman with a preoccupation with the occult. If she made an income from performing blessings, it was in her best interest to leave foreboding little tidbits, warning that danger was on the horizon and that her services were the only thing keeping it at bay. Logically, Margot should have no reason to put any stock in those premonitions.

Except...

She remembered that half-second image of her corpse, staring out of the mirror, meeting her eyes. Shriveled and swollen and bleached a toxic shade of death.

No one had been able to adequately explain her parents' deaths. And Witchety's words were blending with her own moments of panic, thickening and solidifying into something she wasn't sure she wanted to understand.

"Kant…"

He stood at her side, quiet and steadfast and patient as she hunted for the right words, picking the ones that sounded the least panicked, even as her heart insisted this wasn't the time for moderation, that the most frantic phrases might actually be needed.

"Do you…" Again, she hesitated, running her tongue across the inside of her teeth as though to taste the words before giving them voice. "How much faith do you put in Witchety?"

He made a low, throaty noise as he gazed along the driveway, where Witchety was growing smaller, Marsh's tail whipping energetically in their wake. "I've known her a long time. She's reliable. Last Friday was the first time she'd missed her booking in the years I've worked here."

"Oh." Margot's fingertips explored the leather strap from her bag, running along where it had been stitched shut and where some of the stitches were already pulling apart. "I guess what I'm asking is…do you think Gallows Hill actually needs these blessings?"

She'd asked it like it was halfway a joke, expecting Kant to shake his head or smile or comment about how superstitious some people could become. Instead, he gazed down at her, the heavy brows casting shade over his eyes. He was silent a long moment. Margot could only imagine he was testing his own words the same way she had.

"Some people believe Gallows Hill is a piece of the town's history and not much more," he said at last. "Other people feel the deaths have turned it bad. Won't visit. Won't even drive on roads near it. They talk about a Gallows Hill curse and think Witchety is protecting us from something worse."

Margot crossed her arms over her chest. More of her hair had come loose during the walk and now buffeted around her face, itching at the back of her neck and sending minute shivers along her spine. "What side do you fall on?"

Gray eyes searched hers. Then he said, "I'm glad Witchety comes here. I'd better make that phone call. Her neighbor doesn't like the place, but he'll still come and pick her up." He made to step away, then hesitated. "Can you find your way back to the house on your own?"

"Yes. Thanks."

Margot tightened her arms around her chest as she watched Kant pace back toward the staff buildings. His answer had been noncommittal. But it also hadn't been a denial that something was wrong.

She wondered what he'd seen in his thirty years working there.

Margot held her posture—shoulders hunched, arms wrapped around herself—as she followed the drive toward her home. The path was rocky, with weeds and grasses creeping in from the edges, and Margot found herself tracing one of the ruts formed by generations' worth of cars traversing that path.

Her own car waited for her at the hilltop. She could leave if she wanted to. Just climb in and drive away without even saying goodbye. She hadn't quit her old job yet. The city apartment would still be there for her.

The family house stood before her at the top of the hill, tiny glimpses of it peering out from between the trees. Margot stared at it and felt her heart ache.

If she left, she would forever be giving up the answers she'd come here to find. Who had her parents been? What could cause two otherwise healthy adults to die of heart attacks in one night? And why hadn't she been allowed to be a part of their lives?

If there was something dangerous about the property, she could maybe begin to understand them sending a child away for their protection. But

Margot had been an adult for years. They'd never made any attempt to reconnect.

"Think it out." She spoke to interrupt the crunch of her footfalls, which seemed too loud in the otherwise still landscape. "What am I asking myself here? If I got in my car, what would I be running *from*?"

She had no concrete answer, she realized. Witchety had spoken in foreboding generalizations: The ground was turning bad. Margot needed to be careful.

Was it some kind of curse? Bad energy seeping out from the dead buried under the hill? Was she going so far as to consider actual literal ghosts?

Or perhaps, was it something more physical than that?

Margot ran through the events from the previous night. Someone had rung the bells. Someone, perhaps, had pulled the cloth from the effigy. What if her first hunch was closest to the truth? Kant and Witchety had spoken about how reluctant people were to step on the land. Even now, superstitions about the winery seemed to thrive.

Maybe everything they feared could be put down to an individual. Someone who slung old ropes around the house and staged events to give them an otherworldly luster. Someone who, for one petty reason or another, was intent on tormenting the property's owners and those who worked there.

Kant had said it was a coincidence that the ropes had appeared the night Margot arrived. But Occam's razor said the simplest answer was often the correct one: someone knew she was there, and they wanted to make her nervous.

She'd reached the fence running around the house's lawn, and Margot stopped to lean against it to give her tired feet a moment to rest. Although a human threat would be less terrifying than something otherworldly, that was no excuse to take it lightly. She'd been lax the previous night; that wouldn't happen again. Her phone would be charged. She'd have some kind of defense. And most importantly, this time the doors would all be locked.

"I guess that decides it, huh?" She squinted against the sky. Wispy clouds chased one another across the hazy blue, scarcely touching the sun. "If I'm talking about preparing for the night, I guess that means I'm staying."

She'd promised herself four weeks to see if she could handle being the owner of Gallows Hill. At that moment, four weeks seemed like an insurmountable length of time.

She'd try one more night, she decided. If nothing bad happened—if she slept through with no bells or effigies haunting her—then she'd consider the four weeks again.

Margot pushed away from the fence. In the far distance, something chimed. Margot fell still, frowning as she listened. The noise fell quiet before she could catch it properly, but she was fairly sure she knew it. The bells.

Someone's in the house again.

Her heart squirmed in her throat, choking her. She made to turn, to rush back the way she'd come, to catch up to Kant and the others at the distillery, but then hesitated.

The fence was old. Many of the posts were rotting into the ground, and the crossbars were fracturing from wear and age.

But inexplicably, rows of wire ran along the fence. They formed straight lines, positioned just above the horizontal bars, and as far as she could see, covered the length of the fence. Margot reached out a finger and plucked one. Far in the distance, the bells rang.

"Oh," Margot whispered. The chimes seemed to hang in the air for longer than they should, and the following silence left her cold and clammy.

She'd had it all wrong. The bells in the house weren't left over from some centuries-old staffing arrangement. And there weren't levers inside the house to pull.

The wires were connected to the fence. The bells were an alarm system.

16.

Margot's body turned to water. She sagged back against the fence post. In the distant house, bells rang as she put pressure on the wires. They were faint but unmistakable, a grim siren carried on the wind.

The bells warn when someone crosses over the fence line. They rang more than once last night, though. So...someone crossed the fence multiple times? Or multiple people?

Her mouth was dry. She hadn't drunk anything since that morning, and it was beginning to pull on her, a slow, slinking headache forming behind burning eyes.

This doesn't change anything. You already believed someone from town walked to your house last night. This just confirms it.

Her eyes turned toward the opening in the fence. There was a gate, but it was left wide open, wedged in a groove it had gouged in the earth. It had been left open the previous night too.

Why would someone climb the fence when they could just walk in?

She had too many questions, and she kept coming up empty as she tried to craft answers for them all. Margot pushed away from the fence and moved toward the house. She undid the hair clip. More of her curls had sprung free and were turning to frizz in the wind, and she used a band from her pocket to tie them up.

The coils of rope Kant had left near the front door were gone. In their place was a small wicker basket. Margot approached it cautiously, craning her neck to see the contents without letting herself get too close. She recognized the distinct blue of a bottle of milk and moved forward, pulling the cloth back. A note had been tied to the basket's handle, written in a gently sloping script.

A few necessities to make your first day easier.
Welcome to Gallows Hill!
— Nora and Ray

Margot smiled despite herself as she tucked the store managers' note into her pocket. The basket held milk, a loaf of bread, butter that was turning soft, a jar of jam, apples, and a dozen loose eggs. Grateful beyond words, Margot held the basket close to her chest as she pushed her door open and entered the home.

Despite the sun beating on the house's exterior, its insides still felt uncomfortably dim. Margot nudged the door closed behind herself and had to squint as her eyes adjusted to the gloom. Ahead, she could barely make out a set of stairs at the end of the hall.

The kitchen, with its curtained window, was the only well-lit part of the house. Margot moved into it and spent a moment searching the cupboards for a pot, which she filled with water and put on the stove.

She hadn't eaten since the previous night and chewed on a slice of bread to take the edge off her hunger while three eggs boiled. The egg yolks were still runny when she pulled them off the stove, and Margot used another slice of bread to mop them up while she stood at the sink and stared through the window.

In the distance, the fence snaked along the boundary line, slipping in and out of sight as it disappeared behind patchy tree growths. Margot knew there were birds in those trees—she'd seen them the day before—but they were being uncomfortably quiet that afternoon.

At her back, the house felt cold and empty. She had the impression of a historical building, the kind that was too significant to bulldoze but was not wanted or needed for anything more intimate than occasional tours. The furniture was all still there, the plates in the cupboards and the original curtains drawn across the windows, but they'd become fossilized in their neglect; once a daily part of life, now they only existed to be stared at with uncaring eyes.

I need to get out. Breathe a bit.

Nora and Ray's gift basket had tided her over for lunch, but she still needed to go shopping. Discover the town. Maybe meet some of her neighbors. Make a good impression if possible.

She tried not to think about the nooses outside her front door.

Margot grabbed her keys off the kitchen's windowsill. Back outside, parked well away from the house, her small red hatchback caught the sun. She'd need to wash it eventually. It carried a cross-country trip's worth of dust and splattered insects.

The car gave up a muffled beep as she unlocked it, and Margot slid into the driver's seat. It had been given enough hours in the sun that the inside was sweltering, and Margot put the air-conditioning on high before taking a wide turn on the dirt patch and pulling onto the driveway.

Her car rattled over soft bumps in the road. She took the drive carefully, slowing at the bends, and crawled to a stop outside the store.

The lights were on inside the wood-and-steel building. Nora and Ray had to be inside, and she considered stopping to thank them for the gift basket, but there were already two cars parked in the lot. Tourists, she guessed, stopped to taste some of the wine and pick up a bottle or two. She didn't want to interrupt.

The main road appeared ahead, and Margot turned right, toward the town center. She'd barely seen it during her first drive through the day before, her thoughts snarled up by the impending funeral. Now, though, as the gently lilting ground transformed from fields to houses and shops, Margot leaned close to her windshield to examine the area.

It was the kind of town that saw enough tourists to have trendy eateries and multiple gift shops, but it still retained a sense of self. There were no fast-food outlets—probably a choice made by the local council—and most of the cars lining the roads were pickups, like Kant's, or old sedans with blocky bodies and hand-applied tints on the windows.

Margot felt a twinge of self-consciousness. Her bright-red hatchback stood out uncomfortably, just like her clothing choices had that morning. She could have easily blended into any street in her old city, but here she'd marked herself as the stranger. The intruder. The city girl who didn't know how to live in the country.

A low, stress-induced headache began in the back of her head, just above her neck muscles. She flexed her shoulders, trying to give it some relief.

It was early afternoon, and a handful of souls were on the footpaths leading between shops. Heads turned to follow her car as it passed. Margot itched under the cool, unsmiling scrutiny. She'd had some faint idea of wandering between the stores and stopping at a café, but, now, she just wanted to get some shopping done and go home.

She found what looked to be the main—possibly only—grocery store and pulled into an empty space not far from it. A wooden bench stood off to the side of the automatic doors, and a man, his thinning hair hanging across his forehead and tar-stained fingers clutching a hand-rolled cigarette, watched her approach. Margot hazarded a smile. He didn't return it. As she passed him to reach the doors, he said, "You're from the hill." It was a statement.

"Ah. Gallows Hill, yeah." She held her bag against her side with both hands, and even though she knew it made her look anxious and defensive, she couldn't stop. "Just moved in."

He gave a soft, guttural grunt and drew deeply from the cigarette. Margot couldn't tell if he was done talking or not. She made to step away, then he said, "I like some of the people from there."

"Yeah?"

"Place's rotten to its core, though." The cigarette was only half-done, but he dropped it to the ground, crushing it under his boot, then stood. "Take my advice. Keep driving."

Margot stood out in front of the store, heart running fast, as she watched the man walk away, head down and hands in his pockets. Her fingers hurt from how tightly she clutched her bag.

The automatic doors scraped open with a hiss, making her flinch, and Margot shuffled out of the way as an older couple moved past, watching her from the corners of their eyes.

The headache was growing worse. Margot made herself breathe in deeply, her lungs expanding as far as they would go, and then she stepped into the store.

The space smelled faintly of air freshener, moldering fruit, and dust. Only one of the four checkouts was open. A ceiling light blinked, feebly holding on to life. Margot took up a wire basket and entered the labyrinth of shelves.

A dozen shoppers milled, sometimes alone, sometimes in clusters. They spoke to one another in low whispers. Margot couldn't make out any words. She had a horrible, gnawing sense that they were talking about her. She worried she was being paranoid. Worse, she worried she was right.

She didn't labor over her choices but grabbed handfuls of fruit and a packet of nuts as she passed them. When she turned into an aisle, the woman at the opposite end swiveled her cart around and left.

Don't read into that. People move between aisles in a grocery store. That wasn't because of you.

She hadn't eaten cereal in years, but it wasn't a day to be fussy, so she added two brands to her basket and turned another corner.

A boy stood in her path, looking no older than ten or eleven. Blond, windblown hair clung messily above his pale face. Brightly shining, darkly curious eyes looked up at her. "Hi," he said.

"Hey." Margot tried to smile, even though the unexpected presence had unnerved her. There was no one else in the aisle; she didn't know where his mother or father might be.

"Do you live on Gallows Hill?" He tilted his head to one side, eyes narrow in sharp scrutiny, as though he expected her to lie to him. A smudge of dirt or grease marked his chin, and although his clothes looked recently bought, a matching stain ran across his striped shirt.

"I do." She tried to add some feeling to her voice, even though her smile was starting to grow stiff and unnatural and her headache was burrowing into the backs of her eyes. She added, almost in defense of herself, "It's a very pretty place."

The boy flicked his head slightly, as though to disregard that last comment. "My ma won't let me go near it. I'm not even allowed to ride my bike on the road behind it, even though Asher and Deacon both are."

"Oh." There was almost something funny about that. The small jealous bite that can only be experienced in childhood when your friends are given liberties denied to you. "Well, you're not missing much. It's really just a hill with a house on it."

"Deacon said there are ghosts there. From all the people that died." His brown eyes bored into her, eager, hungry. "Is that true?"

Her mouth opened, then closed again. The words shouldn't have startled her as much as they did. But Witchety's hoarse warnings and even Kant's nonanswers were burrs in the back of her mind, leaving her edgy, tense.

Nothing about this encounter—this *store*—felt natural. The fluorescent lights hummed like fat insects. Music played, but she had never heard the song before. The headache was swelling. The boy kept staring at her, unwilling to drop the question, and Margot had no idea what she was expected to say.

And then a woman inhaled sharply. A cart shoved past Margot's side, bruising her thigh, and the woman who had turned away from her in the previous aisle grabbed the boy by his arm. "Levi. What did I *say* about talking to people from—"

The woman's eyes flashed in her direction. The pupils were contracted, tiny dots in an expanse of blue—the fear-lanced glance of prey, facing down a predator. Then she blinked, and the expression was gone, and she pulled the boy at her side as she marched down the aisle. "Don't talk to strangers."

He sighed, a beleaguered noise, but didn't fight her grip. As they neared the end of the row, he threw Margot a look over his shoulder: equal parts intrigue at her presence and frustration at being denied an answer.

Margot felt sick. A cold clamminess flooded across her skin as the headache thrummed in time. Her basket was a chaotic mess of items, none of which could combine into a full meal. She didn't care. She wanted to be home.

A store employee, crouched on the ground to unpack a box, halted his work and stared up at her as she passed. Margot, mouth dry and tacky, asked, "Painkillers?"

He mutely pointed toward the end of the aisle. She followed the rows of shampoos and hair combs until she found the small white boxes and dropped two into her basket.

As she approached the lone open checkout, she saw the mother and her curious son were in the process of paying. Margot didn't want to cause trouble. She doubled back behind some boxes, dropping a bag of chips into her basket for something to do, and lingered there until they were processed and through the door.

"Hey," Margot said, placing her basket on the belt. Bottles of water stood in a display of drinks. She added one to her purchase.

To her relief, the teen behind the counter showed no strong reaction to her presence. Either she hadn't heard the rumors about the hill that seemed to be consuming everyone else in the town, or she didn't care. Her smile was perfunctory and she didn't try to make small talk as she bagged the goods.

The headache was like a drum. Margot leaned on the counter, card clasped in one hand, as she waited for her total. Then she hauled the bags up to her chest and moved through the door, silently cursing even the short distance between the shop and her car.

In the driver's seat, Margot tore the plastic off one of the boxes of painkillers, snapped two out, and unscrewed the bottle of water. She washed them down, then leaned back, head against the headrest, eyes closed, as she waited for her thundering heart to calm.

Kant warned me there were rumors about the hill. I had no idea it would be like this. She squinted her eyes open. A family crossed the road ahead of her. The father said something, and all four heads turned in her direction. Neither they nor Margot tried to smile.

How did my parents cope? Did they get stared at like this every time they came in to shop?

No, she realized. She was new. In a town this size, that would make her a curiosity just on its own.

Her parents' deaths must have been newsworthy. Both owners of a prominent business dead in one night. No matter what explanations the mortician offered, people would want to talk.

Hell, she herself was asking the same questions.

Now their only child—missing for decades—had returned. People were going to stare. It wasn't just about the hill.

She hoped.

The headache refused to abate, and the pain tablets would take a while to work. Margot wasn't sure how safe she would be on the roads with her vision going vague at the corners, but the streets were wide and she didn't want to linger in town any longer than she had to. She started the engine and eased back onto the path leading to the winery.

It will get better. Her legs were still unsteady, wavering on the accelerator and tapping the breaks too hard. *People will stop staring once the novelty wears off. You'll get comfortable here. Make friends. And that's only if you decide to stay.*

She wanted to, she thought. There was a slow kind of attachment growing inside of her. The house was melancholy, the tunnels claustrophobic—but they were *hers*.

And this was the first major significant thing in her life she could say that about. The first home she'd owned…even if, technically, probate was still being processed. The first business where she'd been more than an easily replaced employee.

She wanted to make it work.

The headache was grinding her down, draining her energy. She turned into the driveway, passing the sign advertising the Gallows Hill winery, and then slowed until the car was at a stop. She closed her eyes and breathed slowly as she tried to let some of the tension drain from the back of her neck.

Am I being a sentimental fool?

She couldn't drink wine. She couldn't stand the thought of the tunnels weaving beneath the ground, damp and cold and collapsing.

Was she trying to forge some kind of closure for herself by clinging to the home she'd been born in? Some kind of late-stage replacement for the years she couldn't remember, a false closeness to the parents who were now gone?

Well, would that be so wrong? My life was directionless. A job with no prospects, an apartment I'd have to leave soon regardless. I may not have chosen this path, but now that I've been placed on it, why shouldn't I try to follow it?

She opened her eyes. A car filled her rearview mirror, and Margot jolted. She swiveled to look behind herself. A jeep idled behind her, the out-of-town occupants watching her questioningly, apparently wondering why she'd stopped in the middle of the drive. Margot raised an apologetic hand, then eased onto the accelerator, climbing the hill and allowing the jeep to turn off at the winery store.

The headache was ebbing at least. The painkillers must have begun their work. She pulled onto the dirt patch ahead of the house, slightly closer than she'd dared the day before, and brought out her hard-won prizes from the general store.

With both hands full of bags, Margot had to shuffle in an awkward dance to get the front door open. She tried not to look at the enormous Watcher's silhouette in the living room as she turned into the kitchen.

A distant creaking noise came from somewhere deeper in the house, and Margot hesitated halfway to the fridge. She carefully lowered the bags onto the round table, listening.

There, again. A creak, low and slow and heavy, coming from somewhere behind and above. Like a rope being strained.

It's an old house, mostly built from wood. Margot swallowed and tasted the acrid tang of fear. *It's going to make noises sometimes.*

The noise came again, and this time it was accompanied by something louder. A shuffle, like a footstep.

They're back. They're back and they're in my home.

Margot felt her pocket for her phone, and her heart missed a beat.

She'd left it upstairs, in her room, that morning. Its battery had been dead, so she'd plugged it in to charge while she got dressed and had forgotten to retrieve it after.

The car keys were still in her hand. She could turn and leave before the intruder even knew she was here.

If it had been dark, she might have. At night, with the heavy cloud of stillness that the darkness brought, the world felt like it carried an extra layer of danger. That any risk, even small, would come with a cost.

But it wasn't night. The sun streamed through the kitchen window at her back like courage, and in that moment, the fear was almost—not quite, but *almost*—overridden by her anger. And something more.

Curiosity.

She wanted to know who had slung ropes across her porch the previous night. And why they felt entitled to enter her home. She needed to see their face.

The dense light heated her back as Margot slid a blade out of the knife block at her side. It wasn't large, but it was big enough to do damage. She held it at her side, half nestled in her skirt, as she slipped from the kitchen to the hallway.

17.

The low creaking noise sounded again, distant but unrelenting. She pictured a noose hung somewhere on the higher floors, the dead weight of a body suspended from it, creaking the fibers.

Stop. Don't think like that.

She followed the sound into the lounge room and past the ancient TV and the figure of twisted metal and bones. It loomed, dominating its wall, and she told herself she would cover it with the cloth again.

There was a sound that might have been a sigh. Margot slipped along the hallway, rolling her feet, heel to toe, to keep each step as close to silent as she could make it. Her chest was tight, her breathing low, her headache pulsing in time with each heartbeat. She craned forward to see around the corner.

The stairs were ahead. The same staircase she'd come down the night before. The one where the light had burst and where she'd become convinced that she could see cold lights on the lower landing, like a pair of eyes staring up at her.

She flexed her grip around the knife, feeling the handle heat beneath her hot grasp.

Something was at the top of the stairs. The light was bad. All of the infused courage from the kitchen had been strained and strangled in these deeper parts of the house, its closed doors and drawn curtains smothering the rooms in darkness. Margot squinted against the shadows, trying to understand what she was seeing.

The shape was broadest at its base. From her angle, she couldn't see its top, but it appeared unnaturally tall. Her first thought was that Witchety's Watcher had moved. That it had peeled itself off the living room floor and dragged its way along the hall, the bones and spoons and pebbles chiming against one another as it changed locations. So little else made sense that she might have believed it if she hadn't passed the Watcher just seconds before.

Margot took a step nearer. The knife's blade trembled against her thigh, her skin shielded by the skirt's fabric. She swallowed, wetting her throat in case she needed to cry out, even scream, though there was no one to hear her in the isolated house.

The shape began to move. The higher part of it lowered, like it was folding in on itself. Two heavy feet hit the floor. Then there was the click of a switch, and the upper landing was bathed in light.

"Margot," Kant said. He stood next to a stepladder, a small box in his hand. "Didn't hear you come home."

"Oh," she said, though it came out more like a gasp.

"I came to fix the light. Saw your car was gone and wasn't sure whether I should come in or not." He folded the stepladder and lifted it under his arm. "Didn't mean to startle you."

He moved down the steps, his limp heavy, and Margot took the second of distraction to slip the knife into her pocket where he wouldn't see it. Her heart still thundered.

Kant reached the hallway and set the stepladder down. "It works now at least," he added, nodding up to the bulb that glowed above them. "Call me if any others go bad."

"Thanks for that." She hesitated, fidgeting, then said, "I just went into town."

"Hm."

"The people there don't really like the hill, do they?"

In the bulb's gold-tinted light, his glance looked almost melancholy. "Some are fine with it. Some think it's a bad place. Hugh and Maria used to get their groceries delivered. I can help you set that up, if you'd like."

For a second, she considered it. With work at her doorstep and groceries delivered, she'd never have a reason to leave the estate. She could still go for a drive anytime she wanted, but without a purpose behind it, how often was she likely to do that? She would be a near-perfect hermit.

She wondered if that was what her parents had become—recluses, never leaving sight of their home.

"I don't mind getting out on occasion." She chuckled. "This just wasn't the best first outing. A boy started asking questions I had no idea how to answer. And I got a headache on top."

"Mm." A soft noise, one that carried an apology and something unspoken all at once. "Want me to get you something for it?"

"Thanks, I think I'm good. It's just stress. And, well, lack of sleep probably doesn't help."

"Try a nap," Kant suggested. "You might feel better after."

Margot's mind was stuck with her parents and how they could have gone weeks or months at a time without ever stepping foot off the land. She gave her head a slight shake to get rid of the thoughts and put some life back into her voice. "Never mind that. Did you want something to drink? You came all this way to fix my light, but there's no reason you need to go straight back."

"I appreciate it. Need to catch up on some work, though." He reached toward the stepladder, then hesitated again. "I did have something to ask."

"Yeah?"

"I had a day off tomorrow. Was going to visit my sister. I would have rescheduled, but I only see her twice a year, and we've been planning for months. My nephew is going to be there. She's bringing her new son. Haven't met him yet."

"Oh!" Margot felt a faint rush of relief. This was an easy problem. She'd been in Kant's shoes more than once, asking for time away from work, and had always hated the silently judgmental stare of the business owner. She wasn't going to be that person, she decided. Kant could take as much time off as he wanted. "No, absolutely, you should go. How old is he?"

"Just eight months." Kant hesitated, the unreadable gray eyes scanning the walls around them as though looking for some answer in the paneling. "I know it's bad timing. Only the day after you arrived. Things are still…volatile."

"Don't worry about that. I'm sure I can survive by myself for a day." Margot chuckled, though Kant didn't join in. "I've met the others—Nora and Ray and Andrew—so I can always call in on them if I need help with anything."

"Witchety came through this morning," Kant murmured, and Margot wasn't sure if he intended her to hear. "So that's out of the way. And I'll only be gone for a day."

She turned to put her back against the wall, taking some of the pressure off her feet. "You said you only see your sister twice a year, right? Take a few days off. Spend some time with her."

"No," he said. "Just the one day. I'll leave before dawn, arrive back in the early hours, around three in the morning."

"Are you sure?" She grimaced. "That sounds like a long drive."

"That's how I've always done it."

"Well, if you decide you want to stay longer, you're welcome to it. Otherwise, I guess I'll see you the day after tomorrow."

He nodded, a stiff movement, then picked up the stepladder. "Thank you. I've missed my family."

"Of course."

"I'll put this back in the shed. Anything else you want help with before I go?"

Margot glanced up, along the length of the stairwell, toward the cloistered rooms around them. *Can you dispel some of the bad feelings in this place? Can you make it feel like home?* "I think I'm good."

He gave a soft noise of assent, then turned along the hall. "Take care, Margot."

"You too."

She saw him to the front door. He turned around the side of the house to return the ladder to the shed Margot hadn't yet discovered, and she slowly closed the door behind him. After a second's hesitation, she turned the lock. Then she pressed her head against the cool wood, eyes closed, as she centered herself.

Well…I overreacted.

She tried to tell herself she'd been rational. That the intrusion the night before made it more than justified to be on edge. But as she crossed to the kitchen and slotted the knife back in beside its brethren, she was only grateful that she hadn't embarrassed herself further by calling the police or shouting anything menacing along the hallway.

Margot buried her face in her hands as she leaned against the kitchen counter. She was tired, that was all. The headache, though subsiding, wasn't helping matters. She hadn't gotten a full night of sleep in days, and it was wearing her down, making every stressful situation feel just a little worse.

Maybe some sleep would do her good after all. She checked the clock. It was after four. No one needed anything from her that afternoon. She'd take a nap, hopefully get rid of the last of the headache, then figure out dinner. Based on what she'd brought home, most likely cereal.

She climbed the stairs to her bedroom, her steps heavy. The hallways seemed longer than she remembered.

The padlock still hung from the window frame. Margot found her gaze drawn to it as soon as she entered the room. It was heavy. Thick. So out of place in a child's bedroom. She'd throw it out, she decided. Either that or reuse it on some other door that she cared about locking. She didn't want to have to look at it every night.

Right then, though, she was tired. She drew the curtains across the window, blocking both the padlock and the light, and sighed. The room wasn't completely dark—not *night* dark—but she was fine with that. She wasn't sure she wanted to return to the pitch-black of night anytime soon.

Margot tugged her shoes off, but left everything else in place as she crawled into bed. The blankets felt warmer than they had the night before. The pillows were softer. She closed her eyes and had very few conscious thoughts before her limbs went limp and her mind fell into itself, engulfed by sleep.

For a moment, all she was aware of was darkness. She was upright, walking forward, but nothing was visible.

Then a voice floated through the dark. "We did the best we could, but…"

Margot's stomach coiled at the words. She knew where this led. She tried to turn away, to retreat back into a different dream, but already the scene was forming in the theater of her mind's eye.

The long hallway. The threadbare runner, its color muted, somber. The funeral director. Slight and with gentle hands, an old but clean suit draped from his shoulders, his voice tinged with unspoken apologies.

"It's just this way," he said, and he turned toward her, and if the dream had let Margot cry out, she would have.

His face was no longer the soft, pale visage she remembered. The elements were still there—the eyes and nose and mouth—but they had been smeared, like an artist had taken a cloth to his still-damp painting in a frenzy. All that remained were hazy streaks of color, halfway blended together, striking across the canvas of his face.

And in the dream, Margot could do nothing. She was bound by what had happened that morning: dutifully following the funeral director to that dim, dusty room. The space with the rows of caskets and coffins lined up like sentries. The spaces where her parents lay, inside the boxes that were designed to keep them whole and protected once they were placed into the ground, as though they *should* be whole and protected, as though those faces were something Margot wanted to preserve…

The funeral director fit his key into the lock, and as he turned it, Margot woke with a gasping jolt.

She was breathing hard enough to make her lungs ache. She scrambled to sit, eyes wide but sightless. The world was gone. A horrible thought speared through her mind, sending ice into her veins.

I'm in a casket. He put me in a casket by mistake.

But then her eyes began to adjust, and she saw the bronze bell next to the door, thankfully still, and the faint outline of her phone and its looping power cord beside her bed.

The space was dark. Far, far darker than it had been when she'd lain down. She'd planned for a nap, but both dusk and early night had passed her by. She reached for her phone, squinting in what traces of moonlight reached under the curtains, and tapped to see the time. Nearly one in the morning.

She pulled back, bringing her knees up and wrapping her arms around them. The hour felt dangerous. Like she wasn't supposed to be conscious at such an unnatural time.

That was foolishness, she knew. She'd been awake at one in the morning before. After New Years'. During some holidays and weekends too, when her friends threw parties or had a movie marathon. One in the morning had never felt *wrong* before, just late.

Now, though, the time felt deeply sick. As though anyone who was alert at this hour invited terrible, horrific things into their lives. As though it opened a doorway to a darker world.

It's the house. The land and its history. The stories have gotten into your head. You're not used to living in the country, and it's making you paranoid.

Margot's wide eyes glanced from the bell to the closed curtains. It *was* the land, she thought, but not in the sense that she was letting urban legends upset her. The land itself did something to the hour. Warped it, the way the city never could.

Stop it. This is your home now.

She'd only wanted to sleep for an hour or two. Then she could have eaten while there were still traces of light outside and been in bed before it was truly dark. Now, though, she had the choice of creeping through the building as deep night coated it or forgoing dinner entirely and trying to sleep until morning.

The choice was already made for her, Margot realized. The nightmare had made her tense. She wouldn't be sleeping anytime soon, and reaching a well-lit kitchen would at least be better than lying there, wide-eyed, as the hours ticked by.

She lowered her feet over the bed's edge and slipped her shoes back on, then dropped her mobile into her jacket pocket. She hadn't felt cold when she'd woken, but as she exhaled, a wisp of condensation rose ahead of her.

Margot opened the curtains across her window, inviting the moonlight in, then turned her bedroom light on for good measure. At that moment, she didn't care what the power bill came to. She would turn on every light she passed.

Her phone, fully charged, still did very little to reveal the hallway outside her room. Margot traced her path carefully. Even without the bells, she didn't like the idea of becoming lost in the labyrinth again.

She found a light switch at the end of the hall and pressed it. A bulb shot to life at her back, sending her shadow stretching long and corrupt ahead of her, splashing up the paneling on the opposite wall. The stairs to the main hallway were just around the corner.

Margot found herself hesitating. Her shadow didn't seem right. The hips and chest and shoulders wound in and out according to what surface they fell across—the floor, the skirting, and the wall—but the head was turned at a sharp angle. Pulled to the left. As though her neck had been broken.

It could have come from anything—a distortion in the wall, a quirk of the bulb behind her. Margot raised her hand, watching its mirror flit across the surfaces until it was at the same height as her head. It did not distort.

I don't understand.

She tried turning her head to the right, seeing if she could correct the angle enough to get the shadow's head to stand upright. For a second, it seemed to work. The head rose on the violently twisted neck, reaching a point where it was nearly straight, and then it twisted over, dropping to the other side. Something protruded from the edge of the shadow's neck. A broken bone through skin.

Margot gasped, straightening her head and clamping her hands to either side of her own throat. She felt her pulse leap under her fingertips as they ran across the soft flesh, searching for irregularities. The shadow's fingers mimicked her movements. The head remained violently bent.

A soft noise echoed from behind her. Margot turned fast, her shoulder bumping the wall, but the hall behind her was empty for as far as she could see.

She thought she'd heard the scuff of a shoe. The exhale of a breath. Or maybe it was just the wood sighing. It was hard to be certain with a house that old.

Slowly, her movements measured, she turned back to the wall opposite and to her shadow.

The head was straight again.

She blinked once, twice, forcing back the stinging moisture that stress had brought to her eyes, then shoved around the hallway's corner, racing the stairs to the landing.

It had to be an optical illusion. She leaned her shoulder against the wall, relying on the hard structure to help her feel centered. *Didn't it? I couldn't figure it out right then, but if I'd spent more time, tried moving my head in different ways, I'd see how it worked. Right?*

It was the hour. It made the house *wrong*. Made Margot feel sick and hunted and lost. She breathed slowly, holding her breath a few seconds before each exhale, to slow her heart rate.

Ahead, the hall led to the main entrance. Moonlight came through both the kitchen's and the living room's archways.

She could see the light switches beside the front door. She'd turn them on. Flood the lower levels with brightness, chase back the heaviness of night until she could forget the hour. Then she would make a drink and something to eat. She'd make the meal rich and heavy, more than she should really have so late, so that it weighted her limbs and pulled her eyes closed and let her drift off without any other care.

She pushed off from the wall. Two steps along the hallway, she brought herself to a halt.

Light came from the living room. She'd assumed it was moonlight, like it flowed out of the kitchen, but that shouldn't be possible. The curtains had been closed when she'd passed through that afternoon.

Her eyes traced across the glow on the floor. It was harsher, colder than moonlight. Artificial. A low hissing, spitting sound barely reached her ears. Static.

Someone had turned the television on.

18.

Margot's lungs froze. She inched forward, her feet gliding silently over the floor, as she strained to see inside the living room.

The hissing static grew louder as she approached. The ancient box television's screen was lit up in flickering grays, painting a spreading rectangle of light across the floors and sagging seats.

Someone's in the house.

Her eyes flicked toward the front door. It was still closed. She'd made certain to lock it after Kant left.

That means very little. There are other doors in this building. Ones I haven't even seen yet.

The house felt quiet, though. There was a heaviness to the air that made it hard for her to imagine anyone else disturbing it recently.

She took another step toward the living room. The Watcher was against the opposite wall. Its metals and stones shone in the reflected light, like a thousand eyes blinking at her.

How else could the television turn on? Could a surge in the power spark it to life?

She had her phone in her pocket and let her hand linger over it as she edged closer to the screen. The staticky hiss, though soft, was playing across her nerves, stringing them tight. She slowly lowered herself into a crouch as she looked for a way to turn it off. Then she fell still, the harsh light playing across her hands as she looked down.

A tape protruded from the VCR player beneath the screen. Two words had been written across the label in heavy red ink: *Margot's Tape.*

It felt like a bad kind of invitation, like a fortune-teller asking if you wanted to know when you were going to die. An invitation like that boded only harm and fear.

But she couldn't turn away. Not from her own name, written in a hand she didn't recognize, on a tape she never remembered seeing.

Her fingers trembled as she touched the yellowed, peeling label. She pushed, and the tape shuddered into the inner mechanisms of the player, swallowed up among the gears and spindles like into a beast's gnawing mouth.

The equipment was so old that she half expected it to be broken. But then the static cut out and the screen jumped to life.

The image was grainy and poorly lit. Static still corrupted it, distinct lines traveling up the image in loops. The tape had been damaged. Possibly through time or possibly from being played too often.

The image showed coils of red fabric, like stage curtains. They twitched, then pulled backward in stiff tugs, revealing a painted cardboard backdrop. It depicted a house on one side and trees on the other, both on top of a grassy field. The images were kept simple—almost cartoonish—but had been painted with reasonable skill. It held the atmosphere of low-budget children's programming from the eighties or nineties.

This has to be from some kind of kid's show. Margot, on her knees, face almost uncomfortably close to the screen, stared into the image's details. They held a disjointed, uncomfortable sense of déjà vu. As though she'd once known this tape very, very well.

A woman's voice spoke. "There once was a little girl."

The volume was low. Margot scrambled for the buttons on the television's front, and green bars flashed across the screen as she increased the audio.

A hand puppet appeared on-screen, walking in front of the house. It wore a smock dress and had brown wool for hair. Two marks from a felt-tip pen had been used for its eyes, but to Margot's discomfort, no one had given it a mouth. It stared out of the screen, the eyes wide set and blank.

"The girl lived in a house with her parents," the voice continued. It had become distorted along with the tape, the words stretching and burbling and growing thick like molasses. "All day, she played in the yard around the house."

The puppet danced across the screen, limp arms swinging, blank eyes staring into nothing.

"At night, her parents put her to bed and told her to stay there until morning. You see, the girl and her family weren't alone. Another family lived nearby. And just as the girl played during the day, the other family liked to play outside at night."

The lighting changed, dimming and darkening until the green-painted trees turned to a heavy gray and the sky grew dull. The girl's puppet danced its way back to the house, disappearing off the side of the screen.

There was a momentary pause, then, from the other side—the side with the trees—two more puppets entered the scene. They were taller and thinner, made of gray material, their bodies seeming to sag on the hands that held them upright. Like the girl's puppet, they had been given dark dots for eyes. Below that were their mouths: long lines curving downward at the end.

Three large Xs had been drawn across both of the mouths.

The bodies swayed as they moved across the screen, approaching the house, their limp arms dangling at their sides.

"The other family would play outside from night until morning." The woman's voice had grown further distorted, static hissing across the words, blotting some of them until they were nearly unintelligible. "They didn't like being interrupted. In fact, if anyone tried to disturb their games, they would be very, very angry."

The gray forms moved back and forward, pacing between the homes and the trees. Margot leaned even closer, her breath condensing on the screen. The pixels were painfully bright.

"One night, the girl decided she wanted to play with the other family. Even though her parents had always told her to stay in bed until morning, she waited until her parents were asleep and then left her room."

The girl's puppet reappeared, its cheerful smock seeming dour and cold in the dulled lighting. The mouthless face stared listlessly out at Margot as she tilted toward the gray figures.

"The girl wanted to make friends, but the other family didn't want to be friends with her. They were very, very angry that she'd interrupted them."

The smaller puppet danced closer, wool hair jostling around her head, arms flung out with each forceful step. The gray puppets had turned to face her.

Margot had fallen so still that she no longer even dared breathe. She gripped the television's sides with both hands, as though clutching it might clear some of the heavy static, might make the image clearer.

"The other family was *so* angry that they attacked her." The woman's voice had grown heavy, dark, angry. "They scratched her and bit her and dragged her into the earth."

Margot jolted back from the screen. The gray forms swarmed over the girl's puppet. The three of them thrashed together, limbs shivering, and then plunged downward, disappearing beneath the base of the screen.

For several seconds the image was empty, with only the static and

Margot's own pulse interrupting the quiet. Then, a fingertip appeared from the screen's base. It was covered in some kind of dark paint. It smeared the color across the field backdrop, right where the girl had stood, then lowered out of sight.

The lighting grew strong again, simulating daylight, and the streak of paint became clearer. It was a violent red, fresh and glistening across the painted grass.

"The girl's parents never saw her again."

Margot bit her tongue, watching the image with sick fascination. A thicker section of the paint dribbled downward, then the curtains closed over it, hiding the images from view.

The camera moved, panning back from the curtains, then the screen cut to black. Margot waited, silent, not willing to turn away in case she missed anything else. The VCR player rattled. It ejected the tape, and the screen returned to a wash of speckled white, too sharp and loud. Margot scrambled to lower the volume again.

What kind of show is this? It's made for kids. Young kids. What station approved this? Who signed off on it?

She hunched back, arms folded defensively around herself. She'd seen something right at the end, she thought, as the camera panned away from the curtains. It had only been for a fraction of a second. Almost against her better judgment, she dug through the magazines cluttering around the television set to find the VCR's remote. It was dusty, its keys sticky.

Margot pressed the tape into the player and wound back, then pressed play. The curtains closed over the smear of blood. The camera began to pan backward, a distant mechanical whir barely audible. Just at the last second, the view extended past the edges of the stage. She thought she saw a sliver of the room the video had been filmed in. Then the image cut to black.

She pressed rewind, watching the images twist around one another, then hit play again.

As the camera drew back, Margot waited until she saw just the edge of the space behind the set and hit pause. She was too late. The screen was black.

She rewound again. Pressed play again. Waited, thumb just barely indenting the pause button, and squeezed it down. A fraction too early this time: a line of the background was visible, pencil thin, but it wasn't enough to reveal the image she thought she'd seen.

Rewind again. Play. Pause. Again: rewind, play, pause. Rewind, play, pause.

On her sixth try, she got it. The space beyond the curtained stage was visible. Not by much, but enough. It was dark, and the static clinging to it was heavy, disguising almost all details except one.

A face stared out at her.

Margot, kneeling with the remote clutched in both hands, stared back at it.

A line of horizontal distortion ran across the face, cutting it in half just below the eyes. Poorly lit and grainy, not much of it was distinguishable.

She was almost certain it was a woman, though. Most likely the woman who had been narrating the clip. She hunched close to the miniature stage. Red lipstick created a gash of crimson color among the gray shadows. Something that might have been a pendant hung over her dark clothing.

Margot ran one hand over her face and felt the clammy chill of her skin. The image on the screen, for all its distortion and obscuration, felt uncomfortably familiar.

She dropped the remote and crawled to her feet. The lights on the lower floor were still off. Her mind was too wrapped up in the children's video to care, though, as she crossed the hall into the kitchen.

Moonlight illuminated the table, the shopping bags she'd left on the counter, and the clean plates in the sink. Dozens of magnets dotted the fridge's surface, holding photos and scraps of paper in place. Margot searched the images until she found the one she wanted, pulled it free, and carried it back into the living room.

She crouched back in front of the television, her skin painted in unnatural hues as she held the photo up beside the screen. In it, her mother leaned against her father, red lips lifted into a smile. A bronze, oval pendant hung from her throat, draped over a plum sweater.

The images on the screen were achingly grainy, but Margot was fairly certain they were a match.

She let the photo drop.

It's not studio programming. My parents made this.

Her name had been on the peeling yellow label.

Margot's Tape.

They made this for me.

She ran the back of her hand across her mouth. The film, short though it was, must have taken a lot of effort. They'd painted the backdrop with care. Sewn puppets. Created a small stage with curtains.

For what purpose?

Not as a sentimental gift for their daughter. If that had been their intention, the story wouldn't have featured a young girl dying, surely.

If not sentimental, then...

A parable?

Fairy tales had been created to warn children of dangers in the wider world: Do not trust strange women who offer you treats. Do not approach wolves. Do not wander into the forest alone.

That felt closer to the tape's intentions—a warning, wrapped inside childish visuals to make it easy to watch and absorb.

Warning about what? Another family...that comes out at night?

That had to be an allegory for something. Wild animals possibly. *They scratched her and bit her and dragged her into the earth.*

She pictured the smear of red blood left on the ground where the girl had stood. The gray figures with *X*s across their mouths, dragging the girl's puppet beneath the stage.

On-screen, the line of jagged static ran through her mother's face, quivering faintly even though the image was paused.

She pressed Eject on the VCR. The tape grated through the opening. Its yellowed sticker and red writing seemed alive in the light of the static.

The tape had been made for her, which meant the girl in the smock with the brown wool hair was supposed to represent Margot. That alone would have been enormous work to sew. More effort than someone would go to for a child they didn't want.

Her parents hadn't given her puppet a mouth. Maybe they hadn't wanted her to look happy while she was being torn apart by the gray figures.

Margot moved to lift the tape out, to slide it into a sleeve where it would be protected, but then, instead, pushed it back inside the player. She took up the remote and rewound the video. It was short; it took less than fifteen seconds to reach the start. Then she sat back, her knees pulled up to her chest, as she set it to play again.

She'd seen photos of her parents. But this was the first time she could remember hearing either of their voices. As her mother's bubbled, distorted words began, a lump formed in Margot's throat.

"There once was a little girl," she recited alongside her mother, and it occurred to her that at one time, she may have known this tape's script by heart. She wondered if this was how she'd sat when she watched it: knees pulled to her chest, arms wrapped around them, so close to the TV that the light hurt her eyes.

She watched the doll frolic across the grass during the daylight. Then the stage's light dimmed and turned blue as night set in, the gray figures emerging from the forest-filled side of the screen.

She didn't want to watch the last part again—the girl being killed and the man's finger painting a smear of blood across the grass—but she found herself riveted, unable to look away, until the camera had finished panning back from the curtains and the screen cut to black.

For a moment Margot sat in the cold and the dark, staring into the empty static. Then she rewound the tape to the beginning and set it to play once more.

19.

A chime stirred Margot to wakefulness. She opened her eyes to see tulip-shaped light shades above her head. Her back ached. Her neck was stiff. She groaned as she rolled to her side and faced green patterned wallpaper and a television playing static.

She sat up, grimacing as she moved. The curtains across the windows kept the room dim, but enough light came in through the hallway to tell her she'd made it to dawn.

The tape—*Margot's Tape*—protruded from the VCR player. She couldn't remember how many times she'd replayed the video before falling asleep. At least a dozen times. She'd hated the ending; the girl had only been a puppet, but the simplistic images and words had crawled under her skin in the way even horror films couldn't.

But she'd kept replaying it for one simple reason: her mother's voice. A mother who had cared enough to paint scenes and sew puppets and record a pantomime to keep her daughter safe.

Kant was right, she'd thought as she watched the images dance across the screen. *They may have sent me away, but at one point, when I was very young, they did love me.*

That thought was simultaneously a knife twisting into the center of her chest and a balm. Pain and cure all at once, in a confusing set of emotions that Margot had never felt before and didn't know how to approach.

So she'd watched the tape again and again, until her eyes had burned and she could mouth each line of the script in perfect tandem. And without even realizing it, she'd fallen asleep there.

The chime repeated, and Margot hunted for her phone. It was on the floor, just a few feet behind her. A message flashed on-screen: Hope all's well. Any ETA on return?

That was from her old manager. Margot dug her thumb into the corners of her eyes, clearing sleep, as she shambled to her feet.

She'd made up her mind about this, hadn't she? That she would at least give the new house, the new *life*, a try. As she moved to the kitchen and set the kettle on, she typed out a return message: Parents left a business. Still figuring it out, but probably won't be able to return. Sorry for short notice.

It shouldn't be a shock; before leaving, she'd told the manager that she might be away for a while, possibly indefinitely. Still, the response she got was curt: K.

She turned the phone over so she wouldn't have to look at the text any longer, then leaned on the counter as the kettle heated up.

This is it, huh?

She'd committed. Her old roommates would still need to be messaged, and she'd pay her share of the rent until they found a replacement, but she was slowly cutting ties to her old life.

It was terrifying.

She was fairly sure she'd feel that emotion even more acutely once she'd properly woken. At that moment, it was all happening in a slow haze.

Margot made coffee and cooled it with tap water so that she could drink it faster. The television's volume was low, but it continued to hiss in the living room. She sluggishly crossed the hallway again to switch it off, then gently slid the tape out of the player and tucked it into one of the empty sleeves.

The label was still visible. *Margot's Tape.* She placed it on top of the box, then stepped back, examining the room with a more critical eye now that it was daylight.

The television had been turned on. And she still didn't know how or by who.

It could have been a power surge. A glitch. The tape might have already been in the player, waiting to be played and spat out.

She felt like she was building excuses for herself. Struggling to make this new life work, to justify her decision, to reassure herself that everything was fine.

But she hadn't seen any other trace of someone in her home the night before. That didn't mean she'd definitely been alone, but it left room for doubt.

Maybe she'd jumped in too fast in quitting her job.

The towering statue of nature and metal loomed against the wall behind her, its deer skull's empty eyes boring into her. Margot placed her coffee on a dusty side table and picked up the effigy's cloth. She refused to make eye contact with it as she threw the fabric over it, smothering it.

She could make good use of the day, she decided. Kant had said he'd be leaving early, before dawn, so she wouldn't have a chance to ask him questions until the following day. Still, she could start something that was very overdue: an exploration of the house and the lands.

The coffee smarted her throat as she drank it, but it felt good. She'd never actually gotten the meal she'd come downstairs for the previous night, so she made up for it then, cooking toast and eggs and making a bowl of cereal.

As she washed up, she flipped her phone back over to check the time.

After ten. She couldn't remember the last time she'd slept in that late. It was making up for all of those other days of short sleep, she supposed.

The kitchen window overlooked her car and, beyond that, the grassy slope down toward the trees. She stared through it as she dried the plates, enjoying the way the light moved over the scene. Then her eyes flicked toward one of the nearer clumps of trees. Something seemed to move inside.

Margot, frowning, craned closer to the window as she tried to see. It was no good. The glass was foggy, the sun at the wrong angle to make out any details.

She crossed to the front door and stepped outside, following the porch's steps to the ground. Her neck craned as she tried to see between the sickly branches. The trees there weren't thick. They shouldn't have been able to conceal anything large.

Dead grass crackled under her shoes as she crossed the field. She couldn't hear much else. No insects. No birds. The trees had looked cramped and small from a distance, but as she neared them, they seemed to grow larger.

It's daylight. She tried to smile at the thought, but the expression didn't form quite right. *The video said I was allowed to play outside during daylight.*

There was something among the trees, though. Something that didn't mix properly with the outlines around it.

A post had been left in the ground. It was old, crumbling. Possibly a relic from some old fence that had long ago been removed. Margot let her hand touch down on it as she walked past.

The shape in the trees seemed to move a fraction. Margot hesitated, midstep, eyes squinted against the light as she tried to see. Branches, nearly bare of leaves, swayed in the light wind. But the motion she thought she'd seen was different.

She moved forward, letting go of the aged post as she put her full weight into her next step. The ground beneath her collapsed.

Margot didn't have enough time to gasp. Her hands flew out, clutching at clods of soil as she dropped beneath the surface. The dirt gave out under her hands, falling down with her into endless darkness.

Her left-hand side landed first, jarring her, the impact running along her ribs and through her shoulder. She squeezed her eyes closed, expecting worse, but the stabbing pain of broken bones didn't materialize. Her hip and side stung, but the landing had been padded.

Dirt rained around her. Grains got into her mouth, thick and loamy and sour. She rolled to her side, spitting them out, then carefully opened her eyes.

All around her was nothing but darkness. Her hands and knees pressed into soft soil. The air was cold, at least fifteen degrees lower than the surface temperature, and smelled of earth and old decay.

She lifted her head. A block of light came down from above, marking the hole she'd fallen through. It had to be more than ten feet above her. It was a miracle the drop hadn't hurt her worse.

Where am I?

Margot struggled to pull her phone out of her jacket pocket with shaking hands. The flashlight came on, showing dirt walls reinforced in patches with wood and stone. It wasn't quite a pit—two of the walls pressed tight at her sides—but a passageway led in either direction.

Kant's voice returned to her: *"A network of old passageways…with posts to mark the entrances."*

Margot grimaced. She'd discovered an access point for the old cellars.

This is fine. She held the phone in both hands, afraid that she would drop it and lose her light entirely. *This is okay. You survived the fall, and that's the worst of it over with. If this is an entrance to the tunnels, there must be a way to climb out.*

She found it at her back: a ladder, fixed into the haphazard stones on the walls. It would have been installed when the tunnels were first built, and it looked it: the wood was soft and flaking, and when she pressed her thumb into it, she felt fibers collapse under the pressure. Parts had already decayed away entirely, corrupted by time and underground insects and damp. She was fairly sure it wouldn't hold her weight.

Margot looked up, measuring the distance. Ten feet. Too high to jump.

She still had to try to reach it. She slipped her phone into her pocket, then put her hands around one of the higher rungs. She pulled to test its integrity. It cracked, collapsing in the middle before it had even taken half of her weight.

A low, creeping kind of panic was developing at the back of her throat, turning it tight and aching. She tried another, lower rung by resting her foot on it. Like its sibling, it crumbled with very little pressure.

This is okay. This is still fine. She took her phone back out. Kant's number was in her recent calls list. Only, he was no longer on the estate. He would be hours away by that point and not returning until the following morning.

She bit her lip and tasted dust. The walls were pressing in on her, making her feel crushed and breathless.

Stay calm. She wasn't out of options. She could call the fire department.

She could imagine people from the town watching the trucks turn into the driveway and what sort of stories that would spark. *Only three days on the hill and she's already trying to burn it down.*

That would be worth it, though. As long as they got her out.

Her eyes flicked to the bar at the top of the screen. It displayed a *no service* symbol.

"No," Margot whispered. She clung close to the broken ladder, stretching as she raised her phone high above her head, reaching it toward the opening. The display didn't change. Gallows Hill was already remote; being underground killed any chance of reception.

Margot put her back to the wall, breathing in short, sharp gasps.

How long would it take someone to notice she was missing? How long until someone came near the hole she'd fallen into?

The answer was the same for both questions: tomorrow, when Kant returned.

If he visited the house to check on her. *If* he didn't extend his trip, like Margot had suggested. If, if, if.

No. We have another option.

The tunnels continued through the hill, and their entrances would too. She couldn't climb out through this one, but others might be easier to get out of. Like the stone steps in the tunnel Kant and Andrew had shown her the day before.

She just needed to keep walking until she found an exit.

20.

It's that simple. Just keep walking.

Margot faced the tunnel that would lead down the hill. The dark was immense, intense. It was like looking down a very long, narrow grave. She could taste the soil in her throat.

Just walk.

She did, scraping one foot forward and shuddering as she passed beyond where the column of natural light could reach.

Her skin crawled. Her breath hitched. It occurred to her that her phobia of underground spaces might have been spawned in one of these very passageways. Tightly enclosed areas had never fazed her too much. Only when they were enclosed belowground. Exactly like this tunnel.

"It's fine. You're okay." Her nerves were raw. Every instinct in her body begged her to turn around, to return to the narrow beam of light and the view of the sky. Only, she knew what would happen then. She'd sit, huddled and ashamed, in the cold dirt while she waited for someone to find her.

And that might not be anytime soon.

If she could only keep walking, she'd find a way out. She could hold her fear under control. She *had* to.

They were only tunnels. They couldn't hurt her.

Stones and wood had been used to support the structure in areas, but they were irregular, their placement suggesting spur-of-the-moment decisions, rather than a plan, or sporadic repairs.

In between them, the dirt was crumbling and moist. Clumps of it had fallen from the ceiling to create mounds on the floor, and Margot had to duck her head as she scrambled over them. In other areas, roots had grown through the soil. They hung in thick clumps, stiff and uncomfortably warm under her touch.

Her phone's light caught the edges of a turnoff. She hesitated in the opening, her heart running too fast, as she tried to see down its length. She couldn't make out much. The phone was too bright to let her eyes adjust to the gloom but not strong enough to travel more than ten feet at a stretch.

She took a chance and followed the turn. It tended downward, sometimes as a slope and sometimes with stone stairs embedded. After a dozen meters, it split again. The path to the right led her to an empty chamber: one of the original cellars. Stains and indents worn into the stone flooring showed where barrels had been stored, though they had long since been moved out.

The cellar had a second passageway leading out of it. The Hulls would most likely want an exit close by for easy access, Margot reasoned. She followed the path. It only lasted for a few feet before tree roots, growing densely through the walls and ceiling, blocked her path. She tried to push through, but too many of them had embedded themselves into the floor. She turned back, retracing her steps out of the chamber.

Kant and Andrew said many of the tunnels had collapsed. She forced herself to breathe through the squeezing stress as she reached her light ahead to find the crossroads. *What's the danger of them collapsing further while I'm inside?*

The panic was getting its hold on her, digging claws into her back and squeezing. Her footsteps, originally careful and measured, had become harried. Only her semi-blindness held her back from breaking into an outright sprint.

Stop. Get it under control.

She staggered, one shoulder pressed into a fractured wooden support buried into the wall, and closed her eyes as she tried to reel herself back in.

The tunnels might be a maze, but they couldn't last forever.

Distantly, she wondered if *this* was what her parents' tape had been intended to warn her about. A child could see and avoid the markers over the tunnels during the day, but at night, they must have been all but invisible. It would be easy to fall in, just like she had. In the tape, the girl had been dragged into the earth, never to be seen again.

But then…why add that part about the other family? Why include biting and scratching? To increase fear and make the warning have more weight? If I was too young for a direct discussion about the tunnels, I think I would have been too young for that.

Her legs felt like they didn't fully belong to her. Heavy and slow and as unsteady as stilts, they moved reluctantly as she pushed forward.

The tunnels became more chaotic. Narrower. Her outstretched light flitted over tangled roots and spiderwebs tacky with dust. The dirt walls seemed to bulge, heavily laden, like a dam near bursting.

Margot's vision narrowed to a tight point. Everything outside became blurred, and she kept her eyes focused on the area a few paces ahead of her feet. She didn't dare blink. When she blinked, she felt like the walls were collapsing in on her.

The steady thump of her footfalls began to echo. The sound rang like drums in the back of her ears, too loud, too fast, and she realized it had been nearly a minute since she'd last breathed, but each inhale made her chest hurt until she wanted to cry from it.

Again and again the path split, twisted, reconverged. She couldn't find an exit.

A dark thought invaded her mind, that perhaps there *was* no other exit. That this stretch of tunnels was isolated from the others. That the only way in and out was through the hole she'd fallen down.

And now that she'd left it, she didn't know how to find her way back.

She checked her phone's battery. Forty percent.

How long will that last? How long do I have before I'm left blind down here?

The panic choked her, and she doubled over, trying to get air in, trying not to retch. As she waited for the emotions to slow and ebb, the echoes from her footfalls played in loops before fading out entirely.

Margot blinked, and her eyes burned from dirt and unshed tears. The echoes hadn't sounded natural. They shouldn't have lasted for so long.

Still crouched, she twisted, shining the light around her shoulder. It caught over the twining tendrils of roots shooting out of the soil and...

Hair?

No, she told herself, turning to face the path ahead again, her pulse running like a flood, tearing her sense of control away with every violent tug. No, that hadn't been dirt-clogged hair flowing out between the stones embedded in the wall. It was roots. It had to be.

She was moving again, and it took a second for the echoes to return. They dragged behind her, heavy, not quite in tune with her own pace. They overlapped.

Her steps became longer, faster, as her heart threatened to tear through her chest. She could barely see the path ahead of her; the light zigzagged violently, flashing across walls and floor indiscriminately.

The tunnel turned, and Margot's shoulder grazed crumbling stone as she reacted a half second too late. She didn't slow. The echoes, the footsteps that didn't quite mimic her own, were growing louder. Closer. She didn't dare shine the light behind herself again.

The path tilted upward. Ahead, she caught a whisper of light. Her labored breaths snagged in her throat. She broke into a full sprint, and so did the echoes, loping closer, the ragged gasp of breaths right at her back—

She crossed her arms ahead of herself a second before she hit the trapdoor. It burst open from the force, doors shuddering as they slammed into the dirt, and Margot exploded through, her mouth open in a gasping, silent cry.

Her adrenaline was spent. She collapsed to her knees, forearms braced on the earth, a persistent ringing in her ears.

Warm sun pressed onto her back like a comforting hand.

Slowly, every limb shaking, she rolled onto her side. She was near the base of a steep part of the slope. Behind her, the tunnel gaped open, taking advantage of the earth's natural slant to create an exit that didn't require stairs or ladders to get out.

Margot waited. She didn't know what she expected: to see movement deep in the tunnel maybe, or to hear the scrape of slow steps fading away. There was nothing. No movement. Not even the whisper of a sighing breath.

I was hearing my own echoing footsteps after all. She collapsed back and felt the prickly grass dig into her back. Part of her wanted to laugh. More of her wanted to cry. Her emotions had her now drained, empty, and instead of doing either, she lay there, letting the sun heat her shaking limbs and waiting for the ache in her chest to abate as oxygen flowed through her once more.

She'd let paranoia snatch her up, letting her imagine the echoes were something more. And the faster she'd run, the louder they'd sounded, until she truly believed they were right on her heels.

And all the while, it had just been her, frightening herself in an old, disused tunnel.

She felt embarrassed. Like a child afraid of the dark, panicking the moment they entered a dim room.

The hole stretched ahead of her, as though silently asking her if she would like to take another round through the passages. Even with natural sunlight reaching into it, she couldn't see more than a dozen feet in.

Her chest continued to ache as she moved to her knees and pulled the hinged doors closed. They were at an angle so gravity would hold them in place, and tendrils of reaching grass had begun to wrap over them. When she leaned back, she saw a post positioned nearby and slightly to the side. This entrance was more visible than the one she'd fallen into, but she supposed that wouldn't always be the case. Eventually it would be swallowed up by nature, as so many of its cousins had been.

She stood. The area she'd found herself in was largely clear, but clumps of trees grew to her front, back, and sides. She couldn't see her home, but she knew which direction to go find it.

At least that was one good thing about Gallows Hill: it was hard to get lost. As long as she kept climbing upward, she would eventually reach the house.

Margot sighed as she turned her phone's flashlight off and tucked it into her pocket. Her fingertips were crusted with dirt from when she'd fallen. She could feel grit in her hair and sliding down between her clothes and her skin. She shook herself, trying to clear some of it, but it didn't help.

She was overdue for a shower anyway, she reasoned, rolling the shoulder she'd landed on and grimacing at the low ache that rose from it.

The ground continued to rise. It took her longer than expected to reach the fence boundary. She climbed over the posts, pressing on the wire, and imagined she could hear the house's distant bells chiming.

Then another, slightly closer noise reached her. The low, slow creak of damp rope. Margot faltered. For a second, the world was silent, then the sound returned. Mournful, deep. Like something heavy suspended from a rope.

Her path would carry her near it, whether she wanted to see or not. Margot let her movements grow cautious. The clustered trees weren't dense and didn't extend far, but she found it hard to parse the dappled light and coiling shadows inside.

Something reflected the sun. It was metallic, Margot thought, and about the size of her head. She moved forward, one arm raised to protect her face from branches as she slipped between the closest trees.

She leaned on a trunk to keep her footing stable. Old, crumbling bark collapsed beneath her fingers. It was coated with lichen and dry moss and spiderwebs that were dewy even though the sun had been up for hours. Around another tree, and the metallic shape resolved ahead of her.

She faced an axe, embedded in a fallen, long-dried tree. Logs, already cleaved into fireplace-size chunks, were strewn about.

Someone—most likely her parents—had been interrupted while chopping wood and had never returned to finish the job. Leaves were scattered over the fallen trunk, suggesting it hadn't been disturbed in some time.

The axe was old. The polish on its wooden handle had become dried and cracked, but it still looked sturdy enough to do its job.

Margot tilted her head as she examined it. She'd planned to sleep with a kitchen knife beside her bed that night, but the axe might be an even better solution. It would be hard to feel vulnerable with an axe within reach. Harder to feel like she was at a disadvantage.

And if the late-night intruder returned, she doubted they would be so eager to play cat-and-mouse games if they saw the glinting steel. It wasn't a practical weapon. But then, she didn't *need* it to be. She had no intention of actually hurting anyone unless they tried to hurt her first. But she *did* want to make the point that she wasn't easy prey and that she wasn't someone to be toyed with.

The spectacle of an axe was hard to beat.

She leaned against the handle, fighting it free from the stump. It had become jammed but inched out in painful increments. Margot planted one foot on the fallen tree to hold it still, and with a final shove, the axe jumped from its notch.

The sudden give made her stagger, but she regained her balance, the axe's handle clutched in both hands, its blade lying on the leaf litter. She tried raising it. It was heavier than expected, the rusty head trying to tip over even when she braced herself. She let it swing down to trail at her side.

She thought she could see the house through the trees. She set out toward it, her other arm outstretched to push the dead, clinging branches out of her way. Her fingertips touched something fibrous and soft, and she recoiled.

The axe dropped from her hand, landing heavily, as she stared up, her heart skipping a beat.

A noose was suspended above her head.

21.

The noose turned languidly, revealing strands of fiber or roots or possibly hair trapped in its coils.

It was a sibling of the ropes she'd seen on the front porch—fraying from age, clogged with dirt, the color faded, the fibers losing their stiffness.

And just like the ropes on her porch, it had been tied into a noose, with one end attached to a high tree branch.

Margot reached up. Her fingers closed around the open loop and pulled. The branch, long dead, gave way under the pressure and sent the rope snaking down in a cloud of debris.

She stepped back, letting the rope drop to the ground, and stared up at the canopy.

It hadn't been the only noose. There was another to her left, higher, almost invisible between the leaves. Two more to her right, hanging just about at head height. One straight ahead.

They're probably from the first night, she told herself, picking up the axe and holding it close to her chest. *They left them here at the same time they tied them around the house.*

She pushed through the trees, her pace quickening, eager to get out from under the slowly turning, softly creaking ropes.

Ahead stretched the clearing leading up to the house. Her red car stood out like a marker drawing her to the front door. She could see the kitchen window and frowned slightly as she carried the axe up the gentle slope.

This was the clump of trees I saw through the kitchen window, wasn't it? The trees with something inside?

To her right, she found the post marking the hole she'd fallen through. She gave it a wide berth. The edges of a crumbling trapdoor were visible, surrounding a pit of pure darkness.

Margot hadn't expected seeing the house to feel like so much of a relief. She exhaled heavily as she stepped through the front door and let it swing closed behind her. The space was quiet, faintly chilled.

She left the axe in the hallway. Her scalp itched, and her clothes were scratchy from the dirt she'd collected in the tunnels. She hadn't yet found a place to shower in her new home, but she couldn't put it off any longer.

Margot turned right, moving through the living room, to access the hallway behind it. She opened the first few doors she passed: a sewing room, back from an era when homemade was cheaper than store bought, the machinery and fabric swatches now gathering dust. A formal dining room with high-backed chairs positioned around a dining table. And then a room with only clutter: tables and desks and chairs of different eras stacked around one another, expelled from their original rooms and relegated to this forgotten space.

She spent a moment staring into that room. The furniture would have been expensive at the time it was built: hand-carved wood, the chairs elaborately upholstered in florals and paisley and velvets. There were pieces of the home's history in that room, if she only knew how to put them together.

Some of these pieces must be at least a hundred years old. She traced her fingertips across a nearby dining table. Its edges had been carved into a leaf-inspired design. Kant had said her family had lived there since first buying the land. Each new generation must have gone through the process of shuffling out old furniture to make way for newer styles, though these pieces had been deemed special enough to be kept.

She turned to leave the room, then stopped. There were scratches on the inside of the door.

Margot gently nudged the door so she could see them better. The wood had been stained dark, but its outer layer had been scraped off by hundreds of little scratch marks tearing up splinters of wood.

A quiet nausea ran through her.

Don't overreact.

Her parents had owned at least one dog. Scratch marks weren't exactly shocking in that context.

Except...

She lifted her hand to trace along the scores. They ran from her midchest to head height.

It would've been a big dog.

Margot left, firmly shutting the door behind her. She followed the hallway but didn't try looking into any of the other rooms.

A staircase loomed ahead. She recognized it; this was the staircase at the rear of the house, closest to her parents' bedroom. She climbed it again, and only slowed once she'd reached the landing.

She was fairly sure she remembered the halls around her. Ahead, the master bedroom door was closed. Her mind flashed to her memories of the space. Lying in the stripped bed. Staring up at the ceiling and at the dark, stained cracks above.

Margot shivered and forced herself to turn aside. She moved along the hallway and tried the first door she passed.

It let into a bathroom. To her relief, a shower stood against the back wall. She left the door open as she found her room and retrieved her toiletries.

She hadn't showered since her last night at a motel, and she leaned into the hot water. As she inhaled the steam and let the soap carry away a buildup of grime, she began to feel increasingly in control again. Not normal. She didn't think it *was* possible to feel normal when her life had changed so enormously and over such a short time. But she felt less like there was a typhoon dragging her in its wake.

Normally, she would have spent more time on her hair: adding products, drying it, then adding more products. The whole process took more than an hour, though, and she was burning through daylight faster than she wanted. She'd have to live with frizzy hair for the next few days.

Fresh clothes felt good on clean skin. She traded her skirt for dark jeans and her shirt for a blouse. It was still probably too formal for the region, but she had to work with what she'd packed. She brushed her teeth, relishing the burst of mint, then tied her still-wet hair into a tight bun.

Back down the stairs, then through the front door again. She paused on the porch for a moment, staring at the aged growth of trees she'd emerged from. It was too far away to be certain, but she thought she could make out the nooses twisting there, a dark warning at the edges of her vision.

She left the porch and faced the house. Black, dull windows stared back down at her. The roof tiles, highlighted by the sun, seemed older and more lichen heavy than when she'd first arrived.

The previous day, Kant had used a stepladder to change the light. He'd said he was returning it to a shed. It couldn't be far away.

I can get the answers to one mystery at least.

As long as she could find attic access somewhere in the house, Margot could get into the roof and search for the source of the stain she'd seen above her parents' bed. Odds were that it was just water damage that had never been property patched up. But she needed to be sure.

Margot turned right and began to circle the house's exterior. As she'd thought, it was a winding, wild kind of building. Extensions jutted out at unexpected places. New wings, new rooms, all added as the family grew, and then allowed to molder as the descendants dwindled down to just a few.

She tried to count both the doors and the windows, but there were too many of the latter: broad panes with their views dampened by curtains, narrow glass lattices, and tiny windows, ones so small that Margot might have fit one arm through but no more. Instead, she focused on the doors, trying to form a hazy map of the place in her mind. The doors had been added in strange places, clusters where she wouldn't have thought more than one would be needed, then long stretches with no exit in sight.

A grapevine had been planted along the house's side. It was probably a symbolic touch—a way to connect them to the produce created farther down the hill—but it had been allowed to grow uncontrolled and reached far past the trellises that had been provided for it. Clusters of grapes still grew between the coiling leaves and tendrils. It was late in the season and many had fallen to the ground, where they slowly decomposed into the dead grass, but several bunches held to the vine. She stopped beside them, a low kind of melancholy forming in her chest.

She was the descendant of a family that made its name producing wine. And she couldn't even sample the bottles that her parents had created.

The vine's leaves fluttered as a breeze passed through them. The clustered grapes, deep crimson to the point of being almost black, looked glossy and full.

She might not be able to drink the wine, but she could partake of at least this much, couldn't she?

Margot carefully picked a grape from the end of its bunch. It was still warm from the sun's touch. She raised it to her lips, but the moment her teeth closed around the grape she knew something was wrong. It collapsed under the pressure, spilling foul, sour pulp over her lips.

She heaved forward, spitting the grape onto the ground. In the splatter of split skin and rotted flesh, a thick, white grub writhed.

Margot backed away, her stomach heaving, as she spat and spat again, desperate to purge the sourness from her mouth.

Witchety's words returned to her. *The land feels bad.*

Margot wiped the back of her hands across her lips, then rubbed them clean on her jeans. She began walking again, faster this time, eager to put the rotting vine to her back.

As she rounded the house's rear, she caught sight of old sheds shaded by two large maples. The trees were bare in preparation for winter: dark, twining branches spread outward, scraping on the shed's ceiling, scraping on each other.

She blinked and saw the business's logo again. The hanging tree. Larger than the maples and heavy with age. Heavy with death.

Margot shook her head to clear the image and then crossed the patchy grass toward the sheds. One of the doors had been left ajar. The metal rang out with high, straining wails as the wind pulled it back and forth an inch at a time like a pendulum.

She tried the left-hand shed, putting her shoulder into the door to gain access. Inside was dim and musty and smelled like earth. Margot squinted against the poor light. She hadn't brought her phone, she realized. It would still be in the bathroom, tucked among the clothes she'd changed out of.

She'd promised herself she would be more careful about where and how she spent time around the building, but she was already slipping up, leaving her phone behind and herself caught in the dark.

Still, enough light came through the door that she could make out a tumble of old objects strewn about the place: power tools to her left; old chairs and doorframes, cracked beyond repair; gardening tools caked in rust.

And near the rear of the shed, she caught sight of the stepladder.

Margot stretched to step over a stack of old garden pots. Faintly, she could hear the other shed's door creaking. Inside her own metal echo chamber, the noise sounded distorted. Like a woman releasing low, wrenching wails.

Chills prickled over Margot's skin. She kept her head down to avoid a row of gardening tools hung from the ceiling. As she eased around an old rocking chair, she saw a small, strange scuff mark in the dust-laden floor.

It looked strangely like a footprint.

Not a shoe mark, though; she could see clear outlines for the toes and the curving hollow where the arch belonged. This person had been barefoot.

Barefoot in a shed, in the middle of a field.

Margot crouched, squinting as she traced the outline. It was large. A man's foot, she thought. The first toe's imprint was bigger than her thumb. It was smudged around the edges, though, blurring forward, as though the owner had been dragging his feet while walking.

She tried to guess whether it was fresh or perhaps years old, but the light was too poor. She traced one finger over the impression and it came up smeared in dust.

The other shed's door continued to move, scraping, wailing, and it really, truly did sound like a woman crying. Not just sobs, though, but wails, deep and guttural and howling, raw enough to set flame to Margot's nerves, harsh enough to ache in her teeth.

It's growing louder, isn't it?

Still crouched by the footprint, Margot held her breath, listening. The wind teased at the edges of her hearing as it whistled through narrow gaps in the shed's metal plating. The maple branches scraped across the shed's walls and ceilings. They sounded like fingertips dragging across the surface, asking to be let in.

The door's wails heaved rhythmically. A howling cry, then a stuttering

breath in, repeated. And then, abruptly, the voice cried out "Ezra," followed
by a raw, aching scream of grief.

Margot felt her limbs turn to lead. She swiveled on the balls of her feet,
one hand gripping a broom handle to hold herself steady.

The half-open door created a narrow band of light. The hazy illumination grazed across the edges of shelves, crates, and tools.

And a figure.

22.

Margot felt as though her heart were being squeezed. She hunched, hoping she would be lost in the back of the shed, all but invisible.

Opposite, close to the partially open door, was a woman. She was swallowed in shadows. Only her edges were visible, framed by the light.

Windblown hair framed her head. A dress reached to the floor. She held her hands over her face as the splitting, aching wails rose from her.

Margot didn't move her eyes, but her hand snaked down her side, feeling for the pocket where she kept her mobile. It was still empty.

The wails cracked, unnaturally rhythmic, and she was no longer able to distinguish between the woman's cries and the rusted shed door.

Margot dropped farther back, hoping to bury herself in the dark of the room's corner. The space had no windows and no other doors. The only way out was past the wailing woman. Margot's back pressed into the stepladder.

There was something unnatural about the figure. She wasn't perfectly still; strands of hair and the edges of her dress twitched as the cries shook through her. But the movements felt inauthentic. Rhythmic, even. Like an automaton quivering through a preset series of looping motions.

Margot's heart ached from how hard it was beating. Shallow gasps weren't properly filling her lungs. She fastened her hands across the nearest items—the broom handle and the stepladder—then spoke, her voice dry and whispery with fear. "Hello?"

The woman's silhouette fell perfectly still, like someone had cut the power to her. A second too late, Margot remembered Witchety's words. *Don't provoke anything you don't want to know better.*

Then the woman began to lower her arms. They moved in insect-like twitches, little jolts at a time, horribly stiff, horribly tense.

The head rose, turning toward Margot. With the light to her back and her face clouded by gloom, none of her features were visible. Except for her eyes. Tiny points of light existed where her eyes belonged, sharp and cold, seeming to float in the inky blackness as they flicked toward Margot.

Her throat closed over. She turned her head and covered her face, her arms shaking, as she silently willed the lights to be gone, begging for it to be over.

The grating, wailing noise echoed around her. It was deep, painful. Metallic. Leafless branches tapped on the roof above her head, the walls to her sides. It was impossible to track any of the noises. But they seemed to be getting closer. Closing in on her. Looming right above her, pinpricks of harsh light staring down at her as she cowered—

Margot opened her eyes and drew a rasping, desperate gulp of air in the same second.

Nothing stood over her.

At the shed's opposite side, near the open door, implements and tools and furniture caught the glaring, hazy light. A bale of hay had been suspended from the ceiling. It was almost exactly where the woman's head had been. The wind through the open door tugged at it, making strands of loose hay quiver.

"No," Margot whispered. *No, I didn't imagine it. No, I wasn't mistaking a bale of hay moving in the wind for a woman's hair. What I saw was* real.

And yet, she was alone in the shed. Moving carefully, Margot rose. She took the stepladder with her, holding it against her chest like a shield.

The aching, grinding noise was coming from outside again. Margot stepped over a box of power cables, keeping her back to the wall as she scanned the indistinct clusters of tools. As she got closer to the door, she turned a wary eye toward the suspended hay. It was exactly where the woman had stood. She couldn't have been there without her head passing through it.

I didn't imagine it.

Yet, what had she seen exactly? A woman's outline that moved in a way that didn't seem human. Two pinpricks of light. And the wailing…which had been caused by the open door.

The shed had been very dark. Nothing, including the woman, had been visible with any kind of clarity.

"I didn't imagine it," she said, but there was slightly less conviction in the words this time.

She shoved outside, breathing too heavily. Cold sweat stuck her clothes to her skin. Margot dropped the stepladder from the defensive posture and held it under one arm as she backed away from the shed, scanning its dark insides a final time.

Next to it, the second shed's door, half-buried under the leafless maple branches, groaned as the wind pulled at it.

Margot broke into a jog as she returned to the house. She left the stepladder in the hallway while she turned to the kitchen and dunked her face under running tap water. The cold felt good on her flaming skin. She let herself relax there for a moment, draped over the sink, water pouring across her face and spilling into her hair.

I need to know more about this house. More about the people who lived here. Whether...a woman with windblown hair once grieved for a man named Ezra.

She pulled herself out from under the water, breathing deeply as she used a towel to dry her face.

Kant was her most reliable contact at Gallows Hill. He'd answered almost all of her questions so far. But his answers tended to be short, and he wouldn't be back until the next morning.

There was another avenue Margot thought might be more helpful. Nora and Ray, managers at the store, had invited her to have a chat with them. Nora had mentioned she could tell Margot about the place's history.

Margot went upstairs. As she passed her room, she couldn't keep from glancing inside. Although she'd scattered some of her possessions about the space—clothes in the wardrobe, books on the bedside table—it still felt more akin to a hotel room than something that belonged to her. She found her phone in the bathroom and slipped it into her pocket.

Then she returned downstairs, pressed through the creaking front door, and set herself on the winding driveway that led to the main road.

Her grandmother's home had been in a tightly packed suburb, where there were always children riding bikes along the street and bodies gathered at the bus stop. University had been so crowded it was sometimes hard to find space to be alone, and after her grandmother's death, she'd moved to the outskirts of a city, where she shared an apartment on a fourth floor overlooking a wall of similar buildings.

Her life had been a string of densely populated areas...until now. Gallows Hill felt sparse in a way she'd never known. She could have filled her lungs with air and screamed at the top of her voice and she doubted anyone would hear.

Even as the driveway took her past the staff buildings, they were still far enough away that she couldn't make out any of the bodies moving between the houses and the work areas, and she didn't think any of them were able to see her as she continued down the gentle, swelling slope.

The sun was already at a long angle. Margot checked the time on her phone and grimaced. She'd burned through more of the day than she'd expected. She wouldn't have more than an hour before dusk started to darken the horizon.

Witchety said to stay indoors after dark.

She'd have to keep her visit short. Nora and Ray were probably preparing to close the shop anyway. If it wasn't already shut. She hadn't thought to ask their opening hours.

In the distance, the dark form of the storefront appeared through the anemic trees. Margot thought she saw a glow of light coming from its window and quickened her pace. The parking area was empty, so she ducked around the sign welcoming visitors and skirted the display barrels to reach the door.

"Oh! She's here!"

Margot, still a half dozen steps from the entrance, caught herself at the voice. Nora pulled the door open and leaned through, her smile showing lines of gum above her teeth. "Come on in, come on in! I didn't expect we'd get a visit from you for a few more days yet, so this is very welcome."

"Thanks." Margot ducked into the building, warmed by Nora's enthusiasm and grateful to be with human company again. "I came to thank you for the basket you left. But I wasn't sure what time you close—"

"Oh, the official hours are ten to four, but we tend to hang around for a bit afterward, as you can see."

Nora put a hand on Margot's back and led her toward the counter. The shop was small but modern and clean. The sales counter was kept largely clear except for a point-of-sale system and a row of wineglasses for samples. Ray was behind the counter, shuffling to put a novel away, his sloped shoulders and gentle smile seeming fully at home in the place.

"Take a seat." Nora was all eagerness, her quick, flitting hand movements reminding Margot of a bird. "How about we get started with some samples, hm? Do you like whites more, or are you a reds girl?"

Kant hadn't told them about her refusal to drink wine yet, she realized. Margot felt a small pang of gratitude for his discretion as she lifted herself into one of the four stools spaced along the customer side of the counter. "Ah, actually, I might pass. I just came to have a chat, really."

Nora had already taken a bottle out from beneath the counter. She hesitated, the cap half unscrewed, and glanced toward her husband.

"You go ahead," Margot added quickly. "You're here after hours anyway. I'm pretty sure you deserve it."

"Oh, that's kind." Nora flipped two glasses and poured a generous helping into each. Her hand trembled, sending the flow of wine shivering.

Margot turned on her stool to admire the place. The store was largely built out of warm-toned woods. Golden ceiling lights added to the ambience, lending the place a sense of decadence, even if the actual design was closer to modern-rustic. The counter, made out of a single slab of wood, narrowed and widened in small curves as it followed the tree's natural shape. The shelves behind the counter held what must have been a hundred display bottles, all bearing the same stark, black-and-white design of a dead oak tree on their labels.

On the wall to Margot's left was a menagerie of framed photos. A few were in color but many were grayscale. Old. Pieces of the property's past—exactly what she'd been hoping to find here.

"You'd know the winery's history, I'm guessing?" she asked.

Nora came around to sit on a stool next to Margot, though Ray remained leaning on the other side of the counter. "Absolutely. The history is half the draw for visitors. Some days it feels like we're less salespeople and more tour guides. Isn't that right, Ray?"

"Mm." Ray took a long drag of his glass of wine, draining it. He was breathing slightly too hard when he put it back on the counter.

Something's off.

Margot felt her chest grow tighter as she glanced between the two managers. Nora was fidgeting, her hands moving in quick flicks as she adjusted her wineglass, folded a napkin, adjusted the glass again, and then brushed an invisible crumb off the counter. She held her smile in place, baring white teeth and red gums with an almost desperate surety. But when she looked closer, Margot couldn't fail to notice how red her eyelids were and how, under a light layer of bronzing, her cheeks were blanched.

Ray was silent as he poured himself more wine. His body language was easy—slow movements, gently curving shoulders, one hand resting lightly on the countertop—but his eyes seemed glazed. As though he wasn't actually seeing any of the things he looked at.

They're panicked. Because of me?

No, Margot realized. They were holding close to her: Nora with her seat so near that their knees nearly bumped, Ray hanging over the counter. Almost like Margot's presence was a comfort.

But something had unnerved them. Made them edgy. And Margot was fairly certain it had happened not long before she arrived.

Nora had seen Margot well before she reached the door. She must have been staring through the windows, scanning the landscape around them. Watching for something.

What's happening to the people here?

"Nora…" Margot folded her hands together, pressing the palms against one another. "I'd really like to learn about the people who lived here before me."

"Of course you would." Nora reached forward to quickly squeeze Margot's hand. "*Of course.* This must still be so new to you. We can help with that."

"Start at the beginning." Margot turned toward the photos on the walls. "Kant said my family bought the land hundreds of years ago."

"He's right." The edginess still clung to Nora like cobwebs, but her smile was fuller again. She moved out of her chair, pulling Margot with her as they approached the wall of photos.

Nora reached a hand toward one of the framed images. Her eyes were very bright. "Here are the first private owners of Gallows Hill, Ezra and Louisa Hull."

23.

Ezra. The name was like electricity across Margot's skin. It couldn't be a coincidence. The first owner of the property. The name she'd heard wailed in the shed.

The frame held an ink illustration. Margot doubted it would be an original; from what she could tell, it had been photocopied and enlarged to show the details. Age stains bled across the image.

In it, a family stood ahead of a massive, twisting oak tree, its branches bare. In the center were a husband and wife, the husband clad in a coat that went to his boots and the wife in stays and long skirts. Four children stood to the sides: two boys and two girls, ranging from early teenagers to young adults.

Margot's eyes were drawn to the wife. The illustration, though intended to be a realistic representation of the family, lacked detail. A few strokes implied the eyes. A line for the mouth. The artist had captured the wife's hair, though. Strands of it sailing free from the headscarf intended to hold it down. *Windblown*, Margot had thought in the shed. She hadn't been able to see the woman's face at the time, but now she stared into the illustration's barely represented eyes, fixated by the black pits.

"Tell me about them." Her words cracked. She hated the edge of desperation that was creeping into her voice, but Nora didn't hesitate to oblige.

"Ezra Hull and his family moved into the still-forming town of Leafell to seek better prospects," Nora said, admiring the image with narrowed eyes. "Ezra had always wanted to own land and so, when Gallows Hill was put up for auction in 1761, he bought it with an inheritance he had received from the sale of his late father's estate. The asking price wasn't high. Very few others bid, and Ezra turned his remaining money toward building a home for his family."

"The same house I live in now," Margot guessed.

"A much smaller version of it." Ray leaned across the counter, forearms rested on the old wood. "It's had a few renovations. But at its core, yes. What you have now is built around the original floor plan."

"Ezra Hull chose to use the hill to age wine. Many people in town predicted the business would fail." Nora moved to another frame. This one held an ancient deed to the property, cracks forming in the parchment where it had once been folded. Margot struggled to read the smudged-ink cursive. "People didn't look too kindly on the hill, and the town was small. At that time, wine was a very different business. The wealthy and the aristocracy would have their bottles imported from France. Local-made wine was rare and usually bad. But for Ezra, it worked."

She moved to another frame. This one contained a label, carefully mounted on card stock. The wine's name was handwritten, along with a year: 1768. Above that was an early version of the twisting oak tree logo, faded from age.

"He bought grapes from nearby farms, fermented them, and bottled them. What he had likely intended to start as a hobby quickly grew as word spread and the wine's reputation increased. Within six years, bottles were being bought by socialites and governors in the larger cities. The family became wealthy. They expanded the house. Hired workers. Built additional cellars. For a time, they thrived."

Margot found herself drawn back to the original drawing. It might have been prepared for one of the news periodicals of the day, she thought. She found herself scanning the barely represented faces, looking for some clue to their thoughts, their personalities. "What happened?"

Nora turned away. She eased herself into one of the stools by the counter and picked up her glass. "No one's entirely sure."

There was something haunting about the barely there eyes. They were only illustrations, but Margot found herself fixated by the youngest daughter, positioned at the far left. The illustrator, whether deliberately or by accident, had sloped the girl's mouth. It gave the impression that she was on the edge of tears.

"You're not descended from Ezra Hull, I'm afraid." Nora held the wineglass with both hands, the splayed fingertips lightly balancing the bowl between them, her thumb testing the rim. "They seemed destined to prosper, but…well."

"Go back to the beginning," Ray urged.

"I am, don't rush me!" Her eyes crinkled as she smiled up at her husband. He returned the look, some deep fondness in his gaze.

"Kant said…" Margot, still focused on the illustration, struggled to recall the conversation. It had only happened the previous morning, but it felt like half a lifetime ago. "There was a younger brother."

"That's right. Ephraim Hull. The junior by only a year." Nora stretched her legs out, brown pants grazing her ankles, as she paused to drink. She looked almost relaxed, except for the way her fingertips continued to move around the glass, fidgeting. "The deceased father's estate went entirely to the eldest son, Ezra, which was what allowed him to purchase Gallows Hill. That caused an irreparable rift between the brothers."

"Giving everything to one son sounds like favoritism, but it wasn't unheard of at the time," Ray said. "Wealthy families tended to pass their inheritance only to the oldest, to ensure the family line maintained its land and fortune, instead of breaking it up into little pieces for each son. Only, the Hulls didn't come from a wealthy family. They were from the working class. And apparently, Ephraim had been under the belief that he would receive half of his father's money."

"He fought with Ezra about it," Margot guessed.

"Well, probably, but not in public at least." Nora had finished her glass and placed it on the counter. Ray refilled it for her before turning the bottle back to his own glass. "Historical accounts all agree that a deep bitterness formed between the siblings, though. One that only grew worse as Ezra Hull prospered."

"The inheritance wasn't all that much, really," Ray said. "But Gallows Hill multiplied it many times over. And Ephraim, struggling to make a living in town, saw the winery's success and believed it should have been his."

Nora released a slow sigh. "If the rift hadn't formed, perhaps Ezra would have invited his brother to live and work with him, and they both could have thrived. But there was too much bad blood between them by that point. Ezra had a carriage, employees, nice clothes. Ephraim, who had ten children by that time, seemed trapped in a life of struggle."

The younger brother, feeling cheated at every turn. Seeing that he worked just as hard, deserved just as much, but never got it. The brother I'm descended from.

Margot's voice sounded hollow. "What did he do?"

"Ah." Nora exchanged a knowing look with Ray. "Well. According to him, nothing."

The six faces in the illustration stared up at her, vague but inexplicably filled with heartbreak.

"Ezra Hull, Louisa Hull, and their four children vanished one day."

Ray seemed to slump across the counter, braced on his forearms, gentle eyes faintly glassy as he looked toward the opposite window. "When questioned, Ephraim said he believed his older brother had set out for one of the cities in search of greater fortunes and had no intention of returning. He moved into Gallows Hill to care for the business while his brother was gone. As months passed and Ezra failed to return, Ephraim took over more of the land's work, until eventually his brother was declared legally dead and the estate passed to him."

"Ephraim killed them," Margot surmised.

"Well." Nora laced and unlaced her fingers. "I wouldn't want to speak badly of your ancestors."

"It's fine," Margot said, even though the ache in her heart insisted that it wasn't. "I want the truth. He killed them."

Nora continued to fidget. "Technically, not in the eyes of the law. The house and land were searched, just in case, but no bodies were ever found. All we know for certain is that they vanished."

Margot turned toward Ray. He still held the empty glass, slowly rotating it as though to swirl wine that no longer existed. His smile felt almost apologetic. "No evidence was found against Ephraim or his children. But, yes, even at the time it was fairly widely believed that he murdered his brother, along with his brother's family, and buried them somewhere on the land. Ezra had no reason to leave without saying goodbye to his neighbors. And most agreed that Ephraim wouldn't have moved into his brother's home unless he was certain he wasn't coming back."

Margot nodded and returned to the photos. She was trying to appear sanguine about it. As though the knowledge that she'd inherited the land because of a familial homicide didn't get under her skin like a sickening, crawling insect.

"Ephraim built the business up further," Nora said. "The wine increased in popularity and value, beginning to earn a reputation even overseas. But misfortune seemed to chase Ephraim. He had ten children in total. All but three of them perished before their thirtieth birthday."

"The seventeen hundreds weren't an easy time," Ray acknowledged. "But bad luck seemed to fall especially heavily on Ephraim. Some of his children died from diseases. Others, from accidents around the estate. Machinery malfunctions. Trampled by the family horse. Drowned in the creek. Each year seemed to bring some heavy news, until Ephraim himself perished, by falling—or jumping or being pushed, the details were never clear—into one of the vats used to ferment wine. He wasn't found until the following morning, by which time he'd drowned."

"That's him," Nora said, and Margot followed her finger to another illustration. It depicted a clean-shaven man standing in front of a house. The same house from the background of the first drawing, Margot thought, except the building was larger and the tree was missing. This illustration looked as though it may have been privately commissioned; the lines were cleaner and tighter, and swabs of pastel color had been applied to give it life. She met the man's hard, blank eyes and had to look away.

"That was done the year before his passing, when he was fifty," Nora said. "From there, the estate went to his son and then to *his* son. Each generation has stayed on the land, renovated the home, and expanded the business. And now we've finally reached you."

Dozens more frames ran along the wall. Margot followed them, watching the images turn from illustrations to black-and-white photographs and then, finally, to color. Some images had been taken inside the winery, showing the family stirring the vats of fermenting grapes. Some were taken in the cellar, with rows and rows of dark barrels stacked up behind the posed men and women. She watched each new generation change them subtly. The addition of deeper complexions, Mediterranean features, thickly curling hair, all blending together to form Margot herself.

At last, she reached the final photo: a picture of her parents. It looked as though it might have only been taken a few years before. They were posed outside the house, just like their forebearer Ephraim had been. Her father held his arm around her mother's back. She leaned into him, smiling.

"Your mother was the eleventh generation," Nora murmured. She reached for the wine bottle but it was empty. "That makes you the twelfth."

Margot felt frozen by her parents' likenesses. They were smiling in the image, and it was hard to think of what would happen in just a few short years. Margot swallowed and felt a lump stick in her throat. "The tragedies didn't end with Ephraim, did they?"

Nora and Ray didn't answer, but they didn't need to. As Margot turned back through the images, she saw hints of loss speckled through them: a child in one image that was missing in the next. A man with only one arm. A woman, eyes closed, not from blinking as the picture was taken but from blindness.

"This is why people think the land is cursed," she said, the realization sinking into her like lead poured into her veins.

Ray cleared his throat. "Farms can have a high number of accidents. That's true across the country. Things are safer these days, though. Guards on the vats; protocols to protect workers. It's not like it used to be."

They were pleasing words, calculated to calm her, but they were a deflection, not an answer.

Every new thing I learn about the hill is somehow worse. The hanging tree would have been enough to leave her cold on its own. But the layers kept stacking on: murders, deaths, suffering. At every turn there was some new dark pall draping across the estate.

As though it really was somehow bad.

Cursed.

She had seen the look in Witchety's eyes: the wariness, the reverence. She believed the land had been poisoned by evil. And that evil, now, was returning. Coming to exact a price.

She turned from the photos to face the two store managers. They watched her, silent but expectant. A hint of red was still visible around Nora's eyes, and the color hadn't returned to her face. Ray had finished the bottle of wine. Even while Margot watched him, his eyes flicked toward the window for a heartbeat before returning to her.

"I think I saw someone in the shed behind my home earlier." The words tumbled out of her like water. "Except, when I looked closer, they weren't there."

"Oh?" Nora's smile twitched. She took up the napkin, already folded once, and flattened it before folding it along a different axis. "What do you think it was?"

Margot felt like she was being tested—as though the correct answer would unlock some deeper level of communication, some closer bond where secrets could be shared—but she still had no words for what she'd encountered in the shed. She clenched her hands at her side then forced them to relax. "I...don't know. But I don't think it was...natural." The words hung, unanswered, and Margot pushed further, urged on by desperation. "I think...I think it might have been Louisa Hull."

Nora and Ray shared a glance that lasted half a second. Their faces were blank slates. Then Nora ran her hands over her pants, picking out tiny flecks of lint. "Well, that sounds like a strange kind of experience."

"Oh, it's already dusk," Ray said. His voice was mild, his smile gentle, as though they'd been discussing nothing more interesting than the weather. "We should probably head out. We've been here plenty long enough, haven't we, Nora?"

"I'd say so. Who's best to drive?"

"That would be you." Ray placed the glasses into a tray behind the counter, which already held several others waiting to be washed. "I suspect I'm over the limit."

Margot felt as though she was deflating. She'd been certain that Nora and Ray had seen something, heard something, *knew* something. But they were not only failing to confirm her suspicions, they were ignoring them entirely.

Did I misread things? Something had upset them before I arrived, hadn't it? Reality slipped over her. Yes, they had been bothered by something. But Margot had been presumptuous to assume they were tormented by the same kind of apparitions she thought she'd seen. They might have had an unpleasant customer. An argument. A piece of bad news. There was no reason it had to be supernatural in nature.

"I'm *very* glad you came to visit," Nora said, finding Margot's arm on the way past and squeezing it lightly. "Pop in anytime. I'm always up for a bit of a chat."

"Right." She felt her voice shake with forming tears and humiliation. She knew she must look stupid. Childish. Indulging in superstitions. Leaning into some kind of supernatural narrative the first moment she had the chance. The people who worked at Gallows Hill had been there for years; they were probably tired of the *cursed land* legends that floated through town. And now their new owner was not only listening to them but falling into the rampant paranoia.

But…I didn't imagine any of it. Did I?

Ray gathered their things while Nora fetched the keys from her bag. He tucked his novel under his arm and slung the coat over it. "It really has been lovely to meet you," he murmured as he passed Margot. "Hopefully next time you'll enjoy some wine with us. We can do a full tasting. Give you a chance to try everything the estate offers."

As he stepped through the door, Margot's eyes fell on the book under his arm. The jacket he'd used to cover it caught on the handle, pulling back as he moved through, and for a second revealed part of the cover.

It wasn't a novel like she'd thought but nonfiction. Only one line of the title was visible: *Afterlife*.

Nora and Ray had paused outside, Ray still holding the door wide, waiting. Margot took a slow breath and followed them out.

"Thank you." She forced herself to speak while her mind raced. "Have a good night."

Nora, locking the door, sent her a small, fond kind of smile. Unlike earlier, it didn't extend to her gums. "You too, Margot. Stay safe."

She waited until Nora and Ray had gotten into their car parked behind the building, then turned back to the drive leading to her home.

Stay safe. It was a common enough way to say goodbye, but Margot didn't think she was wrong to read more into it.

She'd gotten some of her answers. But not enough. Not *nearly* enough. She needed to look further, and she needed to do it before the sun failed entirely.

She needed to get into her house's attic.

24.

A hazy sunset spread across the horizon. Margot moved fast, her breathing deep and dragging, as she pushed herself up the hill and toward her home.

My home. A house built on blood.

She tried not to dwell on it, but the thoughts circled back repeatedly like a fly that wouldn't leave her alone.

Where did Ephraim bury their bodies? Did he drag them farther into the land, hiding them beneath the scrappy trees, or did he keep them close to home?

She'd reached the fence surrounding the house. When she leaned on the wires, distant bells rang, calling her closer.

Part of her wanted to delay going inside and to stand out in the waning sun for as long as possible, but she knew that would only make her job worse.

She pushed through the front door. The stepladder waited where she'd left it in the hallway, and Margot hoisted it under one arm as she followed the path to the stairs.

She thought she'd gotten a handle on the house's broad layout, but she still became lost while looking for her parents' room. With the door closed, it blended in with all of the other sealed doors, and she ended up opening four wrong doors before she was finally greeted by the sight of her parents' master bed and, above it, the strange, sickly stain in the ceiling.

Margot shut the door again, refusing to stare at the room's contents—or the mirror—for even a second longer. Instead, she began moving through the halls around it, eyes trained on the ceiling as she looked for an entry hatch.

She found one just around the corner. It blended into the wood ceiling, almost invisible except for the half-moon fingerhold and a silver bolt lock.

A fresh wave of discomfort moved through Margot. She'd seen that kind of sliding lock on almost every apartment door in the city, but never on the underside of a ceiling.

Who had reason to lock their attic?

She shook her ladder open, propping it under the entry hatch, and climbed. The bolt was stiff and took effort to scrape free, but then Margot planted her hand on the wood hatch and shoved.

It was heavier than she'd expected and ground up in increments. Margot, muscles beginning to strain, took another step up and added her other hand to the hatch. It finally reached its tipping point and rocked over, crashing into the attic's floor and leaving a two-foot-by-two-foot opening into the ceiling.

The stepladder wasn't high enough for Margot to walk into the attic, but by standing on the highest step she was able to get her head and shoulders through. She pulled her phone from her pocket and switched it to flashlight mode.

With her other forearm resting on the floor to hold herself steady, Margot raised the phone and stretched it ahead.

It was clear that section of the attic was one of the older parts of the house. Deep fissures ran through the wooden beams. Repairs had been made—sometimes with metal brackets for support, sometimes by replacing whole sections of wood—but the area reeked of age.

She squinted, turning slowly, shining her light as far as it would go. Heavy crossbeams blocked much of her view. Dust motes rotated in the pale light. She craned her neck, her breath held, searching the layered shadows.

Don't stray too far after dark.

Margot bit her lip, then placed the phone on the floor, so that its beam shone toward the ceiling. Then, leveraging both arms, she heaved herself up. The narrow entrance bit into her waist. She squirmed, legs thrashing through empty air, then dragged herself another inch into the attic space, moving her center of gravity onto solid ground. She had to roll onto her back to pull both legs through the opening, then sat for a moment, breathing deeply and scanning the area around her.

The floor had been made solid, as though it were intended for storage, but very little was kept there. Old planks—ones hauled out as they began to rot or crack—had been discarded. Metal brackets had been heaped into a pile from some half-finished repair job. They were all gathering a gentle layer of dust.

Margot got onto her knees. The floorboards groaned beneath her and she hesitated. If the wood had begun to rot...if it wouldn't carry her weight...

She reached for her light and turned it toward the boards. They were old but showed no sign of dampness or crumbling, even when she pressed her weight into them. Previous generations must have been rigorous enough about leaks in the roof to prevent rot from setting in.

Margot rose, testing each movement before committing to it, until she was standing. Then, with one hand on a beam near her head, she tried to orient herself.

Her parents' room wouldn't be far. To her left, she was fairly certain. She crept forward. The aged boards creaked in response but held.

Something scuttled past her foot, and Margot gasped, jolting backward.

A small, shiny spider twitched its way past, thread-thin legs propelling it toward the darkness.

Her breath shuddered as she let it out. The light had begun to waver, and for a second Margot feared that the battery might be dying again, but then she realized she was responsible. Her hands were shaking, sending the beam jittering, rough, and confusing.

Be fast. Get it done, then get out.

The hatch was still visible behind her, a square of light in the otherwise oppressive darkness. Margot tried to keep herself oriented with it as she drifted across the floor, the light pointed downward to scan the dust-laden boards.

There.

Her heart skipped painfully. Ahead, a dark stain spread across the wood, thick and seemingly damp, even under the layered dust.

Margot dropped to her knees as she approached it. The stain was large, broader than her torso and nearly twice as long. It created the kind of irregular shape that would come from pouring a bucket of thick liquid on the floorboards and letting it spread.

She tilted her head up, light pointed to the ceiling, but there was too much insulation in the way to see if there was a gap in the tiles. None of the wood or foam above her seemed corrupted, though. For how large the stain was, she would have expected signs on the ceiling if it came from a drip.

Margot turned back to the mark and bent close, her free other hand braced at her side, careful not to touch any of the darkened surface. She blew on the dust, trying to drive some of it away to get a clearer view, but it stuck there.

What is it?

It seemed to have damaged the wood irreparably. While the boards around her all had clear edges and visible grains, anything beneath the stain had become soft and dense, like it was being melted. It glistened as though still damp. Carefully, Margot moved a finger toward the surface, preparing to touch it.

A soft, breathy sound came from behind. Margot jolted, her heart in her throat, as she swung toward the noise. It had sounded like a sigh coming from somewhere far behind her.

Her shaking light darted across exposed beams and gently spiraling dust motes. She couldn't see the other end of the winding attic space, but there was no sign of any presence.

The wind, maybe? Would it make that kind of noise if it slipped through a crack in the roof?

She didn't know what to trust anymore. Her eyes and ears were sending her information, but superstition had her so tightly in its grip that she couldn't tell if her reactions were measured or unreasonable.

Margot held still until her legs began to cramp and her arm felt too heavy to keep it extended. Slowly, reluctantly, she returned to the stain on the floor. The phone's light shimmered over the moisture hidden beneath the boards. She pressed her fingertip into it. The wood was spongy, like she'd thought; it began to crumble beneath even a light touch. She pressed harder and part of the surface gave way. A viscous, dark liquid bubbled up from the pressure.

She withdrew her hand. Something long and sharp-tipped stretched out of the hole. Margot's first thought was of a splinter, except the splinter was moving, curving up and out, and then it was followed by a spider's body, drenched in the stain's color, its stick legs stabbing into the rotted wood as it wound its way toward Margot.

She flinched back, out of its path, using her elbows and knees to scrape herself through the dust.

The spider continued, undisturbed. She could swear she heard the faint clicking noises of its legs hitting the floor as it roved past the edge of her light and vanished deeper into the attic.

Margot pulled her legs closer to her chest. Her skin was crawling. She raised the hand she'd used to break through the stain and shone her light on it. The stain had been damp after all. The smear left across her finger was a deep, vivid red.

Wine?

No. Blood.

She bit her tongue as she turned her light across the attic again. Every foreign shape was suspect. Every shadow felt like a stranger lurking just out of sight, watching, waiting.

Stop it. Calm down. It can't be blood. No one has been in your attic in years, based on the dust.

That was true at least. She could see her own path through the space: footprints eventually switching to broad scuffs as she'd dropped to her hands and knees. Her marks were the only ones near the stain.

This house has had its share of murders, though. Enough to find blood bubbling out of the floorboards?

It was the paranoia again, digging its claws into her, interpreting every scrap of cloth as a red flag. The stain was slick on her hand, uncomfortably thick and tacky. That didn't mean it was blood.

What, then? What kind of leak could create something like this?

Half against her better judgment, Margot moved back to the discolored smear. Its edges weren't perfect, she realized. The side opposite her was blurred, smears traveling deeper into the attic.

Like something had been placed on the stain and then dragged away.

She gained her feet. Floorboards groaned under her weight, and she fell still again, listening to their echoes, trying to convince herself that the creak hadn't been repeated farther behind her.

She stepped around the stain, moving the light in broad arcs to keep the space around her lit as best she could.

The room's atmosphere felt heavier than when she'd entered. As though a poisonous miasma existed in the air, and it was multiplying with every minute she spent in the space.

Stop it. Stop it!

The house groaned as she moved through it. The smear ran for a few feet, only gradually growing thinner. She bent to trace its path as it lightened until it was almost unreadable between the dust and the wood. Eventually, she reached a point where she couldn't follow it any farther.

Margot took a step back. The streak had been moving in a long, slowly curving arc. She found the point where she could definitively say she lost the path and then followed that trajectory, her light held close to the floor as she panned in circles, searching for clues.

There. A drop of old, dark color had splattered onto the floor. She followed it, and a few steps on was a smudge no larger than Margot's finger. Another half dozen steps beyond that and she found where the stains had been leading.

Another hatch existed in the floor ahead. This one was still closed, only visible because of its raised edges and a crescent-shaped fingerhold. Margot fit her hand into it and pulled, but the hatch only shifted a millimeter before jamming. It was locked on the other side, just as the other entrance had been.

A whisper-soft sigh echoed from Margot's left. She swung her light toward it. A spider crept across the floor, its body shiny black and its shadow stretched long by the artificial light. Margot held her phone still even as the spider crawled past the edge of its glow.

Farther into the attic, masked by darkness so heavy that her light couldn't reach it, were two pinpricks of light.

Margot didn't dare move. The lights weren't a reflection; they shone on their own, two small disks of the harshest, coldest light Margot had ever seen.

Her mouth was parchment dry. It seemed as though the lights were a part of some larger form. Something that stood very still, cloistered in the shadows that hung to the attic like shrouds.

If I could just move a little closer…spread my light farther…

She crept one foot forward but then stopped. She shouldn't be approaching anything she didn't understand. If she was smart, she would back away, follow the stain back until she reached the hatch door.

Her hand holding the phone was trembling. It was impossible to pull back. Not when the eyes stared at her like that. Not when it was so near to being revealed.

I just need to know. One more step, to be certain.

She stretched her foot forward. The farthest reaches of her phone's light grazed over another row of floorboards. It still wasn't enough, though. She moved her other foot, taking a longer step, and the light began to tease at the edges of the thing in the dark—

A horrible crunching, crackling sensation came from beneath her foot. Margot pulled back, her heart in her throat, and stared down at the slowly coiling remains of a spider.

It had been larger than the others. The needle-point legs retracted, curling toward the crushed body. Strands of gray pulp stretched from it to the sole of Margot's shoe, and she bit down on a disgusted cry as she scraped it across the floor, trying to clear it.

She hadn't moved her light from the indistinguishable shape, but she *had* looked away. Now, the pinprick lights were gone. Margot frowned, glancing to either side, then, stepping over the crushed spider, carefully moved toward where she'd seen the figure.

Beams of aged wood came into view. She'd reached one of the walls. The dust hung thicker here, and so did the spiders. Tiny bodies scurried over one another as they raced to escape her light.

Where did it go?

Margot turned in a slow circle, breath held as she strained to hear any movements other than her own. She knew she shouldn't be looking any further for it. She should be moving back to the exit as quickly as she could. And yet…

Something small was wedged into a gap behind one of the support beams. It was very, very close to the place she'd thought she'd seen the figure. Margot lowered herself to one knee to see it better. She'd found some kind of small, leather-bound book. It was aged and dulled by a layer of dust and looked as though it had been there for a long time.

She held the shimmering light above the book as she tried to pry it free. The pages made a crackling noise. Margot poised her tongue between her teeth as she moved more carefully, trying to pull the book out from where its leather had fused into the wood.

A spider scurried out from between the pages. Margot flinched but didn't abandon her work. A fraction at a time, the book came free. Whoever had wedged it into the narrow gap had wanted it to stay there.

A low ripping noise came from the cover as the book finally peeled out. Part of the leather, aged until it was as delicate as crepe, had been left behind, but the book itself was still intact. Margot tried to pry it open, but the pages were fused and threatened to tear. She tucked it under her arm instead and stood.

The attic felt much colder than when she'd arrived there. Gooseflesh ran across her arms as she reached her light out to ward off the shadows.

More spiders fled. Margot held herself rigid as she crept back toward the stain. It looked darker, thicker, than when she'd first found it. She tried not to stare at how the surface glistened at the edges of her light.

She glanced down at the hand holding the book. The index finger, which she'd used to push through the rotting wood, was still streaked with the vivid liquid, though it had started to dry and crust.

When she reached the stain, she paused to reorient herself. The trapdoor hadn't been far away, and when she'd climbed through it, enough ambient light flowed from the opening that it was hard to lose. Now, though, there was nothing but darkness around her. The sun had set. She'd spent too long in this highest level of the house.

It isn't far.

Margot began moving in the direction she thought she'd come. Even the footmarks on the floor had become confusing as she'd crossed her path multiple times.

Wait…no. There are too many prints.

Not all of these are mine.

Ahead, two sets of her shoe marks overlapped: one from when she'd followed the stain and the other, she believed, from when she'd entered the attic. But a third set existed. They showed bare soles, not shoeprints, overlapping her own careful steps.

Fear rose in Margot like a wave. The light flickered as she raised it to follow this new set of prints.

No. No. It's after dark. You need to get out.

She ran her tongue across her teeth and lurched forward, following her own footsteps back toward the open hatch.

Each of her steps sang like a drum on the aged, creaking floor. And yet, the sound wasn't isolated.

It's an echo. She thought it so fiercely, so determinedly, that she almost believed it. Each of her steps was dogged by another sound: a second pair of feet only a few paces behind her.

Her heart was in her throat, her skin damp with cold perspiration. Ahead, the edge of the trapdoor emerged from the gloom. She aimed for it, eyes fixed straight ahead, one horrible thought running on repeat through her mind.

Can't stop. If I stop, they'll catch me.

The echoing, beating footsteps were gaining. She was at the door. Margot dropped into a slide, letting her legs scrape through the opening and into the level below. She threw the book down, afraid for what the harsh impact would do to its delicate binding but even more afraid of what would happen if she didn't have both her hands, and swung around.

Her light grazed over empty air.

Margot, half hanging through the opening, her weight supported on her torso and arms, struggled to breathe. She flicked the phone's light to either side, squinting into the dark, but all she managed to pick up were loosely drifting flecks of dust.

I was so sure... I thought someone was behind me...

She let her head slump, shaking half from the adrenaline and half from stifled, panicked laughter.

She'd done the very thing she'd been trying to avoid: she'd let the attic, and the superstitious fears, get in her head.

The space was empty after all. Empty except for a damp stain she couldn't explain and a book that would probably turn out to be an old repair manual.

Margot slowly lowered herself farther through the opening, legs stretched and searching for purchase, until she touched the top of the stepladder. She placed the phone on the wood beside her shoulder to free up both arms, then reached behind herself and hauled on the open hatch.

It was heavy, and not designed to be shut from that angle, but Margot was not willing to climb back into the attic proper. On her third attempt it swung up and over, and Margot braced it above her head as she reached back to pick up her mobile.

Her fingers touched the cool glass and metal of her phone. And something else. Something cold and spongy and fleshy.

25.

Margot felt as though a knife had been sliced into her heart.

Pinned under the hatch, she could only half turn her body. Her cell phone was still where she'd placed it, but she'd put it the wrong way down, and the light shone into the wood floorboards. Scant traces of illumination escaped around the edges, a whisper of sight all she had.

Her hand rested on top of the phone. And so did another set of fingers.

She could barely see them. But she knew they were pale. Unnaturally warped. Parts of the ring finger and little finger were missing entirely, leaving pale stubs.

Above them, the two disks of light shone, fixated on Margot.

She convulsed backward, a scream catching and dragging in her throat. The phone skittered, sliding over the edge of the hatch and hitting one of the ladder's steps before smacking into the floor.

Margot felt herself losing her footing. The ladder tipped beneath her. The hatch, balanced by one arm and her head, was heavy. Her spare hand scrabbled, trying to hold on, but she was already gone, falling into the dark hall below.

Her shin scraped the stepladder's edge. The ladder fell away, hitting the wall with a crunch, and Margot landed hard. Her ears rang and her knees and hands smarted.

For a moment, she simply hunched there on the floor, swallowed by the darkness of the house, waiting for the pain to register.

It came in smarting strips and dull, throbbing pulses, mostly along her leg but in her hands and wrists as well. It wasn't enough to keep her from moving, though—no broken bones, no torn muscles. She could still stand.

Margot did exactly that. Her legs shook as she fumbled to find the closest door. It creaked as it opened, and Margot pushed it wide, allowing the pale moonlight shining through the window to flow into the hall.

The trapdoor above her was closed. Margot backed up, watching it, daring it to move. It stayed still. Quietly indistinct against the wooden ceiling, as though it had never been opened in the first place.

The fear had left her lungs raw and her body quaking, but Margot forced herself to keep moving. She pulled the stepladder away from the wall. It had left a nasty scrape in the wood. She straightened it under the hatch and climbed two steps. Unsteady fingers found the bolt and drew it home as hard as she could. She tested the lock, checking it again and again, before daring to apply pressure to the hatch. It refused to open. Finally reassured, Margot gingerly returned to the floor.

She found her phone several feet away. It lit up at her touch. A crack ran along one corner of the screen, but after the distance it fell, she was just grateful that it still worked. She opened the *recent* tab. Kant's number was listed there, from when she'd called him after the bells rang. She pressed it.

The phone went straight to voice mail. Kant hadn't recorded a message; a digital woman's voice calmly informed Margot that the recipient was unavailable, but she could leave a message at the tone.

She ended the call before the beep. Kant would still be visiting his sister. He said he'd be back late that night.

Margot slumped her back against the wall as she scrolled through her other contacts. She hadn't thought to get numbers for anyone else on the estate, and except for Kant, no one in her phone lived within twenty hours of her.

She'd had some half-formed idea of calling the winery's manager and asking if she could stay in the staff's accommodation that night. Or anywhere, really, as long as it was away from the house and the *thing* inside of it.

That was still an option. She could walk to the staff buildings and knock on doors until someone answered. She glanced toward the only visible window. Night had fully set in. She'd be walking by her phone's light, and Witchety had told her not to stray too far from home after dusk.

How many of Witchety's words do we take as gospel? Does she know what's actually happening here, or is she just guessing?

Margot wrapped her arms around herself to ward against the cold and turned toward the stairs. Her foot hit something small. The book. She'd dropped it through the hatch first, and it now lay on the floor, its leather cover torn and threads from its binding hanging loose.

She picked it up and carried it carefully, making sure not to damage it any more than she already had.

Once downstairs, the house's layout started to feel more familiar again. She switched on lights as she found them and worked her way to the kitchen. The book went onto the little table, then she turned the sink's water to hot and leaned over the counter as she waited for it to heat.

Her fingers still held a smear from the stain, but it had now darkened into a heavy brown. It truly did look like blood. If she'd had more emotional fortitude, she would have examined it more closely, smelling or prodding at it, but her curiosity had been almost entirely drowned under revulsion. She poured liquid soap onto her hands and plunged them under the water, scrubbing and scrubbing again until the water had run clear for a solid five minutes and her fingers began to sting from the heat.

She dried her hands on a towel as she faced the room and considered her next move.

Someone had known there was something bad in the attic. Maybe her parents, or maybe someone from a generation or two back, had attached the bolt locks to the ceiling hatches.

That meant they had been living with the thing in the roof for years. Based on how old the bolts were, it had been at least a few decades. And they had survived it fine.

No. My parents didn't.

She bared her teeth as she tried to squeeze down the blooming sense of panic in her chest. She pictured the stain in their ceiling, bubbling through the plaster and paint, right above their bed.

They'd survived there for decades, she reminded herself. Decades of living with that thing above them.

Margot could get through one more night. Especially if she was careful. Especially if she was cautious.

That would mean she'd have to return to her room for the night. Try to close her eyes. Try to forget about what was above her at least for a few hours.

But she'd be cautious. She had the axe now. She wouldn't leave the house. She wouldn't open any windows or doors. No more exploring; she would keep to the parts of the house she already knew well. That meant the kitchen and her bedroom and very little besides.

As long as she stayed careful, didn't invite anything else inside, didn't make herself vulnerable, she should be able to get through one more night.

Kant would be back by morning. And she would demand answers from him. Nora and Ray had danced around her questions, but Kant wouldn't. Not if she pressed him.

And at least, if she understood her situation a little more, she might know what was best to do. She wouldn't be staying at Gallows Hill—that much was already certain. But she needed to know whether to sell the business or shut it down entirely.

Margot pressed her palms into her burning eyes. The staff had seemed so nervous to meet her. So polite, so hopeful. Because they didn't want to lose their jobs.

But why would any of them continue working at the winery once they knew what was happening?

Kant will be able to tell me. He's been here for thirty years. He must understand the place better than anyone.

In the meantime...she had one final night to get through.

Margot dropped her hands. A multitude of small aches radiated across her. She tugged up the hem of her jeans and saw she'd scraped a layer of skin off her shin; minuscule drops of blood beaded across it.

Her parents must have kept a first aid kit somewhere. Margot began looking through the kitchen cupboards. She found eight kinds of napkins, three sets of wineglasses, fancy plates and plain plates, multiple strainers, and baking tins in almost every shape imaginable. Her parents had not been fond of throwing things out apparently.

In the cupboard above the microwave, she found a large, clear glass bottle. Its label had been written on with shaky pen: *Holy Water*. It was empty.

Margot didn't know what to think of that. She replaced the bottle and moved on. A box of gauze strips was hidden behind stacks of paper bowls, and she patched two over her leg. At the very least, it would keep her from getting spots of blood on her sheets.

She wasn't going to risk leaving her familiar routes to have a shower that night. Worst-case scenario, she could save it for the first motel she stopped off at on the way home.

Home. It feels strange to call another place that now.

She sagged, the scraps from the gauze clutched in one hand as she stared down at her patched leg.

She could still return to her old apartment. Her job would most likely take her back, as long as they hadn't found a replacement yet. She could slot back into her old life, probably with less effort than she even anticipated.

So why did it feel so much like failure?

Stop. Whatever's happening here isn't your problem. You just need to get out, get somewhere safe.

As she packed the gauze away, she couldn't keep her mind from returning to that thought again and again. *Not your problem.* But it was, wasn't it? This was her house. Her land. They might not feel like it, but her blood had lived here for eleven generations before her.

And she would be the first to abandon it.

Margot kept her dinner simple. Her stomach wasn't easy, and everything tasted slightly wrong, the way it would when she got sick with a cold. No matter how much hot coffee she drank, she still felt cold.

She hunched at the table, chewing a piece of buttered toast. Her eyes landed on the small, leather-bound book. After everything that had happened, she'd almost forgotten about it. Margot pulled it up beside her plate.

It was her first time seeing it in proper light. The shape was warped, the pages rippled with moisture absorbed over a very long time. The leather spine had come free when she pulled it from its nook and now the stitching was visible—gray threads, heavy with dirt, fraying and splitting out of the fragile paper. She opened the cover. It came up without much trouble, but the first page was blank—no title or author name.

Margot tried to turn the page, but the leaves were fused together and threatened to tear. She crossed to the cutlery drawer and brought out a butter knife. Moving in tentative, delicate increments, she eased the knife between the first two pages and slowly peeled them apart.

The words were written in ink. A date was written in the upper-right corner, smudged until she couldn't make out any distinct numbers. The lettering was strange—neat but convoluted and heavily slanted, and though letters stood out to her, the words weren't easily read. Blotches of stray ink had flicked across the margins, leaving permanent stains on the pages.

Margot rubbed her fingers at the back of her neck as she struggled to make out the first sentence. "Today is the…fifth? Firtt? No—wait—"

Firſt. The writer was using an elongated *ſ* in place of *s*. The book was very, very old.

"The first day of summer," Margot read haltingly. She felt like she was a child again, spelling out the letters as she tried to understand the words. "God's bleffing…*blessing*…follows us, joy be given. Papa fays…*says*…I shall have a governess like the girls in the city. He gave me this book for my thoughts. I shall call it my Summer Book…"

Margot bent low over the table, deciphering the words in painstaking increments, occasionally sliding the knife between pages to pry them free. The journal seemed to belong to a young teen. She spoke about her brothers bickering in the field, and wanting to wear a new dress to the town dance. About a friend she made, and then the heartbreak when she found out that friend spoke coldly of her behind her back. The boys she liked. The new plants that went into the home's garden. The way the cook joked with her and gave her treats.

The progress was slow, but Margot found it nearly impossible to put down. The long *S* speckled through the pages meant that the journal had been written sometime in the late seventeen hundreds. That would place it as belonging to a child or a grandchild of the first-generation Hulls. Whether from Ezra or Ephraim's line, she couldn't tell. The unknown girl hadn't signed the book. Except for the first page's numbers, which were unreadable, she hadn't dated any of the entries, only occasionally noting that it was a *Tuefday* or *the feventh* or that harvest had begun to arrive for that season's wine.

Margot was less than a third of the way through the book when she finally stopped and stretched back in her chair. Joints in her spine popped as they released, and she let out a slow, groaning sigh. Her eyes burned. When she touched her phone, she was surprised to see it was after midnight.

I meant to go to my room early and stay there until dawn. Margot carefully closed the journal. The pages she'd managed to separate fanned across the top of the unread section, an easy marker to see where she'd gotten to. She didn't like the idea of leaving the book too far from sight overnight and folded a towel around it for protection before tucking it into her jacket pocket.

A low, melancholy wind bled through the window, and it was at just the right speed to create a whistle-like pitch. The kitchen was lit, but as she approached the hallway entrance, she saw the rest of the house was dark.

That isn't right. I switched on lights as I came down from the attic. Didn't I...? When did they go out?

She hesitated on the kitchen's threshold, staring into the barely distinguishable lines of the lounge room's opening and the edges of the closest couch. In the poor light, it was almost possible to picture a hand lying on the armrest, skin stretched tight across fragile bones, fingertips curled slightly to dig into the threadbare fabric.

Margot took half a step back. The image, caused by poor light and stinging eyes, vanished when she moved, returning the couch to the same forlorn structure it had always been.

For a fleeting moment, she considered spending the night in the kitchen. It wasn't warm and there was nowhere for her to rest her head, but at least it was well lit.

Don't stall. Get to your room. Dawn will be here faster if you can sleep.

She'd roved all through the house on her first night there, unaware of any of its history. Back then it had seemed more like an adventure, each door holding the promise of uncovering secrets. Now, the closed doors felt more akin to a threat. She'd only seen behind a fraction of them. She did not want to open any more.

Margot tied her jacket tightly around herself. She'd grown cold while she sat, and the scrapes and bruises registered as dull, icy points across her body. The mournful notes from the wind dug at her, setting her nerves on edge.

Do it quickly.

Margot fixed her eyes ahead, then stepped over the threshold and into the dark.

26.

The house felt quieter than it should have. Not that there weren't sounds—there were, and a multitude of them—but they seemed unnaturally muffled. The wind through the windows faded into a low, mournful tune that teased the edges of her hearing. The creaks of shifting wood were dulled. Even Margot's own breaths, too quick, sounded like they came from someone several steps behind her, hidden in the darkest recesses of the hall.

And coming from somewhere ahead, barely audible, was a quick clicking, clinking sound.

Is that...? No. Don't. Don't think it into being.

She wasn't going to look in the direction of the effigy. She wasn't going to think about its accruement of spoons and keys and tiny metal talismans, and how the clinking noise sounded so horribly like something brushing past them to set them jangling.

Instead, she crossed to the front door, locked it, and picked up the axe she'd left nearby. Then she faced the passage that led to the stairs. She knew the path to her room. It wasn't far. Only a minute away, less if she ran.

Don't run. Don't let them know you're scared.

Her throat ached as she swallowed. Her legs were too heavy, but Margot forced them to move, dragging her along the hallway, toward the steps she could barely see. The axe was uncomfortably heavy. She'd thought it would be reassuring, but the cold metal pressed against her skin in a way that made her shiver.

She waited until she was well past the living room's archway before pressing the flashlight button on her phone.

The stairs emerged from the darkness, like landmarks in a foggy night. They seemed to lead higher than she remembered them. Margot climbed. The patchy runner crinkled beneath her shoes.

A bell, hidden somewhere in a room above, chimed once. Margot froze, eyes directed upward, but the echoes faded without repeating.

Just the wind.

She wanted to believe that.

Get to your room. Close the door and don't open it again until morning.

She climbed faster. Her cell phone's light flashed across each step ahead, dizzyingly bright on close-by surfaces and paltry on everything farther away. She didn't turn back or shine the light behind herself. Not even when she felt haunted by the sensation that there was something just behind her, something with pinprick-light eyes and cold skin.

Stop it. Stop thinking like that—stop imagining things—

A floorboard several steps behind Margot creaked, and she broke into a full sprint, taking the stairs two at a time, not stopping until she was on the landing and could put her back to a wall.

Her light flashed over the stairwell. It was empty.

She didn't linger but pushed off the wall, her steps hurried, her breathing shallow. Her door was easy to find; she'd left it open that morning. She shoved into it and felt for the light. The switch turned but no power came on.

Margot tried to repress the fear that was creeping up through her, but it was like a living thing, oozing out of her lungs and crawling into her throat, where it choked even the faintest attempts at noise.

The bulb must have blown. Or maybe the circuit breaker tripped; that would explain why the other lights were turned off too.

She flicked the switch multiple times, as though she might breathe life back into it through sheer force of will. The bulb above was unresponsive. She only had her phone and her phone's flashlight to light the space.

She left the axe next to the head of her bed, then turned. The wardrobe door hung open. She couldn't remember if she'd left it that way. The mirror on the door faced her, showing her face lit unnaturally by the light in her hand, throwing long shadows across her eyes and forehead. The image, blurred, felt unreal. Her skin looked too ashen. Like the blood had been let from the veins, and now she stared at an empty husk, an upright corpse.

She turned her head, but the image was still there in her peripheral vision, degrading with each passing second, the skin withering and the lids drooping away from her eyes, and Margot launched herself toward it in three quick steps and slammed the door closed, her breathing rough.

She didn't want to spend the night in this room. But there were precious few alternatives. The kitchen had no guarantee of being any safer. She could still risk leaving the home and running for the employee quarters, but she wasn't certain she could find her way in the dark. Besides that, what was happening on the estate likely wasn't restricted to her home. She'd seen the figure in the shed, and she couldn't discount how unsettled Nora and Ray had been at the store.

Is the poison inside more deadly than the poison that must be out there?

Slowly, her fingertips numb and unsteady, Margot eased the wardrobe door back open. Her reflection was normal. A little desaturated in the artificial light and her features drawn from the late hour and the unrelenting stress, but unmistakably her.

"Damn." She shut the door with a solid click, sealing the reflection away again, and leaned her head against the cool wood. "Damn this whole...*thing*."

She didn't know how much she could trust her own eyes or her own ears. She'd spent hours in the kitchen, undisturbed, while she was absorbed in the journal. It was only once she put the book down and began to focus on the house that things started to turn bad.

Does that mean my mind, too stressed to cope, is conjuring these images?

Or does the house only come alive once I turn my attention to it?

"Just get through to dawn," Margot whispered.

Her bedroom door didn't have a lock. She cleared the lamp and books from the bedside table and pushed it in front of the door. It wasn't as heavy or as sturdy as she would have liked, but it was something.

Then, Margot turned to the window. The padlock was still there. Cold metal stung her raw fingertips as she slotted it into the hasp lock and then turned the key. It clicked as it sealed. She rattled it, tugging and jangling to check nothing would come loose, then dropped it back against the cold panes.

Will locks work against what lives here?

She didn't know the answer. Her parents seemed to believe in the locks, for all the good it had done them.

Finally, Margot plugged the power cord into her phone. It showed it was charging, which meant the house hadn't completely lost power. She placed her phone on the ground, light function still activated, beside her bed. Just on the other side of it was the axe, its blade coated in shadows. It should have made Margot feel safer. It didn't.

She slipped her shoes off and draped her jacket across the bed's cover for extra warmth, then climbed in, still dressed in her clothes from that afternoon.

The sheets were cold. Margot pressed numb feet together as she tried to force warmth into them. The phone's flashlight shone toward the ceiling. It illuminated the room less clearly than she would have wanted but was still better than lying in the dark. It could stay on until morning—a poor man's night-light to ward off nightmares, both real and imagined.

She folded her arms around her torso. It was late. The tiredness was like a heavy weight on her chest, pressing her down. Every time she closed her eyes, though, they snapped open again almost immediately.

The house was too loud. Through layers upon layers of walls, she heard subtle creaks and pops as the ancient wood relaxed in the cool air. A bird far in the distance cackled once, twice, then fell silent. Something small seemed to tap across the hallway. A rat? Something more?

Above, the attic was separated from her by a thin layer of wood and paint. The attic...and the *thing* inside the attic. She wondered whether it was still there. Whether it might have been following her through the house, listening to her footfalls. Whether it might be sitting right above her at that moment, unseen but endlessly patient.

She rolled onto her side, knees drawn close to her chest. A low, throbbing headache had started behind her eyes, which stung. She began to doubt that she could fall asleep at all that night.

Time ticked on relentlessly. The phone's light sent strange shapes across the wall. And Margot, dragged down by the crushing weariness, finally felt her eyes close.

For a long stretch there was nothing but darkness. Shapes bled in and out of the gloom in erratic patches—dreams trying to form, only to collapse under their own weight. And then, a voice: "The viewing is optional."

"No," Margot tried to say. Her eyes opened. She was in the viewing room, surrounded by the sentry wall of coffins. Her parents' caskets were ahead, beneath the only window, bathed in the soft light from a cloud-hazed sun.

The funeral director's face was gone entirely. A smooth, fleshy sheen covered from his hairline to his jaw, unpleasantly flat. An empty canvas. No eyes, no mouth, but still speckled with faint crease lines and pores. The flesh didn't move, but words came from him as he reached toward the casket lids. "We did our best, but..."

"No." The word echoed in her head, but her lips refused to convey it. The funeral director's face had been warped and erased by her memory, but every other detail was as realistic as it had been on the day. The pauses in their conversation. The waxy sheen on the caskets' lids. The dry smell of dust and potpourri. Even the way her heart caught in her throat as she craned her neck to see inside the caskets. "No. No! No! *No! Don't!*"

She couldn't stop it. She'd seen inside on the morning of the funeral, and now her mind replayed those images to her once again, as fresh and sharp and skin-crawling as they had been that day.

Two bodies lay inside the caskets. They had been posed in the traditional way: on their backs, hands folded across their chests, heads resting on low pillows. They were dressed in the best outfits from their wardrobes: a soft purple-and-white dress for her mother, a gray suit for her father. Their hair had been combed. Under their nails had been cleaned. Their faces washed and a layer of natural makeup applied to mask the deathly sallow color of their skin.

The efforts were all intended to make the bodies seem as peaceful and close to life as possible. Ideally, they would have appeared to be gently sleeping.

All efforts had been in vain.

The faces ahead of Margot were stretched, their muscles tight. Although their mouths were closed, their jaws seemed to be straining. As though they were trying to scream.

Their eyes were open. The corneas were cloudy, dulling the colors beneath into a flat sheen of gray. Her mother's eyelids seemed to have been shredded, the skin around her lashes torn into strips.

"I…tried to close the eyes," the funeral director admitted. "First with spiked caps under the lids to hold them closed, and when that didn't work, I tried sewing them shut. But the skin was delicate. I'm afraid they tore—"

A spiral of black thread still clung to the edge of her mother's left eye, its sharp end stabbing into the gray sheen below.

"Why's their skin like that?" she heard herself ask. At the time, like in the dream, she'd felt numb and cold and sick.

"I'm not entirely sure." He moved a hand across her father's cheek, indicating without quite touching the skin. "I…wasn't able to ascertain what happened."

The veins were black. They created dark rivers beneath the skin, threading across their cheeks, their foreheads, their noses. The thickest branches ran down their throats, and the funeral director had tried to disguise them by giving them clothes with high collars.

"They were like this when I received them. It looks like blood, but it's not," the smooth-faced figure before her said. His voice was low, halting, uncertain. "Their blood was drained and replaced during the embalming process. The formaldehyde should have removed any discoloration, but—"

Formaldehyde. He drained their blood and filled them with formaldehyde. The thought was like a punch to her stomach, and Margot felt nausea rise through her.

Everything about this was wrong. Bodies were supposed to relax after death. Rigor mortis should have set in and then faded again, leaving them limp and soft and malleable. Peaceful, even. They were anything but.

The rictus-frozen faces stared blindly at the ceiling. The hands folded over their chests were frozen into grasping claws. Every muscle was taut, stretched to their limits, ready to snap. Their mouths were wired shut, but she was certain, at the moment they died, they had been screaming.

She tried to open her mouth to speak, but in her dream and in reality, words had failed her. She couldn't breathe.

A snap rang through the room like a gunshot. Her mother's jaw flew open. The wire holding it in place had given out, and Margot lurched back. The stretched mouth was unnaturally long, the way that could only happen when the jaw was broken. Inside, pulpy, blackened gums were swollen tight around the teeth.

The funeral director moved forward, slamming the lids down in quick succession.

A gasping cry escaped Margot. The lids were shut, but the image was still burned inside her mind, inescapable. The gaping, silently howling scream. The last time she would ever see her mother in the flesh.

"I am very sorry," the funeral director's smooth face whispered as he leaned, unsteadily, against the caskets. "I think it would be best to keep the lids closed."

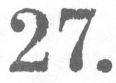

27.

Margot jolted upright, a gasp dying in her throat. Her clothes were drenched in sweat. Her lungs burned, warning her that she'd been holding her breath. A burning, aching headache throbbed.

She was still in her room. The phone's flashlight sent its cold glow across the ceiling, not quite reaching far enough to properly light any of the walls. The window, locked, rattled as a cold wind pulled at it.

Margot hunched forward, breathing in heaving gulps as she pulled her knees up to her chest. She shook. Her body ached. She didn't know how long she'd been asleep, but there was no sign of dawn through the window.

The shivers refused to abate. She rested her forehead on top of her knees as burning tears flooded her eyes.

She hadn't cried at all during her parents' funerals. She'd been too lost, too uncertain. She'd had no memories of them. There hadn't even been any photos; the only image she'd had of her parents were the distorted, broken faces inside the caskets.

Now, tears came hot and fast. For her parents, for Margot herself, and for what they all had lost.

What did this house do to you?

She lay back on the bed, sheets and clothing sticking to her clammy skin, and stared up at the ceiling as she let the tears fall into the hair on either side of her face.

Distantly, in some far part of the house, a bell rang.

Margot closed her eyes and pressed her palms into the aching lids. *Go away. Go away. Go away—*

A second bell began to ring. This one was closer and on the ground floor. Then a third started, along the hall outside her room. And finally, the bell near Margot's own door leapt to life, pealing out its warning as it twitched and thrashed on the end of its hook like a living thing.

She moved her hands from her eyes to her ears, teeth grit and face damp as she waited for the sound to stop. It only seemed to grow louder, ringing from every corner of the house, ceaseless.

And then…it *did* cease. All at once, like the wire had been cut, every bell fell still and silent. Margot watched her room's own alarm. It was barely visible in the shadows, except for the way it faintly swayed.

She rolled onto her side again, facing the window so she wouldn't have to look at the door any longer. The tiredness was still there but worse, stretching her like taffy, pulling a little more with each second to see just how far she could go before she broke. But now that she'd woken, she couldn't fall asleep. Her pulse was alive, jumping as though to keep time with the now-silent bells.

They're not in the house. Not yet. That's only the boundary line warning. But it means they're coming. Whatever they *are. They're on their way, and I don't know how long it will take them to get here, but they're coming for the house.*

She strained to see any trace of light through the window, but the sky was heavy, only a trace speckling of stars to show it existed there at all.

Margot squeezed her hands into fists and held them under her throat.

Her skin was sticky there with still-drying sweat. She forced her eyes closed and willed the darkness to calm her racing heart.

How far away are they now? Half the distance? More?

She squirmed. The knowledge that something was coming beat at her mind. It was impossible to think of anything else.

The bedroom door's barricaded. The windows are all sealed. I have my light. I have an axe.

They were all defenses that had seemed good in the light of day. At night, they felt like nothing. Margot began to believe she'd be trapped like that until morning, stuck in a limbo of suspense, waiting for something that might not ever arrive.

There's nothing you can do about it right now. The bells have rung before, and you've been fine. Think of something else. Anything else.

Her mind flitted across a dozen subjects in a heartbeat. Nora and Ray's smiling evasion of her questions. Witchety and her withered hands holding the talisman. The disk-light eyes staring at her through the darkness.

She pressed a hand across her face, so tired and broken that she felt as though her body could crumble like a sand sculpture.

And then she heard it.

A quiet sound coming from far away. Something at the walls. Fingertips prying at the doors.

She bit her tongue as she waited. The doors were locked. She'd sealed the only entrances she'd used during her time at Gallows Hill, and she'd trusted her parents to have kept everything else locked.

They couldn't get in.

Could they?

Her heart throbbed in her throat as she waited. Slow, shuffling footsteps moved outside, beneath her window. She pictured bare feet slapping into the cold stones, impervious to the cuts and bruises being inflicted on them.

If she went to the window, she might be able to see—

No! Stay where you are. Wait for dawn.

Her light was still on. It had seemed like the wisest choice when she'd gone to bed: keep the room lit, keep the fear at bay. Now, though, she realized there were only two lights left on in the house: the kitchen's and her room's. It was like a beacon drawing attention to where she was.

One hand twitched out, preparing to reach over the bed's edge to turn the light off, but she caught herself. That would be worse. It would confirm that the room was occupied to anyone who was looking.

Instead, she held as still as she could, making no noises, waiting. The footsteps passed along the side of the house. They were slow. Heavy. Each step was punctuated by a pause, and Margot tried to visualize it, the figure below her room, its blank face and wide eyes staring into the darkness, maybe staring up at her window, as it followed its circle along the house's edge.

She listened until the noise had faded beyond hearing.

The doors are locked. The windows are shut. There's no way in.

Her nerves were on fire. Her body had grown tense, until the fibers of her being ached, and Margot was incapable of relaxing. She could only lie there, pantomiming sleep, as she waited and listened.

Then, a scrape.

The noise registered in Margot's head before her ears even had time to process it. She knew that noise. She'd heard it a dozen times a day as a child. No other memories of her earliest years existed, but she knew *this*.

Back then, it had been a good noise. She'd associated it with something she loved.

Now, it spread pure dread through her limbs.

The scrape came from the dog door as it swung open.

Far in the distance, a hand slapped onto the kitchen tiles.

She pictured an emaciated body writhing through the hatch, hands and legs spread out like an insect.

Another slap. A scrape as something heavy dragged itself through the narrow opening.

Then the soft *whoosh-clack-clack* as the flap swung closed again.

Margot's mouth gaped open but she didn't dare make any noise. She felt frozen, locked in place, her body turned to lead as the terror tore through her—

The downstairs floorboards creaked.

Margot rolled over the side of her bed, grasping for her phone. Now that the presence was inside the house, the light was the most dangerous thing in her room. She fought with the button, switching it off, and silently prayed the creature that had paced outside her window didn't remember where her room was.

I could move somewhere else, run into one of the other bedrooms before it gets to the stairs...

That was foolish. She didn't know the house or what she might find elsewhere. At least in this room, she had a weapon and something to barricade the door. They were slim advantages, but they were more than nothing.

She hunched on the floor, phone pressed to her chest, eyes staring blindly at the opposite wall.

The presence didn't keep her waiting. A heavy, dull footfall thumped on the lowest stair. Margot grit her teeth, fear flowing through her veins. It was coming upstairs already. It had to know where she was.

Stay calm. Clear your head. Think!

The stairs groaned under the intruder's weight. It had to be large. Weighty.

Physical. Not a ghost. Not something I can put my hand through.

Each step was slow and ponderous, but they came unrelentingly, each one moving it closer. It was more than halfway up the stairs.

The axe.

She was on her feet before the thought had fully registered. The axe's handle, roughed by age, ached in her sore hands. She raised it. Her legs were unsteady, and she had to stagger to hold her balance.

In that instant, Margot saw herself clearly. She was struggling with the axe, trying to keep it upright, trying to get a measure of its weight. She hadn't built up the muscles to use it. Already, in just a few seconds, her arms were starting to burn from the effort.

It had seemed like an excellent weapon earlier. And maybe if it was only used for show—to chase off teenage pranksters or nosy townspeople—it would have served its purpose perfectly.

But Margot knew, with the same steady certainty as the footfalls that had reached the top of the stairs and turned toward her room, that she would have to use the axe.

And she would fail.

It was too heavy. Too blunt. And her body was already exhausted, its adrenaline nearly drained. She wouldn't be able to put any speed behind the blow or even angle it accurately enough to be sure the blade would hit home.

If she couldn't hit the intruder on the first strike, there wouldn't be enough time for a second try.

Margot let the axe drop onto the bed. The mattress creaked as it flexed under the weight. The horror of her miscalculation ground her insides raw.

The footsteps were in the hallway. Louder now, growing clearer with each one. The intruder had no doubts of where she was. Its path hadn't erred even once.

Margot snatched her phone off the floor. Fear had robbed her of clear thought. She should have called someone on it as soon as she heard the footsteps outside the house; instead, she'd watched its light burn like a beacon.

Shaking fingers dialed the emergency help line. She pressed the phone to her ear. The footsteps were close. How long would it take for police to arrive? Did Leafell even have its own station? She couldn't remember seeing one—

"How can I direct your call?" a man's voice asked.

"Help—" Her voice shook. She didn't need to whisper when the footsteps already traced a path toward her door, but the impulse was impossible to override. "Home intruder—"

Distant clicks from a keyboard came through the speaker. "What's your address?"

"I…" Her head burned. Her heart felt like it was going to burst from the effort it took to beat. "It's Gallows Hill. In Leafell. I don't…"

She couldn't remember the address. Had she even been told? Everyone called it *Gallows Hill*, nothing more. Kant had shown her the way to it. She hadn't paid attention to the street or to the number on the letterbox.

"I need an address." The man's voice was too calm, too uninvolved. "Can you get somewhere you can see a street sign?"

She ended the call. When she blinked, tears ran over her lower lashes, unbidden.

Think. Think! You can't be out of options!

Her fingers felt too slow, too clumsy as she navigated to her recent calls. Kant's number was still there. She pressed it.

The footsteps stopped outside her door. Margot fell still, phone held away from her ear so that the rings wouldn't override any other noises.

Her door didn't have a lock. The bedside table blocking it was flimsy. Her only hope was that, despite the weight of the footfalls and the creaking floorboards, the entity on the door's other side couldn't push through the barrier.

For a second, the world was an unnerving level of quiet, disturbed only by the faint chiming rings from Margot's phone.

Then the door handle turned.

She moved on instinct, lurching forward and slamming herself into the bedside table in the same instant the door began to grind inward.

The door scraped back, but only by an inch. Margot leaned her entire weight into it but it wouldn't move any further.

"Kant."

She still held her phone in her right hand, but the voice, distant and distorted, barely registered. She didn't have the breath to reply. Her bare feet dragged over the floor as the door shifted inward. Something began to reach through the opening.

No. No. No! Think!

The axe was still on the bed. A poor chance, but her last one. She dropped the phone and abandoned the door as she raced for it. Her body was shaking, its energy spent by days of stress and sleeplessness, the last of her adrenaline striking through her in thin, erratic bursts. She heaved the weapon up, its monstrous head held above her own, and turned to the door.

Something was forcing its body through. It was a man. Enormously tall but thin, his head grazing the doorframe.

And he was dead.

His skin was ashen and bruised with old, settled blood. Limp hair clung across his scalp, matted with damp soil. Smears of the substance ran across his naked flesh. His shoulders carried bare strips of what might have once been clothes but had long since rotted into rags. His toes and fingernails were dark with mud.

Margot's eyes fell to his mouth, and she felt her heart freeze. His lips were sealed shut—sewn closed with lines of black thread—but behind them his jaw hung loose, elongating his face. The eyes were a milky white, but there was a presence behind the slack muscles. The eyes, seemingly sightless, had fixed on her.

Margot didn't think she could make her feet move, but they did as a gasping cry escaped her. The axe arced down. She'd aimed toward the creature's neck. It missed its mark and sliced into the arm instead.

The sound the axe made reverberated through Margot's head. It wasn't loud, but it was something she knew she would never be able to forget. Heavy and wet, like a fist slamming into raw meat.

She staggered back. She'd tried to keep her hold on the axe, but it had been too heavy, the muscles in her hands too weak. It hung in the creature's arm, embedded in bone just below the shoulder, for only a second. And then it fell. The jarring clatter as the heavy weapon dented the floor barely registered to Margot. The dead man was climbing through the doorway.

One long arm—the arm that had taken the axe—reached out to shove the table away. The blade had cut through skin and muscle and sinew and part of the bone, but there was no blood. As the arm flexed, the severed flesh flapped open, exposing gray, bloodless veins and off-white marrow. A maggot fell free, its fleshy, white body writhing.

Margot's discarded phone lay on the floor. As the dead man stepped through the doorway, his bare foot landed on it, splintering glass.

He didn't seem to notice that any more than he'd noticed the axe.

Margot backed away. She couldn't breathe. She thought her fear couldn't grow any worse, but then the dead man closed the door behind himself, and it did.

Get out. Get out!

But there was no other doorway. Only the wardrobe, the bed, and...

The window.

She was on the second floor. She didn't care. Margot grasped at the latch. The hasp lock sealed it closed.

No. No, please.

The key was still in the lock. But the dead man was moving closer. Margot fought with it, numb fingers struggling with a key that refused to turn. Floorboards creaked under the dead man's weight as his bare feet dragged his corpse toward her.

Then the key turned. Margot shoved the window open, pushing the rusted hinges to move and forcing herself through in the same movement.

A grave-cold hand landed on her shoulder. Rigid fingers dug into her, long nails biting through her flesh, and Margot screamed. She writhed, half-mad with fear, and her shirt tore as she slid through the window and out of the creature's grasp.

The porch's roof ran beneath Margot's window. It slanted at an angle, just gradual enough for her to cling to it as she slid toward its edge. Hot blood flowed across her shoulder. The edges of her vision blurred. She thrust one leg out and jammed it into the gutter, preventing her from slipping over the edge entirely.

The window frame creaked above her. Margot lay prone on the tiles, fingers digging into the lichen and the cracks to hold her position, the cold wind dragging her hair across her face and half blinding her.

Above, the enormous figure crawled through her open window.

He moved on all fours. Splayed fingers reached out to land on the tiles as he wove his body through the exit. His lips, sewn closed, created a hard line across his face. The dead, white eyes never blinked but fixed on her as he writhed closer.

Margot began backing up. Terror pushed her to go faster, but the roof was precarious, and the drop was high. She pulled her foot out of the gutter. Her legs slid over the edge, dangling. She tried to lower herself farther, so she would be hanging by only her hands and the drop wouldn't be so severe, but when she tried to move, her grip slipped.

She plunged over the edge, the gutter skimming her jaw painfully. She thrashed, arms reaching, legs kicking. One ankle hit the porch railing. She was tipped over, at a bad angle, and put her arms out to shield her head.

A terrible crunching sound came as she hit the ground. She felt the noise as much as heard it; it reverberated through her left arm, followed by a wave of pain that swamped her whole body. Her mouth opened to scream, but she had no more breath left.

Her vision flickered to black, then to red, then to black again. Long weeds scraped across her arms and face. Cold wind fanned over her.

She wanted to lie there, to let oblivion take her, but her mind was running on automatic, screaming at a body that wouldn't respond: *He's coming, move, move, move!*

Above, a roof tile cracked as unnatural weight was put on it.

Margot tried to roll onto her side. The pain in her arm was like a fire licking at the insides of her bones. A groan fell from her. She pulled the arm close, tears burning her face, and clutched it against her chest with her good hand as she struggled to her knees.

Don't give up now. Keep moving. You just have to keep moving.

The gutter rattled as dead hands found it.

Margot got one foot under herself, then the other. She staggered. Her ankle refused to take any weight. She managed three steps, then collapsed back to her knees, the jarring impact sending flames through her body.

Another sound reached her. Bells, ringing. A cacophony of them, rising out of the house. A funeral chorus.

She squinted blurred eyes open. Moonlight battled the shadows that spread across the field. The clumping trees around the property were alive with moving limbs. Long hair. Blind eyes. Dirt embedded beneath their overgrown fingernails. They crawled out of hiding and slowly, painfully, dragged themselves across the fence and its alarm wires.

The dead man dropped from the roof. She felt reverberations run through the ground as he hit it.

Margot let herself slump to one side. She couldn't run from this. More bodies crept into view with every second. There had to be more than a dozen of them. Men, women, their bodies broken, their lips sewn shut. Their circle tightened around Margot like a noose.

And among them, two that were running. A light bobbed between them, cutting through the shadows, putting the grass into harsh relief.

The closest figure moved with a limp.

Kant.

Margot tried to rise to meet him, but her energy was gone. She was slowly turning numb; even the pain of her arm barely reached her. She managed a twitch, to rise an inch higher, but then dropped back.

"There," Kant called, but there was none of the panic in his voice that Margot had expected. "I've got her."

The second figure slowed, turning in a half circle, his heavy flashlight flashing across the field and the long-limbed bodies pacing toward him.

Kant dropped to his knees beside Margot. She tried to speak, but her tongue wouldn't move. He put his arms around her back, pressing her close against him, then lifted her, carrying her against his shoulder like a child.

"Behind you," Andrew called.

"I see it." Kant turned, his gait switching to a loping jog. Each step jarred Margot. Her arm, pressed between herself and Kant, flared with blinding pain.

But they were moving. She watched them pass through the open gate in the flashes of Andrew's light. Her head rolled, limp, and Kant's shaggy hair tangled across her face as she stared back across the lawn stretching up to her house.

The tall man still followed. His unblinking, white eyes never looked away as he paced after her in long, staggered steps, the flap on his arm catching moonlight every time it peeled open.

Then the pain and exhaustion overwhelmed her, and her consciousness dropped away.

28.

Hazy lights bled through Margot's closed lids. Something tugged at her arm as the soft slice of scissors wormed its way into her awareness.

She forced her eyes open a crack. A tall, wiry woman bent over Margot. Her hair had been clipped back tightly from her face, and in the dull light, her skin looked almost like basalt. She worked the scissors along Margot's blouse sleeve, cutting it off.

"Leave it. I'm too tired," Margot tried to say, but the words came out as a mumble.

The woman glanced at her, a tight frown drawing sharp lines around her eyes, then returned her attention to the arm.

Margot blinked, trying to draw the room into focus, but colors and shapes blurred. The space was lit by a gas lamp, she was fairly sure. Opposite, Kant sat, his elbows resting on his knees, hands hanging limp between them. His shaggy hair had half fallen across his face, hiding his expression. Another man—Andrew, she thought—paced.

The sleeve came off entirely, and the woman paused, her head tilted. She ran a fingertip across the skin near the shoulder, and Margot knew she was tracing one of the scars. "Is this from…?"

Kant sounded only resigned when he replied, "Yes."

"You lied to me," Margot tried to say, but her tongue felt like it belonged to someone else. She let her eyes close again and was swallowed by the darkness.

Her dreams were fleeting and strange as distorted images flowed through before degrading into nothing.

When she next opened her eyes, the light had changed. Blinds had been drawn across the room's two windows, but sneaking lines of hazy gray bled through, telling her morning had, at last, arrived.

Kant still sat where she'd last seen him, head down. Andrew was next to him, his arms folded awkwardly around himself as he slept, leaned against Kant's shoulder. Someone had draped a blanket over him.

Margot shifted slightly. She'd expected the webbing of bruises and cuts to set her on fire again, but they were only a dull, distant ache. Her mind felt foggy. More than she could expect from sleep.

Painkillers?

She tried to move her injured arm, but it felt strangely heavy. A blanket covered her. She gingerly pulled her arm out from underneath. A cast had been applied, running from her wrist to just below her elbow, a layer of unexpectedly cheerful blue covering the stiff white structure.

"Morning, Margot." Kant had heard her move. He lifted his head, and his eyes were heavy and tinged with red.

Margot ran her tongue across chapped lips and tasted blood. She sat with some effort, using her elbows to leverage herself up, and put her back to a wall. She'd been placed on a table; layers of blankets had been hastily thrown beneath her to create some padding. A box nearby was filled with papers and equipment she couldn't name, presumably cast off the table to make room for her.

The room looked like it might have been a work area. Shelves ran along the wall above her, and more crates were arranged in the corners, packed with scrap metal.

A sink was set into a counter to Margot's left, and the wiry woman she'd seen earlier that night stood there, washing her tools before packing them away. She was small and bone thin, but her movements were all dexterously quick as her long fingers tucked the supplies into her kit. Her tightly bound black hair was shot through with rivers of gray. She sent Margot a quick, searching look, the whites of her eyes strikingly bright against her dark skin, then returned to the task at hand.

"This is Dr. Maynard." Kant's voice seemed raspier than normal, and Margot wondered if he'd slept at all the previous night. "She's a vet. She treats the Gallows Hill family."

Margot glanced down at her arm and the cast applied there. That wasn't the only work done on her, she realized. Bandages had been strapped around her ankle to stabilize it. A gauze pad was taped across her other shoulder. Tiny spots of pink were beginning to bleed through it.

"A…vet?" she managed.

"I've set casts on animals a hundredth of your size," Dr. Maynard said. "That one's as good as you'd get in any hospital."

Kant's shoulders shifted in something that might have been a shrug, and Andrew, still resting against him, began to stir. "None of the local doctors will make house calls to Gallows Hill anymore. And we couldn't move you."

"Dr. Maynard's been helping the family for years," a soft voice said. Margot turned, squinting in the dull light, and saw they weren't alone. Nora and Ray sat against the back wall, pressed tightly together, holding hands. Nora's smile was tiny and broken. "She's very good."

"Dr. Maynard's misplaced sense of empathy works against her better interests," Dr. Maynard said. She took a quick, deep breath, her chest rising under layers of loose clothing. "I know some of what's going on here but probably not even half of it, and I'd like to keep it that way. Am I safe to go?"

"Sun's up," Kant said. "You're safe."

"Don't get the cast wet." She directed that to Margot. "It can come off in six weeks. I left pain tablets on the counter over there. You can take one in another two hours, and then every four to six hours after that, as needed."

She hitched her kit under her arm and strode to the door without looking back. A block of glaring sunlight came through, cutting around her silhouette and revealing dust and several tiny, fluttering insects, and then Dr. Maynard was gone, the door closed firmly behind her.

"We can open the windows now, right?" Andrew, bleary, rubbed sleep out of the corners of his eyes. Kant nodded without looking up from his hands.

Andrew rose with a sigh. He crossed to each window, and Margot realized the covers weren't blinds but metal shutters. They clattered as they retracted into coils.

Silence fell across the space as Andrew snuffed out the lantern. Margot felt lost. She couldn't stop running her fingers across the edge of the cast, where it looped around her thumb and finished just short of her knuckles. It was *real*. She knew that. But it didn't *seem* real.

Not much did.

Nora was the first to break the silence. She hung close to her husband, both of her hands wrapped up in both of his, her lips pulled down at their corners in a way that didn't look right on her. "I'm so sorry. We...we should have warned you."

"We wanted to, back when you visited the shop. But it's bad luck to talk about the curse," Ray said, his voice gentle and faintly raspy. "No, more than bad luck, really. It...attracts it. Makes it worse. We thought we could keep you safer by not saying anything."

"Can't have gotten much worse than this, can it?" Nora asked him.

"We both know it can."

Nora's face scrunched up, and for a second she looked like she was going to cry, and then Ray pulled her against his chest, his hand running over her hair.

They were talking about her parents. Their deaths. *That* was what happened when it got "worse than this."

Margot shuffled forward on the table so she could let her legs hang over the edge. Her feet were bare; her shoes had been left back at the house. The memories felt frantic, unreal, like she'd dreamed them. A miserable scowl pulled at her face, and she couldn't stop it.

I thought I could sleep through this. That I'd be safe if I pretended nothing was happening. If I just kept to myself and didn't go looking for answers.

"I expect you're angry," Kant said. He hesitated, then added, "You have good reason to be."

Margot didn't respond. What she felt wasn't anger. Not exactly. More like betrayal. He'd led her to her house. Shown her around it. Made her drinks in the kitchen. And he'd never once tried to warn her of what was going to come.

"My job is to help you," he continued. "I'll answer your questions as fully as I know how. You've heard plenty enough rumors about this land. Most of them are true." He closed his eyes briefly, but when he opened them again, his gaze was as steady as always. "Gallows Hill is cursed."

They're not denying it. They're not keeping it a secret any longer. It should have been a relief. A weight lifted. Instead, it felt like peeling a scab and revealing a black and bleeding wound beneath. There was no good here, only ugliness.

"The land isn't right," Kant said. "It won't follow natural orders. Sometimes, you'll see things that shouldn't be there. Like people. Sometimes, you'll hear things."

"Okay." Her throat hurt. Her voice was like a rasp. She couldn't stop touching the cast. "Why?"

"We don't know."

"All the wrong that's happened on the land, most likely," Nora said. The tip of her shoe scraped along dust lining the floor, drawing lines in it. "The executions. Then the original Hull family going missing. But that's just a guess. If anyone knew exactly what caused this, they were lost generations ago."

Kant lowered his head in a gentle nod. "In truth, we don't have all the answers. We have rules to keep us safe, but we don't know why. Witchety's ritual helps, but again, we don't know why."

A quiet, simmering panic was rising through Margot's stomach. The cool light felt too bright in the dim, dusty room. "Tell me what you *do* know. Last night there were…"

She didn't know what to call them. Names ran through her head, none seeming quite right: *Monsters. Corpses, having crawled from their graves. The damned.*

"I saw…*things* last night," she said. "People. Or…something like it."

"Those hung from the tree," Kant said. "And buried in the ground. Back from before the Hulls bought the land."

"Why are they like that? Why are they coming back?"

"We don't know. They just do. Only at night, though."

Margot's chest was too tight. It hurt to breathe. "Their lips were stitched shut."

"That's something they did back then." Ray rubbed his thumb into the corner of his eye, clearing moisture. "There was a myth that the dead would plead for mercy even after hanging, so they sewed their mouths shut to keep their damned words inside."

"And…"

"They'll hurt you if they can get to you." His eyes dropped to the floor, and Margot wondered what he'd seen. "So…we try to keep away from them."

"It's not always like this," Kant said. His gaze was steady, the gray, bloodshot eyes asking her to trust him. "Most of the time, the land is peaceful."

Nora nodded. "It comes and goes. I've never seen it quite as bad as it's gotten right now, mind. But…it should ebb soon. You just have to wait it out. And once it's passed, this place feels no different from any other hill."

"Okay. Sure." A strange, twitchy smile rose in time with a quiet hysteria. "I'm not doing that. I'm not staying here. Thank you…for helping me and for calling the vet. But I'm going to go now. The land is yours. Sell it or let it rot, whatever you want. I'm done here."

"Oh," Nora whispered, glancing at Ray.

Andrew cleared his throat, running his fingers through his dark hair.

"Margot…" Kant clasped and unclasped his hands, running the calloused thumbs across one another. "You can't leave. Not now that the hill has you." He paused, fingernail picking at a scab on his knuckle. "None of us can."

29.

Margot closed her eyes. The words didn't sound quite real. "What…"

"That's part of the Gallows Hill curse," Andrew said. "Stay too long on the property and you won't be able to leave it. Ever."

"No. What do you mean?" Her mind was still foggy, the words hitting her without fully sinking in. "Not able to leave? Are you saying I can't just drive out of here?"

"I'm sorry, Margot," Kant said. "The place chains us to it."

Nora tried for a small, sad smile. "Ray and I have been lucky. It's not as bad for us. We can still live in our house in town, provided we spend the daylight hours here. But the noose is slowly tightening on us too. We've been having to spend more and more time here to keep the symptoms at bay. We'll probably need to move into the employee accommodation by this time next year."

"Symptoms?" Margot managed.

In the window's gray light, Kant's face appeared washed out. As though she wasn't looking at him but at a memory. "It's different for everyone. Some people get nauseous. For others, it's exhaustion or shaking limbs. For others still—"

"Migraines," Margot guessed, and Kant dipped his head into a nod. She remembered the slow, pulsing ache that had started behind her eyes when she'd visited town and how it had swelled to a roar before finally abating as she returned to the land.

"We get little bits of tether," Kant said. "I can still visit my sister a few times a year. But I have to get the trip done in one day; I can't sleep away from the hill. It won't let me."

"The longer you're gone for, the worse the symptoms get, until you can't fight them any longer," Ray said. His wife still leaned against his shoulder, and he kissed the top of her head. "It's like it consumes you, piece by piece."

Margot let her cast-bound hand hang loosely in her lap, while her other arm wrapped around her torso, where bruises were beginning to form. "How many does it...have?"

"Us," Kant said. "The people in this room. Plus a half dozen of the other employees."

Ray nodded. "It takes a while for the curse to take effect. The seasonal workers will be fine; they just can't stay more than one year. We're careful to bring in a new lot each season. Most of them don't even know about the hill's lore."

She felt hollowed out. Like someone had taken a spoon to her insides and carved them out and was still scraping, searching for a scrap or two more. The conversation wasn't making as much sense as it should, and a low throb was starting in her arm as the painkillers began to wear off.

"Wait." She pressed her eyes closed, trying to hold on to her thoughts before they could evaporate entirely. "You said people needed to stay here a while before it affected them. I've only been here for three days. That means I can still leave."

"You're different, though, Margot." Sadness pulled at Nora's features. "You're the owner."

Kant said, "You have different rules from us. You're a Hull. The land is bound to your bloodline. It became yours the day your parents were placed into the ground, and it will remain yours until your death."

A slow, squirming, writhing dread was creeping into her like maggots into a corpse. She took a breath and it whistled on the way down. "I...I can't do this. I can't stay here. I *can't.*"

"Oh, sweetheart." Nora rose and moved to Margot's side. One hand went around her shoulders in a half hug. The other patted Margot's hand, limp in her lap. "You'll be all right. It's hard now, but it will get easier."

"We were hoping this bad patch would pass before you even arrived," Andrew said softly. "They normally don't last this long. We wanted you to move in during a peaceful stretch, give you time to adjust and prepare. But...this one has been bad. It was already going for a week before your parents... Well. And it's getting worse."

"I wouldn't have left if I'd known the bodies were likely to rise again," Kant murmured. "I can't tell you why they're so restless, even after Witchety's visit. They shouldn't be. But this can't last forever. It *will* pass."

There was something unspoken in that. *It will pass...presuming you can survive it.*

Her parents hadn't. And they'd lived there for decades. She didn't know the house or the land, or understand the curse even a fraction as much as they must have.

She already bore injuries from the previous night's encounter. Her left arm was near useless. She was tired, run-down to the verge of breaking. And they expected her to survive however long it took for *the badness* to abate.

Nora must have felt the shudder move through her, because she made soft shushing noises and began to rock Margot. It was intended to be a comfort, but Margot's skin crawled at the touch. She was too hot, too short of breath. She felt like she was suffocating.

"You're not alone," Kant said. "We're going to help as much as we can."

"We've already called Witchety for another cleansing," Ray said. "Things are usually…calmer once she's been through."

Margot blinked furiously and felt wetness bead around the edges of her eyes. "Does she know what's happening here?"

Kant dipped his head. "Part of it. Not much. A few from town—Witchety, Dr. Maynard—know a bit or have figured some out. Most others simply know Gallows Hill as a bad piece of land that they want to avoid."

"It will probably be bad tonight, even with another visit from Witchety," Andrew said. "Talking about it stirs it up. We couldn't avoid that any longer, though, for obvious reasons. So…be careful."

"We'll show you what we know," Ray said. "Help you make a plan for tonight. Help you prepare."

Kant's shaggy hair caught the window's light as he nodded. "Right now, you should rest. You're safe during daylight. Get some sleep while you can. If you don't want to go back to the house, you're welcome to stay here for a bit." He glanced at the others. "There'll be time to make plans later. Let's give her some space."

Ray and Andrew rose, gathering coats. Nora gently pressed Margot's arm one final time, a small gift of comfort even when her words failed. They were at the door when Ray hesitated.

"Ah…" He cleared his throat. "I know this is probably too much all at once, but the funeral home called. I was supposed to pass on a message."

"Later," Kant said.

Margot swallowed. After the previous days, secrets felt like poison. "No. You can tell me."

Ray glanced aside, then cleared his throat. "There was, uh…vandalism. Involving your parents' graves."

Someone from town, glad to see them gone? Her eyes burned. *Someone who wanted to leave me a message?*

"Tunnels were dug down to the caskets. The funeral director is having them removed for inspection now, but he's pretty certain the bodies are missing." Ray fidgeted, shifting his weight from one foot to the other. "He sounded deeply apologetic. Said he's never had anything like this happen before."

Margot's stomach was in knots. She dug her uninjured hand's fingernails into her upper arm, feeling the ache in the back of her consciousness. "That's connected to the curse, isn't it?"

"We're not sure." Kant spread his hands, then folded them again. "I've only been here during your parents' time, and they didn't tell me everything. There's still a lot we don't know. But yes, we suspect so."

"Okay." Margot clutched herself tighter. Nora, Ray, and Andrew filed out, leaving the door open.

Kant reached for something at his side. "You'll have more questions," he said. "I'll get you a drink, and you can ask what you like, but then, if possible, you need to sleep. There might not be much peace tonight."

He drew the object into the light. A prosthetic leg. Margot had felt overheated before, but now she just felt cold as she watched Kant roll up his jeans' leg and fasten the prosthetic into place, below the knee.

"The curse did that to you, didn't it," she guessed.

His glance was brief but not cold. "The hill takes something from most of us eventually."

Margot still felt dangerously empty, like a vital part of her had been stolen away the previous night. Her naivete, maybe. But there was no wisdom or better knowledge to replace it with—just emptiness.

And the others were all acting as though she would be fine. As though *they* were fine. Nora and Ray spoke regretfully of not being able to live outside the hill, but they were already resigned to the idea. And Kant had explained the mechanics of the curse as calmly and easily as if he were explaining a piece of machinery.

This is no longer shocking to him. He's had thirty years to get used to it.

And she, likewise, would have the rest of her life to confront this new existence.

If she was lucky.

Tears burned her eyes. The cast was too heavy. She tried to flex her hand and hated how rigidly immobile it was kept; only the fingers could move, and not far enough.

"You'll do better after a drink," Kant said. He let the jeans fall back into place. Margot never would have known he wore the prosthetic if she hadn't been shown it. "Coffee? Or something else?"

Her mouth opened, then uselessly closed again. The tears were close to spilling. She couldn't breathe. "I need a minute," she managed, and pushed off the table.

Kant stood back so that she could get through the door. Margot paused outside, the glaring sun momentarily blinding her.

She was in the employee building block, like she'd guessed. Either a maintenance shed or a storage room. It was near the outskirts of the cluster, and Margot moved away from the other buildings, toward the patchy trees and the drive leading down to the main road.

Her breathing was ragged. She didn't have any kind of plan, just an urgent, inescapable need to *get out.*

A handful of employees paused as she passed them. She was still wearing the clothes from the day before, she realized, rumpled and bloodstained and with one sleeve missing. Her bare feet dragged through the grass. The band holding her hair back had either been lost or broken, and now her curls ran like a mane behind her, tangled and wild and sticking to her skin.

The stares—pity or curiosity or shock, she didn't meet them long enough to tell—were overwhelming. She turned toward the nearest trees. They would hide her at least.

A bird exploded into angry chattering as she pushed through the branches. The trees were too thin, too sickly. None of the plants she'd seen on the hill had ever thrived. A dozen paces brought Margot out the cluster's other side, facing the long, slow slope of grassy field to the driveway's end.

She wasn't ready to stop moving yet. Her pace lengthened, letting the downward momentum carry her faster than might have been safe. Her sprained ankle ached with each step. Tiny rocks dug into her feet. She still didn't slow. There was an overwhelming, horrific sense that, if she stopped moving, the hill would open up its massive jaws and swallow her like a morsel.

A quiet crunch sounded on the dirt path behind her. Margot flinched, glancing back, but it was only Kant. He followed at a distance, his head raised to watch the sky instead of her.

Leave me alone. She didn't want them to talk to her any longer. She didn't want to hear explanations or commiserations, or promises that she could get through this if she just held on a little longer.

She wanted to be gone. Away from the hill. Forever.

Margot broke into a sprint as she passed behind the store. Long grass slashed across her shins like tiny whips. The building's windows were dark. Nora and Ray hadn't yet returned.

Her lungs burned. Every muscle in her body ached, a slow, grinding soreness that would take days to fade. But the closer she drew to the road, the lighter her chest felt. It was freedom. It was safety. It promised everything she wanted, everything she *needed*.

She burst out between the wooden posts marking the drive's entrance. The hard flecks of road gravel bit into her soles.

A horn blared. Impossibly loud, deafening, and Margot staggered as the car she hadn't seen passed just inches behind her.

She fell to her knees among the long grass and vines on the road's other side. The car, a black sedan, swerved back into its lane and continued on its route. Even with Margot looking how she did—barefoot, streaked in dried blood—the driver didn't stop.

No one questioned what happened on Gallows Hill.

She sagged onto her side, legs spread out awkwardly, the heavy cast resting in the dirt. Her face was wet, but she didn't remember crying. A slow, shaking smile formed as she stared at the fence line opposite.

I'm out. Past the boundary. And I'm not going back.

I don't care if there are symptoms. I'll take pain tablets. A headache can't last forever.

I am not going back.

She closed her eyes, head tilted back, to feel the sun on her face. It seemed different outside the hill. Cleaner. Warmer. She filled her aching lungs as fresh tears trailed down to her chin where they hung for a second before dripping off.

When she opened her eyes, she saw she had company. Kant had reached the fence. He leaned on the highest bar, broad arms folded over it, as he watched her. Unlike Margot, he stayed inside the boundary.

Margot glared at him, defying him to tell her she couldn't be outside the land. He didn't try to speak, though, but only watched her with none of his thoughts showing on his face.

"I'm not going back."

"I won't force you," he said.

Margot let her eyes close again. She had very few plans for what to do next. Her car was still parked outside the house; she would abandon it there. Along with her clothes, her cell phone, everything she had.

She'd hitch a ride away from the town. Or if no one would pick her up, she'd walk. Everything beyond that was hazy. But it didn't matter. All she really cared about at that moment was being away from the poisonous, hateful land and its twisted, broken house.

Being *safe*.

For that moment, it was enough to be outside the barrier. Her feet ached. The throbbing in her arm was starting to awaken. She wanted to rest and think and gather herself.

She opened one eye. Kant was still there, silent, patient. To fill the quiet, she said, "You remember what happened when I was a child, don't you? Why they sent me away?"

"Mm." He took a slow breath. "You were always curious. Asked me endless questions about my work. Always getting into the tunnels and the cellars. Curiosity is good for a child. But not in Gallows Hill."

She shifted forward, trying to ease some of the tension out of her aching muscles. "What happened?"

"When things began to get bad—when the curse woke—your parents would try to keep you safe. They locked your window. Warned you about the dangers of leaving your room at night. But you wanted to understand the strange things you could see from your window. You went exploring. Once, when things were very bad, you got out of the house."

He raised a hand and drew it across his chest, down to his stomach. "The dead ones got to you. Hugh, Maria, and I managed to get them off, but it was bad. You couldn't leave your bed for a week. Maria cried so much—"

His voice cracked. He paused, clearing his throat, then continued.

"The bad patch passed. You healed, though you would always carry the scars. Maria and Hugh thought you would be safe from then on. That you'd be cautious. But four months later, we hit another bad time, and once again you tried to go outside."

Margot's hand fluttered to near her collarbone, where the scars began. She could picture the lines in her mind. A jagged map marking where long fingernails had sliced through her skin.

Even that hadn't been enough to make her cautious. She didn't know whether to laugh or grimace. Her grandmother had always said she was a nightmare to control when she was little. Too much stubbornness condensed in a little body, she'd said.

Even Kant, drained and gravel voiced, smiled. "Even a near-death experience couldn't snuff out your curiosity, I suppose. Your parents talked for days, trying to come up with a way to keep you inside at night. They could lock you in your room, turn you into a prisoner in your own home, but they knew eventually they would slip up and you would find a way out. No matter how many locks and barriers they added to that house, nothing ever worked. It's like…a ship made of rotten wood. You seal one leak and another one springs open. The dead ones *will* find a way in eventually."

She believed him. *Through the dog flap. Through the attic. Through a dozen other holes and forgotten windows I don't even know about yet.*

"It took a while, but they finally agreed that the only way to keep you safe—keep you *alive*—was to send you away. Maria's family had always lived on the land, but Hugh's mother had a house in another state. They didn't tell her about the curse, but she still agreed to take you."

"How did they know it would work?" Margot asked. "I'd lived my whole life there. I should have been trapped already."

Kant sighed, the movement sagging his shoulders heavily. "I can't answer that. There was a lot your parents never told me. I gather that the curse doesn't impact children the way it does adults, though. Maria told me stories about going on holidays with friends when she was a child, so I suppose she had firsthand experience."

"I remember starting at a new school after I moved in with my nana," Margot said. "I remember meeting friends. Getting lost the first time I visited the shops. But I don't remember a single thing from when I lived at Gallows Hill. Is that a part of the curse?"

"Perhaps. I can't say for certain."

She raised her good hand to press at the stiff muscles at the back of her neck. A slow, throbbing headache was starting there, feeding across the top of her skull. It was still fresh. Minor. Barely noticeable, so she pretended she *didn't* notice it.

"They never spoke to me again," Margot said. "I guess visiting was impossible. But…no letters. No phone calls. Not even on birthdays."

"Every generation of Hull before them had grown up on the land and slowly been swallowed into the curse as they matured. Your parents had an idea. They thought that, if they could remove you from the house entirely while you were still a child, remove every single trace of you and never even speak your name, the house might forget about you. That you might be free from it. For a while."

She thought of the photos: she'd been torn out of each one. Her childhood bedroom, cleared empty. They'd tried to scrub out every memory of her so thoroughly it was as if they'd never had a daughter to begin with.

But it hadn't been enough. For all their efforts, they'd left traces. The child's drawing, lost in the back of the wardrobe. The wisps of frizzy hair dancing in from the photos' edges.

"The estate—and the curse—had always followed the bloodline, so they feared it would catch up to you eventually, no matter how well they tried to shield you. I guess they always imagined they had more time. To prepare. To figure things out. But then time ran out and no better plan had been made, and so you inherited the house."

Grass, fluid in the wind, grazed across her skin. She stared at it instead of Kant.

"When we heard you were arriving for the funeral, Nora, Ray, Andrew, and I talked it over. Nora thought we should try to prevent you from getting to the house at all. That maybe you'd spent long enough away to escape the curse, as long as you didn't get too close." Kant shifted his weight, resting more heavily on the wooden bar. "I didn't think that would work. The house remembers blood, Maria had said. Trying to keep you away from the building could only delay it, not prevent it. When you became unwell after visiting town, I knew the land had marked you as its owner."

The headache was still there, mild but slightly harder to ignore now. Margot flexed her neck, as though she could blame stiff muscles for its existence.

"I can survive a headache," she said. "I don't think I can survive Gallows Hill."

"Other people have said the same," Kant noted. "Two in the time I've worked here. If we think someone might have stayed on the land too long—a seasonal worker who didn't move on fast enough, say—we call them up after a couple of days, see how they're doing. If they're sick, we tell them to come back to the land. Sometimes they don't want to. They think they're only unwell with a cold that will pass. Or that we're joking."

Margot pulled her legs up, resting her knees under her chin. The cold, heavy dread was creeping back into her as Kant continued.

"We call back a week after. And then again a week after that. Usually, by the second call, we get a family member. The final call, that family member will tell us they're not long back from a funeral." He paused, letting the words hang, then added, "Two in my time. More in the generations before me. No one's been able to escape it."

Margot put her head down, burying her face into her knees and hiding beneath her hair. The headache was still only lapping at the edges of her mind, but it was growing worse with each minute.

She wondered how long she could hold out against it. Painkillers could only prevent so much. Would she wait until she wept from the pain? Until she couldn't stand, couldn't speak?

Would she, like the unnamed employees, hold out until it claimed everything there was to take from her?

It throbbed again, slightly harder. Not enough to really hurt, but a warning.

"I don't want to do this," she managed.

She wasn't sure if Kant could hear her words across the road, but he replied, regardless, "I'll help you."

She didn't answer but sat for a long while, letting the new knowledge move through her in increments. How the darker side of the estate had fascinated her as a child. Her parents putting together the puppet show video tape to teach her to stay off the land at night. How not even a chest covered in scars had been enough to deter her.

"For most of my life, I thought my parents sent me away because they didn't want me," she said at last.

"Your parents cared for you deeply." Kant's voice was so soft she could barely make out the words. "And they missed you more than I think even they imaged they could."

She pressed the back of her hand to her eyes, wiping tears away before they could fall. The pain her parents had gone through—all the grief and loneliness they'd endured—had been for nothing. She'd ended up back at Gallows Hill after all. And the hill had still marked her.

No. Maybe it wasn't for nothing.

She'd had a life. Friends. An apartment to call her own, a job. Freedom to visit museums and the beach and the theater.

Her parents had given her a gift and she hadn't even recognized it: the gift of a normal life. Of freedom. At least for a few years.

Maybe I'm the reason the curse has been more dangerous lately. Maybe it knew it was missing one of its family. Maybe my parents lost their lives because I wasn't here.

That was a bitter, uncomfortable thought. Margot lifted her head, breathing too fast.

Kant gave her all the time she needed: he, resting against the fence, calm and patient, Margot hunched over in the long grass by the side of the road, weighing up her options as the headache gradually spread across the top of her head and into her eyes.

"Okay," she said at last, and the word felt like it was killing something inside of her. "Let's go back."

The gravel was painful and hot under her feet as she limped across the road. Kant's eyebrows lowered as he watched her. "Wait for a moment. I'll fetch your shoes."

"No," she said, passing through the two posts that marked the entrance. "Don't bother."

Now that she had her momentum, she didn't want to sit, not even for another minute, because she was afraid she might never again get the courage to return to the house.

Kant matched her pace, walking at her side. The headache still throbbed, but it was beginning to slowly recede. She used her good arm to hold her cast against her chest so its weight wouldn't hurt her shoulder.

Kant opened his mouth, then closed it again. Margot looked up at him, expectant.

"The curse is a heavy cost to bear," he said. The words were faltering. "But life here is not empty of meaning. The business thrives. Townspeople are wary, but there are still friends among them. And as bad as the curse grows, there is plenty of joy to be found in the peaceful times."

She knew he had to be right. Eleven generations of Hulls couldn't have survived on the hill if life was entirely bleak. They had married. Had children. Raised up new generations to take on their mantle.

With a small twist of discomfort, Margot realized a lot of them likely saw the curse as a fair price to pay for the prosperity they enjoyed. The business *was* thriving. Their wine won awards, earned them respect, even fame. The house alone was more luxury than Margot had ever imagined owning.

Maybe she could learn to live here, like her parents had.

Margot blinked and saw the dead man entering her room. His lips stitched shut, unflinching as her axe buried itself in his arm.

No. No amount of goodness can make up for that.

They passed the public store. She caught a glimpse of Nora and Ray inside. Nora ran a dusting cloth along the photograph frames. Ray was unpacking freshly washed wineglasses from a tray. It was still too early in the morning for tourist visits, but they had to be on the land until dusk started to set in.

They're playing a pantomime, she realized. *Visitors come and Nora and Ray tell them the history of the land, as though those shocking details are all there is to it. As though the hill doesn't hold a darker secret, one that's silently consuming them.*

The townspeople knew. Or at least guessed some of it. Margot remembered the flash of fear in the mother's eyes as she dragged her son away in the grocery store.

The driveway was hard on Margot's feet. She stepped off it and exhaled as cool grass pressed against her soles. Kant stayed on the drive. The harder ground had to be easier on his own feet. He moved closer to the edge, though, so they wouldn't be so far apart.

"Ah—" Something rose up from Margot's memories. "I tried to call the police last night. I didn't have the address, but I told them I was at Gallows Hill. Will...will that cause problems?"

"No. If a call is made, it will be routed to the local police station, and they'll dismiss it without response. They only come if—" He caught himself, eyebrows lowering.

"Kant?"

"Well, if there's been a death. That's the only thing they'll come for these days."

"Right." Margot swallowed, trying to take that fact in stride.

They said the curse will get worse after we've talked about it. That tonight will be bad.

She realized she was facing the very real possibility that this might be her last day alive. That, by morning, the local funeral home might be receiving a call to pick up her body, just like they'd done with her parents.

"I...I need to understand this. You need to tell me everything you know. What makes it worse. What will keep us safe. Please, I—"

"Soon." He sighed, and the sigh was tinged with heavy sadness. "You only had a few hours of sleep last night. Rest first, then we'll help you form a plan to get through tonight."

She nodded mutely. They were approaching the employee buildings. Voices rose in the distance, calling instructions, then breaking into laughter.

For the staff, it was business as usual. Kant had said that the seasonal employees didn't know about the curse. That, to them, this was just another job, one that would eventually fall into the back of their memories once they moved on, all but forgotten.

"Will you sleep here or back at the house?" Kant asked.

Her feet were sore. Her arm ached. And Kant was right: the exhaustion weighed heavily on her, making it hard to even think. More than anything, she didn't want to be alone in the great home again, or back in the room where the dead man had broken through her door. "Here."

Kant led her toward the small storage room she'd woken in. He held the door open for her, and Margot stepped inside.

Even with the shutters open, it was a dim space. Margot felt a chill travel through her as she gazed across the cluttered shelves and dull, rusted sink.

Kant approached a mug that had been left next to the sink and glanced inside. "Andrew made you coffee."

She accepted the drink from him, and as though he could read her mind, Kant followed it with the bottle of pain tablets. She tipped one into her palm and drank it down while Kant wordlessly shook out the layers of blankets on the table against the back wall. The drink was lukewarm, but she was parched, and she swallowed it all in two deep draws.

Kant fished a pillow from one of the higher cupboards and left it on the end of the makeshift bed. He then moved to the windows and began rolling the shutters down.

"I guess those are more than a stylistic choice," Margot said.

"Mm. This is a place to stay if you find yourself outside during a bad night." He shrugged slightly. "Not completely safe. No area really is. But people like the shutters. Makes them feel protected."

"Hah." Margot filled the mug from the sink and drank that too. As she surfaced, she couldn't help a grimacing smile. "You've had a lot of practice at this."

"My fair share." He finished closing the second window.

The room wasn't perfectly dark—the lines of light under the shutters lent the space a muted glow—but Margot preferred it that way. She didn't want to have to spend any time in the dark at all if she could help it.

"Rest now," Kant said as he crossed to the door. "I'll be back in a few hours."

She waited until he was gone, then curled up in bed. It was hard to slow her mind. The headache was steadily fading, but enough of it remained to be distracting. Every few minutes, someone would pass by near enough to the building that the crunch of footsteps or the murmur of conversation would cause her eyes to snap open again.

But just like the night before, she could only fight her tiredness for so long. Around the time Margot was beginning to think that sleep wouldn't ever visit her, she slipped under.

When she woke, it felt as though no time had passed. She could have thought her eyes had only been closed for a moment except the light had shifted. Instead of running across the floor, the lines of illumination threaded up the wall.

Kant was back on the bench he'd occupied that morning, arms folded and head rested against the wall behind him. His eyes were closed.

Margot moved carefully, drawing herself up to sitting. A plate of food and a fresh drink had been left beside the table. She reached for them, trying to be quiet so she wouldn't wake Kant.

He still heard her. His eyes opened, then he shifted in his seat, sitting up properly with a soft groan. "Andrew made that for you."

She drew the food into her lap. Chicken breast and vegetables, smothered in gravy. She scooped some into her mouth. It was cold, but she was so ravenous that it still tasted like the most delicious thing she'd ever eaten.

"What time is it?" she asked between mouthfuls.

"Near four in the afternoon."

Her heart dropped. Margot lowered the fork, her palms turning clammy. "That's late."

Kant ran his fingers through his hair, pushing it out of his face. He seemed unfazed by the hour. "The more sleep you get, the better you'll do tonight." He paused, then added, "If we are lucky, the curse might have already waned."

That was a thin hope, and they both knew it. Margot understood, with complete certainty, that Gallows Hill wasn't done with her.

She looked down at the plate of food. Her stomach had revolted, turning into a nest of knots, but Margot still forced herself to eat what was there. She remembered how her energy had drained from her the night before, leaving her limbs weak and her mind scattered. Kant was right. She needed to shore up her strength while she had the chance.

"Fetched some things from the house for you," Kant said, drawing them out from beneath the bench. "Your room's light was out, so I changed that too."

He placed her shoes—the ones she'd last seen the previous night—on the floor beside her, and her phone and jacket on the end of the bench. Margot picked up her phone. The screen was shattered into a spiderweb of white lines. To her surprise, it still lit up at her touch.

"We'll get you another of those," Kant said. "Andrew will put it as a business expense."

She managed to smile. Even just a month ago, the cost of a broken phone would have felt like a hurdle to overcome. Now, it barely registered. *Death can put anything into perspective.*

She pulled the coat on to cover the blouse's torn sleeve and the smatters of dried blood. The coat's arm was wide, but the cast still barely fit.

Finally, Kant held up a large white square of fabric. It could have been a handkerchief, except it was wildly oversized. Margot frowned slightly. "What…"

"For the cast," he said, and she felt a rush of gratitude.

Margot stood while he helped her tie the sling around her shoulder. It immobilized her arm further, but at least it took the weight off. Kant stepped back, checking the knot wasn't biting into her, then nodded. "When you're ready," he said.

She glanced about the small room. There wasn't much for her there—but it had given her a chance to sleep without fear of being disturbed. That was a luxury on Gallows Hill. She took up the bottle of pain tablets and slipped it and her phone into her jacket pocket, then turned back to Kant. "Ready."

They left the shed. The work areas were quieter. Margot wondered if Kant had dismissed the staff early. They followed the path back to the main driveway and climbed until the distant house came into view.

A thousand questions sparked through her mind, coming fast and chaotic, but her tongue didn't want to move. Dread was rising in her, growing worse with every ticking second that brought them closer to night. The sun was low. Long shadows speared across the land. And the house, dark and foreboding, stood like an enormous monument ahead, silently waiting for her.

Three bodies sat on the porch outside the front. They rose as Margot neared them, and she recognized Andrew, Nora, and Ray. They smiled at her, but the expressions were tinged with mixes of sadness and concern.

"Witchety's performing a fresh blessing," Nora said, dipping her head to the right. Margot followed the indication and, in the far distance, saw a small body and a large dog moving along the boundary fence. "In case the last one didn't stick."

Margot couldn't take her eyes off the distant forms until they were swallowed behind a patch of trees. "You said the blessings make things better?"

"Oh, yes, usually," Ray said. "Fewer accidents since she started doing them. Fewer bad patches with the curse. We don't know why exactly it works, but it does. We have a regular schedule with her, but she makes special calls if we need them. Like now."

Margot tried to take that as a comfort. After what had happened the night before, though, she wasn't ready to put much faith in anything.

"We promised to help," Andrew said. "And we're going to do that. Our collective knowledge of the curse is far from complete, but we can tell you what we know. And try to help you prepare."

"Daylight's fading," Kant said, and indicated the house's door. "Let's begin."

They moved into the kitchen. Ray made to put the kettle on before catching himself and glancing back at Margot. She nodded to let him know it was okay. He set about preparing drinks while Kant eased himself into a seat at the table. Margot, after a beat of hesitation, sat as well.

"Some elements of the curse we've learned ourselves," Kant said, flexing his broad shoulders as Nora took the table's third seat. "Others are hearsay. I'll try to tell you which is which, because the hearsay isn't always reliable."

"Okay." Margot sat forward. She wanted to fold her hands, to fidget, to run her thumbs across one another, but one arm was strapped to her chest. She made do with picking at the table's white paint with her free hand.

"This part is hearsay, but it's been repeated for as long as I've been here," Kant continued. "The house's owners need to spend the night in the house. The staff need to spend the night in the staff accommodations."

The implications of that hit her like a punch to the stomach. Until then, she'd believed she wouldn't have to be alone after sundown. Either Kant would stay with her, or she could stay with him, and his presence would work like a ward against fear.

The hill wasn't content to let her have that, though. It was going to force her to spend the night alone, isolated. She lowered her head so they wouldn't see the fear burning in her eyes.

"Your parents told me that." Nora's voice was very small. "They didn't say why it was a rule, but I gathered it came from something that happened in a previous generation."

"Abigail, maybe," Ray said, "back in 1836. She fell in love with one of the workers. Slipped out of the house to spend the night with him. They found her the next morning, drowned in a shallow creek, clothes torn and scratch marks over her body."

Nora nodded, her thumb running over her chin. "Maybe. Townspeople assumed the lover was responsible. But the Hulls—Abigail's parents—put pressure on the police to drop the case against him. They knew more about what had happened than they shared with anyone, I'll warrant."

"That doesn't prove she died because she left the house, though." Margot's heart was beating too fast. "It could have been a coincidence. Maybe the rule isn't necessary."

"Abigail's death wasn't the only instance," Kant said softly. "That rule—stay where you belong—was learned at the cost of blood over many generations. Your parents never shared the details with us, but they would have known all the stories. Mostly from their own parents' teachings."

"That happened a lot, I gather," Nora said. "Each generation passed on their knowledge to the next. They probably intended to do the same for you, either in person or in a letter. They just…"

"Didn't expect their time to end so suddenly," Andrew said.

Silence fell over them for a beat. Ray poured water into mugs of instant coffee and passed them out before falling back to rest against the kitchen cupboards.

Kant took a deep breath. "That's part of what's so tricky about this.

Our knowledge is patchy at best. I would never call your parents secretive, except as far as the curse is concerned."

"Mm." Andrew took up his mug and stared into the steam. "I have a theory it's because the knowledge is dangerous. The more you know, the more the curse targets you, maybe."

"Except Ray and I know this place's history better than almost anyone, and we're still allowed to spend the nights off-land," Nora said. "You spent one long season working here and the curse locked onto you. It doesn't make sense sometimes."

Andrew shrugged, indicating he didn't have an answer either.

"I can't sleep away from the house." Margot ran her thumb across the mug's lip, feeling steam condense against her skin. "So…what should I do?"

"It might be easiest to go over everything in three parts," Kant said. "Before the bells. After the bells. And once they're in the house."

"The dead ones don't work on any kind of schedule," Andrew said. He'd been clean-shaven when Margot first met him, but now stubble darkened his tawny jaw. Hints of dark shadows lingered under his eyes. "They might come quickly. Or they might take a long time and not show themselves until it's close to dawn. Or they might not turn up at all. We're hoping for that last option."

"It can't stay this bad for long," Nora said. "It'll burn out. It has to."

Ray dipped his head in a nod. "That's what we're hoping at least. That last night was the end of it. But…it might not be. So it's best to prepare before the dark fully sets in."

"You'll feel like you should lock the doors," Kant said. "And you can do some of that. Whatever it takes to give your mind some peace. But you should know that locked doors won't stop them."

"And don't lock too many," Nora added, her hand darting out to touch Margot's gently. "They get angry when everything's locked up tight. It's better to leave some doors open, even if that goes against what feels like common sense."

"That's a rumor," Kant said, "but, yes, it seems to be the case. A few padlocks are fine. About what you'd expect in a normal house. Not too many more."

Her fingernails ached from how hard she was digging them into the wood. "The house already has a lot of locks. For the attic. And in my room."

"Yes," Kant said. "Human nature. Everyone tries the locks. The dead still get inside. But it's a hard instinct to repress."

"If you've opened any curtains, you should close them." Andrew, standing near the archway, held his mug in both hands. Traces of steam condensed on the edges of his glasses. "It's best if they can't see into the house. Or see you."

"The biggest thing you can do to prepare is going to sound silly." Nora's smile was hesitant. "It's to feel calm. And I know—how can anyone feel calm about this? But it's how you'll get through the night."

"It's why we were eager for you to get as much sleep as you could," Andrew said. "When people feel overwhelmed, they start to panic. And panicking leads to mistakes. And mistakes can cost you everything."

Nora said, "Whatever it takes, try to go into tonight feeling like you're in control. Take a long bath. Cook a good dinner. Nothing too heavy—but enough to sustain you. Read a book or watch some television."

"Are you a deep sleeper?" Ray asked.

Margot couldn't find her tongue to answer but shook her head slightly.

"That's fine, then," he said. "You can nap if you think you're able. The bells are loud. They're hard to sleep through."

"And that's stage two," Kant said. "When the bells ring."

Margot turned her head slightly. The old bronze bell that hung beside the archway seemed innocuous. When she'd first arrived, she'd imagined it hadn't rung for years. Even now, with the bloodred sunset running through the kitchen window and painting streaks of crimson across the metal, it looked like just another faded relic in the kitchen.

"They'll give you some warning," Kant continued. "You'll have at least three or four minutes."

Nora said, "You can keep the lights on until the bells, but once you hear them, you have to turn them out."

"And quickly," Ray added. "This is another part that goes against instinct. You'll feel like you want the lights on. But it just draws them in faster."

"Like moths to a flame." Andrew raised his mug to sip from it. His fingers, tightly clenched around the ceramic, seemed to tremble, but he covered the movement before Margot could be sure. "Except, in this case, the moths aren't the victims."

"Small lights are okay," Nora said. "You'll have to use something if you move through the house. Flashlights covered with fabric or a heavily shaded candle can work. But keep it small, and snuff it out as soon as you don't need it any longer."

Ray, still leaning against the counter, shifted his weight. "Try not to make noise. Or move too much. Once you hear the bells, you'll want to make the house seem completely dead, like no one's home."

"Does that work?" Margot asked.

"We think so." He shrugged. "You see, they don't come into the house normally. In most cases, they'll walk the hill, maybe enter the yard and stare up at the house. It's only when the curse gets very bad that they enter your home."

"It's why I thought it was safe to visit my sister." There was deep regret in Kant's voice. "I believed you'd stay indoors. And I believed that would be enough."

"It only happens very rarely, but once they decide they're coming in, there isn't much to stop them," Ray said. "But it depends on the night. Sometimes the dead ones will take their time coming to the house and then just walk around it, tapping on windows and rattling doors, until they leave again. If you're very quiet and very lucky, you might get through to dawn without actually laying eyes on one."

Her mouth was dry, and even drawing from the instant coffee didn't do much to wet it. "Let's say I'm not lucky. What then?"

"Stage three," Kant said, his voice heavy. "Once they're in the house."

The dread in the back of Margot's mind turned to full-blown static. She lifted her cup just to have something to do, but the bitter liquid caught in her throat. She lowered her head, breathing heavily. Nora fished a mini pack of tissues out of her bag and placed it beside Margot's hand. She didn't try to touch it.

"What do I need to do?" she asked.

"At first?" Andrew took a slow breath. He placed his own cup aside and folded his arms across his chest. "Stay quiet. And stay alert. Listen for them."

"They're not good at being quiet," Ray said. "As long as you keep your ears open, you can hear them coming. When that happens, you need to move. They'll be looking for you, and they're going to be good at finding you. You need to keep yourself a step ahead at all times."

"Don't try to hide," Kant said. "Wardrobes, cupboards, and bathrooms won't protect you. You'll be found eventually, and when you are, closed spaces give you no way out."

Nora cut in. "Use the hallways and rooms with multiple exits. Places where it's easy to get away. You can sometimes lose them for a while and get a chance to rest. Just don't let your guard down."

The information was flowing in too fast, and Margot felt overwhelmed trying to capture it all before it slipped away. "What about defending myself? Or is there anything that will frighten them away?"

"Nothing we've found so far," Kant said. "A bat will knock them back but won't stop them. Same with guns, knives. They'll catch on fire but that makes it worse."

"A flaming corpse will grapple you just as readily as a normal one," Andrew added, a half smile twisting his lips. "Except then you have the fire to deal with too."

Nora gave a short flick of her hand. "If they *do* get into the house, the best thing you can do is keep quiet, keep listening, and be ready to move somewhere else when they get close."

"They'll be gone come dawn," Kant said. "Keep your head. Most people who get hurt were panicking. Finally, remember, you can call us. If you're cornered, if you don't know how to get out, if you're hurt, we'll do whatever we can to help."

Margot grimaced. "The rule about staying in our areas, though…"

"We'll still come," Kant said, quiet and certain. "Just like last night. Call us, and we'll come."

That was the line that tipped her over. She buckled forward until her forehead rested on the table and let the tears flow, her face twisted into a silent grimace.

"You'll be okay," Nora murmured, one hand running over Margot's back like a mother comforting a frightened child. "Everything will be okay."

She couldn't promise that. No one could. The red sunset was turning sour, darkening into a scorched brown as light fell past the edge of the hill.

Ray, at the kitchen counters, cleared his throat. "This is a poor time to interrupt…"

"It's fine." The tears wouldn't stop. They flowed against her will, but Margot still pulled herself up, grinding her palms into her closed eyes as she furiously tried to rub them dry. "You need to leave, I guess."

"It's not that." Ray's words were drowned out by sharp knocks at the door. He pushed away from the counter, an apologetic smile on his gentle face. "Witchety's finished."

32.

The others stood back, clearing the way for Margot to approach the front door. The wood shuddered as she pulled it open, and the tail end of the sunset flooded through, painting them all in its burned shades.

Witchety stood outside, facing the hill. Her long, white hair had been braided, but strands had pulled free and floated like lines of spider's silk snatched up by the wind. Marsh, at her side, panted, his tongue drooped over his lower jaw.

"Well. I've finished." Witchety shuffled around to face Margot. Her skin looked strange in those hues. The dark reds should have imbued it with more color, but she seemed bleached out, desaturated. Her pale lips were drawn into a harsh line. Marsh's leash was woven around one of her forearms; the other arm was bound by the talisman's cord. The bird skull set up a muffled clattering noise as she moved.

"Thank you," Margot managed, and she meant it.

Witchety's gaze traveled from Margot's red eyes to the cast peeking out from her sleeve jacket. "It's bad, is it?"

Margot instinctively touched the cast, but that wasn't what Witchety was asking about. She was asking about the curse. The poison that seeped out of the land at night. Margot wordlessly nodded.

Witchety drew a slow breath. It rattled in her chest frighteningly, and Marsh, sensing her discomfort, leaned against her side.

"I brought extra holy water," she said, slipping the talisman into her pouch. When the hand came out again, it carried a small, unlabeled amber bottle. Margot took it and held it close to her chest. "You'll need it. The ground is bad. Worse than I've felt it before. I don't know what's happened; it's like a poison has gotten into it, and it's spreading. The blessing can only do so much to hold it back."

Margot couldn't find her voice, but she nodded. She understood what Witchety meant now. And she felt faintly ashamed for believing they were the ramblings of a charlatan on her first visit. She wouldn't make that mistake again.

Witchety's expression softened a fraction. "I have one more thing I can give you. It's the strongest talisman I have."

"Oh." Her heart ached. "I'm grateful for anything—"

"Only for tonight, mind." Witchety carefully unwound the leash from her forearm. She extended it to Margot. "I'll want him back by tomorrow."

The ache in her heart started to hurt. She held the bottle in both hands, refusing to touch the leash. "I...I can't take Marsh. I know how much he means to you. It's dangerous..."

A slow, small smile spread over Witchety's face. She tucked the leash into the crook of Margot's arm before she could object. "He's not just a token. The only way to defend against evil is with powerful good. And Marsh is the most good I know of. Keep him close tonight. I'll be back around to pick him up in the afternoon."

She turned and descended the porch stairs with slow, heavy steps. The leash was loose, barely tucked under Margot's arm, but Marsh made no effort to try to pull free. He took up position at Margot's side, apparently recognizing that he had a job. Warm brown eyes smiled up at her. The soft, downy tail thumped against the floorboards. In that moment, Margot understood what Witchety had meant about him being pure *good*.

"Thank you," she managed, taking up the leash. Witchety was already on the driveway leading down the hill and raised one arthritic hand in acknowledgment.

Behind her, Kant spoke, his voice subdued. "Nora, Ray, would you take Witchety back into town with you?"

"Of course," they said in synchrony, and Margot stepped aside as they passed through the door.

"Take care. Be safe," Ray said, a gentle smile his parting gift.

"We'll see you tomorrow," Nora added, and squeezed Margot's arm on the way past. It was a hopeful goodbye. One that promised there *would* be a tomorrow.

Margot watched the three of them until they began to fade into the hazy early twilight, then turned back to Kant and Andrew, her two remaining companions.

"You'll need to leave, won't you?" she asked.

"Sun's just about done." Kant rubbed a hand into his shoulder, grimacing as he stretched it. "That means we have to go, yeah. You remember what you need to do?"

Margot bit her lip. The instructions ran through her head in a stream that became increasingly tangled the more she tried to straighten it. *Stage one, after dark. Stage two, when the bells ring. Stage three, once they're in the house.*

Marsh continued to smile up at her, panting faintly, and Margot felt her heart turn cold.

They're going to get into the house. No amount of false hope or good talismans will change that. They'll get into the house, and there's nothing I can do to stop it.

"How safe is the employee accommodation?" she asked.

Andrew exchanged a glance with Kant. "For you? No safer than the house. Just…more places to become cornered. And the rule says you need to stay here."

"No, I understand that." She frowned, staring down at the smiling golden retriever at her side. "But for you. And the other staff. Are you in much danger there?"

"Less than you," Kant murmured. "The dead ones will come near our homes. But they don't seem as interested in us, unless we interrupt them."

"Good. Take Marsh back there with you."

She held out the leash, but Kant only looked at it.

"I'm not taking the dog."

Her voice caught, half choking her. "I can't let him stay here. It's going to be dangerous. He'll be hurt. I know he will. I can't—I can't do that to him—"

Kant took her outstretched hand, but instead of lifting the leash from it, he folded her fingers closed around it. "Keep him."

"But—"

"The dead ones don't go after animals, unless the animals get in their way." Kant released her hands, and she let them fall, still clutching the leash. "Witchety loves Marsh more than she loves anything, and she still gave him to you. I'm prepared to trust her."

She turned to Andrew, desperate.

"I'm more of a cat person myself," he said, chuckling, as he put his hands into his pockets.

"You can do this." Kant bent forward slightly so his heavy, gray eyes could meet hers. "Remember: when you hear the bells, put your lights out. Stay quiet. Stay alert. When you hear them coming, move. Don't panic."

"Don't panic," she echoed dully.

"That's the important part. Keep your head no matter what. The curse can make you see things. Hear things. Don't fixate on them. Just keep moving."

Margot thought of her reflection in the mirrors. The spiders in the attic. The way her shadow's neck had seemed to break.

The sun was bleeding out on the horizon, its last traces of light dying by the second. Kant gazed through the open door at the twilight landscape and exhaled deeply. His shoulders seemed to droop, as though some of the life had gone out of him. "We have to go. I'll keep my phone beside me. You do the same. Good luck, Margot."

"Thank you," she managed.

"Good luck," Andrew echoed, and he briefly shook her hand on the way past.

She stayed in the doorway for a long moment, watching the two silhouettes as they descended the drive, passing through the open gateway. Both heads turned to look back at her a final time before disappearing behind a crop of trees. Margot raised a hand. They raised theirs in return. And then they were gone.

The lump in her throat ached painfully as she closed the door. Marsh, excited at movement, stood, his tail swishing furiously. Margot crouched beside him and buried her hands and face in the thick, golden fur. His whole body shook as he stomped in place, licking any exposed part of her face, delighted with the attention.

She let the warmth of his body and the sticky, hot breath flow over her, calming her, distracting her. Then she rocked back onto her heels so she could look Marsh in the face. His black nose repeatedly bumped into her cheek and chin as he tried to move closer, and despite herself, despite *everything*, Margot laughed.

"Okay." She hugged Marsh once more, then stood on unsteady legs. "Okay. Stage one. Before the bells."

Nora had said she needed to do whatever it took to feel in control. To eat a good meal. To shower. To distract herself.

She didn't think a shower would do much to calm her. She wasn't certain she would hear the bells if she was under the water, and although Kant had said they would give her plenty of warning, she didn't like the idea of frantically trying to dry and dress herself while the dead were encroaching on her house.

But she could eat. That was easy enough.

Margot unclipped Marsh's leash. He hung close to her side as she moved into the kitchen and looked through the cupboards.

Her parents didn't seem to have any dog food. She was fairly sure they hadn't owned a pet within the last few years. She took her poor, cracked phone out of her pocket and opened the browser, searching up what was safe to feed dogs, then set to work creating a dinner for the both of them.

Marsh was served on human dishware for that evening: a soup bowl for water and a dinner plate filled with boiled eggs, a slice of bread, cashews, and carefully cut apple pieces. It wasn't something he could eat every night, but Margot figured, just for the one day, they could indulge.

She made herself a plate that looked very similar to Marsh's, except her bread was toasted and covered with butter and jam and was accompanied by a large mug of strong coffee. Cooking and eating was awkward with the cast's limited mobility, but much as she hated it, she was slowly growing better at it.

Margot worked through the coffee as she sat at the kitchen table with Marsh licking his plate at her side. Her eyes kept flicking to the bell above them.

They said it's unpredictable. Some nights they come fast. Some nights they take hours. Or they may not come at all.

A grimacing smile emerged as she stared into her mug. *Wouldn't that be ironic? To prepare, to wait, to drink enough coffee to keep me awake all night, and then for nothing to happen at all?*

She would give almost anything for that to be the case. But she also knew she was clinging to a dream. The ground was bad. Witchety had felt it, and when Margot focused, she could too. It was like it was writhing beneath the house's foundations, bubbling, squirming. The pressure building, preparing to erupt.

The thoughts were consuming her. She'd been warned about that too, that letting her fear build would only make it worse once she had to take action. She rose sharply enough that Marsh lifted his head.

"We're going to burn some time," she told him, dropping the empty plates into the sink and running hot water. "We don't know how long it'll take, so we'll keep busy for a few hours, okay? And…"

Her thoughts failed her as she turned and caught sight of the dog door. A relic from her parents' time, set into the kitchen's access to the porch, it was easily overlooked and easily forgotten about.

Except for that awful moment from the night before. The soft *flap-flap* as something entered through it.

Kant had said locks wouldn't keep them out. But she was still allowed to try.

Margot went through the lounge area to reach the halls where she'd found the spare antique furniture. As she'd hoped, most of it was made of heavy wood. She found a narrow chest of drawers that she was just about able to move and pulled it free.

The feet scraped painfully as she dragged it along the hall and finally into the kitchen. When she pressed it flush against the door, though, it fully covered the dog flap in a way that she thought wouldn't be easy to shift.

Marsh, who had happily followed her on her pilgrimage, wagged his tail. Margot grinned at him. "If you need the bathroom through the night, you'll just have to ask."

She leaned back against the drawers and sighed. The kitchen clock said it was approaching seven. There was still a lot of night left.

Margot returned to the hallways, this time following them to the second floor. Marsh padded in her wake, which she was grateful for. She paused outside her bedroom door. It had been left open a few inches, though the space beyond was pure black. She knew there wouldn't be anything inside...but it still took her a very long moment of gathering courage to reach her arm through the opening and turn on the light.

Kant had been in there earlier, to gather her jacket and phone, but he hadn't touched much else. The bedside table was jammed between the door and the wall, forcing Margot to turn her body sideways to slip through. The axe lay on the ground. A thin smear of dried liquid coated its tip. Margot stepped over it.

The only other trace of Kant's presence was the window; it was closed again. Margot circled her bed, which still held rumpled blankets from her disturbed sleep, and retrieved her phone charger from the wall.

She scanned the space to be sure there was nothing else she wanted there. Her books were strewn across the floor, but she didn't think she had the focus for reading that night. Spare clothes were in the wardrobe. The jeans she was wearing would still be fine, but she took a new top and a new bra and tucked them under her cast as she left the room.

Instead of returning straight to the ground floor, Margot circled through the upper level, trying to give herself some familiarity with the layout and which doors would lead to dead ends.

The house had almost been designed to give her escape routes, she realized. There were two staircases on different sides of the building. The hallways looped like a race track. Even many of the bedrooms she looked into shared en suite bathrooms with the room next to them, giving her a path to slip through should she need it.

She wondered how much of the design had been coincidental and how much had been intentional.

That's probably something my parents could have told me. She swallowed thickly and held a hand out to call Marsh closer to her. He'd begun wandering farther down the hall but happily returned at the gesture.

She kept moving, trying to form a mental map of the house. As she paced through rooms, her eye kept being drawn toward hiding places: closets, the narrow spaces under beds, behind shower curtains. She had to force her mind to disregard them.

The others had warned her about hiding places with no exits. She supposed it was still human nature to want to get somewhere small or somewhere with solid walls on three sides.

After circling the second floor twice, she returned to the lower level and did the same there. The layout was slightly more complicated. Doors that she thought would open into another room sometimes led her to the porch instead. She became lost before eventually finding her way back to the kitchen.

As she'd done on the upper level, she turned out all lights when she left an area. By the time the bells rang, she wanted to only have one or two nearby sources of light that could be put out within seconds.

Finally, she ended up back in the kitchen. She ran hot water into the sink and carefully pulled off her jacket and then the blouse.

She used a damp dish towel to wash the dried blood and sweat off. It felt good to be clean again, even if she couldn't get under the cast or the bandages on her shoulder. The cast made it nearly impossible to fasten the new bra, but she managed it eventually, then pulled the top over. It was a soft knit, designed to keep her warm through the night and be flexible if she needed to move. The night was turning cold, and she pulled the jacket back over top.

The old blouse went into the bin. She was normally pretty good about getting stains out, but there wasn't much to be done when it was missing a sleeve. She checked the clock. Only eight fifteen.

It felt later than that. She was already growing sleepy. She set about making another mug of coffee, strong, and carried it into the living room.

Marsh happily flopped onto the rug in front of the television. Margot found the power socket behind the box and plugged her mobile in there. The battery was still at 35 percent, which should have been plenty to get her through the night, but she wasn't taking chances.

A dark figure existed in the back of the room, reaching nearly to the ceiling. The Watcher, the massive talisman Witchety had built for the home, was still covered by its cloth. Her parents had respected Witchety's power enough to keep it. They had not been desperate enough to leave it in plain sight, though. Margot was.

She tugged the cloth off the Watcher. Bones and spoons and sharp metal rattled like chimes as they ran against one another. The massive deer skull atop it loomed far above Margot's head, staring down at her, watching with its black-pit eyes.

Margot threaded her arms in between the wires holding it together. She wasn't sure what she was holding, just that it was solid enough to let her move the effigy. It rattled with each inch, and Margot squeezed her eyes closed, afraid that the dozens of tiny objects scratching at her arms and cheek might extend their claws at any second and sink into her. But she didn't stop. Not until the Watcher was positioned in the hallway, facing the front door.

Breathing heavily, Margot backed away and slumped down beside Marsh in front of the television. The main hallway seemed like the right place for the talisman. A precious ward at the front of the house, refusing entry to anyone who might try to knock at the door.

She'd hated the Watcher before. Especially for the way it seemed to stare at her when she turned aside. Now, though, she was only grateful to have it. She felt less vulnerable with it there. Less alone.

"Want to watch something?" she asked the golden retriever. His head tilted slightly at her voice, though he seemed more than content to relax.

Margot sipped from her mug, then returned it to the floor while she selected a tape. She chose an old romance, one where the woman's hair was bobbed and the man wore expensive jackets. She pulled her knees up ahead of herself and let her eyes fix on the grainy, slightly off-color images. She couldn't follow the plot as well as she should have. There was something about a fake relationship and an inheritance. Her eyes kept moving toward the bell hidden in the room's back wall, behind the overstuffed couches, and it was hard to pull her focus back. She turned the film off after forty minutes.

Most of the tapes had handwritten labels, but one in particular stood out with its faded red words: *Margot's Tape.*

She slid it into the player and rewound it to the start. After a second, the curtains flickered onto the screen, and her mother's voice began narrating.

The other family. It's so obvious now that I know. The gray puppets are less an analogy and more just…a simplification. They play outside at night. They get irritated if they're interrupted. They even have Xs across their mouths to represent the stitches.

She watched the girl's puppet leave the house at night and sway toward the tall, gray figures. Her mother's voice dropped lower, growing darker, more menacing. "The other family was so angry that they attacked her. They scratched her and bit her and dragged her into the earth."

Margot knew the tape by heart, but she still flinched, squeezing her eyes until they were nearly closed, as the three puppets twitched down and disappeared off the screen.

At her side, Marsh exhaled heavily. She reached out and dug her fingers into his fur as the narration finished and the red curtains drew back across the screen. She took up the remote and rewound it again.

Margot hadn't meant to fall asleep, but Marsh was pleasantly warm at her side, and the coffee was doing little to stave off the tiredness, and sometime around the tape's fourth replay she slipped under, curled on her side on the rug, the golden retriever's flowing fur grazing across her face.

She didn't wake until the bells rang.

Margot gasped as she came to. A shudder ran through her, prickling her skin into gooseflesh and settling into her bones. She lay curled on her side. The television behind her played static, pouring a stream of gray, sickly light across the room.

As she stared into the dark, open doorway in the room's back, she felt sure there were lights there. Bright, shining, piercing eyes, fixated on her. Then she shifted, and the lights vanished, leaving the doorway empty once more.

The bells were ringing. That fact took a second to register, and then her heart thumped, heavy and loud, like a drum beating through her veins. The bell in the dim back of the room leapt like it was on fire. She scrambled to her feet. Her mind was fogged from sleep, leaving her scattered and slow to react. A hundred discordant thoughts flashed through her before catching on the one most important: *The lights. Turn out the lights!*

She mashed her thumb into the television's power button and watched the hissing static die. Then, across the hallway, into the kitchen. She had to skid to the side to avoid hitting the Watcher on her way through, then she smacked the light switch and paused for a second, her shoulder against the doorframe, as she soaked in the darkness.

The kitchen curtains were still open. The others had said to keep them closed, to make the house look as cold and empty as possible. They had also said not to let herself be seen. She crept toward the window, keeping her body low and to the side, where the moonlight couldn't graze over her. The kitchen bell screamed at her back, a rattling, shrieking chime, mirrored by dozens of others across the house. Then, abruptly, they all fell silent.

She strained forward, daring to look through the window. Moonlight touched the grass. Beyond that, the closest crops of trees. She thought she could see the fence in the far distance. Nothing moved within her line of vision. She reached out and dragged the curtains closed.

Now, the house truly was dark. Margot's wide eyes fought to see through the pitch-black. She reached out her good hand, fingers questing for the table, but couldn't find it until her hip grazed it on the way past.

She felt along the edges of the archway to orient herself, then crossed the hall, moving in an arc to avoid the Watcher. She missed her target by a few inches, her shoulder bumping uncomfortably into a wall before she found the archway to the living room.

They said I would have a few minutes until the dead reached the house. She lowered herself to her hands and knees as she crawled along the living room. She found the rug first. Then, moving her hands in wide arcs, touched cool metal and cracked glass. Her phone's screen came to life at her touch. Full battery. *How much of that time have I already used?*

Margot unplugged the phone. With just the screen's light, almost nothing was visible, not even her own arm. She raised the phone, using it to see her way as she crawled toward the windows, then froze, a gasp running through her.

Two enormous, glinting eyes filled her view. They weren't quite human.

The shape was wrong; the colors were wrong; the way the light glistened off them was wrong. They blinked, and a quiet huff accompanied the movement, and Margot collapsed forward, burying her face into Marsh's fur as she struggled to catch her composure.

The bells had made her panic so badly she'd forgotten about Witchety's final gift.

"Good boy," she whispered, patting the side of his head. Then she let him go and crept up beside the television, to where heavy curtains blocked the windows. Moving with incredible slowness, she inched one corner of the curtains back, exposing a sliver of glass, and pressed close.

The corner of the window gave her a very narrow view of the outside world. In the distance, a bird screamed, then fell silent again. She strained, trying to trace distinct objects in the disorienting moonlight.

Something horribly tall stalked across the grass toward her house. The light was to its back, leaving it silhouetted.

Behind it, another two followed. Then more behind that.

She slowly, carefully lowered the curtain back into place. She undid the sling around her injured arm, letting it fall free. Then, with her thumb pressed over the light to blunt it, she activated her phone's flashlight.

Margot slipped it inside her left jacket sleeve, between the fabric and the cast. Dulled by the cloth, it was barely stronger than a struggling candle. That would be enough. She tested the setup, jostling her arm to make sure the phone wouldn't fall free, then pressing it against her side to ensure she could smother the light entirely in an instant if she needed to. It worked. And it kept her one good hand free.

Margot turned back to Marsh. He sat patiently, smiling, quietly curious about why they were moving about in the late night. She found his collar and nudged him to stand.

"Come on." Her voice was a raspy whisper, too quiet for even her own ears to make out the words. "We've got to hide you somewhere."

Kant had wanted her to keep Marsh through the night. She just couldn't. Even if it meant the difference between life and death for her, she couldn't put the beautiful animal ahead of her in the firing line.

Kant had said the dead things wouldn't bother with animals as long as they weren't in the way. That meant she just needed to find a secure, tucked-away room for Marsh. Somewhere he'd be safe. Somewhere he'd be found the following morning if Margot didn't get through to dawn.

She chose the sewing room. Swiping piles of fabric off a shelf, she nudged them into the vague form of a bed and encouraged Marsh to lay down. Then she kissed the top of his head, whispering "Be safe" as she did and slipped out of the room, closing the door behind her.

Her heart ran at a thousand miles a minute. Even when she rolled her feet, each time her sneakers touched down, she heard it echo in the back of her head. She bent, fumbling with one hand to undo the laces, then slipped them off and carried them in her good hand.

With socks muffling her steps, she crept back toward the living room. It seemed like the best place to wait. There were multiple exits, windows to watch the outside, and she would be near the door as a last resort. Kant and the others hadn't mentioned leaving the house. Their advice had only circled around how to stay safe *inside*. That likely meant the outdoors was an even riskier prospect.

Every few steps, Margot paused, breath held as she strained to hear any trace of the encroaching figures. The world seemed quiet. She moved with agonizing care into the living room and placed her shoes on the floor near the television.

Then, back to her hands and knees, left arm pressed to her chest to douse the light, she crept back to the window.

The curtain was heavy under her shaking fingers. She lifted its corner in slow increments, her heart beating too fast, too loud. A sliver of the outside world came into view. A slice running across the porch and over the long grass leading down to the driveway. The figures she'd seen farther down the hill were gone now. Her eyes darted toward every small trace of motion, but they were only being drawn by a swaying patch of grass or a distant tree.

Her breath misted across the glass, blinding her for a second before the mist faded. Her ears strained, but the outside world felt perfectly silent. She couldn't hear the wind. Or insects.

A body moved in front of the window. The foot landed with a slam so heavy that she felt the reverberations along her spine.

Terror flooded her veins. She'd flinched at the motion but managed to keep her hold on the curtain. At that height, Margot could only see its thigh. Gray skin, puckered and mottled, tiny holes bored into it by countless insects. Muscles twitched underneath.

She held her breath as she lowered the curtain back into place, desperately afraid that the movement might draw the dead figure's attention. She wanted to crawl back, to put some space between herself and the horrible, gray form. If the wall hadn't stood between them, she could have reached out and touched the clammy skin.

Instead, she held herself still, muscles cramping from the position, her pulse like a torrent through her veins.

The world was silent for a moment. And then, above her head, a muffled *tap* against the glass. There was a second of silence, then the sound repeated, louder.

She could picture it. Spongy fingers missing their nails, stabbing into the window, looking for a way through.

The urge to run was overwhelming. She held where she was. *Don't panic*, Kant had repeated to her. Panicked people act rashly. Panicked people make mistakes.

One of the porch's wooden boards groaned. Then, a heavy thud sounded out as the body moved forward. Margot, her light still pressed against her chest, let her head droop and her eyes close as she listened to the body circle the porch in painstaking, measured paces.

More sounds began to register at the edges of her hearing. The creak of someone climbing the porch's stairs. A low, slow clicking noise coming from somewhere to her right.

Then the groan of heavy rope not far outside her window.

The footsteps stopped outside the front door, and the sounds repeated. Dulled fingers stabbing into the wood. Knocking. Seeking a way in. After a moment, the figure turned, and its slow march across the porch continued.

Margot waited until the footsteps were at the kitchen window before lowering herself to sit. Her muscles ached from holding one position for so long. She put her back against the wall and slowly stretched her legs out to give them some relief.

They said that the dead might spend the night just walking around the house, knocking. That they might not come in at all.

If she stayed very quiet and very still, she might be lucky. Margot kept her arm pressed tight against her chest, where not even a whisper of light could escape. And she kept her ears open, tracking the corpses' movements. There were at least three. The largest one—the one that had been outside the window—paced back and forth at the house's front. Sometimes it stopped and stood still for minutes at a time. Sometimes it turned around the side of the house, only to return again.

The other two moved more freely, running along the house's side, questing fingers probing at every door and every window.

Maybe they won't be able to get in after all. I sealed the dog door. All the other main entrances and windows are locked. What if that's enough?

The slow, pacing footsteps kept coming in waves. Moving closer. Stopping. Moving past her. She didn't dare lower her guard. With the phone's light covered, she was as good as blind, except for a whisper-thin line of light that came in beneath the curtains at her back. Her eyes began to grow unsteady as they stared into the chasm of gloom surrounding her. Robbed of stimulus, her brain began to create its own phantoms: ethereal shapes that danced through the dark, teasing her vision, promising movement where there was none.

She couldn't close her eyes, though. The hour was late. She'd been sitting still for so long that her limbs began to feel heavy. Tired. If she let her eyes close, even for a minute, she was afraid they might not open again on her command.

The footsteps wouldn't stop. They weren't fast, but they were dogged. Floorboards creaked under them. Each pace was measured so that Margot could count three heartbeats between footfalls.

When the dead ones grew close, Margot's skin would prickle and her muscles would tense in preparation. But the figures always kept moving, never lingering outside her window for more than a second, and she would relax again, the tension draining from her limbs.

The more often they passed her by, the less pronounced her reactions became. Her mind was growing tired. Not just from the desire to sleep, but from the exhaustion of tracing each of the bodies as they looped the outside of her house. She didn't know how long she'd sat there already. Her feet were numb. Even with the jacket, the cold was starting to set in, seeping into her back where it was pressed against the wall. Each time she blinked, her eyelids felt heavier. Her mind started to drift.

And then, it happened. Footsteps began trailing toward her once more, and she was halfway to dismissing the sound before it registered.

The footsteps were coming from the wrong direction. No longer circling the house or at her back, these sounds moved toward her from the kitchen.

One of them was inside the house.

34.

Margot's mouth turned dry. The heavy tiredness evaporated. Adrenaline ran through to replace it, pulsing fast, setting her body on fire.

Keep still! Don't panic. Don't run.

Bare feet slapped against the wooden floor. Margot stared toward the sound. In her mind's eye she could picture the open archway no more than eight feet away. She visualized the body approaching it, arms limp, feet dragging with every step.

Can they see me? I can't see them. If I keep very quiet and very still, will they pass me by?

She held her breath suspended. Her muscles had locked up, rigid with the vicious desire to lurch away, to run, but she forced them to be still.

The footsteps paused in the room's entrance. For a heartbeat Margot thought that might be it, that the dead one might look into the dark and then turn away, that she would be safe. But then the figure moved again, and it moved directly toward her.

The dark might disguise her. But it would not save her.

Margot scrambled to gain her feet. Her legs were chilled and full of pins and needles. She grit her teeth, trying to keep quiet as she moved blindly.

The entrance to the hallway had to be ahead, but she couldn't see where. The dead thing was already drawing nearer, its heavy, unsteady footfalls becoming faster as it sensed Margot was close.

She couldn't afford to scramble through the dark. Margot's arm shook as she lifted it from her chest, and the phone's flashlight sent a pale shimmer of illumination through the sleeve. It grazed over the open doorway, and Margot skirted around the furniture as she raced toward it.

Just as she reached the exit, she threw a glance behind herself. The dead one stood in the place where Margot had been sitting. Her view of it was only a microsecond long, damped by heavy darkness and disorienting stress. It was like a snapshot of the scene, blurred and barely discernible, but the image stuck behind her eyes as she slipped through the open door and, breathless and silent, raced along the hall.

It had been a woman. Tall. Age was hard to tell when the body was that distorted, but Margot thought she must be past fifty. Long hair hung about her breasts. Scraps of her old clothes draped from emaciated shoulders. Her arms were stick thin, the bones prominent lines beneath the skin, bulging out at her elbow and wrist joints.

Old, dry dirt smeared her body, clinging to her clumping, stringy hair. Her eyes were glazed white.

In the brief glimpse Margot had gained, she'd seen the hands twitch. Bulging, knotted knuckles spasmed as the too-long fingers flexed out at her side. Her mouth was pressed in a thin line, no lips visible. Black thread wove through the skin, loops of it sealing her mouth shut.

Margot kept her own mouth open, drawing air into starving lungs as silently as she could. She wanted to break into an outright sprint but forced herself to keep her pace slower. Slow enough that her thumping footsteps wouldn't give away her location too easily.

She passed the door to the sewing room and heard Marsh drag his claws against the door, snuffling as he asked to be let out.

Stay quiet, she mouthed, not even daring to speak out loud, then she was past the door and flying into the back quarters of her home.

This was the section she'd become lost in when learning her routes earlier that night. Remembering her path was harder in the dark. The light under her sleeve only revealed glimpses of the house. A flash of the stairwell banister as she passed it. The outline of paneled walls. An open doorway here, and she couldn't for the life of her remember where it led, but when she moved through it, she entered a new hallway with more open doors.

She turned right and found herself in the laundry. The room only had one other exit. A curtain hung over the door's small window, telling her it opened onto the porch.

A narrow closet stood at the room's back, and Margot's instincts told her to crawl up inside of it, to pull the doors closed behind herself, to hide. She repressed the thought with a shudder and instead came to a halt in the room's center.

She felt vulnerable to a dangerous degree. Especially when she pushed her left arm into her chest, blotting out the light. She was exposed on all sides. Unable to see anything that might be approaching. Unable to even see the open doorway she'd come through.

Use your ears. They're not quiet.

Margot forced her breathing to be low and slow. One arm clutched to her chest, the other stretched into the crushing darkness, she listened.

Echoes reverberated through the house. Footsteps, slow, moving toward her but not following the route she'd taken. They were at her back. Margot turned her head slowly, giving her ears a better angle. One of the bodies from the porch was coming around the side, approaching the laundry's door.

Farther away, another set of feet dragged. She couldn't identify whether it was the corpse inside the house or the third one on the outside.

They weren't the only things she could hear, though. In the stillness of the laundry, there was a strangely rhythmic, rasping noise.

It was so quiet she could barely make it out, but it was unmistakable. The sound of muffled breathing.

Margot clenched her teeth. The noise wasn't coming from her. She tilted her head a fraction and was able to pinpoint its source. It echoed from the space just a few steps behind her right shoulder.

Rough breathing. Gasping. Stifled, as though the owner had covered their mouth with their hands.

Margot didn't dare let herself breathe. Slowly, she brought her arm away from her chest, letting the dull light radiate around her. Dust motes danced in it. There was a glint of metal: a sink. The cold white of a washing machine. A shelf.

She rotated silently, turning her arm across the room. There was no one else there.

But she could still hear the breathing. It stuttered. A hiss of air through teeth. Distressed. Trying to be quiet but not quite able to smother the sounds entirely.

What is this? It's not the dead ones. What am I hearing?

Kant's words flashed through her mind. "The curse can make you see things. Hear things. Don't fixate on them. Just keep moving."

A deep wash of dread moved through her. Margot pressed her light back to her chest. She desperately wanted to leave the room. She couldn't afford to. Not when the dead one outside the laundry door was growing closer.

The curse can make you see things. Hear things. He hadn't said it could hurt her, though. Not like the dead creatures that were creeping around her home. She had to keep still. Keep quiet. Or she risked drawing more of them inside.

The breathing was growing closer, though. Margot kept her eyes closed as she pressed her own hand across her mouth. Each shuddering breath left hot condensation across her fingers. *Don't panic. Don't panic. You'll make mistakes if you panic.* But the sound was nearer again, as though someone stood just behind her shoulder, close enough to wrap their arms around her, close enough that she should have felt the breath on the nape of her neck.

A voice whispered into her ear: "I don't want to die."

Her legs nearly buckled. Margot bit her tongue hard enough to taste blood as she staggered away from the words. Her shoulder bumped into a shelf. It rattled. The footsteps out on the porch fell still.

There's no one here. No one.

She didn't dare lift her arm, though. Didn't want to see what the insipid light might reveal.

Her shoulder pressed into the shelf, its sharp corners bruising her skin as she forced herself to stay still and silent. The figure outside the door had heard her. She just prayed none of the others had.

Scraping footsteps moved through the house. Faster than they'd been before. Drawing nearer to her hiding place.

Margot's heart plunged.

Move. Move quickly!

She ran for the door leading back to the hallway, desperately trying to keep quiet as she raced for a fresh place to hide. She couldn't remember which of the doors were a dead end and which led to a new path. She tried the first door to her right. Her light flashed over the cold tiles of a cramped bathroom.

The footsteps were growing closer, heavier. She backed out, reaching for the door on the hall's opposite side instead. It opened to a formal dining room. She couldn't remember it if had another exit.

Margot glanced back into the hallway. Even with her eyes adjusted to the gloom, she was barely able to see more than a few inches past her arm. There was something there, though. Deep along the hallway, far past where she should have been able to see. A looming silhouette. Dark, muddy hair hanging across a naked torso. Bare feet with overlong nails dragging over the floorboards.

She backed into the dining room and shut the door in her wake. Her heart was running at a furious, unstoppable tempo. Kant's warnings ran on a loop through her mind, the words becoming strung out and distorted, like her mother's voice on the video tape's damaged audio: *"Don't panic. Don't panic. Don't panic."*

She was very close to it. A screaming terror was boiling up inside of her, threatening to spill out, and for every time she repeated *don't panic* inside her head, the urge became worse.

A door to her right slammed open. The laundry. The creature that had been outside had found its way in.

35.

She backed up and raised her phone, praying the light wouldn't shine through the gap under the door, praying the dead woman hadn't seen her enter the room. The formal dining space was long. A large table—not ornate but solid and heavy—took up the room's center, with fourteen chairs tucked in. There was no tablecloth, and the wood had gathered dust. This was a space for a much, much larger family. It likely hadn't been used in decades.

Footsteps converged on her location, merging from two directions. Margot skirted the table. Large windows ran behind it. She dragged back the curtains from the nearest set and nearly choked.

Thick bars ran up the window, barely wide enough for Margot to fit her arm through.

Everyone tries the locks. The dead still get inside. But it's a hard instinct to repress.

She clenched her teeth as she dropped the curtains back into place. One of the dead was at the door. The handle rattled. Margot backed away, her breath held, her arm raised high as she tried to see her environment.

There—!

The dining room had a second door. Tucked away in the back, behind a cutlery cabinet, it blended into the wall nearly perfectly except for its bronze handle. Margot wrenched it open.

A narrow passage stretched forward. Margot hadn't seen it before, but there was no chance to examine it or to wonder where it led. The dining room's main door groaned as it opened. A dry, rattling breath creaked out of the dead woman's lungs.

Margot pulled the door closed behind her, wincing as she heard the latch click home. She crept backward on padded feet.

Something thin and scratchy grazed her throat. She flinched, biting down on a gasp, as her good hand flew to her neck. Cobwebs tangled in her fingers. Her breathing was low and ragged as she swiped them away.

She wanted to hide in the passageway. To crouch down on the floor, arms wrapped around herself to protect from the cold air, as the dust trickled around her.

But she couldn't. The dead ones would find her eventually. The others had been clear about that: hiding wouldn't save her. Having an exit to slip through would. And she didn't know where this passage led or if its other door was even unlocked.

Her right hand traced along the wall to hold her balance as she lifted her left arm to light the path. The cast was heavy. Her ankle and arm throbbed, but she'd left the pain tablets in the kitchen. The stress was starting to burn inside her head, aching behind her eyes.

She could still hear the footsteps, only now they echoed. Above her. Behind her. To all sides. The tunnel distorted any noise, and she couldn't tell where the dead ones were any longer.

Up ahead, an open door caught at the edges of her light. Margot moved her hand across the phone, not entirely blotting it but muting it further. Her toes were numb, but she still kept her steps light as she edged nearer to the entrance. Another hallway, this one running perpendicular to her current one. Margot stepped out, squinting as she tried to orient herself, and turned right.

An immense figure loomed through the dark. Margot's heart froze, the bubbling sense of panic rising and filling her throat with bile. Begging her to run. To no longer heed the directive to stay silent but to race, wild, into the night.

She might have if she'd had any strength left in her legs. Her shoulder hit the wall as her legs turned to water.

No. No. It can't be one of the dead. They're not quiet. I would have heard them. I would have...

The body faced away from her, but its edges were ragged, as though it had been torn into shreds. Something glinted across its form. *Blood? Exposed bone? No—*

Metal.

A faint gasping noise escaped her throat against her will. She was looking at the Watcher. The monstrous effigy still faced the front door. She'd found a back passageway that led her to the area beside the kitchen.

A dry, rasping inhale came from somewhere across the hall. The thump of a dirt-crusted foot. The scrape of fingernails against a closed door.

She clamped her hand over the light, blotting it out, and turned.

Don't panic. Don't panic. Don't.

Her feet were moving faster, though, the soft taps of each footfall growing louder as her steps turned uncoordinated. She bit down on her lip, using the spike of pain to pull some focus back, but her mind was still running out of control, and her muscles still twitched in response to every jittering shadow and creaking floorboard as she flew through the house.

The stairwell appeared ahead. Margot was on it before she could even question if this was a good idea. It put her farther from the front door. Farther from escape. From help. Placed her behind two staircase bottle-necks. But in that second, all her mind knew was that the corpses were all on the ground floor, and the stairs would put some distance between her and them.

She didn't stop moving when she reached the landing. Cold air burned her lungs with each low, gasping breath. The old floorboards groaned beneath her feet, and Margot flinched, knowing it would be drawing attention to her, but unable to make it stop.

She rounded a corner and then another, no longer conscious of where she was or with any plan about where to go. It was only when she turned one more corner and saw a familiar door at the top of the second stairwell that she let her frantic dash slow.

The master bedroom door was still closed. It was only when that thought registered that she realized so many of the downstairs doors had been open, when they shouldn't have been. The dining room door. The entrance to the hallway. When she'd explored the house earlier that night, she'd been excruciatingly careful to shut the doors behind her.

Locks don't hold them back. Closed doors wouldn't either.

A sharp, achingly harsh chime broke through the cold night air. Margot flinched. An unseen bell farther down the hall began to dance, and it was quickly followed by the one in Margot's own bedroom, and then another somewhere on the floor below, and within seconds the house was alive with the ringing, sharply discordant alarms.

Margot darted forward, her movements disguised under the furious assault of noise, and shoved through the door to her parents' room. She shut it harshly behind herself and pressed her back to the wood, her jaws clenched until the teeth ached.

The master bedroom had its own bell. It danced on its hook, adding its voice to the cacophony. Margot stared at it, willing it to be silent, but it only moved faster.

Cool moonlight came through the open window. It streamed over her parents' bed. She crossed to it, crawling onto the mattress, and pulled her knees up to cover her face as she folded her arms over her head to muffle the noise. The cast was heavy and uncomfortably hard.

She couldn't think through the sound. She tried to count her breaths, to ground herself, but she couldn't focus on even that. She wanted to scream.

And then, all at once, the bells cut out. Echoes hung in the air for a second, and then intense silence took their place.

Margot lowered her hands. The moonlight washed over her, and she realized this was the first time she'd been able to see an entire room at once since turning out the lights.

The bells meant more of the dead were coming over the fence. She didn't want to think about how many there might be or what it meant for her.

Her arm ached. Her ankle felt swollen. Each breath made her lungs hurt, as though she'd been running for hours. She blinked at the room, disoriented. The mirror across from the master bed showed her reflection. She sat huddled in the center of the bed, her socks putting dirt on the mattress. Her hair was wild, pulling free from the clip she'd used for it, drifting in strands about the edges of her face.

The reflection showed her in death, her face shriveled and withered and somehow swollen. The outline of her skull was visible beneath her jaw and cheeks. Her skin was deathly gray.

Margot's mouth twitched into a grim smile, and the corpse smiled back. *The house will show you things, make you hear things, but they can't hurt you.*

Faintly, she could sense the dead ones moving below her. It was hard to pinpoint where in the house they were. Or how close to the stairs they might be. Or whether the third one had gotten into the building.

She ran her hand across her face and felt a sheen of cooling sweat. Her pulse still leapt, but her mind was starting to clear.

I panicked.

She'd done what she wasn't supposed to. She'd gotten desperate. Bolted. Reacted on instinct. She blinked at the room. It was the place she most closely associated with her parents, and it had drawn her in: a promise of comfort, of protection, even if the promise was hollow.

The room only had one exit. That was a second rule broken.

A dead end. If they catch up to me here, I have nowhere to go except through the window, and I only survived that *last time because Kant came for me.*

It wasn't too late. She'd made mistakes, but they hadn't cost her yet. She could get back into the hallways. Return to the plan.

Is this how my parents spent their final nights alive? Moving through the dark in their massive house, unable to stop, as the dead hunted them down?

Her eyes trailed down toward the double bed. *No*, she realized. They'd been in their room, lying under their covers when they died.

That meant the bells hadn't rung that night.

Then what…?

A flicker of motion drew her eye to the window. Something moved in the distance. Margot crawled to the edge of the bed, then hesitated.

I need to go back. Get into the hallways. Do it before they start climbing the stairs.

The shape had looked strange, though. Too close to the ground to be human. Margot crossed to the window. She didn't dare stand in the opening, in full sight of the world outside, but clung to the curtains, using them as a shield as she glanced around the edges.

A shape was moving across the blue-washed field surrounding the house. Margot inched back, knowing she should leave the curtains, shield herself better, avoid being seen. But it was impossible to look away. The long shadows and polarizing light were disorienting, but the silhouette didn't move like the others had.

No. That's not a human.

A golden retriever's tail swished once, twice, through the night air, as it trailed toward the trees.

36.

No. No. Marsh, no!

The fear was immediate and ferocious. Margot felt like she was choking on it as she abandoned cover and pressed herself against the window.

The golden retriever raised his head to smell the wind, then turned into one of the copses of trees at the fence line. He'd disappeared within a second.

He was supposed to be safe. I locked him in the sewing room. I blocked the dog door. How did he get out? He should have been safe—

She remembered what Kant had told her: she was allowed to use locks if they made her feel safer, but she couldn't rely on them.

That was because things turned wrong when the dead ones emerged. Lights broke. Locks failed. Latches opened.

They corrupted the house's defenses, slowly breaking them down until they were useless. It was how the dead had gotten into the house. It was how Marsh had gotten out.

She bit her thumb, grinding into the soft flesh as she thought. Kant had said the dead ones normally didn't go after animals. But this wasn't a normal night. The curse was bad. The dead figures were more active, more violent.

As she watched, two of the dead ones moved in from the edges of her view, walking with purpose toward the trees where Marsh had vanished.

No.

Margot turned. Belatedly, she realized the distant footsteps had changed. One of them was louder. Heavier. They had started to climb the stairs.

Her chance to be quiet was gone. Margot ran. Each footfall seemed to boom like a drum through the night. She shoved the bedroom door open as she flew through it and choked down a cry.

One of the dead was at the top of the stairs. Only his silhouette was visible until Margot lifted her arm and shone the phone's pale light into his face. One eye was missing entirely. Maggots filled the cavity, roiling, squirming through the flesh. Nostrils flared as his head turned toward Margot. The mouth twitched, pulling against the black threads.

He wasn't yet blocking her path, though. Margot skidded on the wooden floor as she changed direction, turning herself toward the passages that led to the second stairwell.

She passed her bedroom, the door still hanging open, the carnage inside still visible. The idea that the axe might be useful flashed through her mind, but she didn't stop to retrieve it. At best, it could only slow the dead. At worst, it would slow Margot. And she couldn't afford that.

The corner appeared before she expected it, and her shoulder scraped the wooden panels as she took it too fast. Her arms swung to keep her balance, and the light, weak to begin with, swung along with them, revealing the pathway in sparse flickers.

She was at the stairs, though, and took them two at a time, spasms of pain jarring through her ankle and her arm at each step. Then she was back into the hall leading to the front door. She caught herself on the corner to the kitchen and snatched up Marsh's leash from the table. Then back into the hallway. The Watcher blocked her way, guarding the entrance, and Margot thought maybe he *did* do some good because when she reached the front door she discovered it was still locked. She scrambled to unseal it, then darted out, leaving it open behind her. So many of the dead were already inside, it seemed futile to try to block them.

Margot was at the porch's top step before she saw the figure climbing toward her. A third member of the dead was on the stairs, reaching up, his cheeks billowing as his jaw tried to stretch past the limits of the black thread.

She leapt away. The dead man's long fingernails snagged in a lose lock of hair. Margot threw herself back, and a muted cry escaped through her clenched teeth as hairs were torn from her scalp. She was free, though, and racing along the wraparound porch, the wooden boards booming beneath her feet.

Dark, thin shapes hung from the ceiling. Margot ducked to avoid one and realized she was seeing nooses only when they creaked, heavy and slow, behind her.

Ahead, the porch turned a corner. A gray arm reached around the house's edge, stretching toward her. Margot turned toward the railing instead. It came up to waist height, but the drop over the other side was longer. She draped her torso over the railing and lifted her feet over first. If she'd had more time, she would have lowered herself slowly, but time was thin; the dead converged from each direction, so Margot let go, and gasped as the impact rocked through her.

A spark of pain ran up from her ankle, but it wasn't enough to keep her from running, so that was what she did: away from the house, through the gathering fog, and toward the darkly silhouetted trees in the distance.

She recognized that this choice was significant. It would most likely decide the remainder of the night and decide whether she lived or died.

And every strand of logic she'd managed to cling to warned her that this decision was not a *good* one.

But she was helpless to do anything else. She couldn't leave Marsh outside while the dead surrounded. If she had even a small chance of protecting him, she had to try.

She lengthened her strides. Her feet seemed to catch every sharp rock and dead clump of grass.

The words from her parents' tape danced through her mind. *The other family would play outside from night until morning… They scratched her and bit her and dragged her into the earth.*

Still, she didn't let her feet slow but flew across the sparse field. Early dew soaked into her socks. Her breathing was ragged, aching. The wind tugged at her clothes and at her hair like a thousand tiny hands raking across her.

She only came to a halt when she was nearly at the trees she'd seen Marsh disappear into. Then she pressed her fingers in between the jacket's left-hand sleeve and the cast and pried out the phone.

Its light cut through shivering branches. She opened up her list of contacts and selected Kant but didn't activate the call. Instead, she held it there as insurance while she raised the phone up, slicing through the darkness.

The trees weren't thick. It shouldn't have been so hard to see between them. But mist had set in, and her light didn't reach as far as she wanted. She stretched it higher, trying to get a better angle, as she took the first step between the branches.

"Marsh!" Her throat was dry, her voice a rasping whisper. Dead branches scored along her cheek. More snagged at her hair. She pressed forward. Some kind of animal chattered in the branches above her, but when Margot flashed her light upward, she couldn't see it.

The fence ran through the trees. Margot climbed over it, awkward with her cast, and heard the distant bells ring. She was nearly at the end of the growth. A quiet terror was rising. She couldn't have missed Marsh between the spindly trunks.

Unless the dead got to him first.

She pushed through the final layer of branches. The gradual, grassy slope spread out ahead of her, an undulating ocean of shadows and light, the grassy knolls shimmering like waves.

In the distance, drowning in mist, a dark shape lumbered down the path. Smaller than a human. A long, fanlike tail waving in its wake.

"Marsh…" She coiled the leash around her wrist and broke into a run again. To her left, she thought she saw a shape through the fog. It was bent almost double, its arms hanging close to the ground, long hair creating a screen around the face that twisted to follow her movement.

She blinked as cold air stung her eyes. Her feet were growing unsteady. She was so tired. When she glanced at her phone, it displayed a time: four thirty. Dawn was still a while away.

"Marsh!"

She knew she shouldn't raise her voice, but she was desperate. The dog's head twitched when she called him, but he didn't slow as he entered a new bank of trees.

"Please," she hissed.

The ground dropped into a shallow ditch, the kind that likely only carried water when there was rain. The grass grew taller at its base, making it seem less deep than it actually was. Margot scrambled down the slope, her center of gravity lowered and arms stretched out for balance. As she neared the base, her socks slipped on damp grass. She landed with a grimace, the phone sliding out of her hand, liquid soaking into her jean legs and the edges of her jacket.

She scrambled to catch her phone before she lost it in the grass. Her fingers touched something damp, and she recoiled.

Don't panic. It's just groundwater.

She forced her hand into the soggy, spongy grass, afraid the water would get into her phone and shut it down entirely. Her hand closed around metal, and she breathed a sigh as she lifted the phone out.

Both its screen and her hand were smeared in red.

Bile rose in the back of her throat. Margot scrambled back, trying to pull away, but the arm with the cast plunged deeper into the spongy ground, and beads of viscous red liquid welled up from the pressure, bubbling over her fingers.

Blood. It's blood. The ground's bleeding.

She bit her tongue to keep herself from gagging. The ditch wasn't deep, but its soil was soft, and Margot crawled on hands and knees to get herself over the edge. She crouched on the other side, panting and shivering, as she stared at her red-drenched hands.

Fresh nausea washed through her. She ran her hands over the dewed grass, desperately trying to clean them. There was too much. It was on her jeans, her jacket, the leash, and it soaked through her socks. There was not much she could do to escape it. Not until dawn.

It might not actually be blood, she tried to tell herself. It could be wine. She would be able to tell the difference if she had the courage to taste it, but nothing in heaven or on earth could compel her to put the crimson liquid near her mouth.

She dried her hands as much as possible on her jacket, then scrambled to her feet again. She'd lost sight of Marsh. She wasn't alone, though. Thin, dirt-clad figures were visible in the distance, no more than dull-gray blurs through the mist. Their heavy footsteps echoed, inexorably growing closer.

What will they do if they catch me?

Margot thought of the girl, Abigail, that Ray had mentioned. Found drowned in a shallow creek, her clothes torn and scratch marks coating her body. Would the dead hold Margot's head into the ditch, pushing it under until her lungs were filled with viscous liquid and churned dirt?

She didn't want to find out. Her legs shook and the dampened leash hung like a noose from her hand as she stumbled toward the trees.

Margot pressed through the scratching branches, eyes straining, heart thundering. She dried the phone's front on her jacket multiple times, but the light seemed to have been imbued with a red tint. A soft huffing noise came from ahead. *Marsh.* She quickened her pace, barely reacting as a dead branch scored the back of her hand.

She stepped into a gap between two patches of trees. Saplings grew there, quivering in the cold air, fighting for survival as the taller trees dwarfed them.

Marsh was there, facing away, his head lifted to look at something Margot couldn't see. Her heart almost burst from relief. She crouched, arm extended to catch his collar, to pull him back around, then hesitated.

Something didn't feel right. The hairs across Margot's arms rose, the skin prickling. Marsh still wouldn't face her. His tail no longer swayed but hung low. His fur didn't seem right.

"Marsh?" she whispered, and he finally responded, turning to look back at her.

His eyes were empty, dark pits, squirming and alive with maggots.

37.

The dog shuffled toward Margot. His fur was darkened and clumping, as though he'd been dragged through mud. His jaw hung open. The tongue was black. The gums pocked with holes. The rank stench of death rolled off him, wet and heavy and like an unbearable knife through Margot's heart. He blinked. Maggots spilled from the hollow eyeholes, tumbling over his muzzle and writhing on the ground.

A scream tore from Margot, building and winding until she thought she would go deaf from it. She scrambled backward, but her shoulder hit a trunk, blocking her path.

The golden retriever's tail swung once, twice, and strands of fur fell from the decaying flesh beneath.

Her heart felt as though it had stopped. She couldn't bring herself to look away from the dead, squirming eyes.

It's not Marsh.

It wasn't Marsh; it couldn't be. She was going to find him and save him and everything would be okay again.

But then the thought hit again, harder, and this time with a ring of truth.

It's not Marsh.

Marsh's collar had been blue to match his leash. An orange collar hung around this dog's neck, decayed and faded and almost falling loose. It had once held a name tag, but it had been lost at some point, a bent metal loop all that remained.

This was another dog. Its body shape was different. Broader. Even through the caking mud sticking its fur into clumps, she could see its coat was darker than Marsh's.

A thought came to her mind, spawned by the shade of orange the collar must have once held.

"Clementine?" she whispered.

The dog responded, lifting its head, its peeling paws carrying it a step closer.

She knew this dog. Marsh's ancestor, the golden retriever her parents had owned when she was a child. The source of her love of dogs.

Dead for more than a decade. Somehow not yet gone.

Queasiness ran through her in waves. She sagged, lowering her head, trying not to choke as her lungs filled with the wet scent of death and rot.

The dog's black tongue smacked over its tattered lips as it turned away again. It was decaying before her eyes but somehow didn't seem to notice.

It wasn't suffering. That was a small mercy but one she was grateful for.

Something moved through the trees at the opposite side of the clearing. One of the dead ones emerged. A woman, her hair matted from dirt, grime crusting beneath her fingernails and in every crease of her skin.

She was different from the others, though. She wore a formal purple-and-white dress. Although it was muddy and torn, it wasn't yet decaying off her body, not like the other corpses. Her mouth was stitched closed with black thread. Her wide eyes, the lids shredded, had a sheen of gray across the corneas, but they weren't entirely bleached. A dark pupil and iris were visible beneath the surface.

Margot choked. She'd seen that dress before. Once several days before and then again in her dreams. Both times inside the funeral home's dim viewing room.

A man stepped out behind the woman. His thin face was sagging and gaunt and tallowy. He'd lost the jacket from his gray suit, and the shirt was stained and tearing at the seams.

Andrew said their graves at the cemetery had been dug up. The bodies removed.

It wasn't vandalism.

Margot's face was wet. She hadn't realized she was crying until salty tears dripped from her chin. Even in death, the hill wasn't going to let her parents go.

Her mother, Maria, moved first. Swollen ankles shuffled her closer. Arms rose, dirt-caked fingernails reaching for Margot's face.

"I'm sorry." Margot closed her eyes as a sob broke out of her. She wasn't going to run. And she wasn't going to fight. She couldn't. Not anymore. This night had extracted more from her than she'd thought she was capable of giving. More than she could endure. She was done.

Spongy, cold fingertips touched Margot's throat. She quivered but didn't recoil as she waited for the bite of nails digging into her flesh.

It didn't come. Her mother's thumb trailed over her jaw, wiping back the tears.

Margot keeled over, howling cries breaking out of her. She hadn't cried during their funeral. But she made up for it now. The small traces of what she knew about them combined into something achingly bittersweet. How the curse had chained them to the hill. What they'd sacrificed in sending her away. How, even now, they were denied peace. Those thoughts mingled with the pain forged through years of loneliness, years of believing she hadn't been wanted, until she couldn't see, couldn't hear, couldn't do anything except wail.

Arms encircled her, holding her up. They were as cold as the grave. Her mother was solid in the wrong ways and soft in the wrong places. She smelled of mildew and fetid water and formaldehyde and rot.

A second set of arms moved around her, stiff, too heavy. These corpses were wrong. *Bad*, Witchety would have called them. But Margot leaned into them, clinging to them, and in that moment, she had never wanted anything more.

Faint panting sounds echoed from her feet. Clementine, the golden retriever, paced around them.

Stiff, clammy fingers trailed over Margot's hair. Her mother pulled away first, and Margot tried to hold her there, to not let her go, but when her father also released his grasp Margot raised her head to look at them.

Their broken, sallow faces could not even smile at her. Their lips had been sewn shut. That was wrong, Margot knew; she'd seen them in the viewing room. The mortician had wired their jaws closed, and he'd tried to stitch the eyes shut as well, but he hadn't sewn their lips. That was only for the convicts, the ones who had been hung.

Margot reached up to touch the threads on their mouths but hesitated just shy, afraid the caress might hurt them. "I'm sorry. I can fix this. I—let me find some scissors. I can get these out—"

Her father took her outstretched hand and shook his head. He pointed to the ground behind Margot. She followed the signal and saw her mobile laying there, facedown, its light diffused into the grass.

Then her father pointed behind himself, into the trees.

Something was coming toward them. It crackled through the dead branches, fallen leaves crunching underfoot.

Even without words, Margot understood. Her parents wouldn't hurt her. But the others would. She needed to leave before they caught her.

"I don't want to go," she whispered. A thought occurred. She grasped their hands. "Come back with me. I…I don't care. Stay with me in the house. At least for tonight."

Her mother's eyes filled with longing and sadness as she gently shook her head, and once again, Margot understood.

They didn't belong in the house any longer. They were part of the land, the soil. They couldn't leave it.

The girl plays outside during the day, and the other family plays outside at night.

They belonged to different worlds now. Their paths were not supposed to cross like this. It was a fluke, a mistake that they had even found each other.

The footsteps were growing nearer. Three pairs, coming at her through the trees. In the pale fog and the heavy moonlight, she could barely make out the forms: tall, wild eyed. Gray skin. Quivering fingers.

Clementine wove about her legs. Her mother pressed her hand, pointing again to the phone on the ground and then toward the rise in the hill that would lead her back to the house.

"I'm sorry," Margot said a final time, and it encompassed everything: an apology for not knowing them better. For what had happened to them after death. For the life that had been dealt to them.

She picked up the phone just as the dead ones broke through the edges of the trees. Three of them, their cold, empty eyes fixed on her, their skin sliding unpleasantly across their bones. Margot's mother and father backed up, spreading their arms, trying to slow the twisted forms. They shoved through like her parents didn't even exist, and Margot only had time for three parting words: "I love you."

And then she turned and ran.

Climbing uphill was harder than the descent. Her lungs ached and her legs shook. A shadowy shape moved in from the side, and Margot had to swerve to keep out of its reach.

Dead sticks cut into the soles of her feet. The air was growing colder as the night grew longer. Enormous plumes of condensation rose from her lips with every breath, and they merged into the fog around her, adding to the heavy screen. Her face felt swollen and damp from crying. But at the same time, she felt like something bad had been drawn out of her, like a toxic growth being carved out of her chest. It wasn't healing. Not yet. But it was the first step.

She heard the ditch before she reached it. When she'd first crossed it, it had been damp, the soil spongy and ready to give up its offering under pressure. Now, though, it flowed.

Margot stretched her phone above the writhing snake of a brook. Bubbles swelled and burst as eddies formed in the violently red liquid. Drops of color squeezed out of the banks on either side, joining the flow.

The liquid still covered her hands and clothes, drying in smears and damp in other patches. She wasn't willing to step into the flow a second time. Margot followed the divot until it narrowed, then leapt across the gap. The impact sent spasms of pain raking through her, but she gained her feet almost instantly and continued.

Behind, the river continued to flow, a soft gurgle rising as eddies collided. The imagery hung with her far longer than the sounds.

Like a gash in the ground, cutting through arteries and veins. As though blood runs under every inch of the soil.

Ahead, the house's silhouette cut a sharp line against the night sky. Margot slowed as she neared it. All of her instructions had said to stay inside, to wait out the night under her own roof.

Why? Is that just what the previous families have done?

She glanced across the hill. Shapes moved in the distance, converging toward her. They were easier to see outside. Easier to run away from, with less risk of being cornered.

The curse is bad right now. The previous families might have only needed to deal with one body at a time, not multiples. And I don't know the house's layout. It's possible that staying outdoors will be safer.

She'd have to keep moving, keep herself ahead of the slow corpses, but that was true inside the house too. Margot checked the time on her phone. Less than an hour to go to dawn. Her body shook from exhaustion, her muscles aching, her knees wanting to buckle, but…she could keep moving, she thought. It was life or death. She'd *have* to.

Ahead, the house's front door remained open. Nooses hung from the porch's beams, and their slow, painful creaks bled through the night air. They really did sound as though bodies were strung up in them. Maybe the ropes remembered their last use, even though they now hung empty.

She couldn't see any bodies on the porch. No sounds came from the house. The corpses might have left to follow her down the hill. It might be safe enough to retrieve the one thing she wanted to keep close until dawn.

Marsh.

She needed to be certain he was still safe. And then she needed to keep him at her side. Witchety had been right. She needed something *good* with her, and Marsh was the most *good* she knew.

Margot took the stairs lightly, her ears straining for any signs of motion in the house. The enormous Watcher towered in the entryway, blocking her view of the hall behind it. Margot clung to the passage's right, stretching her light forward, fighting against the impenetrable darkness.

The house was so quiet she could hear every thud of her heart and every dry, crackling breath. She slipped along the wall, tentative, cautious. Her light caught on the living room's bell. It stayed silent.

She darted her tongue across her cracked lips. Each step left a dark, smeared footprint to mark her path. Her fingers were growing numb. She adjusted her hold on her phone so it wouldn't slip.

She stepped into the hallway leading to the sewing room. The door was still closed. Even in the house's deathly quiet, Margot couldn't hear any sounds from inside the room.

Quiet fear stuck to her like cobwebs that she'd been mistaken, that Marsh had gotten outside after all.

Worse, that the dead ones had gotten *in*.

She gripped the door handle. Turned it. Braced herself. Then opened the door.

Marsh leapt at her, dancing at her feet, his tail slapping the doorframe as he came through. A choked, grateful laugh escaped Margot. She bent, hugging the dog tightly, but only for a second. They needed to get back outside. She still had the leash wrapped around her arm, and clipped it onto Marsh's collar. His eyes smiled up at her, showing how much he had missed her.

"Good boy," she whispered. "Come on. Let's go."

The house remained perfectly still. As she led Marsh back along the hall, his nails clicking on the wood with each step, she experienced a pang of uncertainty.

Maybe this really *was* the best place to hide. If the dead had all left to follow her down the hill, she might be able to close the doors and blot out the lights and spin out her final hour of night undisturbed. The dead had spent longer than that roving outside the building when they'd first arrived.

No. They won't take their time like that again. Margot entered the lounge room, her breath held as she darted the light across the scene. *The house isn't a sanctuary. It's a trap. Don't let it trick you into thinking otherwise.*

Her path to the front door was clear. She moved forward, preparing to slip past the Watcher, but felt a sharp tug on the leash.

Marsh had backed up. His eyes, normally so gentle and warm, had turned as hard as slate. His back was raised, fur prickling up around his neck and spine.

"Marsh?" She gave him some slack on the leash. He backed up farther, and his lips peeled back from his teeth. A low, rumbling growl echoed from deep in his chest.

Margot looked back to the hallway, her own chest feeling the press of dread. Moonlight flowed through the open door, pouring across the floor and rising over part of the Watcher. Long shadows trailed behind the effigy. Across from it was the kitchen, darker. She could barely make out the glint of the fridge's edge in the distance.

Low, rumbling growls continued to flow in a continuous stream from Marsh. She couldn't hear any of the dead. No thumping footsteps in the hall. Nothing from the porch except the constant, low creak of old rope. Her light didn't pick up any kind of movement.

"What is it?" Margot whispered. She kept her hold on the leash firm as she lowered herself to Marsh's side. His eyes barely flicked toward her. She traced his gaze and saw he was staring at the Watcher. "You don't like the statue? Your owner made it, you know."

He wasn't calming. The fur across his flanks grew tenser. More teeth were exposed as the warning growls became deeper.

She switched the mobile to her left hand, holding it awkwardly around the cast, then tucked her good hand's fingers underneath Marsh's collar. She could feel his prickling fur on her knuckles as she led him toward the hallway. "Please, Marsh. We have to go."

He obeyed this time, but with each inch they gained, the growls grew louder. Lines of saliva ran from the corners of his mouth. The pitch-black eyes were as cold as ice as they fixed on the effigy.

Margot had barely gotten through the archway and into the hall when her feet faltered.

Marsh was here before. He watched me drag the effigy across the room. He lay down with it ten feet away without making a peep. Why now?

She turned, the press of dread in her chest growing heavier, to face the massive sculpture.

The dark pits in the deer skull were no longer empty. Clouded gray eyes stared out at her.

38.

The effigy's body had been hollow, made up of a convoluted mesh of wires and braced shards of driftwood. Now, though, it held something solid inside. A body. Wrapped around by metal. Pierced *through* by metal. The dead eyes stared through the holes in the deer skull mask as its long, twitching arms reached toward her.

A thousand trinkets rattled as the effigy moved. Light flashed across spoons, across bones, across needles and sharp knives.

Margot tried to jolt back. Her socks, damp, slid on the wood in the same instant that Marsh lunged away, robbing her of her balance. She felt herself fall. She landed hard, her hand pressed over the phone, her legs unresponsive, her lungs unable to draw air as fear overrode her mind.

The body had been incorporated into the effigy in the most nightmarish way. The loops of wire that were supposed to hold the trinkets together now threaded through its flesh. Each movement pulled sharp angles in its skin as a thousand piercings were pulled taut. The arms stretched forward, run through with metal, hung with Witchety's gifts, and it was hard to see where the wire ended and the flesh began.

A low, rippling bellow rose from behind the deer skull, and Margot thought that, behind the stitched mouth, the dead one must be screaming.

Margot's voice died before it could reach her throat. She scrambled, legs and arms moving wildly, slipping on the wood. The mantra ran through her mind on a loop—*Don't panic, don't panic*—but she was well past that point, her head empty of everything save raw terror.

The effigy pulled forward, skin peeling up from bones with each shift, puckering as hundreds of piercing wires pulled on it. Bones and wood and talismans clinked. The heavy, closed-mouth bellow grew louder as it bent down to put its face above hers. The arms were coming to encircle her, and with a sickening jolt of horror, Margot knew what was going to happen.

She would be drawn into the web of metal, just as the dead one had been. Pierced. Threaded through. Torn to shreds inside the cold, cutting lines of steel.

One of her arms rose in a desperate effort to guard her head, and the metal pressed into her, and she felt drops of blood trail over her arm as the skin began to split.

Then the dead one jolted back. The gray eyes stared, wide and blind, toward the ceiling. Its bellow rose, reverberating inside its sealed mouth.

Margot scrambled another foot back. The pain in her arm registered but only dully, overridden by terror and shock.

The effigy was slow to turn. Its skin stretched. Rattles moved through the form as the accoutrements shook violently.

Marsh, eyes wild, fur spiked in terror, grappled with the dead thing. He'd bitten one of the corpse's few exposed patches of skin: the back of its right leg. Skin and muscle tore as the dog's teeth clamped down ever harder.

The effigy raised one of its arms, and Margot's heart turned to ice. Angular shards of metal and the ends of wires radiated from the limb. And it was aimed at Marsh.

"No!" She lurched forward. There was nowhere to grab the form that

wouldn't shred her skin. Margot moved on blind instinct as she extended her left arm, using the cast like a battering ram to slam into the creature's legs.

It tilted violently. A paring knife, protruding from a flap of torn skin, came close to scoring the back of Margot's neck as she ducked.

Marsh released the leg as it twisted away from him. His jaws opened for a fresh bite. Margot hurled herself toward him and grabbed him by the collar. A bark rang free from him as she hauled them both back.

The effigy lurched toward them, the eyes behind the skull round as disks. One of its feet landed on the end of Marsh's blue leash. Margot gripped the cord, pulling, but it was pinned in place. She reached for the back of Marsh's collar instead and unclipped the leash.

Then she was clambering backward, dragging Marsh with her. She hit the open threshold to the porch, and Marsh, recognizing freedom, took over. Margot clung to his collar, scrambling her feet against the floor to give them extra speed as Marsh dragged her to the steps.

A cacophony of ringing metal cut through the dead one's bellow as it staggered after them. It wasn't fast, though; the pinching, pulling wires restricted its movements, and Margot was able to get her feet under herself before it had reached the door.

"*Go*," she called to Marsh, but he needed no encouragement. Together they flew onto the field surrounding the house. The scene was drowned in mist. Gray forms blurred in the distance as they converged toward the house. Margot, bent double, kept one hand on Marsh's collar.

Dawn can't be far. Please. It can't be.

She tried to track the forms about them, but their ferocious pace made it hard to see anything. Marsh, dragging her in his wake, chose a gap between the gray figures. Margot had a second-long glimpse of twisted faces, hollow eyes, and black-threaded mouths, and then they were past, racing down the hill.

To where? The employee accommodations? Off the land entirely? I can survive a headache for a couple of hours if it means the dead ones aren't able to follow.

She thought they were, though. Witchety had been so particular about not taking a car, to protect against bringing unwelcome things home with her. The dead were tied to the land, but they weren't restricted to it.

Still…she just had to survive a little more. The sky was the heavy, intense kind of dark that told her dawn couldn't be far away.

More of the dead figures were emerging, though. Every time she glanced to her sides, she saw new ones. Wearing the scraps they'd died in, their bodies sallow and withered by death, their gaits growing long and eager as they caught sight of her.

How many?

Hundreds, Kant had said. Hundreds of lives cut short on this very hill, just outside her front door, then interred in the toxic ground.

She couldn't recognize the land any longer or even tell which side of the hill they were on. Marsh led her according to some arcane plan, weaving around the trees, his tongue rolling free, froth at the edges of his mouth.

A stitch formed in Margot's side. Each breath hurt more. She pulled on the collar, begging Marsh to slow, and he finally did. Black eyes peered up at her, unfathomably worried, his own pants echoing through the mist. She didn't have the breath to speak but ran her hand through his fur, telling him she was okay, that he'd done a good job.

She'd lost her phone in the house. Without its light, she couldn't check his muzzle properly, but there was no sign of blood, and when she peeled back his lips, she couldn't see any punctures to his gums. He'd managed to escape the worst of the effigy, then.

Margot couldn't say the same for herself. Blood trailed down her fingers, dripping from the cuts on her forearm, blending with the stains from the flowing creek. She tried not to look too closely.

Her legs shook. Her side continued to ache. She didn't think she could run any longer, but she couldn't stand still. Already, the dead ones were tightening around her, their creaking joints and heavy footsteps sending prickles of stress along her back.

"Good Marsh," she whispered, putting her hand under his collar again so she wouldn't risk losing him. "Let's go."

The tail waved once, twice, then the eyes began smiling again, and Margot couldn't stop herself from marveling at his resilience.

They moved down the hill, Marsh trotting, Margot staggering. She didn't have a clear idea of where they were going, just that they needed to keep moving.

In the distance she caught a trace of faintly glowing yellow light, and both Marsh and she instinctively adjusted their path toward it.

Dawn?

The word sparked a flicker of hope through Margot's chest before dying out again. It wasn't dawn. The light was too sharp, too focused, too small.

Flashlights.

They were growing closer now, and Margot could see the outline of Kant's shoulders. She didn't understand. He shouldn't be here. She hadn't called him.

Unless...?

Through the breathless ache in her side and the haze flooding her mind, Margot flashed back to the moment she'd realized the effigy wasn't empty. Falling backward onto the floor, her phone had become pinned under her hand. She'd had the screen open to Kant's number just in case.

Did I press the call button? I wouldn't have heard it ring, not through the rattling of the Watcher's trinkets.

Kant wasn't alone. Andrew jogged behind him, and farther back, two more bodies moved close together, their own lights flitting left and right as they traced the dark shapes clinging to the mist. Nora and Ray.

Kant raised his hand as Margot neared him, his voice hoarse as he called, "Okay?"

"Fine," she replied, even though she was anything but. "I dropped my phone, that's all."

Kant's light ran over Margot. She could barely make out his features, except that his eyes seemed a shade darker than before. His eyebrows lowered, his jaw twitching.

"The hell," Andrew muttered from just behind Kant.

Margot looked down at herself, and at the way her body had been painted in red. Blood dripped from her hand. Her hair was a wild mane, matted with the crimson liquid and dirt and cobwebs. She had to look like she'd crawled out of a nightmare. That didn't feel too far from the truth.

Then Kant said, "Come on," and extended a hand to encourage her forward. "Back to the path. Night's almost over."

She staggered forward, and Andrew took Marsh from her. Nora and Ray hung just behind, their backs rigid, pressed close to each other. A glint of metal hung at Ray's side, and it took her a second to recognize it. He was carrying a rifle. They'd never experienced the hill at night when the curse was active, Margot realized. They hadn't yet gotten used to it like Kant had.

In the erratic movements of the flashlight, she saw they were at the driveway. Kant had come within an inch of the edge but refused to step past.

"You don't like leaving the driveway, do you?" Margot mumbled. Now that she'd become aware of it, she realized the only time she'd seen him step off the track was when he accompanied Witchety on her first blessing.

"Mm." He placed a careful hand at her back, silently offering her support as she limped. "Soft dirt is dangerous for me. How I lost my leg. Cheated death once, which means now I always have to watch my back."

"Oh." Margot squinted, one hand held to the stitch in her side. She felt like she'd been given an explanation, and yet understood nothing.

It could wait. Everything could. She was tired down to her very bones. Her body hurt. Her emotions had been stretched and strained and beaten until she couldn't feel much at all, just a numb, heavy kind of weariness.

Her experiences from that night would catch up to her later, and she'd have to figure out how to process them. But not yet. She needed warmth first. Rest.

They formed a narrow procession on the dirt track. Kant stayed at her side, his pace matching her own. Andrew led, Marsh's collar in one hand and his flashlight in the other. Behind her, Nora and Ray brought up the rear, their own lights darting across the landscape. Margot looked over her shoulder and saw the pinched paleness to Nora's face and the grim set to Ray's jaw.

"I thought you'd be back in town," Margot managed.

Nora's laugh was weak, stressed. "Not anymore. We got as far as home before we started to feel sick."

"Had to come back," Ray finished for her. "We thought we'd be able to sleep off the land for another eight months or so before it fully claimed us, but…well. We're here now."

Margot didn't know what to say except for "I'm sorry."

He shrugged. "It was going to happen eventually. This is just sooner than we'd hoped."

They walked downhill, and although Margot had followed the exact same path a dozen times since arriving at Gallows Hill, it felt alien to her. Thick fog flowed around their path and moved in eddies under their feet. Noises encroached from all sides. The sharp trill of a disturbed bird. The whisper of grass. The creak of aged limbs.

"They're coming in from the right," Andrew said.

"And from behind." Nora's voice, soft, faded into the cold night air. "They're closer than I thought."

"We'll need to be fast." Kant glanced at Margot. "Can you?"

Her energy was spent. But she'd gotten this far. She nodded. Their pace increased, and Margot pressed a hand to her stitch.

Ahead, Marsh's happy panting had become tense, stressed. "How many are there?" Ray asked, the exact question Margot had posed herself earlier. She frowned into the mist, picking out dark smears through the fog. They were growing more distinct. Their outlines gaining definition and their footsteps ringing out clearer as they drew near.

"I've never seen this many," Kant admitted. "They usually come one or two at a time."

"We're very close to dawn." Andrew, bent double to keep his hold on Marsh, panted as he spoke. "Once we get back to the employee area, we can—"

He pulled up short. Marsh, recoiling at his side, released a single heavy, booming bark.

One of the dead ones blocked their path. It stood in the center of the driveway, head lifted to point toward the sky, its empty, white eyes unseeing. Its arms were spread wide, as though waiting for them to walk into its embrace. The fingers were broken. They twisted at unnatural angles. They twitched.

"This isn't right," Andrew murmured. "What's it doing?"

Kant's hand, lightly touching Margot's back, felt unsteady. "It's blocking the path."

"It shouldn't be, though, should it?" Andrew backed up a step, Marsh hanging close to his side. "They don't...*wait*. They follow. They search. They don't set traps or linger or whatever *this* is."

"No," Kant agreed. "They shouldn't."

Nora and Ray were shuffling closer to Margot, their lights darting across the environment. The dead ones were drawing in, narrowing their net. Faces were beginning to grow visible through the mist. Lips twitching beneath the dark threads.

"We can't stop," Andrew said. He threw a look back toward Kant. "Should we go off the path?"

Kant didn't answer. His expression was heavily shadowed, nearly unreadable, but Margot thought she saw a flicker in his eyes. *Fear?*

"Kant?" Andrew asked. His voice grew tighter as the bodies around them pressed inward.

"Yes," Kant said, and the words seemed to cost him. "Leave the path."

They moved as a group, breaking into a jog as they went left, swerving around the figure with the broken, twitching fingers. Its head turned to follow them, nostrils flaring as they passed.

Dew-laden grass flicked across Margot's ankles. Her breath came hard and raw, rasping through her lungs. Kant loped at her side, holding pace with her. Distantly, she thought she could make out lights. *The employee's area.* It wouldn't be an easy run, but she could make it that far, she was sure.

Then Kant stumbled. Margot's reflexes were slow, and she reached out to him a second too late. He hit the ground with a muffled grunt, his shaggy hair covering his face. Margot turned and grasped his arm, trying to pull him back to his feet. She couldn't move him.

That was when she saw it. A long, gray limb reached out of the earth. It had clamped around his leg, just below his knee, its knuckles bulging as it dug into him.

The earth seemed to bubble. Margot lost her own footing, collapsing in the spongy soil, the air knocked out of her. More arms rose from the ground, rising up around Kant, latching onto his legs, his back.

Pulling him into the earth.

No. Margot scrambled forward and grabbed Kant. She wrapped herself around his shoulders and pulled, desperate, trying to drag him free.

"*Go,*" he rasped. "*Run.*"

The ground was no longer solid. It churned, grass and grubs and damp soil boiling like lava. Pulling Kant into it. It was at his chest already. His breathing became tight, labored, as the pressure intensified.

Margot felt her own legs sliding into the earth as she pulled against him. *Help me*, she wanted to yell, but there was no air left in her lungs.

Andrew yelled something. A gunshot fired. Out of the corner of her eye she saw a gray body stagger from the impact, then continue walking forward.

Guns can't stop them. Nothing can.

Cold fingers wrapped around the back of her head. Jagged fingernails dug into her scalp, tangling in her hair, as the dead one dragged her back. Margot couldn't even scream. She lost her grip on Kant. She reached above herself and felt a brittle, clammy wrist. She beat her hands against it, trying to break it, to get free from its hold.

The gun fired again, then again. Nora screamed. Marsh was barking, wild with terror. The gray one's fingers tightened around Margot's head as its other hand clamped over her mouth, her nose. She thrashed. Her eyes were wide, unblinking, as she stared toward the sky.

The stars were fading. The first trickle of dawn's light touched the hill.

A cry escaped her as the pressure on the back of her head vanished. Margot dropped onto her hands and knees, air whistling in her throat, tears burning her eyes.

Andrew was struggling to his feet not far from her. Nora bent over Ray, holding on to him. His gun lay discarded some distance away.

The dead were gone.

So was Kant.

Nearly.

His arm rose out of the churned dirt, from the elbow up, reaching toward the dawn.

The fingers twitched.

Margot heard herself scream. She felt herself drag her way across the broken earth. Watched, like she was watching a stranger, as she began to feverishly claw dirt back, trying to dig him free.

Andrew was at her side, gripping the hand, pulling, yelling. The dirt was too heavy. Too dense.

Tears drenched the dirt as Margot's fingers plunged into the soft, damp sods with growing desperation.

Digging.

Digging.

Digging.

39.

They scratched her and bit her and dragged her into the earth.

Dr. Maynard made very few comments and asked even fewer questions. She worked with brisk efficiency, her slender fingers stitching and cutting and bandaging her way through them.

Margot sat outside the small workspace for most of it, her back against the wall, her feet stretched ahead of her. With her good hand, she picked at her cast. It was stained and swelling around the edge, and she was able to pull little shreds free.

Sometimes employees moved past her as they caught up to their morning's work. Quick glances were thrown her way when they thought she wouldn't see, but someone must have warned them against staring.

She'd seen her reflection, briefly, in a window. Blood smeared up to her elbows. Blood smeared across her face, from when she'd tried to wipe her tears away. No shoes. No life left in her eyes.

There were soft voices inside the room. Ray, answering questions. He was conscious at least. Strips of skin had been torn from his stomach and chest.

Margot tilted her head back and let the sun soak across her. It was the first time she'd felt warm in hours. The first time she'd felt *safe*. She wanted it to last forever. It was a cruel twist that the sun could only ever last for so many hours before it was dragged back beneath the horizon.

The door behind her opened. Dr. Maynard stepped out and stood over her for a second, then carefully lowered herself to sit at Margot's side.

"How are they?" Margot asked.

"They would benefit from at least an overnight stay in a hospital." Her dark eyes were heavy as they scanned Margot's face. "But I gather that's not an option."

Margot grimaced. "No."

"Then let's take a look at you."

"I'm fine."

A soft scoffing noise escaped Dr. Maynard's throat as she picked up Margot's hands. "You're very much not. The cast will need to be replaced. Is this blood yours?"

"No." Margot carefully withdrew her hands and folded them around herself, as though she could keep from falling apart with enough bracing. "A couple of scrapes. I can take care of them myself. And I'll make do with the cast for another day."

"But—"

"You'd just have to redo it again tomorrow morning." That was a half truth at best. Margot didn't know if there would *be* a tomorrow morning. But she was fairly certain Dr. Maynard's efforts would be wasted if she tried to replace the bandages that day.

The doctor turned, her slim, dark face glistening in the light as she scanned the area around them. "I don't want to know any more than what I've been told," she said, speaking carefully. "But I *do* want to know if there's anything in my power that will prevent my services being needed like this again."

Margot tried to smile. She didn't think she could form the right expression. "No."

"Then at least let me give you a proper exam."

"Thank you. I'd really prefer to have some space, though."

Dr. Maynard exhaled slowly. "I understand. Call me if you change your mind."

She rose and returned to the room, and Margot listened to the distant sounds of her cleaning and packing her supplies away. A moment later, she slipped back outside and gave Margot a brief, curt nod before turning to the driveway.

Margot continued to pick at the cast. She needed to go into the room, she knew. But the sun was warm, and the sun was safe, and she couldn't find the energy to stand.

The door opened again. Nora moved out first, supporting Ray on her shoulder. She smiled when she saw Margot, but it was no longer the full-bodied expression that lit up her face and revealed her gums. It was small, strained. Troubled. "There you are."

"Holding up okay?" Ray asked, and a lump formed in Margot's throat. It was a question she should have been asking *him*. He was pale, his normally neatly combed hair slick with sweat, his feet unsteady as he leaned on his wife.

"I'm fine," she managed, and she thought that if she repeated the phrase enough she might even begin to believe it. "Are you…"

"The doctor patched me up." He patted his stomach beneath his shirt. A faltering, cautious movement. "Got some painkillers. Going to take a few days off, close the shop while I get some sleep, but then it'll be back to business as usual."

There was an unspoken addition to that final sentence. *We don't have much of a choice.*

"Thank you for last night." The words had been lying heavy on her tongue all morning, but she didn't feel any relief to speak them. "Thank you for helping. And I'm sorry about what happened."

"Well, it's no one's fault, really." Ray looked down at Nora, but the smile she returned was strained. "We're all in the same boat together, aren't we?"

Nora took a quick, short breath, then patted the arm hanging over her shoulder. "Come on. Andrew says we can have the empty cabin at the back of the row. It's not far."

"Sleep well," Margot said as they left, but they didn't respond.

She continued sitting as they vanished behind a block of buildings, then slowly, unsteadily rose to her feet. Dr. Maynard had given her a pain tablet when she'd first arrived, and it worked to reduce the worst of the aches, but the bruises across her body still felt stiff and cold. She hesitated outside the door for a second, then gently knocked.

"Come in," Andrew called, and she entered.

The shutters had been opened to let the light in, but the space was still dim. Andrew stood, his back to the wall, arms folded over his chest, dark shadows falling heavily around his eyes.

Marsh lay under the table Margot had woken on the day before. One sleepy eye opened to watch her, then he huffed softly as he dropped back into his nap. Andrew had brought him bowls of food and water earlier, while Ray was being stitched.

Margot shut the door behind herself and took a step in, turning to face the bench near the door. She'd had a script before. She'd worked out exactly the words she wanted to say. They had been good, sincere. They entirely failed her.

Kant sat on the bench. "Margot," he said, giving her a brief nod.

A sharp white patch had been taped across his right eye. It had been removed, she knew, from what she'd heard while sitting outside the door.

Unbidden memories resurfaced. Digging, digging, spit flying from between her teeth, the muscles in her arms screaming but refusing to stop.

Her fingers had plunged deeper into the soft, churned earth. Deeper than she'd thought was possible. And then deeper still. Until she had stabbed into something horrifically soft.

She turned aside, feeling like she was on the verge of being sick.

Kant waited, silent, his expression inscrutable. Score marks from her fingers ran across the bridge of his nose and his forehead. Those would heal. He wouldn't get his eye back.

She struggled for words of any kind. "I'm so sorry."

"What for?" One of his large hands flicked up, as though to brush her apology aside, then dropped back to his lap.

"Your...your eye."

"Yes," he said. "I lost my eye. I kept my life. That seems like a small price, considering."

His voice was raspy. He'd inhaled soil particles, Dr. Maynard had said. That, too, he could recover from.

"You look like hell," Kant said, and the words were softer than she'd expected. "Sit a moment. Andrew, can you get her something to drink? Something hot?"

"Yeah, can do." Andrew pushed off the wall and crossed to the door. Before leaving, he pressed Kant's shoulder, a familiar, tender touch.

Kant waited until the door was closed, then leaned back against the wall, exhaling heavily. "Have you gotten any sleep yet?"

"No." She pulled up a chair from the desk and positioned it opposite Kant, then sank into it, relieved to take the pressure off her feet.

"You should. This bout of the curse shouldn't be able to continue after last night, but you should still be prepared." At her look, he continued, "The curse wears itself out. It gets worse, building like a storm cloud, but it can only sustain so much before breaking."

Margot felt cracks in her lip form as a genuine smile emerged. "I can't believe you're so sanguine."

He inhaled heavily, and a rasping cough formed as he let the breath out. He wiped the back of his hand across his mouth. Most of the dirt had been washed off his skin, but it still clung in his wrinkles and around his fingers. "You have to figure out how to be a bit sanguine, living here. And I've been waiting for the ground to take me for a while now. An eye is not much to lose, all considered."

Margot leaned forward in her seat. "Last night…this morning…you said something about that. About how you didn't go on soft ground."

"I cheated death once," he said, and his hand rested on the knee connected to the prosthetic leg. "Dug where I shouldn't have, late at night, when I shouldn't have. I disturbed something. The arms came out and tried to drag me in. I stabbed them with the shovel and got away, but lost the leg for it. And they've never forgotten."

"Which is why you don't leave the driveway," she murmured.

"They got a taste of me when they took my leg and now they're waiting to finish the job, whether the curse is active or not. They can't reach through compacted soil. Only the soft parts." His broad shoulders rose in a slight shrug. "It's usually safe during the day too, but I don't take chances. I'm not as young as I was back then."

"Will they do that to anyone else? Should I stay on the drive too?"

"No. You're fine to walk on soft ground. This is something different from the curse we're all under. I provoked them, and they put a mark on me for it. That happens sometimes. You'll know if it does."

Margot let her eyes close as she bent forward and rubbed the stiff muscles at the back of her neck. At that moment, the exhaustion felt like it would never abate.

Something pressed against her hand, and Margot flinched, her eyes snapping open. It was Marsh. He'd come out from his nap under the table and nudged his muzzle into her hand. She ran her fingers through his fur. It was flecked with mud and decaying leaves, but he'd made it through the night unscathed—something she was overwhelmingly grateful for.

The door creaked as it opened. Andrew had brought three hot cups, balanced precariously, and passed them out. Kant murmured gratefully as he took his. Margot accepted her own mug of coffee and stared into her distorted, fractured reflection.

"Last night was the worst I've seen it," Kant said. "It will get better. Easier. Most of the time, you can forget the curse even exists."

They kept promising her that, as though it was supposed to give her hope. Margot smiled, even though she felt like she was going to cry.

"Witchety's coming later to pick up Marsh," Andrew said. "I asked her for another blessing. For all the good it did last night, it's still the best help we have."

"Good." Margot lifted the coffee to her mouth. It scorched on the way down, but she welcomed the heat. Not even the sun had been able to abate the chill that had settled into her core.

Kant thinks it will have spent itself last night. I truly can't imagine how it would get worse.

"You need rest," Kant said, as though he could read her thoughts. "It can be here or it can be at the house, but you should try to sleep."

She nodded. Her limbs felt heavy. Her eyes burned. The idea of sleep—of oblivion—was seductive. Hours away from this world. Hours where she wouldn't have to worry about what the next night would bring. She drained her mug and left it on the countertop next to the sink.

"If you're staying here, I can bring in some spare blankets," Andrew said.

"No." She rubbed her palm into her closed eyelids. The skin was gritty and sensitive. "I'll go back to the house. Shower. Fresh clothes."

"Sure."

"Thank you. For everything." She rose, sighing at the ache in her feet. "What about you both? Is there…anything I can do?"

"I'm fine." Kant sighed deeply. "Might visit Ray later. You'll be able to find me around if you need me. Take care, Margot."

"I'll walk you out," Andrew said. He followed as Margot stepped back into the warming late-morning air. She squinted against the sun as she turned to face the house leading to the hill.

"Will you be all right?" Margot asked as Andrew came up beside her.

"Yeah. I'll keep an eye on him. Make sure he eats something." Andrew took his glasses off and polished them on the corner of his shirt. His eyes glanced across the grass, the buildings. Anywhere that wasn't Margot. "Look. I…might be speaking out of turn here."

She faced him. "Go on."

"Don't ask any more from Kant. Please." Andrew looked uncomfortable to even say it. "He'll try to help, because he's Kant, and that's just what he does, but…"

"Yeah." She felt a prickling, miserable kind of pain in the center of her chest. She knew what Andrew was saying. The hill had already extracted such a high price from the manager; she couldn't ask for more. Not even when she desperately needed it. "I understand."

"Right. Thank you." He took a step back, replacing the glasses. "I'll see you later, I guess."

"Yeah." She turned, her throat sore, and began the slow climb back to the house.

The front door still hung open, shifting in increments as the wind played with it. Dust and fallen leaves had blown into the entryway, coating the smear of blood she'd left as she scrambled for the door.

She didn't know what she'd expected to find there. The Watcher, upright, the way she'd originally left it? Or maybe a tangle of metal wires and bones and river stones, collapsed onto the floor, irreversibly broken. Or, worst of all, the Watcher, still containing the dead one, even after dawn was long risen.

Instead, there was nothing. A single bird skull lay broken on the floor, crushed underfoot by either her or the Watcher itself, to prove the creature had once stood there. She found her phone, kicked into the room's corner, and tucked it into her pocket.

Margot closed the front door and turned into the kitchen. She took her bottle of pain medication from the cupboard and swallowed a tablet, along with two large glasses of water.

She could have fallen asleep right there, draped over the kitchen table, but she made herself climb the stairs instead. There were likely other spare bedrooms that would be more comfortable, but Margot made for her old room instead. The axe still lay discarded on the floor. The bedside table had been crushed into the wall, leaving a dent in the plaster. She ignored all of that and crawled under the bed's blankets, fully clothed. It didn't matter how the room looked. And it didn't matter how the stains on her arms and dirt in her hair would get through the sheets. She was too exhausted to care.

Sleep came easily. There were no dreams—not of the funeral parlor and not of the dead ones. Only a single thought ran through her head as she drifted under. *What now?*

It clung to her over hours, and when she woke, it was still there, heavy and dense like a physical thing clouding the center of her mind.

The shadows had moved across the walls. Margot shifted and felt the bruises and scrapes across her body spark back to life. Flakes of dirt crumbled from her hands and beneath her fingernails. She brought her phone out to check the time. Three in the afternoon. She crawled out of bed and staggered to the bathroom.

Her cast made showering difficult, but she ran warm water into the bathtub as she peeled her clothes off, dropping them on the floor.

What now?

The water turned a muddy shade of red as she washed herself. Gradually her skin became visible again. She picked around the edges of the cast the best she could as she waited for the water to drain and poured a fresh tub.

The marks on her arm became clear as she rinsed blood away. They were punctures more than cuts, already scabbed with dry blood. She'd had a tetanus shot just eight months before, so should be safe at least as far as that was concerned.

Once her body was clean, she wrapped a towel around herself and rinsed her hair in the sink. There wouldn't have been time for a full routine, even if she'd had the energy, so she focused on getting the dirt out and then let it lie, damp and dripping, over her back as she returned to her room.

What now?

She chose new clothes from her wardrobe and used a thick elastic to tie her hair back into a bun. In the hazy wardrobe mirror, her scars looked like lightning against her darker skin. She covered them with a knit sweater.

Then she returned downstairs. Her sneakers were in the living room. She'd left them there after the bells rang, which meant they'd stayed relatively clean. She pulled them on, then retrieved the cloth Kant had given her for the cast.

The triangle was awkward to tie one-handed, but she managed it, taking some pressure off her shoulder. She crossed to the kitchen, where she found the first aid kit and wrapped gauze around the cuts on the back of her other forearm. She ate cereal out of the box and stared through the window. Heavy clouds made the space feel cold, robbed of its colors.

Still, the question wouldn't leave her. *What now?*

Now, she supposed, assuming the worst of it was over, she would have to learn to adapt. Begin cleaning up the mess. Learn how to live her life at Gallows Hill. The others had promised her it wouldn't be so bad.

Everyone keeps saying this is the worst the curse has ever been. There must be a reason for that, surely. Something that provoked it. Is it because I moved in? Does it get worse when the ownership changes?

No, she thought. Her presence wasn't a catalyst. It had been bad before she'd even arrived. Bad enough to claim her parents.

Then, what? Kant didn't say anything had changed. From what I can gather, the business has been running the same way it always has. The same routines, the same habits. Even down to using lanterns in the tunnels.

She wished she'd been able to ask her parents about it. Kant, Nora, Ray, and Andrew had tried to step in, to coach her through how everything worked, but they'd admitted they knew relatively little about the curse compared to her parents.

The curse. And the blessing. Because there are two sides to it, aren't there?

Margot lifted her head to look at the house around her. The Hulls had prospered. More than they had any right to on a windswept hill and with disaster nipping at their heels. She had to think that wasn't coincidental. The curse and the prosperity were tied together: two sides to a coin.

So…what now?

She could make a life here for herself, just like her forebearers had. Lock the doors and cover the windows during the bad bits. Order in groceries. Make friends with the people who worked there.

Her parents had done it. From what she'd heard, they'd managed to be happy a lot of the time.

And then?

She would try to make the best life she could.

She didn't have a choice.

Even in death, the hill wouldn't release her.

Margot's mouth twisted as she searched through the drawers for large plastic bags and tore one off the roll. She'd need to wash some of the clothes she'd left in the upstairs bathroom or she'd risk running out of things to wear. Not that there would be much salvageable.

Dregs of dirt still lingered in the bathtub, even after rinsing. That could be left for another day. She crouched to pick up the discarded clothes.

They were all stained. She'd put them through a spin in the washing machine, just to see whether they could be saved. As she moved to stuff the jacket into the bag, she felt something solid in its pockets. She pulled out the bottle of holy water—entirely forgotten the previous night—and a small parcel wrapped in a dish towel.

The journal.

Margot took care as she unwrapped the book. One corner had become dampened when she fell in the ditch, but the damage wasn't extensive. She placed it on the bathroom sink as she carefully flipped through the pages.

I wish she'd thought to write her name or even the date. I don't even know if she's one of the original Hulls or whether she comes from Ephraim's line. My own line.

Margot lifted her head. Dark, sallow eyes looked back, filled with weariness, filled with resignation, and Margot felt an unexpected stab of frustration at herself. She didn't want to think she was the kind of person who just *gave up.* And yet, wasn't that what she was doing? Accepting her lot in life and trying to find a way to bear it, just like the past generations.

She looked back at the book. It had been lost for hundreds of years, but it was a snapshot into the winery's earliest days. It had to be able to tell her something, surely. Some little clue about what was happening.

The hill was under a curse. And curses could be broken, couldn't they?

She held the journal close to her chest as she turned and jogged for the stairs.

40.

Margot chewed her lower lip as she entered the kitchen. She retrieved a butter knife from the drawer and sat at the table, just as she had on the night she found the journal, and began prying its pages apart.

> I afked for fugar plums but papa faid we are faving them...

> The rain feems to never end...

> I feel bleffed to live on top of the hill, thofe in town cannot fee half fofar...

Margot rubbed her palm into her eyes. The journal entries were engrossing in a strange kind of way. They were all small and self-contained. The writer rarely talked about the town meetings or news arriving from across the country. Instead, she documented her life. The little things. The hopes, the disappointments, the small treats she snuck from the kitchen.

Margot had kept a journal of her own for a few years while living with her grandmother. She'd lost it long ago, but she imagined it would read very similarly to the unnamed girl's. It was almost uncomfortably intimate how well she was growing to know the young teen.

At the same time, she wished the journal would give her something more substantial. Names, instead of *papa* and *my brother*. Dates. Any mention of a curse or of having to lock her windows or of seeing strange people outside.

Maybe she didn't. Maybe she lived through a period when the curse wasn't active.

Margot peeled another page. The writing style abruptly changed. What had been painstakingly neat—the kind of hand being maintained by a girl who had tutoring lessons—suddenly became larger, rougher, looser. At first glance Margot thought the journal might have been picked up by someone else, but she recognized the strange lilt to the *E*s. This was still the same person… She just no longer had the time or space of mind to focus on form.

As Margot read the entry, she understood why.

"Papa is dead…" Margot leaned over the table, her elbow propped on the white surface and her hand bracing her head. "We were asleep when there was a loud banging at the door. Uncle. He hit Papa with an axe."

Margot let her eyes close as understanding washed over her. The journal belonged to one of Ezra Hull's two daughters, most likely the youngest. The original Hulls, the family who had first bought the hill and prospered.

She knew what fate awaited the girl. Part of her didn't want to read any further. But another part of her desperately needed to know.

"Mother told me to run, but I saw lights outside the home. Our cousins have surrounded us. I got into the attic. I am here now, with my candle and my book and enough ink to finish this page. I do not know what will become of us. Mother ran to the shed. I saw Uncle follow her there. He came out after a minute. Mother has not."

The writing was growing messier, more frantic. The letters wavered as the girl's hand shook.

"Jeremiah went for town. The lights followed him a little way down the hill, then they stopped. I pray he made it away from them. I pray he was fast enough. I heard Giles yell at someone downstairs, and then there was an axe, and he has been quiet since then. I do not know where Constance is."

I can't imagine what that must have been like. Hidden in the attic while your family is killed one by one. Knowing they'll begin to look for you soon.

"I fear Uncle Ephraim will hide us all and take the house. He has wanted our home for a long time, Papa said. I fear he will hide us in a place we will never be found."

That was an uncomfortable strike of perceptiveness. There had been a search of the property, but the original Hull family had never been uncovered.

"I am writing this all down so that, should this night be my last, he will not be able to escape from his crimes. I hear them on the stairs now, opening doors as they search for me. I will hide my journal here and pray that someone might discover it. When you do, bring it to the town. Let Uncle Ephraim's wickedness be known. May God be with us."

There was a date beneath. November 26, 1772.

Margot slid her knife beneath that page, prying it free, but she already knew that would be the last entry in the journal. The rest of the book was empty. The youngest daughter had achieved what she'd wanted: hiding the journal in a place her uncle wouldn't find it. But that had come at the cost of the message remaining hidden for more than two hundred years.

More than two hundred years...

She stared at the date in the journal, then opened her phone to double-check the date there. "Oh," she managed, then she was on her feet, journal clutched protectively under one arm as she pressed through the front door and raced down the hill.

Sore muscles in her legs ached as she pushed them to jog, but Margot barely noticed. Her mind ran in circles, picking at the problem that was Gallows Hill, a furious pit of hope burning in her chest even as doubt tried to flood over it. Doubt that she'd gotten it wrong. Doubt that this was bigger than she could handle.

At the staff buildings, she turned right to find the accommodations. Nora said she and Ray would be in the final house along the row. They were small but tidy buildings, modern and with space for a small garden around them. Margot followed them, arms folded around herself, until she came to their end.

The last house had its lights on. Soft conversation floated through an open window, which abruptly cut out as Margot climbed the front step. The door opened before Margot even had a chance to knock.

"Margot! What a surprise!" Nora was smiling, but Margot could tell it took effort.

"I'm really sorry to disturb you." Margot cleared her throat. "Especially with…everything that's happened. But no one knows the estate or its history as well as you do. And I think I've found something."

A chair creaked, and then a familiar voice said, "Margot."

Nora moved aside so Kant could join her in the doorway. He'd showered and changed into clean clothes, like her, but he looked bone weary. She didn't think he'd had any rest since she'd last seen him.

"I thought you'd be asleep," she said.

"Can't." He ran his fingers through shaggy hair, then said, "What were you needing?"

She bit her lip. She'd promised she wouldn't involve him any further. But she needed to know more about the estate, and Kant had lived there longer than anyone.

"I don't need people walking on eggshells around me," Kant said, a hint of roughness to his voice. "What's brought you out here?"

Margot raised the book. "I found something in the house. And I need to know more about its history. About the curse. Records, photos, dates."

Nora glanced up at Kant, fidgeting at the door's edge. "It gets worse when we talk about it…"

"I think I figured something out," Margot said. "And…it might help. I hope."

Nora met Margot's gaze, a crease running between her eyebrows, then took a slow, deep breath. "Right then. We'll want to go down to the store. It has a lot of the old photos. It'll give Ray some peace too."

"Mm." Kant reached for his sweater, which he slung around his shoulders. He shut the door behind himself as he joined them on the drive.

"Are you sure you want to come?" Margot asked him. "You should get some rest—"

"You sound just like Andrew," he said, sighing, and fell into pace next to her.

Margot kept one eye on the sun's angle as they walked. It was lower than she would have liked. There were still a few hours to go until dusk, but that felt like an uncomfortably narrow margin to play with.

The sign on the store's front door read *Closed*, but Nora pulled a set of keys out of her pocket and slipped them into the lock. Lights flickered on overhead as she turned switches.

"Right," she said, setting the keys down on the counter and indicating the stools. "I'm at your disposal."

Kant took a seat, resting one arm on the wood, while Margot gently laid out the journal. "I found this in the attic a few days ago. And I finished reading it today. I'm almost certain it belonged to Ezra Hull's youngest daughter."

"Esther," Nora said, and crossed to the gallery of photographs. She took down the ink drawing representing the family and laid it on the counter ahead of Margot. Six faces looked out at her. Ezra and Louisa stood in the center. Two sons to their right. Two daughters to their left. Margot found her eyes drawn to the youngest. The ink drawing was sparse, implying shapes more than detailing them, but she still found herself fixated by the dark blots used to represent Esther's eyes.

"She and her family were killed by Ephraim after all." Margot turned to the journal's final page and leaned back while Kant and Nora examined the writing. "She wrote about it. And look at this. The final paragraph. *I will hide my journal here and pray that someone might discover it. When you do, bring it to the town. Let Uncle Ephraim's wickedness be known.*"

"It may be too late for a formal conviction, but we can grant part of her wish at least," Nora said. She leaned close over the book, squinting to make out the jagged, scrawled words. "We can show it to the town, so to speak. Scan the pages and put it up on display here. Let visitors read about what happened. If that's what you want."

"Yes!" Margot drew a slow, ragged breath. "I think this is why the land's cursed. Esther lived on it for years and never once mentioned strange happenings in her journal."

Nora glanced up. "We don't see the Hulls at night, though. We see the early townspeople who were hanged."

"I know. But I think…" Margot hesitated, trying to put the disjointed, fragmented idea together in her head. "I think they're a part of it. If you want to believe that death leaves a bad energy in a place, the hangings did exactly that. They poisoned the land over more than a hundred years. Turned it bad. But that alone wasn't enough for a curse. That came with the Hull family murders. Because to have a curse, you need someone *to* curse."

"The descendants," Kant murmured.

"Exactly. Until the journal, people suspected Ephraim was responsible for his brother's disappearance but had no proof. Esther has not only given us the answer, but also told us something else: Ephraim wasn't alone. He brought his sons."

Nora turned the book, reading the blotted pages quickly. "Oh. You're right. Ephraim had a large family. Six sons, four daughters. By the time Ezra's family vanished, the boys would have been teenagers and young adults."

"The hangings poisoned the land," Margot said. "The murders gave that energy a channel to focus on. Ephraim and his children. His descendants. For as many generations as it took to see justice."

"Eleven generations," Nora said, one hand over her mouth. "Twelve counting you."

"We always believed the curse came from the hangings," Kant said. "That Ezra Hull and his family were victims of it."

"That might still be true," Margot said. She shrugged, uncomfortable. "I might be wrong about the curse starting with the murders. And that's why I wanted to talk to Nora. To reference some dates."

She pointed to the date written below the entry. *November 26, 1772.*

"Ah," Nora murmured. "Yes, that's the last day the family was ever seen. We celebrate the winery's founding each year, but I've never paid that much attention to the date the original Hulls went missing, except when guests ask."

"Turns out it might be important," Margot said, and the words tasted bitter on her tongue. "It's the twenty-sixth of November today."

41.

"Today's the anniversary," Nora said, frowning at the faded pages.

Margot nodded. "And that's something I needed to check. Was the twenty-sixth the day the family was last seen or the day they were reported missing?"

"Last seen," Nora said, glancing up.

"Okay." Margot tried to smile to hide the deep uneasiness running through her. "That's what I was afraid of. Esther used the previous day's date in her journal. She went to bed on the twenty-sixth but died in the early hours of the twenty-seventh. Which means, if I'm right, the curse is going to reach its peak tonight."

"The anniversary of the deaths." Nora, frowning, turned away from the journal. "It makes sense. Does this happen every year? I would have thought we'd make the connection before now—"

"No," Kant said. "I've noticed things become slightly more tense toward the end of the year, but nothing like this. Not in the thirty years I've been here."

"I think it's because this year's anniversary is more important than most," Margot said. "Seventeen seventy-two. That's exactly two hundred and fifty years ago. A quarter millennium since they died."

"Oh" was all Nora said. Kant turned aside, his eyes heavy.

"It's the connection I was looking for," Margot said. She pulled a stool out from under the counter and perched on its edge, feet crossed at the ankles. "I wanted to know why the curse is so much worse right now. And, well…it's because my ancestor killed a family and stole their land exactly two and a half centuries ago."

Nora turned away, disappearing into the store's back room. Margot heard a filing cabinet open, then Nora returned, carrying a thick binder. She opened it on the counter, next to the journal, and began thumbing through.

Kant nodded toward it. "Is that…?"

"Births, deaths, and marriages." She kept thumbing. "We have a summary somewhere. Ah—here. Yes."

Margot craned forward. Nora had opened to a ledger filled with small, neatly written names and dates. Nora ran her fingertip down the plastic protective screen, lips twitching as she silently read. Margot glanced toward the window. The sun was growing low.

Nora took a heavy breath as she looked up from the paper. "I think you're right. The Hulls have always been followed by death. It's sometimes hard to tell what comes from the regular kind of misfortune and what comes from the curse, since they're all given natural causes: *Fell into machinery. Drowned in creek. Kick to the head by a horse.* But Ray and I have gotten pretty good at guessing which ones weren't actually accidents. And a lot of them—a *lot* of them—are clustered at the fifty-year marks. Five in 1822, from illness. Another group in 1872: six died in a fire."

"We never noticed the pattern," Kant said softly.

"Because we never talk about the curse." Nora, still bent over the page, frowned. "And the Hulls always had large families to make up for the deaths. In some ways, they had exceptional good luck. There were almost no recorded deaths during childbirth. Almost no infant mortality either, even back when it was more common. There were multiple lines of Hulls living in the house at a time during the eighteen hundreds."

The blessing and the curse, wrapped around one another. For generations, my family has accepted that price.

"Tonight is the night Esther and her family died," Margot said, speaking carefully. "Which means it's going to be as bad as it can get. Unless I can find a way to break the curse."

Nora glanced at the still-open journal. "You think she wants us to fulfill her last wish, to show her journal to the town?"

"That's what I was hoping." Margot swallowed thickly. "But I'm not so sure now. Six of the Hulls died that night. And I'm pretty sure all six of them brought this curse into existence."

They were silent for a moment, staring at the old, age-faded pages. Then Kant said, "Trying won't hurt."

"No," Nora said, suddenly decisive. "If there's even a small chance—Margot, it's too late to get people into the store to read the book today, but we have a website and social media pages. I can put the journal up on those."

"Good." Margot pushed the book toward her. "Scan the pages and write a transcript as well. Put it on the website's front page. Boost the social media posts. She wants people to know what happened. We'll spread the word as far as we can."

"I'll do that. Just wait a moment." Nora took the book, holding it gently as she half walked, half ran into the back room.

The sounds of a scanner rose in the background. Margot ran her fingers across her still-damp hair as she tried to think.

Esther wanted the world to know the truth. But that wasn't all the curse was based on, surely. The family had been killed, their home stolen. Their murderers had stepped into their shoes, claiming the wealth and respect they had been robbed of. An announcement on a website felt inadequate in the face of that.

What do they want? What would it take to break the curse?

Margot thought she knew the answer. It was achingly simple, and nightmarishly complex all at once.

They wanted justice.

But how did you give a family justice two and a half centuries after their deaths? The killers were long gone. So were their children, and their children's children.

There was only one descendant left. Margot.

She could tell the truth to anyone who would listen. She could arrange for gravestones to be placed in the cemetery. She could donate the winery's proceeds.

It still didn't seem like enough.

Ephraim stole the land and the house, so in retaliation, the curse holds his descendants here. Squeezes them. Kills them.

Until they're all gone.

Ezra's lineage had been snuffed out in a single night. The curse was going to kill Ephraim's line in return.

That would be justice.

The scanner continued to whirr in the background. Nora must have been capturing earlier pages from the journal too. The noise was starting to ache in the back of Margot's head, and she abruptly found it hard to breathe.

"I need some air." She made it as far as the door before hesitating. The sun was low. The sky's blue was beginning to turn dusky. Chills crawled over her skin, leaving her feeling vulnerable and cold, and she glanced back at Kant.

"Want some company?" he asked, and Margot nodded.

He followed her outside. They only traveled a half dozen paces from the store until they reached the signpost. There were decorative barrels there, and she and Kant leaned back on them. Margot crossed her arms over her chest, staring toward the trees lining the driveway and, beyond, the sky.

Kant waited beside her, silent, patient. Margot was grateful for it. She felt like she needed to get some of her thoughts out of her head, but the words were difficult to gather.

"Do you think my parents knew the curse was caused by the murders?" she asked.

Kant rolled his shoulders, loosening the muscles, then said, "I can't say for sure. But they knew a lot they never told me."

She nodded. There was something else weighting on her, though. Something that felt almost petty compared to everything else but was hard to shake. She dabbed her tongue across her lips, tasting the tang of old blood where they'd split.

"I never thought my family were heroes. But I didn't believe they were, you know, evil either."

She glanced up at him. He was as inscrutable as ever, but he didn't try to interrupt, so she continued.

"When I was younger, I tried to imagine what sort of people my parents might be. And I wanted to believe they were just human. A little selfish. A little stubborn. Flawed but no worse than most of us. But now I'm starting to think I was wrong. How do you cope with knowing your family might have been a part of something truly horrific?" She glanced aside. "Not just Mom and Dad, but…Ephraim. I keep trying to think of him as someone I'm not connected to. Someone I can look at from a distance and judge. But…he's my ancestor. This is what I'm built from. Every generation until me, *including me*, has benefited from what he did back then. And there's nothing I can do to escape it."

Kant breathed in slowly, held it for a moment, then let it out in a lingering sigh. Together, they watched a pair of birds fly overhead, darting and diving as they made their way to the next patch of trees.

"Some people believe you can't escape what's in your blood," Kant said at last. "That evil lives on in our genes or something of the sort. But I don't think we're shackled like that. We can change our legacy when we put good into the world to replace the bad. Sometimes it takes a lot of work. More than you, personally, should have been responsible for. But it can be done."

Margot's throat felt too full for her to speak, so she only nodded, dragging one of her sneakers through the dirt to form lines in the sand.

Kant scratched around the edge of the patch over his eye. His voice dropped lower. "For what it's worth, your parents weren't bad people. They were what you said. A little selfish. A little stubborn. They inherited a problem bigger than either of them knew how to deal with. If they were guilty of any crime, it was of just going on as they were. They never tried to fix any of it." A glance. "You might be able to, though."

The door behind them clattered as Nora forced it open. She held the journal reverently as she approached Margot. "I've scanned everything in there. The final pages are up on our site and on social media. I'm going to start work on the transcription now and add that as soon as I can."

"That's perfect. How long do you think the transcription will take?"

"Shouldn't be more than ten minutes. It's not long."

Margot glanced toward the horizon. The sun was getting low, but they still had time. "Do that, then go straight back to Ray. You should get indoors before the sun sets and stay there until dawn."

"I'll do that." Nora glanced down at the journal. "Would you like this back?"

"No. Keep it somewhere safe in the store. We'll find a way to preserve it and display it. In a frame, maybe."

Nora nodded, then disappeared back into the shop. Margot looked up at Kant. "The same goes for all of us. We should get indoors before nightfall."

"You think the journal won't be enough," he said.

She turned back to the drive, feeling the shadows from the trees' dead branches graze her as she slowly began the climb. "No."

Kant stayed beside her. "You have your phone."

"Yes." She already knew, with complete certainty, she wouldn't be calling Kant that night. Or any of the others. Whatever came for her after dark, she'd have to face on her own.

As they neared the path leading to the winery, two figures appeared on the road ahead. Andrew, his hair combed and a new, cleaner vest in place, walked beside Witchety. Her loose, layered, moss-green dress billowed in the wind as Marsh, leashed, trotted at her side.

"I didn't know you were here!" Margot called as they drew closer. "I thought you must have picked up Marsh hours ago."

"I've been tramping all over looking for him," Witchety said, a twist to her lips. "Went up to the house first. Utterly empty. Thought for a moment you might have whisked off in the night and taken my dog with you."

"It's a temptation." Margot bent to kiss Marsh's silky head and was rewarded with eager, humid licks in return. "Thank you for letting him stay with me."

Witchety made a soft scoffing noise. "Of course. But I'm taking him back now. I don't mind lending things out on occasion, but I missed this one too much."

Margot's heart hurt at the thought, but it was for the best. Marsh had been a small glimmer of comfort through the night…and she was fairly sure she had her life to thank him for. But Gallows Hill was not safe for dogs. Not even ones as good as the golden retriever. He leaned into her pats, adoring eyes gazing up at her, as she whispered a goodbye into his soft fur. Then she stood, breathing slowly to hide her growing anxiety.

"The Watcher's gone," she said. Witchety deserved to know, even if Margot couldn't tell her what had happened to it. "I'm sorry."

Beneath the cataracts, Witchety's eyes were sharp as she scanned Margot's face, and Margot thought she guessed more than the words implied. "I suppose your parents didn't show it much respect."

"Well…" She didn't know what kind of respect a monstrous effigy was supposed to be given, but it seemed to have spent most of its life tucked away and hidden beneath a cloth.

"Talismans lose their power eventually." Witchety reached under her shawl, to the small bag she kept there, and pulled out her threaded trinkets. "You have to cherish them, value them, if you want them to keep working. Otherwise, all the strength bleeds out of them and they become just another pile of junk. Your parents had the Watcher for years. I hoped it would last longer than this, but…"

Margot swallowed, knitting her fingers together. She hoped she wasn't asking too much. "Witchety…could I borrow your talisman? Just for tonight? And could you show me how the blessing works?"

Something that might have been a raspy chuckle escaped Witchety but was swallowed by coughs before it could fully form. She slipped her talisman back into her bag as she caught her breath. "This won't do you much good. You'd be better making one of your own. It's got to be something special to you, understand? Keys to things or places you care about. Your favorite spoon, the one you use every morning. Bones from animals that lived free and wild around your home. Buttons that belonged to a good friend."

"I…" Margot's mind was racing. She swallowed. "I don't have any of that."

"Child, it doesn't have to be those *exactly*. Just whatever has meaning for you. Small things that make you feel something. They can be happy feelings or bittersweet ones, just as long as they're strong. Thread them together with love and care. Treat it like it's powerful, and it will *be* powerful."

"Thank you. And…the blessing. Is that something I can learn to do? I still have the bottle of holy water."

Witchety's laughter was loud and rough this time. One of her bony hands came out to grip Margot's wrist to steady herself. "Mercy. There's no method to it. If you try very hard, and if you believe it works, it does. I never studied these things. They tend to run on instinct more than anything, I've found."

She gave Margot's wrist a final squeeze, then pushed away, Marsh at her heels as she turned back to the drive.

"*There's no method to it…*" Andrew muttered as soon as Witchety was far enough to be out of earshot. "And all these years I really believed she knew what she was doing."

"The blessings *do* have an impact," Kant said mildly. "So maybe she does."

"Mm." Andrew's eyes narrowed behind his glasses. "I thought *you* were resting."

"I am. In my own way." Kant gently patted his shoulder, then glanced back at Margot. "Would you like some company until sundown?"

That was less than twenty minutes away, by her calculation. She hated the thought of being left alone, but she'd also feel better if she knew Kant was sheltered in his own place for the night. "Thanks, but I'll be all right. I've got a lot to think over. Can you update Andrew on everything? And make sure everyone gets somewhere safe before nightfall?"

"I'll do that. Call us if you need us."

She made to step away, then hesitated. "Kant?"

"Yes?"

Heat rose across Margot's face. She didn't know where to look. "Could I...have one of your buttons?"

His eyebrows rose lightly. He fixed his hand around one of the large, black sweater buttons and pulled. It broke free from its threads with a snap, and he passed it to Margot without comment.

"Thanks," she managed, holding the button tightly. "I'll see you tomorrow."

"See you then," he said as he and Andrew turned back to their homes. "Good luck, Margot."

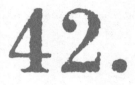

42.

Margot paused on the threshold of the Gallows Hill house. She held her good hand tight against her chest, the button clasped inside as though it were a gem. Treat the items with care, Witchety had said. She intended to.

Ahead of her, the hallway stretched, growing dim as the closed doors and curtained windows blocked out all natural light. Far in the distance, she thought she caught the glint of something. Two lights, very much like eyes, hidden in among the shadows. She blinked and they were gone.

"Ezra Hull," Margot murmured to herself. "Killed in his hallway with an axe."

She began to walk through the house, speaking out loud. "Louisa Hull, killed in the shed. Jeremiah, attempting to run to town, caught and killed in the trees."

She remembered seeing a hint of movement in a block of trees, near where she'd found the axe. She'd been so focused on it that she'd misstepped and fallen into the underground passageways.

The axe she'd found hadn't been used to kill him. It was old, but not enough to have lasted outdoors for two hundred years. That was a very small relief. She wouldn't have wanted to think about it being in her bedroom, otherwise.

She reached the laundry and paused there, letting her eyes adjust to the dark. "Constance?" she hazarded. "Or Giles?"

The room was silent, but she could still remember the rapid breathing, the muffled whisper of *I don't want to die*. Giles, she thought.

She turned back to the hall, and as she traced her path back to the kitchen, she turned her eyes toward the ceiling.

Constance had died in the hallway behind the living room, then. And Esther, of course, had been in the attic. Her blood had spilled on the wood, and although Ephraim and his family must have cleaned the house thoroughly before anyone arrived to search it, they had not been able to eradicate all traces of the youngest daughter from the house's highest floor.

Six Hulls. Six spirits, still lingering in the home, still haunting the halls they had once called their own, their eyes shining out of the shadows as they watched the usurper's descendants take it over.

She shivered as she returned to the kitchen. One of the drawers held a small box of string. She placed it on the table, along with the button, then went in search of other items that might have enough significance to act as a ward.

Margot's Tape was still in the VCR player. She lifted it out and carefully, painstakingly peeled the label off, tongue pressed between her teeth as she fought to not damage the sticker. It was old, its glue weak, and it gave way easily.

Upstairs, she found her hair clip. It was one of the few claw designs that would hold on to her hair, and she wore it almost every day.

Her travel cases still stood against the bedroom's wall. She opened one of the zipper pouches. Inside was her most valued possession. Wrapped in a small silk handkerchief was her nana's wedding ring. Living in an apartment, she hadn't been able to keep much from the woman who had raised her, but that was the keepsake she'd always clung to.

Then, at the window, she removed the key from the padlock. Witchety said the emotions were allowed to be bittersweet, and she hoped the key would count. It represented the night she learned about the curse, about her family, and about her new life. It represented her parents and their efforts to keep her safe.

Finally, she returned to the kitchen and chose one of the photos from the fridge. It was the picture Kant had shown her on her first day there: her parents, leaning into each other, a fragmented wisp of Margot's hair visible at the torn side. One corner held a stain from where she'd spilled coffee on it.

There weren't many items, but laid out together on the table, Margot's heart ached to look at them all.

She pulled up a chair and unrolled a length of string. Dusk had set in, heavy and dark beyond the window, and she was hyperaware of the press of passing time. She didn't hurry, though. Witchety said the talisman needed to be woven with love and care. She lingered over each item, her fingers trembling as she tied careful knots through and around them.

The video tape's label formed a neat scroll when she rolled it up, with the string cinching its middle. The button glittered as she wove the string through its holes. The photograph was the hardest to tie; she didn't want to fold it or damage it and finally settled for puncturing small holes in opposite corners and running the string through them, so it bobbed on the line like a flag.

When she finished, she raised it up. The loop of string held each precious item at an interval, like jewels on a necklace. She wrapped the string around her wrist, tying it there so that its talismans hung over the back of her hand. Then she stood.

Night had arrived. She hadn't made any of the preparations she was supposed to—closing windows, snuffing out lights. And she didn't plan to.

"I think…" Her voice broke. She moved into the hallway and faced the house, the rectangle of light from the kitchen washing over her, a spotlight in a void of darkness. "I think I know what I need to do to give you peace."

She didn't speak loudly, but her voice echoed through the house. She hoped the spirits would be listening. And she hoped she was right.

The curse would exist until the last of Ephraim's line died.

Or until the spirits found justice.

Margot ran her fingertips across her talisman, touching each item in turn, gathering strength from them. The original Hull family had died here, in this home, but their bodies had never been found.

Not during the initial searches. Not during the renovations.

Their bones were still somewhere on the hill, buried in unmarked graves. And Margot thought she knew where.

Her legs had gone to water. She closed her eyes, waiting for the wave of fear to wash over her, until she thought she could speak again. "I'm going to try to find your bodies. I'm going to search the underground passageways."

Her mind conjured images of them. The dark. The damp. Far underground, layers of dirt above, pressing down on her, threatening to collapse.

But it was the only location that made sense to her. The original Hull family had constructed most of the underground chambers before the formalized, official cellar had been built. They were a labyrinth of bare soil and collapsed paths.

Nora and Ray had said the police searched the property after Ezra's family was reported missing. They wouldn't have just looked in the house; they would have searched the hill for recently disturbed soil. For signs of a hastily dug burial site.

Ephraim had hidden his murdered relatives in a place where none of the searches could have easily located them. And the only place that presented that opportunity was the underground maze.

No one used the old passageways since the larger, airier cellar had been installed. They were deemed unsafe. Blocked off. The bodies could have easily languished there for two hundred and fifty years, hidden in some easily forgotten corner.

Margot exhaled slowly as she turned to the door. She knew how foolish this was. She didn't know the tunnels. Many of them had collapsed. Her chances of finding the bodies were slim at best.

But she still had to try.

She placed the bottle of holy water into her pocket and switched on her poor, abused cell phone's flashlight function. Then she stepped outside, carefully closing the door behind herself.

The tunnels were supposed to weave right through the hill, even underneath the house. Margot circled the building, aiming for the sheds behind it. Her light caught on the grapevine, promising bounty but delivering rot. Insects flicked through her beam, tiny beads of light set against the dark. It was almost shocking how quickly the last of the daylight had faded.

The two sheds waited for her beneath leafless, spreading trees. The loose door rocked on its hinges as its sharp, metallic wails cut through the night. Margot put her head down as she stepped into the other shed.

She raised her light high, darting it across the tangling storage heaps. At the back, near where she'd found the stepladder, was a shovel. She stepped over old planters to reach it.

The wails were growing thicker, discordant. Margot kept her face to the shed's back as she lifted the shovel. She tucked it beneath her cast arm, wedging it against her side, and then slipped the bottle of holy water out of her pocket.

It had a small cork sealing its top. She pulled it out with her teeth, then, holding it in the hand that was wrapped in the talisman, turned back to the door.

Two piercing white eyes stared into her, less than a foot away.

Margot's voice choked. She grit her teeth and slowly, carefully, let several drops of the water fall. "Please show me mercy tonight." Her words were rough, gasping, barely audible, but she pushed on. "I want to help. I want to make this right."

She didn't aim the phone's light at the specter, no matter how badly she wanted light. It felt as though it would be disrespectful. Margot directed her beam at the floor instead.

She could see the body's ragged edges against the open doorway. The long, windswept hair, tied back by a headscarf. The outline of the dress. The shoulders, quivering with each wrenching cry.

"I want to do the right thing for you and your family," Margot whispered.

The eyes shone, narrow points of light in a void of darkness, then blinked out. The path to the door was clear again. Margot's breath choked in her lungs as she moved forward, tripping over unseen debris on the shed's floor. As she stepped outside, she heard the rusty, whining metal noise break into a shriek: *"Ez-ra."*

Louisa had died weeping for her slain husband. She must have entered the shed knowing she wouldn't be coming out again. Ephraim had been close behind her, pursuing her, still carrying the axe that dripped red with her husband's blood.

Margot clutched the shovel against her chest, one thumb pressed across the bottle of holy water's open top, phone clutched in her cast hand's clumsy fingers, as she ran from the shed. She only slowed when the wailing metal had fallen out of her hearing range, then doubled over, breathing heavily.

Think it through. Ephraim was working with his sons. They would have helped him move the bodies out of the house. But he wouldn't have wanted to carry them too far. There must be an entrance to the tunnels somewhere close by.

Her phone's light couldn't reach far. She covered it, blotting the light out, as she let her eyes adjust to the moonlight.

A thicker bank of trees grew around the house's back. As Margot scanned them, she glimpsed something that didn't mesh with the trunks. It was too far away to be certain, but she thought it might be a post. A marker. She set out toward it.

Even at that point, she felt doubt. The curse would reach its pinnacle that night. If she could just survive—hide well enough, outmaneuver the dead ones, just as she had the night before—she would be granted relative peace afterward. It wouldn't grow that bad again for at least fifty years, by which time she might already be gone from natural causes.

But that was exactly what every other generation of Hull had done. Accepted the curse as the price to pay for wealth. Endured it. Passed the home and the business down to the next in line.

She couldn't—wouldn't—live like that.

She wasn't sure she would even have the option to.

Death had nipped at her heels the past two nights. She felt its touch across her body: in the sprained ankle, in the gash across her shoulder, in her broken arm. She'd pushed her luck and her strength as far as they could go and had run out of both. This wasn't just a chance to right past wrongs—it was her final chance to escape the fate that had been scripted for her.

Kant believed a person had the power to change their legacy. Put good into the world to outweigh evil. She hoped he was right.

Even if it meant descending into the dark pits, knowing she might never come out again.

Margot reached the post. It stood alone, rotting from age, listing at an angle as the earth beneath it sank. She shone her light at the grass and found an area that grew thin and sickly. When she scraped her shoe over it, she uncovered decaying wooden boards beneath.

Her skin felt alive with electric shivers. She placed the shovel, bottle, and her phone on the ground, nestled into a clump of crabgrass, then knelt. The wood's outer layer flaked away under her fingernails as she felt around for its edge.

The wood groaned as she lifted it and sent showers of dirt flowing into the dark pit below. Margot put her shoulder under it to tip it fully open, then sat back, panting, as she stared into the hole.

You have to do this.

Her fingers were turning numb. She picked up her phone and angled its light into the hole. She could only see down a few feet. A wooden ladder, decayed, was set into the wall, but very little else was visible. Margot slipped the phone into her pocket, along with the corked bottle of water. Then she pushed the shovel over and flinched as she heard it hit the base.

Do it. Now. Or you never will.

Already she could feel the fear locking up her limbs, making her chest tighter. Her mind and her heart begged in tandem for her to just stay where she was. But that wasn't the promise she'd made.

She lowered her legs into the dark pit, then shuffled forward, easing herself over the edge in increments, until she was supported only by her arms.

She didn't know how deep the drop might be. Her light hadn't been able to reach the bottom. Margot squeezed her eyes closed, each breath coming as a narrow gasp as her arms lowered her as far as they were able.

And then she let go.

43.

Her stomach lurched into her throat as she dropped into free fall. Her legs kicked at air. Her outstretched hands grasped at nothing.

Then she hit the ground. The breath rushed out of her as she rolled to her side. Margot lay for a second, shivering as the hundreds of tiny aches across her body flared and faded, then cautiously sat up.

A square of moonlight hovered above her, like a window to the real world. It was the only thing that was visible. Margot couldn't even see her own hands when she lifted them, and it was possible to imagine the drop had blotted her out of existence, erased her from the earth.

She pulled the phone out of her pocket with shaking hands. Its beam of light trailed over the shovel, laying at her side. The passageway continued to her left and to her right. Opposite were rough stone walls. Farther along, though, the tunnel changed to bare dirt, crumbling and uneven.

An arm hung from the soil.

Margot's mouth was dry. She held still, her light fixed on the shape, not daring to move.

The limb emerged from the wall at waist height and hung down, bending at the elbow, so that its old, cracked fingers grazed the floor. It was old. Gray. The fingernails were overgrown and caked with dirt.

Margot stomped her foot on the floor. Echoes traveled down the tunnel in both directions. The arm didn't move.

She crept forward, holding the holy water in her cast hand and the light in her other. The flesh was sallow and wrinkled. The soil around it didn't look disturbed. It was as though it had grown there, like a root pressing out through the damp ground.

Margot reached out and touched the forearm with her index finger.

It was as cold as the grave. But it wasn't dead. At her touch, the arm twitched, then abruptly writhed back, withdrawing inside the hole, the long nails inches from Margot as it moved.

She flinched back, her teeth clenched as her heart thundered. The light shook as she tried to focus it on the arm-sized hole in the wall.

Something shifted inside. Against all wisdom, against all better judgment, Margot crept forward again.

A mass of flesh writhed behind the hole, twisting, squirming. It came to a halt with a blanched white eye fixed in the opening, staring out at her.

Margot's hands shook as she fought to remove the cork from the bottle. She tipped it, letting just a drop fall outside the hole. "Please forgive the intrusion. Let me pass in peace."

The face didn't shift, but the eye twitched to follow her movements as Margot backed away. She retreated to the square of light beneath the open trapdoor and picked up her shovel, tucking it back under the arm with the cast. Her whole body felt clammy and sick. She did her best not to look back as she continued along the passage, away from the thing inside the dirt.

The path led downward. Long stretches of bare soil pressed in at either side, sometimes interrupted by wooden supports, sometimes torn open by heavy, tangled roots. She found an offshoot to the right and followed it, only to find her way blocked. The tunnel had collapsed, clumping soil and rocks larger than her body filling the space. She turned back.

What am I hoping for here?

She ran her tongue across her lips and tasted the sour dirt particles gathering there. She'd had some faint idea of following her instincts. Of being able to guess which passages Ephraim would have chosen during his quest to hide his murdered relatives. Of knowing where to dig.

The passage split, and Margot chose left. It continued to slope downhill, sometimes rapidly enough that steps had been added.

This is a maze. I could spend days down here and still fall short of searching every hall and every chamber.

Her skin crawled, keeping her hyperconscious of how far she'd drifted from the surface. Still the path led farther down, drawing her deeper, dragging her into the hill's darkest recesses.

These passages couldn't all have been built by Ezra, surely. She stepped into a cellar and faced bare walls and bare floors, stains marking where barrels had once stood. *Ephraim and his descendants must have continued them, expanded them. I need to find the original parts. The oldest areas.*

As her eyes glanced over the endless tracks of bare earth and rotting wood supports, all of them vague and flickering in her weak light, she wondered how that would be possible. The passageways were starting to blend together. Sometimes they narrowed. Sometimes they took strange turns and seemed to double back on themselves. All the while, splits and offshoots robbed Margot of her sense of direction.

She just knew she was deep. She could feel the soil's weight above her, heavy enough to crush even her bones if it were to collapse.

Margot staggered, eyes closed as she drew in sparse, aching gasps. The panic was rising again. Clawing up through her chest, slicing up her insides as it tried to strangle her throat.

In between her gasps, she thought she heard something coming from the passageway behind her.

Something metallic.

Her first thought was of the bells at the house, signaling that the dead were awake, that the fence line had been breached. But there was no way she could still hear that at her depth.

She put her shoulder against the crumbling, rocky wall and bit her tongue as she listened.

Metal jarred together, like a drawer full of cutlery being tipped out. It fell silent for a heartbeat, then the sound repeated, fractionally closer, fractionally louder.

Margot's heart turned to ice. She raised the phone and pointed it to the passage at her back.

It wasn't strong enough to reveal anything except the nearest ten feet of cold, damp earth.

She switched to the camera and set it to flash, then raised it toward the passageway again. A burst of light glared across the tunnel as she took a photo of the void ahead of herself.

Margot had already known what she would see there, but the actual presence itself was so much worse. She lowered her phone, her heart hammering. The screen still displayed the photo she'd taken. Twenty feet of bare, cold tunnel, and at its end, the outline of a deer skull grazing the ceiling, and the distorted glimmer of twisted metal beneath.

"Please, leave me alone." She turned the bottle, letting drops of water fall across the compacted soil. Her hands shook so badly that the string of talismans rattled over her wrist. "Show me mercy. Leave me alone."

The metal rang together as the effigy took another step nearer.

"I'm trying to do the right thing." More water. She'd meant to conserve it, but her muscles had grown as tight as bow strings as she was racked by shivers. She couldn't control the pour. "Please, let me have peace tonight."

The metal rang out again and again. It seemed to be growing faster.

Margot couldn't take it anymore. She clamped her thumb across the bottle's top as she turned and ran.

Her pace was too fast. She couldn't see the changes in the hall in time and hit a corner hard enough that her teeth rattled. Clumps of dirt rained down from above, and Margot hunched, fighting the overwhelming, primal urge to scream.

The metal chimed again and again, unyielding, unstoppable.

She shoved away from the wall. The passageway split. Margot chose the left side and pressed her phone against her chest, blotting out the light, hoping she might be able to lose the unnatural creature in the dark.

She stumbled as she put out her good arm, her fingertips tracing along the wall. Her breathing was loud, panicked. She only hoped the effigy wouldn't be able to hear her under the chimes of its own hideous hide.

Blind but unwilling to slow, she pressed through the dark, feeling her way with her fingertips. They stubbed against wood, then grazed over stone, but she kept moving. The metal rang out behind her, closer than she would have liked, and she couldn't tell whether the effigy had reached the turn yet.

Then her fingers touched something spongy. Soft. Fleshy. Margot jolted backward. She hit the opposite wall. Her panic was a living thing inside of her, choking her, as she turned the phone around to light the pathway.

One of the dead ones loomed out of the wall. He was entirely bald. Holes had been bored into his scalp, revealing a shallow layer of red flesh and then the white of his skull beneath. His jaw twitched, even as the black threads kept it sewn shut.

Only his chest, shoulders, and head were visible. He seemed to loom out of the wall, as though the dirt had spontaneously appeared around him midstep, trapping his arms and legs behind. The blind eyes stared at her, unblinking, black veins creeping in at their edges.

Margot's mouth opened and closed. She knew she was supposed to continue the blessing: pour water, ask for mercy. But her hand wouldn't tilt and no words would leave her mouth. She was locked in perfect terror, her heart threatening to give out from it, every muscle in her body rigid.

And then the man moved forward.

The dirt appeared to bubble around him as he drew one withered leg forward, stepping into the hall. His arms pulled free as they reached toward Margot. She scrambled, but with her back against the wall, she was only able to move to the side. Her feet slipped on loose soil. She fell, landing hard, the bottle of holy water spiraling out of her grip and pouring its contents across the soil.

The dead one continued toward her, and Margot realized she'd fallen between the advancing figures. Metal rang out at her back. The man from the wall blocked the path ahead. She was trapped between the two dead ones, in a passageway barely wide enough for a single person.

"Show me mercy." The words flowed from her in a stream, almost unintelligible, as she repeated every phrase she remembered Witchety using. She clamped her hand around the talisman across her wrist, feeling the smooth button under her fingers, the sharp edges of her nana's wedding ring. "I wish you peace. Show me mercy, please!"

The man from the wall reached out, one enormous, pocked hand grasping for her leg. Margot kicked back, felt her shoe connect with soft flesh, and dragged herself backward as he lunged forward again. The metal was almost deafening. She tilted her head back and saw, upside down, the monstrous deer skull swaying as it moved over her.

The hand fastened over her ankle. He dragged her closer, the atrophied muscles unnaturally powerful as he hauled her across the floor. She bit down on a scream as the fingers dug into her skin, threatening to crack the bones in her foot. His second hand reached out, aiming for her face.

"I'm sorry!" she yelled.

The metal rattles fell silent. The hand froze, inches from her head.

Margot hung there, eyes squinted as she stared into the creased, soil-darkened hand. She couldn't breathe. Pain radiated from her ankle where the dead one pinned her in place.

"I'm...sorry." That was what had stopped them. She didn't understand why. The hand slowly, achingly withdrew. The grip on her ankle loosened but didn't entirely let her go.

They want...an apology?

She stared into the blind, disfigured face ahead of herself. It stared back, the jaw straining behind the black threads. She barely had enough air in her lungs to breathe, but she forced herself to speak.

"I can't imagine what it was like to be hung like that and left on the tree, in full view of the town and the people you once loved." Her mouth was dry. She swallowed to wet it. "Even after your life was taken, you were denied a proper grave. You were forgotten. No matter what you did during life, you deserved more than that. And I'm sorry for it."

The pressure left her ankle entirely. The dead one stood, joints moving slowly, and took a step back from Margot.

She turned, carefully, to see the effigy behind her. Its skin was pulled taut by the threading, agonizing wires. The deer skull stared down at her, unmoving.

They had been hung as criminals. But Kant had said many of the crimes were as petty as stealing to put food on their table. They had not been perfect people. No one could be. But they deserved more than they had been given.

An apology isn't enough, she realized. *They need something sincere. Remorse. Respect. They want the dignity and humanity they weren't afforded during their death.*

She moved, carefully, to pick up her fallen phone. As she stood, both heads turned to watch her. Margot swallowed thickly.

"I wish I could do more to make this right." She blinked. Her eyelashes were powdered with dust. "I don't even know your names. I'm sorry."

She took a tentative step along the hall. The dead ones made no effort to stop her. She squeezed as close to the wall as she could, but even then, she grazed against the dead man's cold flesh as she passed him.

The bottle of holy water lay on the ground, nearly emptied. She placed it into her pocket. Then she glanced back. The two gray forms were still, silent, watching.

"Thank you for showing me more kindness than you were given," she said, then faced forward again. Her ankle ached with each step. The darkness pressed in around her, excruciatingly heavy.

But she was alive.

44.

The path ahead held a passageway to the left. As Margot neared it, she saw a dead one in the opening. She was a woman, old, her breasts sagging, her gray hair thin. She stood like a sentry, watching Margot as she passed.

"Thank you," Margot murmured. "And I'm sorry."

The image of the black threads running through the mouths hung in her mind as she moved still deeper into the passageways. Ray had said the townspeople sewed them shut as superstition. They believed the hanged would continue to plead for mercy even after death.

Maybe that's the truth. Maybe they weren't even pleading for an escape from death but for some small kindness. A proper grave. Their name to be recorded. Someone to remember them after they died. Respect.

Her throat ached. Even hundreds of years later, they had been unable to find peace. Each of them would have had lives that were likely fuller and more difficult than anything Margot had experienced. They had eked out an existence on harsh land. They had laughed, shared stories, made friends. They had been fully realized people, as real and varied and fascinating as anyone Margot knew. All of that was taken from them. Now, they only existed as shadows of themselves. Robbed of names, of identities, of their sense of selves.

She passed through an abandoned cellar. The path split. Another of the dead stood at the right-hand turn, blocking the passage. Margot murmured her thanks as she turned left.

Her father had loved humor. She could picture her parents, late in their lives, making jokes about the dead in the comfort of their kitchen. That was human nature, in the face of fear. Defang it by mocking it. Make light of a threat. Rob it of its power over you.

She could imagine every generation had done that eventually. Live on the hill for long enough, see the dead ones trailing outside the house on enough nights, and it would be easy to grow cavalier about it.

Until the dead finally caught up to them. And then they would stitch their victim's mouths closed, just as theirs had been. Never again allowed to laugh at their suffering. Never again allowed to argue their own relative virtue. Death made an equal out of everyone.

Steep stairs led her down. She reached one hand out to steady herself on the wall, and that was when she realized she'd lost her shovel. It would be with the effigy and the man from the wall. She glanced back. The path behind her was blocked. Three of the dead filled the space, their bodies caked in soil, their white eyes silently observing her. She shivered, then continued on.

Another split in the path appeared ahead. Once again, one of the passages was blocked by a dead sentry. It solidified the thought in Margot's mind that she was being shepherded toward a destination.

Witchety's blessings had worked because she treated the hill with reverence, Margot realized. She both feared and respected the dead. And it had been enough to calm the ones who lived under the earth, at least a little.

The passage turned at a sharp angle. It felt older than the others Margot had passed through. Roots trailed through the ceiling, scraping over her shoulders and tangling in her hair as she pushed through. She raised her light on the other side and felt herself grow cold.

Her path was blocked. The passage had collapsed, a tumble of rocks and soil and broken wooden supports thoroughly sealing the way ahead.

The dead had led her on a path that was clear of blocked passages until that point. Margot reached forward, trying to climb the pile to see if there might be a gap somewhere she could squeeze through, but no matter what angle she held her light at, she couldn't find enough space to fit an arm, let alone her body.

Should I dig? I wish I hadn't lost the shovel—

Cold skin grazed against her arm, and Margot flinched. The dead that had been trailing her now pressed forward, their slow, measured footsteps carrying them around Margot. She held still, arms clasped at her chest, the talisman gripped tightly, as bodies walked past her. Men and women, young and old, at least a dozen of them.

The first body stepped into the piled debris. Instead of hitting a wall like Margot had, it moved into it. The soil seemed to come alive, churning, moving, closer to a liquid than a solid as the body passed into it. Just like the earth that had swallowed Kant.

More bodies walked into the soil, their steps unhurried. It churned around them, almost bubbling.

Margot thought she understood. The dead were a part of the land. The hill had molded them, and they, in turn, molded the hill.

As the last body disappeared, Margot realized she was no longer looking at a solid wall of dirt and stone, but at a narrow passageway carved through it.

"Thank you," she whispered, and moved forward.

The path was tighter than anything she'd gone through until then. Margot turned her body sideways, her breathing shallow, as she squeezed between the rough walls of crumbling soil. It didn't mold itself around her like it had for the dead. Her cast scraped across it. She felt dirt tumble through her hair and under her clothes.

As she neared what looked like the channel's end, her hip hit something solid. She struggled to angle both her head and her light to see.

A table?

The surface was wooden and far more solid than any of the collapsing structures in the passages. Margot was wedged so tightly that she didn't have any way to climb over it. Instead, she shoved it with her hip, feeling the wood bite into her flesh with each inch it crept forward, until she had enough clearance to straighten.

It was a desk after all. An unlit lantern stood on one end. Stacks of neat paperwork on the other.

She raised her light, giving as much color to the room as possible. There were two doors, one to her left and one to her right, both locked. And ahead…

Margot's heart felt like it was going to break. She knew this room.

The chamber.

Six ancient oak barrels stood against the back wall, carefully positioned on a wooden stand that locked them into place. They had been carved from the wood of the hanging oak tree. The tree that had claimed every life that followed her through the passages.

Margot put her phone down while she crawled over the desk to reach the room proper. She'd entered through the passageway she'd seen when Kant had first showed her the chamber. It had been collapsed then. But it was the only way into the room that wasn't locked.

She found a box of matches and carefully lit the lantern. The light was warmer and stronger than her phone's, so she turned the mobile off and tucked it back into her pocket to preserve the battery.

A speck of dirt fell down before Margot's eyes. That had been commonplace in the neglected, abandoned pathways, but the chamber was supposed to be maintained meticulously. Margot lifted her eyes.

There was a crack in the ceiling. It was small, but as she watched, it grew larger. Jagged lines spread outward, widening. Color seeped from its center. A dark, poisonous, staining liquid, the shade of rot, the shade of death.

Fingertips emerged through the widening crack. Margot pressed her back against the desk, her heart in her throat, as she watched the fingers curl around. They weren't natural. They didn't have the gray hue of the dead ones, but they weren't *alive* either. Their edges were sharp, but the centers were vague. As though she was looking at a silhouette of a hand.

Clumps of dirt rained as the crack grew. The color darkened as toxic liquid flowed into it. A single drop fell free, and then another, and then more, until the crack was dripping like an overflowing drainpipe.

Another hand reached through the opening, this time stretching to its shoulder. Margot thought she could see something beyond. A pinprick of light. An eye.

This is how my parents died.

The thought felt as sharp and harsh as a slap. She knew it was the truth, though, as the dead hand reached toward her, and the head—horrific, long dead, cleaved in half by an axe—forced its way through the opening.

"Esther," Margot whispered.

She would have come through the crack in her parents' ceiling like this. Crept down to them as they lay frozen. Reached the rotting fingers into their mouths, into their throats, and drawn the life out of them.

Margot couldn't move. She could only stare, her mouth open, her heart skipping beats.

She knew what was coming as the fingers reached for her lips. They touched her, and she felt death itself in those fingertips. And she still could not move.

The pinprick lights for eyes stared into her, too wide, split apart by the axe.

And then they vanished.

Margot dragged in a ragged, coughing breath as the paralysis left her body. Something heavy landed at her feet. She clutched her side as she stared down at the floor. At the axe that had been dropped ahead of her.

"Oh," Margot whispered, breathing hard. She looked up. The crack was still there, its edges stained, but it had shrunk again. Now, it looked no different from simple water damage marring the ceiling.

Esther had dropped the axe through that hole, though. And it wasn't the axe Margot herself had brought to her room to keep her safe.

This one was far older. Far wickeder. Its handle curved. Its steel edge looked painfully sharp. This was not designed for cutting wood. This was a weapon.

The axe Ephraim owned. The axe that killed the Hull family.

She understood. She knew why she had been brought to this room. What she needed to do.

Margot picked up the axe. The handle was slick with Esther's death and crusted in dirt. Margot flexed her hands around it to fix her grip. The head was heavier than she was prepared for. She raised it. She aimed it toward the first of the oak barrels.

She brought it down.

Wood splintered. Vivid red wine, the shade of blood, poured free. It gushed across the floor, over Margot's feet. The air was thick with its scent. Sweet and cryptic and nauseating.

Margot raised the axe again and then again. The wood was old. It broke easily. The barrel's front cleaved away, its produce gushing out.

Through the lantern light, Margot could see something inside the barrel.

Fabric drifted in the currents of wine pouring away. A wash of pale hair tangled through splintered wood as it flowed out of the opening. Behind that was uncanny flesh.

Ephraim needed a place to hide the bodies. Somewhere he was certain no one would think to look.

Margot let the axe slump as she stared at Esther's corpse. Nearly perfectly preserved, and horribly transformed by the wine. Her skin was taut and wrinkled and puckered in strange places. Her lips were pulled back from her teeth, discolored gums glistening as wine trickled out of her open mouth.

Margot had seen that skin before, on herself, in her parents' mirror.

The body was coiled up, the knees to the chin, rigid hands clasped under the jaw. Bare feet grazed the barrel's back. She sagged, limp and heartbreakingly small in the shallow pool of remaining wine, but Margot could imagine how she'd looked when she was suspended in the liquid: her nightdress floating about her, her hair like a halo around her split face.

Margot squeezed her eyes shut as tears turned her vision hazy. Then she braced herself and lifted the axe again, bringing it down on the second barrel.

Shards of wood burst away under the impact. Each chop of the blade released a torrent of wine. Flecks of it splattered across her face, her clothes, and her arms. It pooled around her shoes and then soaked into the ground, only for the next barrel to replenish the flood.

The smell—of heady, powerful wine—made Margot sick. Sweat covered her body, both from the exertion and from nausea. She was panting, her hair sticking across her drenched face, before she finally stepped back from the shattered row of barrels.

The row of caskets.

Six barrels. Six slain members of the Hull family. Each body coiled up inside its tomb, knees drawn up to the chest, mouths open as though to cry out one final time.

Margot lifted her eyes. The lantern's light couldn't quite reach the darkest area behind the broken barrels, where the shadows seemed to cling heavily.

The faintest outlines of silhouettes hung there. Margot might not have even seen them except for six sets of shining eyes.

Louisa's windswept hair, tied down with a headscarf. Ezra, taller than the others, his shoulders broader than the shriveled remains inside the barrels. Jeremiah and Giles, standing beside their father. Constance, next to her mother. And Esther, the smallest, her expression as unreadable as the ink drawing of her had been.

They stood there for a moment, lined up behind the barrels, watching Margot, watching as the dregs of wine soaked her shoes and drained into the soil.

Then, as one, they faded like smoke.

45.

Margot sat on the step outside the fermentation room. Just like the day before, she was painted in red. Only, this time, the liquid was wine. She thought she would have preferred blood.

She heard Kant before she saw him. His limp seemed more pronounced as he slowly, haltingly left the room and lowered himself onto the step next to her. He'd come from the chamber and the scene that Margot had left there.

His skin was pale. His one remaining eye was glazed as he stared across the field, toward the employee buildings. There was an air of quiet shock, of resignation, about him.

Margot was grateful. She'd been afraid that he might have known what was inside the barrels.

She was fairly sure her parents had.

Someone would need to empty and refill the casks. Even if the lids never came off entirely, it would have been difficult not to notice that they required so much less wine than the other barrels.

The barrels from the hanging tree. Ephraim must have taken some dark delight in the choice. They were the barrels Ezra had carved by hand. The barrels that had made his family wealthy. And so, Ephraim had chosen them to be the Hull family's tomb.

It had been a clever choice too. When the family went missing, the police would have searched the house, the grounds, likely even the tunnels.

They were less likely to break open every barrel in the winery.

And so it had continued through eleven generations. The family's darkest secret. The family's source of wealth. The vintage that won awards, that sparked delighted discussion, that sold for six-figure amounts. Each generation would have been shown what existed inside. Each generation would have realized they could never tell a soul.

To bring closure to the murdered Hulls would have meant losing everything. Their business. Their reputation. The curse exacted a heavy price, but it also brought prosperity they were loath to lose. Each owner in turn had deemed the cost of justice too high.

And it had fueled the curse.

People who worked closest to the barrels were the quickest to be chained by them. Andrew, originally hired as a seasonal laborer, had likely helped prepare the wine that went into the hanging tree casks.

Nora and Ray, responsible for the public store, had managed to stay at their house in the town for years. The store only sold midrange wines to tourists and locals, aged in the regular cellar. The priceless hanging tree wine was by special order only.

Kant, the manager, had overseen all projects, and the dead had tried to drag him into the earth for it.

Most of the curse lay with Margot, though. She had become sole owner of the casks after her parents' deaths. They were her responsibility.

"The police are on their way, as you asked," Kant said. His voice was low and still slightly shaken. He rubbed his wrist. "I told them there was a death. Six deaths, I suppose."

"Good." Margot leaned forward, hands clasped between her knees. She hesitated, then said, "You might want to visit your sister for a few days. Things are going to get messy here."

He turned his head slightly, a silent question.

"You can now," Margot added. "Leave, I mean. I tried walking past the property's boundary, just to be sure. No headache."

"You broke the curse," Kant muttered, faintly shocked, faintly amazed.

"I mean..." She rolled her shoulders. "I'm pretty sure I still have work to do, to make it permanent. But yes. We're on the road there."

"Work." He stretched his legs out, exhaling slowly. "What kind?"

"The bodies can't be kept a secret any longer. Not who they are and not where they were kept." She'd run over the mental list a half dozen times. It never seemed any less daunting. "The public will need to know. Which, obviously, will destroy everything. The business. The business's reputation. The reputation of everyone attached."

Kant made a soft grunting sound of agreement. "It'll hurt at first, but it's better to get the ugliness out where everyone can see it."

"That's what I think. And it's what Ezra's family deserves." She took a slow breath. "Then I need to create a memorial to the men and women who were hanged here. If there are any kind of records from the time— names, dates, anything of the sort—I'll need to find them. And if I have any money left over after the media circus and lawsuits that today is going to spawn, it'll go to excavating parts of the hill, looking for remains. And giving them formal burials."

"You might have more money than you expect," Kant said. "You never asked Andrew what your financial situation was."

She shrugged. "I'll find a way to put it to something good. It doesn't seem right to profit from this kind of thing."

He nodded.

"After that..." Margot raised her shoulders and let them drop again.

"You'll always have a home here if you want it. I'll offer that to everyone who was working here. But I can imagine you'll want to go somewhere else, after being chained to Gallows Hill for so long. In the short term, at least for the next couple of days, you and the others might want to clear out. The bodies are old, but I'm sure the police will still have plenty of questions. And I figure I have until this afternoon before the news vans arrive. I'll probably want to ask you some questions later—the best way to wind up the business and the best places to start searching the land—but that won't be for a while."

"That is a lot of work," Kant murmured.

"Well, I might not have made the mess, but it's mine to clean up." The talisman was still threaded around her wrist. Margot ran her fingertips over the precious items she'd tied there. The photo of her parents, soaked through with wine. Her hair clip. The key. The label from her tape. Her grandmother's ring. Kant's button. "I never really had a purpose before this. When I came to Gallows Hill, this wasn't the kind of responsibility I was expecting. But I think I'm able to do it. And it'll mean something to a lot of people who have been waiting a very long time."

Kant turned his face toward the sun. His gray beard and shaggy hair were lit through with shocks of gold from the light. He was silent for a minute, lost in thought, then said, "I've always been happy working here. Even with the bad parts. I like the work. I think I'd like to take on some more of it, if you wouldn't mind the company."

Margot, surprised and touched in equal measures, felt herself smile. "Yeah. I'd like that."

"Mm." He breathed in deeply. "Looks like we're ready to start."

They stood, drenched in the morning's first light, freer and lighter than they had been in a long time as they faced the flashing lights turning into the driveway.

ABOUT THE AUTHOR

Darcy Coates is the *USA Today* bestselling author of *Hunted*, *The Haunting of Ashburn House*, *Craven Manor*, and more than a dozen other horror and suspense titles. She lives on the Central Coast of Australia with her family, cats, and a garden full of herbs and vegetables. Darcy loves forests, especially old-growth forests, where the trees dwarf anyone who steps between them. Wherever she lives, she tries to have a mountain range close by.